Time was running out on ~~~~
No time to wonder. Escape was, sim-
ply, her only chance. She moved to
the window and discovered that most
of the tiny panes of glass had been
broken long since. There would be no
shatter of glass below. Now!

Already she was on the windowsill,
with the rope burning her hands. She
landed, jarred but unhurt.

Any minute now, the men would go
upstairs and find her gone.

She kept moving steadily away from
the house, and felt something trickling
down her face. Blood.

How much longer could she go on?
Madness to think of resting. No—at
all costs she must find help, shelter. . . .

She turned off the road past the
dark shape of an outbuilding, and
moved toward the house. Suddenly she
whirled at a movement behind her.
But she was not quick enough. She felt
a violent blow on the back of her head
and fell into blackness. . . .

Jane Aiken Hodge

Watch the Wall,
My Darling

A Fawcett Crest Book

Fawcett Publications, Inc., Greenwich, Conn.

Five and twenty ponies,
Trotting through the dark—
Brandy for the Parson,
'Baccy for the Clerk;
Laces for a lady; letters for a spy,
And watch the wall, my darling, while the Gentlemen go by!

From: A Smugglers' Song by RUDYARD KIPLING

A Fawcett Crest Book reprinted by arrangement with
Doubleday and Company, Inc.

Library of Congress Catalog Card Number: 66-17398

Printed in the United States of America

Chapter One

RAIN BEAT against the carriage windows. The light was fading fast. For the third time since they had left Rye, the coachman stopped to ask his way. For the first time, Christina admitted a qualm of anxiety. At this rate, it would be full night before they reached Tretteign Grange. She shivered. "The Dark House," the landlord of the George in Rye had called it. "They don't much like strangers at the Dark House. Best stay the night here, miss, and go on in the morning." At the time, telling him firmly that she was expected, it had seemed mere common sense to continue her journey. Now, as the carriage lurched forward once more along the lonely marshland track, she was not so sure. Suppose her grandfather had not had her letter? But of course he must. She had stayed an extra day in London, partly to finish her business there, partly to make sure it arrived before her.

The coach was going more slowly now, the driver feeling his way along the strange road in the dusk. She had tried to persuade the landlord to send one of his men as guide, but he had been oddly reluctant. Pressed, he had hedged. "We don't go on the marsh at night much, miss. They don't like it."

"They?"

He seemed to hesitate for a moment, and yet, when it came, his answer was reasonable enough. "The guards, miss . . . the soldiers." And then, indulgently, "Course, I keep forgetting you're a Yankee. You speak so clear, just like the rest of us. Maybe you don't even know. Any night now, Boney may land his army here. There's guards waiting, all along the coast—beacons ready for lighting. Reckon you must a' seen some of them on your way down from London."

"Of course I know an invasion's expected." During the short time she had been in England, she had been constantly irritated by this assumption that as an American she must be totally ignorant of European affairs. "I'm glad to hear the coast *is* guarded—from what I heard in London . . ." She broke off. "But surely that is no reason why I should not drive to my own grandfather's house?"

"Your grandfather? Mr. Tretteign? Why didn't you say so in the first place?" Oddly enough, this seemed to settle everything—except the question of a guide. Here he was obdurate, shifting his ground now to say that he was sorry, but had no man to spare. The instructions he had given her London coachman had seemed lucid enough, but they had missed their way just the same, and had lost valuable time.

It was very nearly dark now. The wind was rising, and she could hear a new sound too, the sullen roar of the sea. Well, at least that should mean they were near their destination, since Tretteign Grange was almost on the shore. Perhaps she would not be so very late after all. She leaned back, purposely relaxed in her corner of the carriage, and wondered for the thousandth time what her grandfather and cousins would be like. Should she have waited for an answer to her letter? In London it had seemed nonsense. Now . . . in the dark she wondered. . . .

The carriage lurched to a sudden stop and she heard the coachman and groom shouting. What now? Another missed turning? She lowered the glass and leaned out to feel the whip of the wind and to taste salty rain on her lips. "What's the matter now?" Her voice blew away on the wind. The coachman, on his box, was fully occupied in holding his horses; the groom had run forward to their heads. She could just see him in the dim light from the carriage's lanterns, and beyond him—what?

"It's clear across the road," his voice came back faintly over the roar of the wind.

"Damnation take it," said the driver. "And no room to turn."

Christina swung the carriage door open, judged the distance as best she might by the uncertain glimmer of the carriage lights, lifted her skirts, and jumped. She landed on soft grass, and just managed to keep her balance on the edge of a deep ditch that ran beside the track. Recovering herself, she moved forward. "What's the matter?" she called up to the driver.

"Road's blocked," he answered tersely. And then, "How the hell did you get out?"

"Jumped." She went on to where the groom had succeeded in steadying the horses. Now she could see that the lane was indeed blocked by a barricade of hurdles and brush. "What on earth?"

The groom started and turned at the sound of her voice. "I reckon landlord's right. They don't like strangers on the marsh," he said.

"What do we do?"

"God knows. Can't go on. Can't turn. Ditch this side, shingle that. Take the carriage on to that, we're here for good. Frank," he raised his voice, "what's to do?"

The driver's only answer was a string of curses. He'd been a fool to come, and it would teach him to put himself out to oblige a lady.

"You were paid well," said Christina, "and promised more." She moved forward to examine the barrier. "If we can't go back, we will just have to go on." She pulled a bit of brushwood clear of the obstruction and threw it in the ditch. "It will take a bit of time, but we can get this down easily enough, if you will just leave swearing and help."

She thought the groom muttered something about Yankees, but he left the horses and came forward to join her in removing bits of prickly gorse from the improvised barricade. "I don't reckon we should," he grumbled as he did so. "Suppose it's part of the invasion defenses?"

"If it is," said Christina, "heaven help us if the French really land. It wouldn't hold them five minutes. . . . Oh!" Strong arms had caught her from behind; a hand covered her mouth on the beginning of a scream. Vainly struggling, she saw that the same thing had happened to the groom, while a group of dark figures had surrounded the carriage. It was all over in a moment. Her captor now had her hands held behind her in one of his, while the other still covered her mouth. She bit it as hard as she could.

"Damnation!" The voice was a gentleman's. The hand had been whipped away and she drew in a deep breath. "Scream if you must," he went on, "there's no one to hear."

It was too obviously true. She let the breath out again on a long, angry sigh. "What is the meaning of this outrage?"

"A lady!" The hand she had bitten moved casually down the front of her warm pelisse and she tensed inside it, grateful for the protection of the heavy unfashionable worsted. "A young lady!" He went on. "What the devil are you doing, wandering about the marsh at night?"

"What business is it of yours?"

"Suppose I tell you we are on coast guard duty here?"

"I shall say you go a very odd way about it." Tartly. "You will tell me next that these ruffians of yours are in Volunteer uniform."

"I shall tell you nothing. And, if you are wise, you will ask no questions. There are times when might is right."

"Too many." She felt that his grip on her had slackened and wondered whether to make a break for it.

"I wouldn't." He seemed, disconcertingly, to have read her thoughts. "Not if you like living."

A chill shuddered through her. It was no casual threat. He meant it. Held close against his body, she could feel the tension in him, steel-taut, ready to snap. With an effort, she made herself relax, lean more easily against him. "I like living very much." Her light tone pleased her.

"Good. Then answer my questions. Your name, and your business here."

"Christina Tretton." She felt a shock run through him. "I'm on my way to visit my grandfather, Tretteign of Tretteign Grange. I come from America, where, I may say, only Indians would use travelers thus. Why—what's the matter?"

Absurdly, fantastically, he had burst into a great guffaw of laughter. "I might have known," he said. "Trust a Tretteign! You're on your own land, my dear. . . . Yes—what is it?" One of the other men had approached to whisper urgently to him, the strong Sussex accent more effective than the whisper in preventing her from understanding. "You're right, we've wasted too much time already." And then, in answer to a further remark, "No." Curtly. "Did you not hear? She's a Tretteign."

"I don't care if she's the devil walking." This was another member of the gang, speaking much more intelligibly. "The sea's the place for her. And for the men, too. It's the only way, and you know it."

"I know nothing of the kind." It was odd that the hand that held hers in so ruthless a grip should contrive to convey reassurance. "I said—she's a Tretteign."

"And I say she's a danger to us. And them two, still more so. Londoners both . . . stands to reason." There was a little growl of approval from two or three other men who gathered around, uncomfortably close.

"So we kill all three, do we? And have the Bow Street Runners down here, looking all over the marsh for them? Just what we want! Your brilliance is such, my dear friend, I wonder you do not take over as captain in my stead."

"Who'll know they were here?"

"I expect Miss Tretteign can answer that best. Who will know you came here?" Hands and voice alike conveyed a warning.

"Plenty of people. The landlord of the George at Rye. He advised us not to come tonight—and, I begin to think, misdirected us on purpose. We have asked our way three times—they cannot help but remember. And—I wrote my grandfather that I was coming."

"You see." This for the others. Then, to her, "Miss Tretteign, I would rather not have to kill you, but, believe me, I will, if necessary. Have I your word of honor that you will forget what has happened tonight? Not woman's honor . . . word of a Tretteign."

"Yes. Word of a Tretteign." For the first time, a warm little thrill of pride in her family. "But what about the men?"

"I have no doubt they'll promise too."

"But will they keep it?" growled someone. "I say death for the lot of them."

Once again there was a low mutter of agreement. Amazingly, her captor had let her go. The hand that had been holding hers now held a gun. "Am I captain here, or not? Those against, speak up now, and I'll shoot you where you stand."

The show of force worked. "Oh, very well," muttered the ringleader, "but you'll regret it, mark my words."

"It's a risk, either way. I prefer it like this. Right. Clear the road, some of you. Miss Tretteign, you will be hostage for your servants' good behavior. You will be here on the marsh. If there is trouble, we will know where to look for you. Do you think you will be able to shut their mouths?"

"I hope so." She had stood stock still since he let her go.

"So do I. I'd be sorry to have to kill you." His orders were already being obeyed. Two or three of the men were hauling the remaining hurdles off the road, muttering as they did so. He took no notice. "You will excuse us, I am sure, if we leave you the task of untying your servants. This road takes you directly to Tretteign Grange. So—*bon voyage*, Miss Tretteign."

"Good-bye, sir. And—thank you."

But they were gone, as silently as they had come. Christina gave a little shiver. It had been a very near thing, she knew, and—they might change their minds. She hurried over to where the coachman and groom lay by the roadside, and began, with hands that trembled, to loose their bonds. An outburst of unfamiliar curses celebrated the removal of the gags and she listened unmoved as she struggled with the cord that tied the coachman's hands, and then, while he rubbed them angrily, the groom's. Only when she had finished, did she speak. "I have promised, on your behalf, as well as my own, that we will say nothing about tonight's work."

"Say nothing?" Another outburst of swearing. "I'll have the law on them if it's the last thing I do."

"It very likely would be. They swore they'd kill us all if we talked. Besides—could you describe them? Would you even know them if you met them again? And a proper pair of fools you're likely to look if you do tell the story. You told me you were armed—a fine showing you made of it! Surrounded and disarmed by half a dozen men, without so much as a shot fired. Least said, soonest mended, I think, for all our sakes. They warned me, if the least whisper gets out about tonight's work, they'd reach out to get you, even as far as London." This seemed to her a very much more powerful argument with two self-proved cowards than any talk of danger to herself. "And now, let us get on before they change their minds and come back for us. The gang wanted to throw us in the sea, by the way. It was only their captain who prevented it."

"And you expect us to be grateful?"

"Well, I know I am." He had let down the carriage steps for her, and she climbed in, then turned. "Our road lies straight ahead. They cleared the barricade for us."

"Mighty obliging, I'm sure," growled the coachman.

As the carriage moved forward, Christina sank back against the squab and gave way, for a moment, to the great involuntary shivers that ran through her. Then, angrily, she steadied herself, sat upright, took off her bonnet and began to tidy her hair as best she could in the dark. It was over. She was safe. Think forward, she told herself, not back. She peered out the window, but it was impossible to see beyond the uncertain pools of light cast by the carriage's lanterns. Leaning back again, she deliberately composed her thoughts for the coming meeting with her unknown grandfather. Would he be glad to see her? It seemed unlikely. But—she had promised. A deathbed promise, doubly binding. She shrugged in the darkness. Too late to be indulging in qualms now.

The carriage was going more smoothly, and slowing down. Once again she pressed her face close to the window and saw a range of low buildings to the right, dark against the darkness of the sky. No lights anywhere that she could see, but the carriage was still moving forward, so presumably they had not reached the house itself. On the thought, it turned and stopped, and now she could see the bulk of a higher building, with lights showing here and there. There was none at the entrance, but the carriage lamps showed her a flight of steps leading up to a big doorway.

The groom had opened the door and let down the steps for her. "It don't much look as if you was expected," he said.

She had thought the same thing herself, but took it lightly. "I expect they keep early hours down here in the country," she said, "and have given me up for today. Here," she had the money ready in her hand. "This is for the two of you—to make up for what you've gone through tonight. And, remember, not a word, for all our sakes. Particularly, not here. Who knows what spies that gang may have."

"Aye," said the groom. "I've heard, often enough, that half the countryside, down in these parts, is involved in smuggling, one way or another."

"Smuggling," she said thoughtfully. "I suppose that must be what it was."

"Course it was. It's the last time I come down this way near the dark of the moon—or any other time, come to that. But thank you, miss, just the same." He had just recognized the magnitude of the tip she had given him. "And—mum's the word."

"Good. Now, knock on the door for me." It was raining hard, but she jumped down from the carriage, pulling up the hood of her traveling cloak to cover her bonnet. She had got very wet and must be able to explain it. While the man knocked loudly on the big door, she looked about her: a broad carriage sweep, buildings ranging away to right and left, the huge entrance portico looming above her. . . . She had had no idea that Tretteign Grange was so imposing a mansion, but then her father had seldom talked about his home or his family.

The big door was opening at last. She climbed lightly up the shallow steps to stand beside the groom and meet the amazed eyes of an old man who was shrugging himself into his livery coat.

"Yes?" He looked, oddly, at once surprised and relieved at sight of her, and seemed to be peering beyond her into the dark. "What brings you here so late at night, miss? Have you lost your way?" He held the door carefully ajar and looked at her around it.

"Not at all. This is Tretteign Grange, is it not? I am Miss Tretton. I begin to think my grandfather cannot have had my letter."

"Miss Tretteign! It can't be true." He put down the lamp he carried and swung open the door. "Miss Tretteign!" he said again. "All the way from America? And—all by yourself? No, there's been no letter—but then, no one's been to Rye all week, you see. How could there be? But, come in, miss, if it's really you. Lord, what a day this is. But—where are the others? Where's your father? Where's Mr. Christopher?"

"Dead." It was still hard to say it. "Will you tell the men what to do with the carriage? They'll have to spend the night here. I'm sorry to come on you so unexpectedly—and so late. We lost our way on the marsh."

"Yes. Yes—I see." He raised his voice to shout. "Jem, Jem! Where is the boy?" And, to her, "Mr. Christopher dead! I can't believe it. And your mother and sister still in Paris?" He made it sound worse than death. "And you lost on the marsh—and in the dark, too. You—you're all right, miss?"

"Of course." Why did he shake so? Surprise, no doubt, at

her arrival. After all, he was an old man; must be, to remember her father. But—what had he expected when he opened the door and peered out so cautiously around it?

"You're wet, miss?" It was a question.

"Yes. I had to have a look at the place. It's huge—I had no idea."

"But not much of it lived in, you'll find. Ah, there you are at last, Jem." A boy had emerged from somewhere at the back of the big dark wall. "Here's Miss Christina, come from America. Show the men round to the stable yard, will you? They're to stay the night, of course."

"Tonight?"

"Yes, tonight, looby." He followed him out the front door, giving him some further instructions that Christina could not hear, then returned to her, full of apologies for keeping her standing.

"I don't know whether I'm on my head or my heels, miss, and that's God's truth, but, lord, what a happy day this is—and what a sad one. But—Mr. Christopher's daughter!"

"Parkes! Parkes! What is it?" The agitated whisper drew Christina's eye upward to where a candle flickered at the stairhead. The woman who held it was leaning over the banisters, peering anxiously downward. "Who is it, Parkes? What's the matter? What's happened? Is it Ross?"

"Nothing's the matter, ma'am." His tone was oddly repressive. "As for Mr. Ross, he's away tonight, as you know. But here's Miss Christina, home from America."

"Christina? Christopher's girl? What in the world's she doing here?" She picked up the skirts of her blue negligée and came down the stairs toward them, the candle lighting up blond hair around a faded pretty face marred by the drooping corners of the mouth. "Christina Tretteign?" She put her candle down and advanced on Christina, her manner as unwelcoming as her words. "What brings you here?" And then, on a still sharper note. "Did Papa send for you?"

"Who? Oh—my grandfather? No. And Mr. Parkes tells me he has not had my letter. I am sorry to come on you so unexpectedly and so late, Aunt . . ." She paused expectantly.

"Tretteign. Verity Tretteign. I'm Ross's mother." A curious mixture of pride and complaint in her tone. "I wish he was here. He would know what to do. Parkes—"

"No, ma'am." Once again that oddly repressive note. "May

I suggest that Miss Christina sleep in Mr. Richard's room for tonight? It's always kept ready for him. It's but to put a warming pan between the sheets. And you'll be needing some supper, Miss Christina."

"Parkes, I'm famished!"

"And cold, too, I'll be bound." His voice warmed at her use of his name. "Come you in by the library fire, miss, and I'll wake the girls and have them warm your room and get you something to eat."

"But, Parkes," objected Mrs. Tretteign, "suppose Papa should not approve? You know what names he calls Christopher—"

"My father is dead," said Christina.

"Oh, I'm sorry, I'm sure, but just the same, if Papa did not invite you—and, besides, how do we know you really are you? If you see what I mean. Parkes, do you really think . . . ?"

"I think you had best go back to bed, ma'am, and let me look after Miss Christina. Then if Mr. Tretteign should be angry, it's no fault of yours."

She clapped her hands in a gesture that must once have been attractively girlish. "Parkes! How clever you are. That is just what I will do. Good night, Miss Tretteign, if you really are . . ." She let it hang. "Parkes will look after you admirably, I know."

"Don't mind her, miss." Parkes led the way into a big dark room where the embers of a wood fire glowed on a huge hearth. "She's not a Tretteign, of course, only by marriage." His tone dismissed her. "Sit down, Miss Christina, and warm yourself." He picked up a huge pair of bellows and began to blow life into the fire.

But she moved forward and took the bellows from him. "I'll do that, Parkes. Do you find me something to eat. I'm ravenous. I could eat a horse."

"It's not fitting, miss." He surrendered the bellows reluctantly to her wilful tug. "A young lady like you blowing the fire—"

"An American young lady, Parkes. I have begun to see that it makes a great difference." She picked up a couple of small logs from the pile beside the fire and placed them exactly where they would do most good. "But perhaps I should not be asking you to find me food. Is that it?"

"Miss! I'd die for you! Mr. Christopher's girl . . ."

She laughed and went to work once more with the bellows. "I do hope that won't be necessary, Parkes, but in that case—"

"Absolutely, Miss Christina." He was lighting a range of candles as he spoke. "Some cold mutton, perhaps? It's marsh grown—you'll never have tasted anything like it. And a glass of our own mead—there's a welcome home for you—if so be it ain't too strong for you."

"I doubt that, Parkes. Not tonight, at any rate." She had turned toward him, fire- and candlelight alike on her face.

"Miss! You're hurt! You're bleeding!"

"Nonsense!" But her hand went up to her face and felt dried blood on her chin. "Good gracious!" She must have bitten the smuggler harder than she realized. And then, thinking fast, "Oh, that. It's nothing. I bit my tongue when the carriage hit a rut. There are plenty of them on your marsh."

"You should not have come at night, Miss Christina."

"Do you know," she said, "I rather think you are right, Parkes."

Chapter Two

CHRISTINA AWOKE next morning to a familiar, delightful sound. It was the sea, of course, not deeply growling, as it had last night, or sullenly threatening, as on the voyage from America, but contentedly murmuring to itself. The wind had dropped in the night and autumn sunshine illuminated the pattern in faded red curtains and shone around them to pick out here a gleaming piece of mahogany and there the rich brown backs of a shelf of books. Pulling herself farther upright among soft pillows, she looked about her and thought that her cousin Richard might be congratulated on his room. Nothing, it was true, was new, or particularly elegant, but everything spoke of care and comfort and enough money well spent.

But what a strange household . . . Her thoughts were interrupted by a light tapping on the door, and a girl about her own age looked in. "May I light the fire, Miss Christina? Mr. Parkes said not to last night, you being so tired, but there's a proper autumn nip in the air this morning. You'll need it while you breakfast."

"In bed?" The idea appalled her.

The girl had crossed the room to draw the heavy curtains and flood the room with sunshine. "Mrs. Tretteign always does, miss."

"Well, I'm not going to." Christina sat farther up in bed, preparatory to getting out.

"But, miss!" Genuine horror in the girl's voice now. "You ain't got no maid, and Mrs. Emeret—she's the housekeeper, you know—she ain't decided yet who's to do for you. Till your own comes on, of course." She was back at the fire now, busy with flint and tinder.

Christina laughed. "If Mrs. Emeret waits till my maid arrives, she'll wait forever. I've never had one."

"Never?" Shocked. "Oh, miss, please don't let on! Mrs. Emeret is bad enough this morning, and Mrs. Tretteign, and her Rose, about your coming all on your own like—and in the night too. Please don't let them know you never had a maid. There'd be no end to it. Please, miss, do stay in bed till Mrs. Emeret sends someone."

"What's your name?" Christina settled back among the pillows.

"Betty, miss." She had the fire going now and moved nearer to the bed, showing a broad friendly face under the mob cap. "I'm the second housemaid. I do all the fires."

"Do you? Well, today, you're going to be my maid. Can you find me some hot water, do you think?"

"Your maid! Oh, miss—I don't know what they'll say." And then, chin up. "I don't care, neither. Hot water? Right away, miss. And I'll tell Parkes, shall I, that you'll be down for breakfast?"

"Do." Christina jumped out of bed as the girl closed the door behind her, and crossed the room to look out the window. As she had hoped, it looked across a paved terrace to a range of brown shingle, and then the sea, gray-blue and quiet in morning light. On each side the shore swept around in a great curving bay, ending on the right in a far-off cliff, hazy with distance, and nearer on the left, in a long low promontory. Almost directly ahead, far out to sea, a ship was making slow way on the light morning breeze.

Christina turned as the girl re-entered the room with a big steaming can. "What ship's that? Do you know?"

Betty put down the can and joined her at the window. "Oh, that. She's a French privateer, miss. Been hovering offshore this week or more."

"French! And so near."

"Oh yes, they're fast, you see, miss, and can show anything but a frigate a clean pair of heels." She turned to look to the left, toward the long low spit of land. "Yes, you see, the wind's from the east. The Dungeness squadron's sailed for Boulogne roads—and while they're there, keeping an eye on Boney's army, his privateers come over here and snap up what they can. Took a cutter almost within sight of Hastings last week—just think, miss, those poor sailors, prisoners of war for goodness knows how long—or, very likely, forced to serve in a French man-of-war. Boney's mad for sailors, Jem says. He'd have been here long ago if he could only beat our fleet, but Lord Nelson's too many for him, thank goodness." She shivered dramatically. "Ain't you scared, miss, coming here to the invasion coast?"

"Not nearly so scared as I was crossing the Atlantic, I can tell you. But what time's breakfast?"

Thus reminded of her new duties, Betty poured water from her can into the heavy basin. "Well, Mr. Ross being away, and his mother always having it in her room, and the old master too, it's only you. Mr. Parkes said to tell you, miss, he'd see yours was ready sharp at nine. Best not meet old Mr. Tretteign till after his, he said, excusing the liberty, miss, but he's a proper tartar till he's had his cold meat and ginger tea. I don't reckon Parkes means even to tell him about you till after."

"Goodness! Is it as bad as that? Then we had best lose no time. Look in the big box, would you, Betty, and find me a fresh gown."

Coming down the wide stairway twenty minutes or so later, she found Parkes anxiously hovering in the flagged hallway. As he came forward to greet her, a huge grandfather clock wound itself up with much groaning and creaking and struck nine times. "Good morning, miss. I do hope I didn't have you called too early."

He was old, she saw, white-haired and shaky in his immaculate black. "No, indeed, Parkes. I hope I don't inconvenience you by coming down. I hate breakfast in bed." And then, turning to look at the big clock, "Is that the one where father hid?"

"That's it, miss. He told you about that, did he? This way, if you will." He turned and led the way into a shabbily comfortable breakfast parlor.

"Yes, he talked sometimes of his childhood. But I had no idea Tretteign Grange was such a place. It seemed huge when we drove in last night."

"So it is, but little of it lived in, you'll find—or livable. It was an abbey, you know, even more prosperous than Battle in its day—and more ruthlessly sacked in the Reformation.

The Tretteigns built this house out of the debris of the abbey —well, you will see for yourself." He had seated her, while he talked, at a big oval mahogany table with only one place laid. "I hope you eat a proper English breakfast like your father, Miss Christina." And then, surprised, "Why, Mr. Ross, I didn't expect you so soon."

"Entertaining on the sly, eh Parkes?" The drawling voice made Christina swing around to face the speaker. A tall man, he was leaning nonchalantly against the doorpost, surveying her through a quizzing glass. He was dressed in the scarlet coat she had learned to recognize as a Volunteer's uniform and his broad shoulders and great height combined with this martial outfit to present an odd contrast to his dandy's voice and manner. His thick dark hair was cut short and curled irrepressibly around a face tanned almost as dark as an Indian's. His gaze, at once languid and piercing, had now taken her in from her own softly waving brown hair to her kid slippers and, on the way, had contrived to make her dark stuff dress seem even more unmodish than she had thought it. Now he turned back to Parkes. "Some relation of yours, perhaps, Parkes?"

"Mr. Ross! Sir!" The old man was very much on his dignity. "This is your cousin, Miss Christina, come from America."

"Good gracious!" There was something absurd about the mild exclamation from this formidable figure. "A thousand apologies, Cousin, but how was I to know?"

"How indeed?" Infuriated by the cool scrutiny, she checked an impulse to rise and greet him, and, instead, made a little business of pouring herself another cup of tea. And as she did so, an odd thought struck her. She was perfectly certain, all at once, that his entry had been prepared—that he had known all about her before he entered the room. Then why the deliberately insulting pretense of ignorance? To make her angry, of course, as it had. But why? Well, he should at least find her difficult to rouse. She looked up at him, her glance as coolly appraising as his own. "May I pour you a cup of tea, Cousin Ross?"

"I thank you, no. Parkes, coffee, and breakfast, at once. And none of that catlap you seem to have served to my cousin. If you are my cousin, . . . did you say Christina?"

"I said nothing, sir." Parkes had left the room. "But yes, I

am Christina Tretton." Keep it short, let him do the talking,
perhaps she might gain a clue to his inexplicable hostility.

"You can prove it, eh?" He pulled up a chair and sat down
astride it, facing her. "Admit, coz, if coz you are, that it would
be a devilish neat idea to turn up here at this stage of the
game and claim kin with the old man. But I warn you, there's
nothing second childish about him. You'd best be able to prove
your claim."

"Believe me, Cousin, I can." Once again she refused to be
drawn.

"Splendid." Mockery in the drawling voice now. "It would
make a play worthy of Colman himself, would it not? *The
American Claimant*—or do you prefer *The Return of the
Prodigal?* But, forgive me, you have probably never heard of
our English dramatists."

"If you want to call that second-rate playwright a drama-
tist."

His laugh was oddly attractive. *"Touché*, coz. So there are
actually books in those United States are there? I'd never have
thought it. But what, I wonder, moved you to leave. Thought
you'd be in at the death, did you? Well, I can't say I blame
you. It's not every day one has a chance at an abbey, though
I doubt there'll be much else. So your father decided it was
time to kiss and be friends, did he, and sent you with the
olive branch? Not a bad idea either, I'll say that for Uncle
Christopher." His glance, sweeping her once more from head
to toe, suggested that this was intended as a compliment.

"My father is dead." Angry at last, she rose from the table
and stood tall above him for a moment, an Amazon in gray
worsted. "As for your other insinuations—I will not waste
your time, or mine, in trying to convince you how unwillingly
I decided to come here."

"Left you without a feather to fly with, did he? Well, I'm
sorry about Uncle Chris. I don't remember him, of course,
but by all accounts he was the best of the family. Come,
Cousin, forgive me if I spoke out of turn, and kiss and be
friends. You'll need friends here, I warn you."

"Oh?" She had made herself sit down again and drink tea
as if that was all she cared about. But—what was it about
that last speech of his? He had forgotten his quizzing glass
now, and, with it, seemed to have lost much of the drawl and
the foppish manner with which he had entered the room.

While he had spoken, with obvious sincerity, about her father, a mask had slipped, revealing . . . what? It was fantastic. She must be imagining things. And yet . . . her glance fell on the hand that had held the quizzing glass. "You have hurt your hand, Cousin."

"It's nothing." He looked down at it carelessly. "A trifle. One of the dogs bit me."

"A bitch, perhaps?" It was impossible. It seemed to be true. Brown eyes met brown eyes squarely, met and held.

"Perhaps." His tone admitted nothing, denied nothing. "And here, in good time, is Parkes with my breakfast. Surely you will stay and pour my coffee for me, Cousin Christina?"

"I believe you are very well able to take care of yourself, Cousin." And with that she got herself fairly out of the door and ran, oddly breathless, upstairs to her own room.

However impossible, it seemed to be true: her cousin Ross had been the leader of last night's gang of smugglers. And, apparently, he took it quite for granted that she would keep his secret. Well, of course, she had promised, last night. And, of course—odd to have so little doubt about this—she would. But—infuriating to have him so sure of it, so sure, in fact, of himself. Did he think his charm so great, with his airs and his quizzing glass? Not to mention the Volunteer's uniform. A smuggler in uniform! Fantastic. But then her father had often talked with surprising sympathy about the smugglers down here on the marsh. "Bad laws make bad customs," he used to say, drawing a parallel between British smuggling and the Boston Tea Party. No time now to be thinking of Father. Or, rather, remember that it was at his insistence that she was here. "Wrongs on both sides," he had spoken with difficulty, weak from his wounds. "Go home, Chris, make it up—for me, for all of us. Promise?"

Of course she had promised—promised other things too while his life ebbed slowly away with the blood she could not stanch. So here she was, and, judging by Ross's reaction, everyone was going to think she had come to curry favor with her grandfather in hopes of inheriting the Abbey. For a moment, irrationally angry, she had been on the point of betraying herself and breaking her promise to her father, down there in the dining room. Well, her smuggler cousin would not find her so easy to draw another time. Of course—she prowled over to the window—it had all been contrived so that in her anger she would fail to recognize him. She laughed a little angrily to herself. I beat you there, Cousin Ross. It would take more than an assumed drawl, a dangling eyeglass, to make her forget the hands that had held her so hard last night. Hot color flooded her face at the thought, making her angrier than ever. But, she promised herself, it would be the last time. In future, she would be ready for this self-confident cousin of hers who took her connivance so easily for granted. Oh yes, she would keep his secret, but keep her temper too. And if he thought she wanted the Abbey— now, at last, she smiled to herself—in six months he would learn his mistake.

She turned from the window as a scratching on the door heralded Verity Tretteign, a vision this morning in rose-colored muslin and cherry ribbons. "There you are, my dear." She gushed her way into the room, her manner in almost ludicrous contrast to last night's suspicion. "See how early I am got up on your behalf! Ross says it is my place to break the news to Papa." Odd to think that this fluffy creature was his mother. But Mrs. Tretteign was looking her over dubiously. "You will forgive me, I am sure, my dear Christina, since we are aunt and niece—how strange it sounds. Being a mamma has always seemed quite bad enough. . . . But, as I was saying, Papa is a great stickler for female elegance. . . ." She dwindled into silence, her eyes reproaching Christina's uncompromising gray gown.

"You think I won't do? I'm afraid my wardrobe is not very extensive. There was not much dressing where I am come from."

"No, no . . . of course not. Quite out in the wilds, was it? You must tell me all about yourself one day, but the question is, what's to do now? My lavender-colored muslin, perhaps? But, no, absurd. You are quite a head taller than me are you not? Such a big girl . . . I expect it is the American climate or something. Why, I really believe that you are taller than your cousin Richard."

"Richard Markham? Is he here?" Christina was not prepared to discuss her unfashionable size.

"Oh no. He hardly ever comes. He's so busy, you see, in London. He has a most important position . . . let me see, is it at the Foreign Office, or the Board of Control? I never can remember. But the fact remains that he can hardly ever be spared. What a pity you did not know to get in touch with him while you were in London. He would have seen to everything for you and prevented your arriving in such a scrambling sort of a way. Oh dear!" She started to her feet. "There's Papa's bell. Oh, what in the world shall I say to him?"

"Let me go," said Christina. "He might as well see the worst at once."

"Child! You don't know what you're saying. He'd never forgive you—or me neither. You have no idea. . . . Yes, Parkes?"

"Mr. Tretteign is asking for you, madam."

"Oh, thank you, I was afraid, I mean I expected. . . . Tell Mr. Tretteign I will be with him directly, Parkes . . . and not a word—"

"He wishes to know what all the commotion was last night," said the old man. "It roused him from his first sleep, I'm sorry to say."

"Oh, Parkes! Is it very bad?"

"It will be, ma'am, if you don't go to him directly." And then, as she fluttered out of the room, "The men who brought you last night are asking for a word with you, Miss Christina."

"The men? But why? I paid them off last night and thought them gone long since."

"And so they should be, miss, but sitting in the kitchen is what they're doing, drinking our best home-brewed and talking mighty queer, if you ask me—and asking your pardon, miss."

"Of course." Odd that a tacit alliance should already exist between them. "But—what are they saying, Parkes?"

"Why, nothing to the purpose, but a deal of hints that I don't quite like the sound of. Did something . . . happen to you on the way here?"

"Happen?" Thoughts flashed through her mind like lightning. But no need, really, for thought. Her decision was taken. Ross must be protected, the men silenced. Well then, how? Quick . . . think. No chance, surely, of the men recognizing Ross. They had never been near him; most important of all, they had no way of knowing she had bitten him. The telltale mark on his hand would mean nothing to them. "Happen?" she said again. "Why, nothing to signify. We lost our way.

There was a barricade across the road and we had to take some time pulling it down. You know how late we were. . . . But, why, Parkes, what do they say?"

"It's not what they say, miss, so much as what they don't say. A lot of talk about never coming into these parts again . . . and shrugs and groans, and something about needing danger money to come on the marsh . . ."

"A lot of talk, in fact." She had come to her decision now. "If you ask me, Parkes, they had a couple of flasks along and were drunk as owls last night. It was lucky for me they got me here at all. And now they are talking big because they are ashamed of themselves."

"It might well be that." He took it with evident relief. "But, a barricade, you say? Whereabouts would that be, miss?"

"Not far from here. I thought it must be something to do with the coastal defenses. I hope there won't be trouble about our taking it down."

"I'm sure there won't. As for the men, will you see them? I'd be glad to see the last of them, I don't mind telling you, and so would Cook."

"Of course. I'm only sorry they have been such a trouble to you. But . . . do you think my cousin Ross would help me deal with them? They think me a crazy Yankee, I'm afraid, and might pay more attention to him."

"Mr. Ross?" Was he taken aback by this apparently logical suggestion? "I—I think he's still in the breakfast parlor, miss. Shall I ask him?"

"No, thank you, Parkes. I'll ask him myself."

Ross had finished what looked to have been an enormous breakfast and was sitting, very much at his ease, reading a three-day-old copy of the *Morning Post*. He made as if to rise when Christina entered the room, then settled back into his chair and smiled at her over the paper. "You see, Cousin, I treat you quite as one of the family. Have you come, after all, to pour my coffee for me? I am desolated to disappoint you, but I am afraid you are too late."

Impossible not to admire the coolness of it. "No, Cousin." She kept her voice cool as his. "But I am glad you treat me as family, for I am come to ask a favor of you."

"A favor?" Did something close in his face? But, "Granted, of course, Cousin Christina."

"Thank you. But I wish you would call me Chris—my father always did." Now why in the world had she said that?

"Chris? Why not? It's certainly less of a mouthful. But—this favor?" Again that shuttered look. Women—favors. He clearly did not like the connection. His mother perhaps? Did she always want something?

No time to be thinking about that. "Yes," she said. "The men who drove me here haven't gone yet. Parkes says they are sitting in the kitchen throwing out dark hints of strange doings on the marsh, and danger money, and I don't know what all. Of course, what they want is simply money. I gave them quite enough last night."

"How much?" And, when she told him, "Just right. What makes them ask for more?" His bright eyes held hers in a look full of speculation and, surely, amusement.

"I told Parkes I thought they were drunk last night. We encountered a . . ." She paused, watching him.

His eyes were brighter than ever. "Yes, Cousin? You fill me with curiosity. Something out of Mrs. Radcliffe perhaps? A ghostly monk, for instance?"

"Nothing half so interesting. Merely a kind of barricade across the road. Not very well built. It did not take us long to pull it down, but of course it did make us late. I think what with that and all they had drunk they have dreamed themselves into some fantasy of adventure—lord knows what, I didn't trouble to ask Parkes."

"Quite so. And now you would like me to knock their heads together for you?"

"Precisely. I don't intend to give them any more money. I can't afford it, for one thing. And, besides, I think it would be a mistake."

"I am so sure you are right, Cousin. Were they maudlin, would you say, when you arrived?"

"I was too tired to notice. But Parkes would know."

"Of course. Our invaluable Parkes. I will have a word with him, and then—dispose of them for you. Do you wish to be present?"

"Not in the least. But I think perhaps I should." Once again their eyes met and locked and then his flickered down, just for the shadow of a second, to the red mark on his hand. She smiled at him warmly. "Your bitch bit hard, Cousin. I hope you have disposed of her."

"You think I ought to?" He had risen now and pulled the tasseled bell rope. "I wonder . . ." And then, to Parkes, who must have been hovering outside the door, "Miss Tretteign and I will see her driver and the other man in the Great Hall. Were they pretty far gone last night?"

"Oh, half seas over." Parkes seemed to take a cue. "And so Jem will testify who had to help put them to bed. They ended up on our mead, you see."

"Did they so? No wonder if they had delusions. Thank you, Parkes."

Chapter Three

THE GREAT HALL lived up to its name. Long, high, dark and draughty, it was furnished only with an immense trestle table and a few chairs. Even on this mild October day, the air struck chill and lifeless, and Christina, shivering a little in a dress that had seemed unreasonably warm elsewhere, was not surprised that the two men who awaited them already had a slightly diminished look. Her cousin had calculated well. The mere size of the room had had its effect on the two cockneys, and the sight of him, tall and commanding in his scarlet uniform coat went far to finish the business. They had expected to bully a girl, a stranger; they found themselves knuckling foreheads to one of their hereditary masters.

Their rout was swift, complete, and, Christina thought, probably lasting. Ross asked curtly what they wanted, and the coachman stammered out something about being benighted, assaulted, in terror of their lives. Some small compensation. . . . His voice dwindled away under Ross Tretteign's contemptuous stare.

"Moonshine!" said Ross. "Assaulted, were you? A strange thing that my cousin here remembers nothing of the matter. And how, pray, did you get away? Put up a gallant resistance, did you, and overpowered them without receiving so much as a scratch yourselves? A likely story to tell your friends in town, but don't be surprised if you get the name of a couple of lying drunkards and dwindle into hackney coachmen for lack of custom. I've heard about the inroads you made last night on our mead. Well, I don't blame you. They

27

should have warned you how strong it was. . . . But even so,
I know I'd not hire a coachman who suffered from delusions."

"Delusions, sir?" The coachman plucked up a bit of spirit.
"But the young lady must remember—she paid us to say
nothing."

"And thus you reward her? But . . . did you, Cousin?"

"Of course not, any more than I remember anything about
this so-called assault. I may have tipped them a little more
highly than I should have, being a stranger, but, if so, what
are they complaining about?" She could not help feeling
sorry for them as she saw the ludicrous change in their
expressions.

"Precisely." Ross took it up. "What are you complaining
about? You'd best be off before I look into the amount she
overtipped you and complain to your employers. You're from
the Bolt in Tun, in Fleet Street, are you not? I thought I knew
your hangdog faces. I don't suppose you'd want this absurd
story to get back there. Well, I'm a humane man, I'll say nothing about this piece of work, and my cousin, I know, will be
ruled by me. So, if you can but bridle your own tongues—
which, frankly, I doubt—you may not be ruined yet."

The reversal of positions was complete. The two men who
had begun by considering blackmail, found themselves thank-
ing this formidable young man for his forbearance, and shuf-
fled their way out, speeded by his Parthian shot, "I often put
up at the Bolt in Tun when I come to town. I must remember to look out for you there and see what new fantasies you
are indulging in." And then, as they pulled the huge nail-
studded door to behind them, "Well, so much for them."

"Poor things. It hardly seems fair, somehow . . ."

"Fair? What's fair in this world?"

She sighed. "Nothing, I suppose. But I do congratulate
you, Cousin. You certainly routed them, horse, foot and
guns. And now—I'm to be ruled by you, am I?"

His laugh sounded older than his looks. "I thought I saw
you rise to that one. Yes, Cousin, you are. You, too, are
going to forget that anything out of the way happened last
night. If you know what's good for you."

"Threats, Cousin?"

He shrugged. "If you wish to take it so. Or, a request, as

from one long-lost cousin to another. Should I play-act it for you. 'Dear Cousin, as a favor to me . . .' "

She could not help laughing at his ridiculous falsetto. "Oh, very well, but I hope you know what you are doing."

"Better than you do, that's one thing certain."

"Now what, exactly, do you mean by that?"

"Why, anything you like." Impatiently. "And now, if you will excuse me, I have better things to do with my morning than to be trying conclusions with a girl."

"You don't like women much, do you, Cousin?" Now why in the world had she said that?

But he only laughed his oddly cynical laugh. "You've met my mother. Tell me, why should I?"

It was not the best possible moment for Mrs. Tretteign to pop her blond beringletted head around the big door. "Oh, there you are Christina. And you, Ross?" Amazement, and something else, in her voice now. "Are you showing your cousin the house? But what an odd place to begin." Her glance dismissed the high hammer-beamed roof and intricate paneling of the big hall as beneath contempt. "Besides, she must be quite perished with cold, even in that"—a significant pause—"dress." Her own airy muslin made further description unnecessary.

Surprisingly, Ross filled the angry little pause. "She's certainly dressed more suitably for a tour of the Abbey than you are, Mamma, so why not leave us to it?"

"You mean, you really are showing her the place?"

"Why not? She must see, sometime, what a white elephant she has come home to, and what better guide than I?"

"Well, of course, if you put it like that. . . . But don't expect me to come too—and don't let him take you in the cloisters, my dear, not even in the daytime. It's not safe."

"Not *safe?*" asked Christina. "But surely in that case they should be repaired."

This time Ross's laugh was entirely gay. "You quite mistake my mother, Cousin. She does not mean that a coping stone will fall on your devoted head, merely that you may take a private haunt away with you."

"A private . . . you are laughing at me, Cousin."

"Nothing of the kind." This, sharply, from Mrs. Tretteign. "I suppose you cannot be expected to understand, child, being from such a new country, but there are things here in England that must be treated with respect."

"Well, of course . . ." she said, puzzled.

Once more Ross's harsh laugh echoed from the beamed roof. "She don't mean the king and queen, Cousin, nor yet the mother of parliaments. She's talking about the ghostly monks in the cloister."

"Ghostly monks! You cannot be serious!"

"Who, I? Well, that's another question, but, just look at my mother—she is. And, it's true, odd things have happened to people who walked in the cloisters at night—or, for the matter of that, sometimes in the daytime."

"You don't understand, my dear." Mrs. Tretteign again. "There were terrible things done here at the time of the Reformation . . . and in the cloisters, particularly."

"And, I'm afraid, by a Tretteign, among others. Some say the Tretteigns are immune to the curse on the cloisters . . . because they have a private doom saved up for them. Others that it is more risky for them to go there than for anyone else. Personally, I don't believe a word of it." Christina sighed with relief at this belated note of sanity. "But, just the same, you will save my mother, and even more so, the servants, some anxious moments by keeping away from the cloisters. Which, by the way, are also in a most lamentable state of disrepair, since no stonemason will go near them, so that in fact you might easily be killed by a coping stone before you'd even had time to be frightened by a ghostly monk."

"Ross!" His mother sounded genuinely shocked. "You must not speak so."

"No? Poor mother." And then, impatiently, "Well, Christina, do you wish to see the Abbey, or not."

"Of course I do. But . . . Grandfather?"

"Oh, I clean forgot," said Mrs. Tretteign. "That's what I came to tell you. Papa says he has no intention of seeing you until he has had time to study the letter you sent him. He doesn't seem quite sure . . ." She paused.

"Whether Christina is Christina?" put in Ross. "To be expected. Nor were we, remember?"

"But you are now?" Christina could not help asking.

"Oh yes. No one but a Tretteign . . ." He let it hang. "So have we sent for the letter, Mamma?"

"Yes, of course. . . . I should think by after dinner—"

"A pleasure postponed." Sardonically. "Well, in that case, Cousin Christina, there is nothing to prevent your enjoying a conducted tour of the estate."

"I do wish you would call me Chris."

"Chris?" said Mrs. Tretteign. "Most unsuitable."

"Well, come along then, Chris," said her son.

"You're sure you can spare the time?" Christina picked up her skirts, ready to follow him.

"But, Christina," said her aunt in an awful voice, "you surely cannot be proposing to go out without your bonnet?"

"Oh dear." She stopped in the doorway. "Must I really? Just about the place like this? I never did—"

"What you did in America," said her aunt in quelling tones, "is entirely beside the point, and the less said about it the better. In England you will, I hope, try to conduct yourself as much like a young lady as is possible. Besides, I had hesitated to mention it, but really your hair . . . I tremble to think what Papa will say."

"All Lombard Street to a china orange he says it suits her," said Ross, who had been waiting impatiently in the hallway. "And so it does. If you let them frizzle you up into modish curls, Cousin, you're a greater fool than I think you. And if you want to see the property, you will come now. I cannot be waiting all morning."

"In that case . . ." With a lingering, apologetic look for her aunt, Christina yielded to temptation and followed him.

In the hall he looked down at her soft slippers. "Pattens, however, you will need," he said, "but there are plenty of those in the back entry. The rest is mere nonsense."

She had worn pattens only once, on a brief visit to Boston, and was grateful when he exclaimed, "What a barbarian!" snatched them from her fumbling hands and put them on for her, his hands as brisk and impersonal as if, she thought wryly, he was shoeing a horse. "There, you'll soon get the knack of it." He took her arm for a second to steady her down the steep step into the stable yard, where she saw her carriage was almost ready to leave, the two men busy about harnessing up the horses. She felt, suddenly, an odd qualm. Those two were her only link with London, the outside world. What would it be like, left alone here in what, by all the evidence, seemed to be a den of smugglers?

Late in the day, though, to be thinking thus. She smiled a

carefully casual farewell to the two men and followed her cousin across the yard.

"Was it really an abbey?" she asked as he bent his head to lead the way through a low arch into what seemed total darkness.

"Good God, did your father tell you nothing? Best not let my mother hear you ask questions like that. She'd start all over again trying to prove you an imposter."

"She really thought that?" It was hard, somehow, to believe.

"Of course, since it suited her." Dismissing it. "Now, here we have one of the chapels of the abbey church. Not much left of it, as you can see."

"No." Her eyes, used now to the half light, took in the bricked-up windows, the rough floor, the general air of dissolution and decay.

"Our Great Hall," he went on, "was once the presbytery. It's the only part of the old building that's still in use. The rest is as you see. What remains at all, that is. The greater part of the old buildings was torn down to be used as materials for the Grange."

She shivered, partly with cold. "A ruthless business. And the monks?"

"Some of them settled happily enough into lay life. Some of them . . . well, I'll leave my mother to tell you those stories. But I suppose you are longing to see the haunted cloister?"

"Indeed I am. But is it really . . . ?"

His laugh was mocking. "Afraid?"

"With *you*, Cousin?" Her voice matched the mockery in his.

He made her a little, burlesqued bow. "I am inexpressibly flattered. We will not, however, tell my mother we have come here, nor will you come again, without my permission." As he spoke, he took a key from his chain to unlock a small, inconspicuous door in a corner of the gloomy room.

Following him through it, she noticed that it was a modern improvisation, strongly if roughly made; then she stopped to gasp with pleasure at the contrast on the other side of it. The cloisters were a ruin, but a beautiful one. On three sides they were open to the sky, and sunshine slanted down to make shadow patterns on gray stone. In the center, green grass, rankly growing, was filigreed here and there with the purple of wild asters. Where they stood, the walk was still roofed in a succession of bays, each with its central gargoyle, some laughing, some sad, all fantastic.

"But it's beautiful. And so quiet . . ." It was true; the heavy outside walls seemed to protect them completely from the sounds of the household, and even the voice of the sea was nothing, here, but a contented background murmur. He had stopped, as if expecting her merely to look and then return by the same door, but she moved forward, studying the gargoyles. "History," she said. "I never saw anything like this before. May we make the round?" she turned back to ask him.

"I suppose so." Reluctantly. "There's no other way out—now."

"What are the doors at the other corners, then?"

He flung open the one they had reached, which hung crazily on its hinges. "Doors to danger." His voice sounded oddly loud in this quiet place. And then, as she peered past him into darkness, "Careful!" His violent movement of the door had dislodged a big stone high up in the roof and it fell with a crash, uncomfortably close to them. "You see." He closed the door. "I think that's really why the cloisters got their bad name. They were used for a storehouse for a while. There were . . . accidents. Easy to blame a set of ghostly monks for the results of human carelessness. But, just the same, we keep them locked now."

"How sad. It's so beautiful," she said again.

"Beautiful—and dangerous. Don't decide this is a romantic place to come and indulge in maiden meditations."

"But the cloister itself seems safe enough." She had indeed been thinking what an oasis of quiet this might prove in a strange household.

"It may be." They were back now at the corner they had started from. "But, aside from anything else, we'd have the servants leaving in a body. You may be too modern a young American to believe in ghosts, but the servants are terrified. They think I bear a charmed life."

"You come here then?"

"When it's necessary." He pulled the door shut behind them and locked it. "But you will not even try to, Christina. Is that understood?"

"I should find it difficult, I can see." She watched him replace the key on his watch chain.

"Yes, so don't try. Your word?"

"Word of a Tretteign?"

If he noticed the echo of his own words the night before, he gave no sign. "Precisely." He led her back through the forlorn little chapel and out once more into the stable yard. "Your friends are gone, I see."

"So they are." Once again that odd little qualm.

"So—here you are." Disconcertingly, he seemed to have read her thought. "And now what would you like to see?"

"Oh, the sea, please. It seems odd to be so little aware of it."

"You won't think so when you've been here through the winter. I don't know what pious freak made the monks build here in the first place, but of all the barbarous situations . . . well, come along and you shall see." He turned and led the way, not through the house as she had expected, but under the arched entrance of the stable yard and so around to the front entrance. "Odd, isn't it?"

"It certainly is." She had not seen this view of the house in daylight and was surprised to find that the drive by which she had arrived last night was the dividing line between grass and a sea of shingle. On its left, a few sheep were nibbling at short marsh turf, on its right lay the desolate shingle waste, with beyond it the sound of the invisible sea. The house itself was just a little higher than the surrounding country.

"We're on the tip of a spit of higher ground," Ross explained. "The story is that when the monks built here, soon after the Conquest, it was a peninsula, like Dungeness now. They were Normans, of course, perhaps they felt safer so. But the sea betrayed them and here we are, between the marsh and the shingle. A bleak home you've come to, Cousin. As you see, Mr. Tretteign does not exactly believe in landscape gardening."

After her many glimpses, on the way down, of gentlemen's mansions lurking in Palladian splendor among carefully landscaped grounds, she had indeed been surprised by the way marsh and shingle alike were allowed to come right up to the house, but a few stunted bushes, blown permanently sideways by the wind from the sea, provided at least part of the explanation. "It does seem a pity about the cloisters." She spoke her thought involuntarily.

"You will forget about the cloisters." Iron in his voice now. Once again with a little qualm, half fear, half pleasure, she recognized last night's bandit. How strange it was. . . . "You wanted to see the sea," he went on, "so . . ." And, turning, he led the way across the broad carriage sweep, around the corner of the house and up a few steps to the paved terrace she had seen from her bedroom window. "There's your sea."

She joined him at the gray-stone wall, leaned her elbows on it and gazed across the shingle waste. "But can't one get down to it?"

"Not in pattens. It's farther, too, than you think."

"Oh." She could see a ridged path running from somewhere to their right. "Where does the path start from?"

"From the other side of the Great Hall. I'll take you one day, though you'll find it disappointing enough. Sand, at low tide, and weed, and, if you're lucky, a preventive officer."

"Preventive? Oh—against smugglers." Furious, she felt herself going fiery red. Why should the subject embarrass her, not him?

But he had pulled out his watch. "And now, if you will excuse me, I have a company of the rawest marsh boobies you ever dreamed of to drill into some kind of shape."

"And I've been keeping you? I am so sorry, you should have said . . ." And yet, how fantastic: smuggler at night, captain of Volunteers in the daytime.

"No hurry." He shrugged. "They can wait. One does not greet a long-lost"—why the pause?—"relative every day. Surely you must have more questions, Cousin?" A touch of mockery now?

"Of course I have. What's that point?" She indicated the long low spit of land on their left. "And that one?" This time it was the higher cliff far off to the right.

"Dungeness—and Fairlight. Rye, where you came from last night, is set back on the marsh. You can't see it from here, but there is Rye Harbor, its port since the sea retreated."

"What are they doing there?" From her bedroom window that morning she had noticed and wondered at the signs of activity.

"They plan to build what they call a Martello Tower to keep Bonaparte at bay."

"You think it won't?" There had been no mistaking the irony of his tone.

"I think it a great waste of time and money, like all the other panic preparations. Boney won't land, Cousin. I doubt if he even means to try. No need to imagine yourself fighting a gallant rearguard action from your bedroom window. You're as safe here as you were in America. Safer, I expect."

"So do I." She thought of her father's death, shivered, and made herself go on. "But they talk of nothing but invasion in London. Is it really all a hum?"

"I think so. What's he got at Boulogne? Flat-bottomed boats! Thousands of them, I grant you. But who cares whether he really has three thousand boats and a hundred and twenty thousand men ready to invade, as he claims, since his chances of getting them over here are negligible. Give him a flat calm and a thick fog and he might manage—always provided that the Channel Fleet had been miraculously stricken with the palsy, but otherwise . . . no, Cousin, if you want to fret, think of a serious subject, like how your grandfather will receive you."

"Our grandfather, you mean?"

Now, oddly, when she did not mean to, she seemed to have touched him on the raw. He colored. "Of course." He turned and led the way back around the house.

The boy Jem was waiting on the carriage sweep, holding the reins of a big gray horse. "Oh, there you are, Mr. Ross. I was beginning to wonder . . ."

"Thanks, Jem. . . . You'll excuse me?" This to Christina, and then without more ado he swung himself up into the saddle and trotted away down the drive.

Left alone, Christina stood for a little while, gazing after him. Was she quiet mad? How could she have accepted, so easily, this tacit complicity in his crimes? No use, by now, to try and pretend to herself that she might be mistaken. Several times he had as good as admitted to being last night's brigand. Why was she not already on her way to the nearest magistrate? But, of course, from what she had already learned of English country life, the chances were high that her own grandfather held that position. And Ross was out, this minute, drilling the Volunteers. It was all fantastic.

Go to the preventive officer on the beach? She remembered the glint in her cousin's eye when he mentioned him. It had been almost a challenge, but one he had been sure she would never accept. No doubt, with his tall good looks, and his expectations, he must be the beau of the district and used to charming his way with females. Well, she must endeavor by her manner to show him that American young women were less easily bamboozled; that if she was prepared to keep his secret, it was merely from family feeling.

Having come to this satisfactory conclusion, she found herself impatient to put it into practice. The morning dragged out interminably. Her aunt was absorbed in trying to make herself a silver-gilt reticule according to the instructions given in *The Lady's Magazine* and making, Christina thought, a sad botch of it. At last she sighed and dropped it disconsolately on the table. "It's no use. It will never do. I can't think where I have gone wrong. And I was counting on carrying it if ever we go to a ball again. Papa is so mean—oh, Christina, you won't tell him I said that!"

"Of course I won't." Useless to be angry with the poor, grumbling creature.

"I'm sure you won't." A sharp little glance. "Nor would it be the best way to his favor. Of all things, he says, he hates a talebearer."

Inevitably, Christina found herself wondering about the occasion for this remark. She picked up the poor little travesty of a purse. "Let me see." Anything to change the subject. She bent over to read the instructions but found the fine print almost impossible to decipher in the dim light of the room. "This is the darkest house I ever saw." She moved impatiently over to the window. "Why do you not ring for working candles, Aunt?"

"Working candles? In the daytime? Papa would have a fit. You'll get used to it—the house, I mean. Of course it is dark —I remember how gloomy it seemed to me when I first came here . . . lord, what a long time ago! It's on account of having as few as possible windows facing the sea—and you'll understand that when the winter winds begin to blow."

"It seems a pity," said Christina absently, "with that splendid view of the sea. Ah, now I have it. It goes like this." Her deft fingers twisted the giltwork first this way, then that.

"There." And then, cutting short her aunt's enthusiastic thanks, "Will my cousin be back before I see Grandfather?"

"Ross? Why did I never think of him! Of course, he is gone to Rye too, to drill his Volunteers. He will doubtless fetch your letter and Thomas will have his journey for his pains. And Papa will be so angry if he finds out. Of all things, he abominates waste. He really is—between ourselves and since I see I can trust you, my dear—well, just a little mean. If you knew what I have to live on! I only hope he sees fit to give you a proper allowance, because how we are to outfit you suitably otherwise is more than I can imagine." Once again an expressive glance told Christina what her aunt thought of her plain gray dress. "I hope, in a way, that Ross *does* bring the letter, because if anyone can, he will be able to make Papa see sense, much more so than Richard. It's the strangest thing . . ."

"Strange? But why? His heir?"

"Ross!" Bright spots of color outlined the rouge on Mrs. Tretteign's cheekbones. "He's not Papa's heir."

"Not? But, Father said . . ."

"Oh, you're thinking of the entail. Of course, there is no way you should know, or your father either, since he never saw fit to tell us where he was—the entail was broken, years ago. . . . At least, well, there was an understanding, and of course Ross—such a stubborn boy—I never thought it should be considered as binding—signed under duress, but I might have known—Ross honored it as soon as he came of age. And now Papa has absolute right to dispose of everything as he pleases. You really did not know?" Another of her sharp little glances.

"As you say, how could I have?"

"You are come most timely, just the same. Since Papa's last illness he has actually been talking about making a will. He even got his lawyer down from London once—and then felt better, changed his mind, and sent him back again. Good gracious!" She gave a little start as the clock on the chimney piece struck twice. "Two o'clock and not a sign of the nuncheon I ordered for us. I don't know what this household is coming to. Mrs. Emeret takes no more notice of me than if I was . . ." She stopped for a moment. "It would be different if Ross were here . . . they all dote on him. But I should have thought in your honor. . . . Ring the bell, there's a good girl."

Christina did so and a parlor maid presently appeared, looked scared in answer to Mrs. Tretteign's question, and then stammered out, "Please, mum, Mrs. Emeret says the master's given strict orders about no more midmorning snacks—he calls them, mum. He says dinner's good enough for him and must be good enough for his household. If you please, mum, and excusing me." And she got herself out of the room in a way that suggested a healthy respect, at least for her mistress's temper.

"Well! What did I tell you!" Mrs. Tretteign's color was unbecomingly higher than ever. "You never saw such a household! And as for Mrs. Emeret, there's no reasoning with her."

Christina could hardly believe her ears. "But surely, you, as the mistress of the house—"

"Who, I? Don't make me laugh. When Ross signed the waiver to the entail, he signed away any rights I might have had here. I might as well be dead, for all the consideration I get. Sometimes I wish I was! And as for Ross, he just stands by and sees me insulted."

"Well!" Suddenly Christina found herself angry. "I, for one, am famished." She gave the bell another firm tug, and when the girl reappeared, looking more frightened than ever, she said simply, "Tell Mrs. Emeret I would like a word with her, if you please."

"Christina! You can't!" Was it the first time her aunt had addressed her by her Christian name?

"Can't I? Just watch, Aunt. Father told me, when I took over the housekeeping, that the one thing I must never endure was insolence from the servants . . . it's quite a problem where I come from, you know, since they are all quite as good as oneself. But . . . it can be dealt with . . . Ah, Mrs. Emeret?" A portly black-gowned figure had swung open the door and sailed into the room like a man-of-war to battle. "Allow me to introduce myself. I am Miss Tretton—and, I am hungry."

If Mrs. Emeret had been wondering how to greet this interloper, she found herself somehow decided. A low curtsy, and, "It's good to see you home, Miss Tretteign, but, the master has given orders—"

"Very nonsensical ones," said Christina coolly, "and so I

will tell him when I have the opportunity. In the meantime, are you or are you not the housekeeper?"

"Of course I am, miss."

"Then there is nothing to prevent you, I take it, from serving a light nuncheon to Mrs. Tretteign and me. Something quite simple will do—I don't suppose your household rises to anything more. A little cold meat, perhaps, some fruit? A glass of wine would do me good, and you, too, Aunt, I am sure."

"Wine!" Horrified.

"What, have you none?" asked Christina sweetly. "I am so sorry to lay bare the defects of your housekeeping."

"Oh, as to having it—"

"Well, then—and quickly, if you please. I am hoping to see my grandfather shortly and should be sorry to have to tell him I was starving in his house."

The threat was decisive. Mrs. Emeret, bridled, started to say something, changed her mind and withdrew.

"Christina, how could you?" asked her aunt, somewhere between awe and terror. "Beyond question she will give in her notice, and then what shall we do? You have no idea how hard it is to get anyone to come and live here on the marsh."

"I devoutly hope she does," said Christina. "A mannerless woman and a deplorable housekeeper. Look!" She ran a finger across the face of a big, gold-framed mirror and left a shining mark on the dull surface. "I cannot imagine why you have borne with her so long. As to the housekeeping, I have been wondering what on earth I should find to do here. Now I know. I made my father comfortable. I hope I shall be able to do as much for you."

She spoke more cheerfully than she felt, and a long, gloomy afternoon confirmed her fears about life at the Grange. Over their nuncheon, her aunt embarked on a cross-examination about her life in America that she found at once difficult to answer and hard to bear. It was no better when Mrs. Tretteign turned to the subject of her mother and sister. "You hear nothing from them?" Her eyes were bright with curiosity.

"From France? Not for years." The tears she had shed years ago, over the letters that never came, made her aunt's inquisitive sympathy still less endurable.

But the meal was over at last, and Mrs. Tretteign retired to

her room, leaving Christina to her own devices. Rain was
beating against the window panes. She abandoned her hopes
of continuing her outdoor exploration and wandered instead
through the high, dark downstairs rooms of the Grange. They
were dreary enough in the half light of small panes and wet
October and her heart sank at the idea of a lifetime spent
moldering here. No, she told herself firmly—not a lifetime,
six months. After that she would be her own mistress, free of
her promise to her father. But at the moment, with a wet afternoon stretching endlessly before her, six months seemed
like a lifetime. The morning room, where a fire provided the
only cheerful note, offered no prospect of occupation beyond
her aunt's collection of fashion magazines. She looked further
and found, at the end of the hall, a smaller room, half study,
half office, with one wall given over to bookshelves. It
seemed, at first, a discouraging collection enough, composed
mainly of sermons and odd volumes of *The Spectator,* but at
last, in a dark corner, she hit upon a gold mine—the complete works of Henry Fielding.

Two hours later, her aunt found her curled up in a chair in
the morning room, her book held up to catch the ebbing
light. "Reading?" She made it sound a most unusual activity.
"What can you have found worth spoiling your eyes for?"

"Oh—just a novel," Christina closed the book, anticipating
trouble.

"A novel?" And then, on a note of horror, "Good God,
you cannot be reading *Tom Jones!*"

"Why not? Father let me. He said Mr. Fielding was a considerable moralist in his own way."

"You cannot be serious! I can only say, I was never so
shocked in my life. But I suppose it's all of a piece—I can
only warn you, miss, that no young lady of any breeding here
in England would ever mention such a book, still less think
of reading it."

"I wonder," said Christina. And then, "I'm sorry, Aunt. I
promise I won't be caught reading it, but it is so entertaining."

"Christina!"

"I'm sorry," she said again, and then, to change the subject, "It's getting dark already." She put her book down and
moved over to the window. "Ross must be back," she said,
"there's his horse. I never heard him come."

"You don't hear things in this house," said her aunt. "The walls are so thick. It's quiet as well as dark. They call it that, you know?"

"What?"

"The Dark House. The marsh people do. Most of the living rooms look inward, you see, on to the stable yard, so there are seldom any lights showing at night."

"And a very absurd arrangement it is," said Christina. "Unhealthy, too, if you ask me."

"Don't say that to Papa when he sends for you. . . . Ah —yes, Parkes?"

"Mr. Tretteign will see Miss Tretteign now." The old man was at his most formal.

"Does he want me, Parkes?" Mrs. Tretteign sounded nervous.

"No, ma'am." Oddly uncompromising. And then, "This way, Miss Christina."

Old Mr. Tretteign occupied a whole suite of rooms on the second floor at the back of the house, and Christina, following Parkes through a dark little antechamber, saw that they too must look out on the stable yard. But there the likeness to the rest of the house ended. When Parkes opened a second door, it was to reveal a blaze of light. The big room was aglow with candles in branched, glass candlesticks. Deep-golden curtains, already drawn against the gathering dusk, intensified the mellow light, as did the fire on the hearth. A big, winged armchair drawn up close to it had its back to her, and facing it, negligently leaning against the chimney piece, her cousin Ross seemed to dominate the room. Her heart gave an odd little lurch at the sight of him. Well, of course, she had assumed that her first interview with her grandfather would be tête-à-tête.

"Well, don't just stand there. Come in, girl, and let's have a look at you." The invisible occupant of the armchair showed no sign of rising to greet her.

"Yes, Grandfather." She moved forward to stand beside Ross and look down at the withered old man, who sat, wrapped in a knitted shawl, tiny in the huge chair.

" 'Yes, Grandfather!' " the harsh voice mimicked hers. "Expect me to welcome you with open arms, I suppose." His thin right hand tapped angrily on the letter he held in his left. "Wrote me a letter full of pretty phrases, eh, and thought to turn me up sweet? And signed it Tretton!" His voice cracked with anger.

"That's my name. I'm sorry if you don't like it, but Father changed it, years ago. He said fancy spellings and America didn't suit."

"Just like his impudence. Nothing was ever good enough for Christopher. Not his home, not his family, not even his name. Well, miss, you'll change it back now, d'you hear."

"I'm sorry, Grandfather, I'm afraid I can't."

"Can't? Won't, you mean!"

"If you prefer it that way. But—can't was what I said. Father left his estate to me as Christina Tretton. That's my name."

"His estate, eh? That's rich!" A harsh cackle of laughter shook him. "A log cabin, five cows and his rifle, I suppose. And, besides, what about your sister—your mother for the matter of that?"

"They went back to France, you know, sir, four years ago, after Bonaparte seized power in '99. My father is a friend of his wife's."

"A Frenchwoman and a friend of Joséphine de Beauharnais! There's a striking recommendation for you. Trust my son Christopher to make a fool of himself."

"I wish you will remember, sir, that you are speaking of my mother. And—my father is dead."

"And the more fool he for trusting the Indians. Or for going there in the first place." And then in response to a little angry movement on her part, "Oh very well, we'll say no more about it. Your mother had more sense when she went back to France, and took your sister. Why didn't you go?"

"I preferred to stay with my father."

"Preferred!" Once again he contrived a falsetto parody of her voice. "And now you prefer to come here and be a charge on me—and begin your visit by getting rid of my housekeeper, who has served me faithfully for twenty years. What have you to say about that, hey?"

"Why, that I didn't discharge her, Grandfather, though if she has seen fit to give in her notice, I'm glad to hear it. Her manner to Mrs. Tretteign left me no alternative but to speak as I did. I am only amazed that you have tolerated her so long." Here a glance part explanation, part apology, for Ross, but his brooding face was turned toward their grandfather.

"And as for serving you faithfully—if insolence and dirt are your idea of good service, they most certainly are not mine."

She stopped, taken aback both by her own vehemence and by his reaction to it. Once again he had gone off into the long, wheezing laugh that shook his whole body. "Listen to her!" he appealed to Ross. "A proper spitfire, ain't she? Turns up bold as brass in the middle of the night and starts telling us all our business first thing next morning. Well, now, Miss Know-all, having got rid of Mrs. Emeret for me, how do you suggest I set about finding a replacement for her? Have you heard what they call this house on the marsh? The Dark House. They don't come here willingly, I can tell you. And —for our part—we don't much like strangers, do we, Ross?"

"Not overmuch." Ross turned a darkling stare on her. Then, suddenly, he laughed. "I wager I know what my cousin has in mind, though. Going to take us over, Cousin Chris?"

Now, suddenly, she felt herself ill at ease. "Well, I had thought of it." And then, impulsively, to her grandfather, "If you would let me try, sir. I have looked after my father— ever since Mother left. I would do my possible to have everything as you wish it, and, truly, I do not wish to be merely a charge and a burden on you. And, besides, it would be something to do."

"Find it dull already, do you?" The thin voice was sardonic. "Well, remember, no one invited you to come here. What do you think, Ross? Shall we risk discomfort and spoiled dinners, or shall we go on our bended knees to Mrs. Emeret?"

"I doubt if it would answer," said Ross dryly. "Jem tells me she has her boxes packed already!"

"In that case, girl, you had best see to it that you get her keys from her before she goes. And now, I'm worn out with all this chatter. You may go, both of you. Oh"—an afterthought—"what did we pay Emeret, Ross?"

"Fifty pounds a year, sir, and her keep."

"Hmmm . . ." A long pause. "By rights, Christina should have less, being a novice. But since she is a member of the family. . . . What do you say to forty-five pounds my dear?"

Christina could hardly help laughing. "Thank you, Grandfather," she managed meekly.

Chapter Four

THERE WAS nearly mutiny in the servants' hall when Christina took over the housekeeping. Lazy and venal herself, Mrs. Emeret had had two blind eyes for the corruption of others. Christina had to dismiss two housemaids and a groom in the first week she was there.

"And what if you can't replace them?" Mrs. Tretteign, too delicate, she explained, to concern herself with domestic affairs, had done nothing but grumble at Christina's activities; had done so, Christina suspected, where it did most harm—to the servants themselves.

"We'll still be better off." Christina was checking through the household accounts. "The amount of work they did— Betty and I could get through it in a morning."

"Most unsuitable," said Mrs. Tretteign.

"Well, I've got to do something. It's no use, Aunt, I wasn't raised to be a lady and do nothing. I'd far rather clean out the stillroom. D'you know, we found quince preserve dated 1794!"

"Was it any good?" How quietly Ross moved. She had had no idea he had joined them.

"Delicious. . . . Ross, you're drenched. Does it rain still?"

"Of course. It always does in November." His dark hair was sleeked down close to his face, his cheeks flushed with exercise. "Do you see now, Chris, why the house was built facing away from the sea?"

She laughed. "I do indeed. As it is, the wind gets in everywhere. It's no wonder there are stories of ghosts and hauntings."

"And you are attacking the ghosts, like a colony of spiders, with a New England broom and scouring powder?" Ross had crossed the room to look out at the stable yard. Now, over his shoulder, "I had a complaint about you today, Cousin."

"I'm not surprised."

"No. I have no doubt you were right to dismiss those two girls, but of course it's hard . . ." He left it at that.

"Hard! It's monstrous!" Mrs. Tretteign put down the book of fashion plates she had been studying. "Sally's mother came to see me this morning. She says they're starving."

"For lack of the five pounds Sally used to get a year?" Christina asked. "Or because they miss the perquisites she used to take home? Now that I can believe, Aunt. I know now why we could never afford working candles. If they had but been lighted for five minutes, they'd be out of their holders next morning and shared out in the servants' hall. We must have been keeping half the marsh in wax candles."

"Well—and why not? That ever I should live to see such cheese-paring Yankee ways at Tretteign Grange. No, wait a minute, miss. Try to show a little respect for your elders. I know I'm only a useless invalid, whom nobody minds, but I've a warning for you just the same, and I consider it my duty to give it. You're making enemies, you know. Don't blame me, girl, if you run into trouble one of these fine days, on those walks of yours to the beach. And don't expect me to be sorry for you either. It will serve you richly right. Walking alone! Miss Tretteign of Tretteign Grange!"

"Not Tretteign, Aunt. Tretton. And as to walking alone, well, I'm a Yankee, remember, and used to taking care of myself. I've walked in places where you'd not like to go with a regiment of guards."

"I believe you." Mrs. Tretteign shuddered. "And the less said about it the better. Ross, cannot you persuade your cousin?"

"No, ma'am." To Christina's relief his voice was firm. "You know we've been into this before, many times. Since we've no horse for Chris, and since she's such an active young lady, the only thing left for her is these walks of hers along the beach. I promise you, no harm will come to her. She's made friends as well as enemies. Your medicines seem to be powerful ones, Chris. From what I hear on the marsh, my worst fear for you is that you'll end up burning as a witch."

She laughed. "If that's the worst! Yes, I've some useful things with me, and lord knows they're needed here on the marsh, with no doctor nearer than Rye. My nurse was an Indian woman, you know. She taught me a great deal—"

"Ugh!" said Mrs. Tretteign. "Don't talk about it. Unspeakable things, I have no doubt!"

"Just herbs, Aunt. If it would only stop raining, I would go out and replenish my supply."

But the wind and rain continued, day after day, night after night, worrying last leaves from the stunted bushes that grew all sideways on the marsh. Even in the house, the wind seemed to get in everywhere. Frayed old tapestries lifted from the walls as one walked by; curtains blew out unaccountably over closed windows; even the thin carpeting in some of the rooms seemed alive on the floor.

"Invasion weather again." Ross took the cup of coffee Christina handed him across the breakfast table. "Are you alarmed at finding yourself in what may prove the front line?"

"Should I be?"

"You'd think so if you'd come to Hastings with me yesterday. They were taking a census of wagons suitable for evacuating women and children when the enemy lands. Delicious coffee, Chris. What magic have you used on the cook?"

"Simple. I let her use enough of the beans. But—you don't seriously think the French will come?"

"I don't know. I thought not, this summer, but these bungling attempts of ours on Boulogne and Le Havre must have put new heart into them. There's been no more talk for a while of disaffection in their troops over there. I know one thing—if I was Bonaparte, I'd come tomorrow. Look at us! Piles of bricks where there should be fortresses . . . pikes in the churches . . . volunteers without muskets . . . cavalry without horses! Yes, Parkes?"

"Mr. Tretteign would like a word with you, sir, if you please."

"The royal summons." He finished his coffee and rose to his feet. "I hope you've not been overspending on the housekeeping, Chris. The food's so good these days I've been expecting a complaint."

She laughed. "Don't worry. What I've spent in one place, I've saved in others. I hope to show a profit over the month, and so you can tell Grandfather, if he asks."

"What an economist! I cannot imagine how we struggled on without you. Indeed, it seems already as if you had been here forever."

"Does it? How flattering!" But he had gone. She sighed and finished her own coffee. It should be satisfactory to be taken so comfortably for granted by this tall cousin whose dislike of women was, she knew, something of a byword in the district. "Here forever," indeed. Angrily, she poured coffee she did not want and then made herself drink it so as not to hurt Cook's feelings. And yet she, too, sometimes felt as if she had been here forever, fighting her battle with dust and carelessness in the dark house that had seemed so sinister and had proved so dull.

Had it all been imagination, then? Had she dreamed that her cousin Ross led a band of smugglers? She paused, the cup halfway to her lips. How did he know there was no talk now of disaffection among the French troops around Boulogne? She had certainly seen nothing about it in the papers, which she read quite as thoroughly as he did.

"Chris! Oh, there you are still." Re-entering the room, Ross looked oddly disturbed. "A message for you from your grandfather. My cousin Richard's room must be prepared . . . he arrives this evening. And another room—one of the best guest chambers—for our lawyer, Mr. Foxton."

"Oh?"

"You may well say, 'oh.' It could not have come at a worse time. Bound to happen of course, once you arrived. But today of all days." He took a restless turn across the room, then came back to stand over her. "Do me a kindness, Chris?"

"Of course." Absurd to be so pleased.

"You've been using Richard's room have you not?"

"Yes." She had been thinking about this.

"Don't turn out for him. He's merely a visitor. Stay where you are."

"I hardly like to. And—why?"

"As a favor to me. And—blame it on me, if you like. Put him in one of the wings overlooking the yard. Say I told you the northeaster gives him the migraine. Very likely it does.

You never saw such a man for looking after himself. Say anything you like. But don't put him on the front of the house. Or Foxton either. And"—a hand up in warning— "don't ask me why."

"Will he be angry?"

"Not Richard. He's far too complete a lady's man. Such a perfect gentleman! And such a gossip. Don't say anything to him, Chris, that you don't mind having all over town when he gets back."

Was this another warning? She smiled up at him. "You make me quite long to meet my cousin. But what's it all about, Ross?"

"The old man's will, of course. He hasn't changed it for quite six months." He smiled his sudden, heart-warming smile. "No use looking so mutinous. He's quite right to want to put you in. You deserve it for the coffee, if for nothing else."

"Thank you." She returned his smile a little tremulously. "But, believe me, I don't want anything."

He laughed. "Oddly, I believe you. But try to convince my mother."

It was another warning. And indeed Mrs. Tretteign was more than usually fretful all day. Christina had begun to hope that she had grown used to her presence and had even begun to forgive her for taking over the housekeeping, and, worse still, making a success of it. Today's stream of complaints and criticisms undeceived her. Nothing she did was right, nothing she said was welcome. The last straw came when Mrs. Tretteign learned she was not intending to move out of Richard Markham's room.

"Put Richard in the west wing?" she exclaimed. "What can you be thinking of? He and Ross have had the two front rooms ever since they were tiny. You cannot mean to oust him from his own room." Not even you, said her tone.

"Ross says the northeaster gives Richard the migraine. Besides, there's so much to do today. And he'll be here only a day or two, Grandfather says. He can't be spared from the Board of Control for longer."

"Dear Richard." Luckily, she was easily diverted. "Such a hard worker. Not at all like my Ross. Idling around at home as if the world was his oyster. I warned him that if things go wrong today it will be entirely his own fault."

"But Ross works harder than anyone. You know he has the entire running of the estate now Grandfather's confined to his room. And his work with the Volunteers—"

"And his nights out with his drinking friends in Rye," interrupted his mother. "I know how often he uses the side entrance below his room, if you don't. I suppose it was his idea to put poor Richard way off in the west wing for fear he prove a less incurious neighbor than you. If word of his carryings-on were to get to Papa I don't like to think what would be the end of it. Not, of course, that Richard would lower himself to tell tales on his cousin, but it's just like Ross to think he might. Of all the careless, inconsiderate, reckless sons a mother might be plagued with—"

"Who, me?" Ross sauntered into the room and dropped a letter into Christina's lap. "For you, Cousin. I did not know you had friends in town."

"Nor have I." She opened the short letter and read it rapidly. Then, aware of Mrs. Tretteign's inquisitive glance, she felt bound to explain. "Merely some business connected with my father's estate."

Ross laughed. "Don't tell me you're really an heiress, Chris."

"Don't you remember? The log cabin and the five cows? Will Richard and Mr. Foxton be here in time for dinner, do you think?"

"I'm sure they will, since Grandfather told them to."

"He must be a rich man if even London lawyers jump to his bidding."

"You'd think so, but—I wonder . . ."

"What do you mean, Ross?" His mother's voice was sharper than usual. "What are you trying to suggest?"

"Why . . . that Grandfather's famous meanness may have a more practical basis than we have suspected. I don't altogether like the way things are going on the estate. It's not like him to starve his land."

"And he has been? Ross, you alarm me unspeakably."

"I rather thought I would," said her son.

To Christina's amazement, her grandfather sent for her that afternoon and announced that he would come down to dinner for the first time since she had arrived. "Are you sure you are strong enough?" she asked.

"Of course I am, girl. I've always been strong enough for what I want to do. When I'm not, I hope I'll be dead. You've ordered a full dinner, I hope, that won't shame us before those Londoners? I won't have it thought we don't do things in proper style, even if we do live miles from anywhere. Tretteign Grange has always had a name for hospitality . . . it shan't lose it under me."

Since these were the first visitors who had entered the Grange since her arrival, she could not help but find this faintly comic, but "No, Grandfather," she said meekly.

" 'No, Grandfather.' " It amused him to exaggerate her faint trace of an accent. "Sound meek as a mouse, don't you, miss? And keeping your own counsel all the time. I've seen you sit there and think about us . . . don't think I haven't. What have you decided, hey? What d'you think of your Cousin Ross?" And then, mercifully, before she had contrived an answer. "What do you think of me, for the matter of that? And—I wonder—what will you think of our city beau, Richard? As for the dinner—I will say for you, it won't shame us, no need for me to ask. D'you know what we've saved since Mrs. Emeret left?"

"Yes, Grandfather." Her sparkling eyes challenged him to imitate her.

"I thought you did. No fool, are you, girl? Worth both your cousins put together, and you can tell 'em I said so. Can't think how your father came to get you, but I'm grateful to him just the same. Never thought I would be. Oh, tell Parkes we'll have the champagne from the far end of the wine cellar—he'll know which one I mean. And plenty of it. You're going to need it. And now—I'm tired."

She was too busy for the rest of the afternoon to waste much time in speculation about what he had said to her. By the time the rooms in the west wing were ready and the table laid in the big draughty dining room they had never used since she came, the shadows were closing around the house.

"It's lucky we keep town hours." She had met Ross in the main hall.

"Yes, they're later than I expected. Perhaps they have lost their way, like you."

She flashed him a darkling glance. "I do hope not! Grandfather orders full dress by the way." For Ross was still in blue coat and buckskins.

"I was just about to say the same thing to you."

"Thank you! I am on my way to change now." She brushed past him and ran lightly up the stairs to her room. Why did she let him irritate her so? She lit the candles on her dressing table and surveyed herself impatiently in the glass. Her stuff dress was as plain as a dress could be, and as uncompromising. Well, she had intended it to be. The muslin Betty had laid out on her bed was little better and she shivered as she thought of the draughts in the big dining room. With a little, impatient gesture she picked up the dress, moved over to the big mahogany wardrobe and reached far to the back. There! She brought out a calico bag and tenderly removed a deep-red velvet dress from the hanger inside it. Holding it up against her she returned to the glass. Yes, champagne might not help, but this would.

Betty tapped at the door ten minutes later. "I'm so sorry I'm late, miss . . ." And then, "Ooh, just look at you!"

"Do you like it?" She had finished brushing her dark hair and smiled at Betty's reflection beside her own in the glass.

"Like it, miss? I should just about think I do. You look different, somehow"—she reached for a word—"stately."

"Thank you." She picked up a thin gold chain from which hung a miniature of her father. "Fasten this for me, would you, Betty?"

"Gladly, miss, but won't you be cold in the dining hall?" Her glance rested on the white expanse of shoulder revealed by the low-cut gown. "Take a shawl, do."

"No, thank you. I've worn this dress on colder nights than this." For a moment, her eyes clouded with tears as she thought of the last time she had worn it. But she had promised herself not to look back, not to think about Father, most of all not to think about his death. She rose from her stool, and the heavy velvet sighed around her. "What's that?"

"It sounds as if they've come, miss. They won't half have to hurry changing if they're not to be late for dinner. And the fur'll fly if they are."

"I'd best go down and hurry them. I'm sure my aunt is not ready yet."

"Not her." And then, on a note of pure joy, "I just can't wait till she sees you, miss."

Pausing at the top of the big stairway, Christina saw that Ross had changed even more quickly than she had. He was below her in the hall, greeting a large man and a slight one, both heavily coated against the cold November air. Now he looked up and saw her. "And here is our cousin. Chris! You will make me ashamed not to have gone the whole hog and worn knee breeches."

If she was disappointed at his reaction, she took care not to show it, and imitated his rallying tone. "Nonsense. You know perfectly well you said the other day your court dress no longer fits you."

"Ross never would take the trouble to look a gentleman!" The slighter of the two strangers advanced to the foot of the stairway. "Cousin Christina, I am enchanted to make your acquaintance. But why did nobody tell me?" With a courtly gesture, he picked up her hand and kissed it. "If I had known, I should have been down here long since to pay my respects."

"Known?" She was still a step above him on the stairs, which accentuated her impression of his neat slenderness.

"That you were a beauty, Cousin. I can understand that my aunt might not have thought fit to tell me, but I take it ill of you, Ross."

Christina laughed. "Don't blame him, Cousin Richard, he never noticed."

"Shame on you, Ross! But I can believe it. He thinks of nothing, that great cousin of ours [why the little pause on the word cousin?] but mulch and drill and the price of wool. Am I not right, Cousin Christina?"

"Entirely right."

She turned from greeting the lawyer, who was a large middle-aged man with a look of professional competence. "And now, if you gentlemen will excuse the reminder, we dine at six, and my grandfather wishes to see Mr. Foxton first."

"Does he, by Jupiter! Then we must make haste, Foxton. I hope that man of mine has my things ready for me. The usual room, Cousin?"

"No. A million apologies. I am in your room. I have put you in the west wing, with Mr. Foxton."

"I am honored beyond measure. Come, Foxton, I'll show you the way."

The food was delicious, the champagne flowed freely, but the dinner could hardly be called a success. Old Mr. Tretteign, huddled in his huge, draught-excluding wing chair at the head of the table, ate only a mouthful here and there and sipped at his champagne as if he thought it might poison him. Mrs. Tretteign, sitting on his right, was terrified of him as usual and could merely stutter answers to the few questions he barked at her. Christina, on his left, had her cousin Richard Markham on the other side, and found herself the object of his assiduous attention. Full of praise for the cuisine, he pressed her to try a bite of this or that side dish with the composition of which she was already extremely well acquainted. And all the time he kept up a continuous flow of what she assumed to be London conversation—and very small talk indeed it seemed to her.

He knew exactly when the king had last quarreled with the queen, and which of the princesses he liked to have about him. He had a new version of the story of the mad king going to open Parliament and proposing to address them as "My lords and peacocks." "I had it from an absolutely unimpeachable source—he'll never be right in the head again." He was full of unimpeachable sources and Christina was content to let him talk on until he turned to the subject of America. "You must be glad to be safe away from there, Cousin."

"Oh, why?"

"Well . . ." He looked about him importantly. "All friends here, of course, and it's pretty much of an open secret anyway. A friend of mine's a close friend of Anthony Merry —our ambassador at Washington, you know. He thinks Civil War may break out there at any moment."

"Civil War? In the United States? But how fantastic! Why, pray?"

"Because of this incredible bargain President Jefferson has struck with France over Louisiana. What is it the Federalists say? I have it: 'A stack of dollars three miles high for an enormous desert.' They don't like it, Cousin, and can you wonder? What with that and a freak of a President who knows no better than to receive our ambassador in an old coat and moccasins! I have it on the best authority that Merry thought him some kind of a servant at first."

"The best authority?" She kept her voice sweetly cool. "I suppose you must mean Mrs. Merry, Cousin. I have heard stories about her, too. But we won't go into that. As for Louisiana, do you realize that Mr. Jefferson, a great man, moccasins and all, has secured a million acres for us at three cents an acre? And without shedding a drop of American blood?"

"Dear me." He looked comically taken aback. "I had no idea you were a political bluestocking, Cousin. And one of Mr. Jefferson's democratic republicans, I take it? And, doubtless pro-French as well? Ross, do you think it is safe for you to harbor such a firebrand here on the invasion coast?" His voice was only half teasing and Christina felt bound to answer him.

"Just because I am devoted to Mr. Jefferson does not mean I like Bonaparte any better than you do, Cousin. Though if you ask me, there's not much to choose between French and English so far as we Americans are concerned. You both stop our ships and take our seamen—not to mention our goods. But, just wait—I tell you a time is coming. Do you know we are building three hundred ships a year? Well, work it out for yourselves."

"Not warships, I hope, Chris." Ross had been following the conversation closely from his end of the table.

"No, not warships, trading vessels. Jefferson is a man of peace, everyone knows that. Though, mind you, we showed what we could do when the dey of Algiers insulted our flag."

"Yes," said Ross thoughtfully, "you did at that. I can see you're right, Richard, we've a dangerous politician in our midst. Let us by all means respect the Stars and Stripes or who knows what ghastly fate may befall us?"

Mrs. Tretteign had been growing increasingly impatient with the line of conversation. Now she leaned forward across old Mr. Tretteign, who seemed to have dozed off in his chair. "Politics!" she said. "Most unsuitable in a young lady, my love, and so, I am sure, your cousins would agree. But tell me, Richard, what's new in London fashions? I'm positively starved for information down here."

He was delighted. "You could not have come to a better source, Aunt Verity. The dear Duchess of Devonshire was talking to me only the other day about the changes she has seen in her time. Poor thing, she's breaking up fast. They say she is oceans deep in debt again. Well, no wonder, the way she plays!"

"But what changes, Richard? We are quite Gothic, you know, down here in the country. I have been trying this age to persuade Christina that she should order herself some new gowns, but she is almost as obstinate as Ross—just look at him!"

"But that is quite the thing, Aunt. I have only put on full dress out of deference for my grandfather. It would be considered quite antediluvian to wear it in town for a small family dinner like this. Delicious though it is . . ." This for Christina, just as his previous remark had been carefully aimed at his grandfather.

Old Mr. Tretteign opened his eyes. "If you have nothing better to talk about than clothes, Mrs. Tretteign, I suggest that it is time you and Christina left us to our wine. As for you, Richard, it is news to me that you are coming out as a Whig."

"A Whig? Why, Grandfather, whatever gave you that idea?"

"The general tenor of your conversation, to which I have listened with considerable interest. Spending your time—and your money, I wager—at Devonshire House, are you? And picking up their bits and pieces of gossip as gospel? Well, don't come crying to me for an increased allowance when you run into debt. I suppose you want the Prince of Wales for regent, hey?" And then, while Richard was still searching for an answer, "No, no, don't tell me. I'd rather not know." With an effort he rose from the big chair. "Your servant, ladies. We will join you almost at once for a family conference."

Inevitably, it was Richard who sprang to his feet to open the door for his aunt and cousin, while Ross merely watched quizzically from his side of the table. "We must talk more, much more." Richard contrived to delay Christina for a moment as she passed him. "You must enlighten my ignorance about your remarkable country, Cousin Christina. In the meantime, allow me to thank you for the most delightful meal I have ever eaten in this house."

"Thank *you*, Cousin." Bending her head in stately acknowledgment, she could not help finding him faintly ridiculous. But then, it was not his fault that she was so much the taller. It was rather as if a mere gunboat should try and carry on a flirtation with a man-of-war.

She smiled a little at the idea of herself as a man-of-war, and Mrs. Tretteign saw and, inevitably, misinterpreted the smile. "A most delightful young man, is he not? Such a con-

trast to my poor Ross! Such polish, such address, such *savoir
faire.* I knew you could not fail but find him charming."

"I find him entertaining, certainly." Christina was too wise
to take up the cudgels, as she would have liked, on Ross's
behalf. But why did his mother underestimate him so?

Mrs. Tretteign's grumbling voice went on, "And Ross
would not even take the trouble to change into full dress,
though he knows how his grandfather feels about these new"
—a coy look—"inexpressibles, I believe they call them."

"We call them pantaloons in America."

"My dear, that puts me in mind of something I had been
intending to say to you. Of course your feeling for your father is an admirable thing, and quite what one would expect,
but is it really necessary to drag America into the conversation quite so often as you do? I was really afraid your grandfather would have a spasm when you took poor Richard up
so sharply."

"Were you, Aunt? Now is not that a strange thing? I
thought he was pleased. Grandfather and I understand each
other quite well these days, you know."

"Do you?" A sharp calculating glance. "I confess I was
amazed when he did not make more of an issue of your in-
sisting on calling yourself Tretton."

"It happens to be my name."

"Fiddlestick. If you had the slightest wish to oblige us—
and most particularly your grandfather—you would not have
been so obstinate."

"But why should I wish to oblige you, Aunt?"

"Why? Give me patience! Have we not taken you in,
housed you, fed you, clothed you?"

"Grandfather has, it's quite true. And in return I am running his house for him better, he says, than it's been done for
years."

"I see how it is." Her aunt had recourse to a lacy pocket
handkerchief. "I might have known that sooner or later you
would be giving yourself airs because of running the house
—and in a most improper way, too. My maid tells me you
were in the kitchen half the afternoon, advising the cook
about sauces. Most unsuitable!"

"But the sauces were delicious, were they not? Come,
Aunt, let us not quarrel. Perhaps my way of doing things is
a little odd by English standards, but try to bear with me, and

remember that I am an American, though I will try not to harp on it, as you ask. And as for you, think what an ornament you are to the household, which is more than I can ever be, a mile high like this, and built to match. Where would I get as a swooning miss in a drawing room? My line must be usefulness, and I intend to stick to it. Do you look after the refinements of life and I will see to it that the machine keeps going."

"Well, if you put it like that . . ." Mollified. "And if you will not mind my giving you a little hint now and then——"

"I shall like it above all things. Good gracious, can this be the gentlemen already?"

Old Mr. Tretteign entered the room first. "Tea?" he barked in answer to his daughter-in-law's anxious question. "No, I do not wish to take tea, and nor, I should think, do these gentlemen after the inroads they have been making on my port. I shall have my second glass later, in my room, when this is all over. You may offer the rest of the party tea then, if you still wish to." He had settled himself, while he spoke, in a huge armchair close to the fire. "Now, sit down where I can see you. Why the devil aren't there more lights? No, don't ring, Richard, aren't you capable of lighting a few candles yourselves? Not you, Christina, you must learn that English young ladies stay still and let themselves be waited on. And don't hide yourself in that corner either, come here and sit by me. That's better." She had pulled a low chair up close to his while her aunt settled herself with a petulant swish of skirts on the sofa. Mr. Foxton had withdrawn to a discreet corner where he sat watching the rest of the party with an expression at once anxious and disapproving. Now Richard and Ross finished lighting the remaining branches of candles and came forward to take their places in the circle around the fire.

"Well now, we're all here." Old Mr. Tretteign was sitting up very straight in the big chair, surveying them in turn with his dark-circled eyes. "All the family—such as it is. And with the exception, of course, of your mother and sister, Christina."

"Yes, sir."

" 'Yes, sir,' " he mimicked her. "So far as I am concerned, they left the family when they returned to France—they can stay out of it. Is that understood?"

"You make yourself very clear." She had no intention of arguing the point with him.

"I intend to. Mr. Foxton is here in case there should be any legal point you—any one of you—wishes cleared up. He knows my intention and has protested against it as much as he dares. He admits, however, that there is nothing to stop me doing as I wish. Right, Foxton?"

"Right, sir, but I must protest—"

"No, you must not. You have had your opportunity for argument. Now it is my turn. So, first, you will confirm, I know, that since the breaking of the entail, there is nothing to prevent me leaving my property as I wish."

"Nothing but your own good sense, Mr. Tretteign. You know how I felt about the breaking of the entail."

"That will do, Foxton. The matter of the entail was a long-standing agreement, which, I will say for him, Ross chose to honor. And was rewarded for his co-operation by the purchase of his commission. Have you anything to say, Ross?"

"No, sir."

"Good. So, here I am, eighty-nine, in full possession of my faculties, and ready to dispose of my estate. Such as it is. You, Ross, have suspected for some time, I think, that we are not so rich as we were. It's true. I'm not going to apologize, or explain. Why should I? I'm entitled to do what I like with my own. If I've been unlucky in my investments—well, there it is. There's no reason why I should be accountable to you —to any of you. You, Ross, and you, Richard, have had your schooling at my hands. You, Mrs. Tretteign, have had your jointure regularly paid, and houseroom here as well. Have you anything to say at this point?"

Ross looked up. "What about Christina, sir?"

"I owe her nothing. Her father chose to abandon his home, and, worse still, his country. He could have starved in the streets before I helped him. . . . Don't interrupt me, girl. What's past, is past. It's the future we are thinking of tonight. And you, Ross, hold your tongue. From now on, I'll have no more interruptions. This is not a pleasant task for me . . . I want it over. As I have told you, I consider myself in no way accountable to any of you, but, in order that you may understand what I intend to do, I must explain the position in which I find myself. You will be quiet, all of you, and listen. First of all there is the Abbey—or the Grange, if you prefer it. It has been in the family since Henry VIII gave it us. Its title is free and clear as it has always been. I intend that it shall remain so. You, Ross, have tried to persuade me to sell some of the outlying part of the estate in order to feed the rest. I won't have it, do you understand?"

"So I have found."

"Nor yet will I have it said that I did not provide properly for my descendents. So—in addition to the estate, I have sufficient capital to take care of your jointure, Mrs. Tretteign, so long as may be necessary, and to produce, in addition, an income of a thousand pounds a year. This is what we are living on, and why I am not exactly lavish in the articles of wax candles and tea. When I die, I propose that the income shall be divided equally between Ross and Richard. . . . Quiet, Ross, I am coming to Christina. She gets everything else . . . the Abbey, the shingle, the marsh, the sheep—on two conditions. First, that she keep her aunt here as long as she wishes to stay. Second, that she marry either you, Ross, or Richard." A lifted hand compelled silence. "No, I'll not be interrupted! And, if it's Richard, he's to change his name to Tretteign. At least, thus, the name continues." He stopped, surveying them broodingly from the depths of his chair.

"But it's absurd," said Ross.

"Fantastic," said Richard.

"I won't," said Christina.

"Quite so." He was unexpectedly patient. "That's what Foxton said—at first. So let me explain a little further. And do, I beg, remember that I have absolute control of it all. And—I flatter myself that I have provided for everything. If, when my will is proved, you, Christina, are not married either to Richard or to Ross, Mrs. Tretteign's income remains the same, the rest is divided between the three of you, and the Abbey goes to the Patriotic Fund. Think what an admirable army camp it would make, Ross. Imagine the convenience for Mr. Pitt, Richard. I don't know exactly how any of you will contrive to live, but that will be your own affair. I only hope, for all your sakes, that Christina can be prevailed upon to marry one of you."

"Sir, it's not fair," said Richard.

"Fair? Who said anything about fairness? And, if you mean, as I suppose, that Ross has had first chance at the lady —well, surely you—Bond Street beau that you are—can afford to give him that slight advantage." He had pulled himself to his feet as he spoke. "Now—I'm exhausted. I've made up my mind. The will is to be drawn up tomorrow . . . signed, sealed and witnessed. Mr. Foxton takes it back to London with him. So, if you want time to make up your mind, girl, you had best take care of me. Ring for my man, Ross, I'll not have any of you helping me upstairs and arguing all the way. Trouble out of any one of you, and it goes to the Patriotic Fund at once. Is that understood? Then, good night . . . and pleasant dreams."

"It's monstrous." Christina had jumped to her feet and spoke the moment the door closed behind her grandfather. "Can he do it, Mr. Foxton?"

"I'm afraid so, Miss Tretton—"

"Fantastic," said Richard. And then, "Now I see why he told me to plan to stay as long as I could. Cousin Christina, I don't know what to say."

"Then don't say it," said Ross.

"But, what about me?" wailed Mrs. Tretteign.

"I'm going to bed," said Christina.

"At eight o'clock?" Ross laughed. "Well, I can't say I blame you, Chris. At least it puts off our proposals till the morning, eh, Richard?"

"How can you speak of it so lightly, Ross. Cousin Christina, how can I find words to convey my feelings for you, placed in a position of such delicacy—such—"

"In the morning," interrupted Ross. "Here is your candle, Chris."

"Thank you." She could only hope that its wavering flame did not reveal treacherous tears in her eyes. "Good night." She was safe away.

Chapter Five

RESISTING THE TEMPTATION to storm in and
tell her grandfather what she thought of him, Christina hurried
to the asylum of her bedroom and threw herself into its one
armchair. Useless to go to bed—she was far too angry to
sleep.

Plan after furious plan chased through her head, to be re-
jected one after the other. Comic, in a way, to think how the
old man had unwittingly outgeneraled her. But—she did not
find it funny. Inevitably, her thoughts came back to Ross.
"At least it puts off our proposals till the morning." He had
meant it, too. Intolerable. . . . She shivered, not entirely
from cold, though the fire had burned low on her hearth. The
house was quiet; her candle was flickering in its socket; it
must be very late indeed. "Till the morning." Ross's mocking
voice. Mocking her, or himself, or both of them? She jumped
to her feet. She would need her wits about her in the morning, if she was to refuse two proposals, and keep her secret.

Her candle was almost out now and she lit the two on her
dressing table from it. Old Mr. Tretteign would be appalled
at such an extravagance. The idea pleased her for a moment,
and then, irritated with herself, she moved away to push her
window open behind the heavy curtains. Wind caught it and
almost wrested it from her hands before she made the bar
fast on its nail. As she did so, she thought she heard movement below. Was that a groan, or merely the wind worrying
around the corners of the house? Holding the window steadily now, she pushed it farther open and leaned out to peer
down into darkness.

As she did so, a whisper came up to her, just audible in a temporary lull of the wind. "Chris? Thank God! It's me—Ross. Can you come down to the side entrance—quickly? And quietly? Bring some rags . . . anything . . . an old sheet." And again the groaning, unmistakable now.

"You're hurt?"

"No—not me. Quickly, Chris. And—wake no one."

"I'm coming." She had no thought but to obey him. A shawl around her shoulders; basilicum powder from the chest in the hall; a clean but threadbare sheet from the linen cupboard; and she was hurrying down the side stairs, the candle flickering in her hand. The big bolt was shot to in the side door and she had to put down the bundle she was carrying to unfasten it. To her relief, it moved easily, as if it had been recently oiled, and the door, too, swung open silently.

"Bless you, Chris." Ross stooped, so that the head of the man he carried would clear the low door. "Watch there's no blood, will you? And—light me to the cloisters."

"The cloisters! But—he's hurt." Like him, she spoke in the lowest possible whisper as she closed the door silently behind him.

"It can't be helped. Quietly, now." They were passing the steep stairway that led to the servants' quarters. The man he carried hung limp over his shoulder and Christina thought he must be unconscious. An ominous dark patch had spread on one sleeve of his light-colored greatcoat and, once, as Ross moved him to get under the low door into the stable yard, she saw something dark splash on the doorstep.

"Ross!" She put down the candle and bent to scrub at it with a corner of the sheet, and as she did so the candle blew out.

"Never mind. I know my way. Keep close behind me." He was edging along the side of the yard toward the entrance of the chapel. In the archway, he paused. "The keys," he said. "On my chain. Can you?"

Her hands shook as she felt inside his heavy coat, found the keys and fumbled them off the chain. "There."

"Keep near me—and, quickly. I don't know how long we've got."

The chapel was an even blacker dark than the night outside, and she was glad to keep close behind him. A brief pause, as he found the lock of the door on the farther side, and they were in the cloisters, where a sickle moon gave just a hint of light, after the pitch blackness of the chapel.

"This way." He turned to the left, to edge his way carefully along the side wall. "We can talk now." His voice, pitched normally, sounded oddly loud.

Equally strange, she found, for a moment, that she had nothing to say.

"We left no traces?" He had reached the first corner of the cloister and was using the other key on one of the doors he had told her led nowhere.

"I don't think so." She followed him through the doorway.

"Good. Feel above the door, will you? You'll find a tinder-box and candle."

Her hands felt cold stone, dust, and then the box. It seemed to take her a very long time to get the candle alight, but he stood, silently, in the darkness, his breathing, rather quick from the burden he had carried, the only sound.

"There." At last the little flame grew in her hands and the room came to shadowy life around them. It was small, square, windowless, deep in dust and furnished with a cot, chair and table.

While Christina moved forward to put down the candle, Ross eased the man he carried down onto the bed. Standing again. "I'll have to leave you with him," he said. "You're not afraid?"

"Should I be?"

"He'll be more so, if he comes to, which I doubt. He's French. You speak it of course. Tell him he's with friends. Bandage his wound if you know how, keep him quiet. He's bled a great deal. I'll come back as soon as I can."

"When will that be?"

"How can I tell?" Impatiently. "We are bound to have . . . visitors. God knows how soon. They'll want higher authority before they come here—it depends on many things. I must be there to receive them . . . they would hardly disturb you in bed."

"You expect a search?" Was she mad to be helping him?

"Yes, of course. No time to explain. If you hear us coming, put the light out and keep him quiet, at all costs. And I mean at all costs. And—trust me, Chris?"

"I suppose I must. There's blood on your coat. Best leave

it here. And—look in the back entrance, there was blood there. I may not have got rid of it all."

"Thank you. You'll need this to cover him." He dropped his heavy coat on the chair. "I'll have to lock you in. Do you mind?"

"Does it make any difference?"

"No. I'm sorry, Chris. And . . . thank you." He closed the door gently behind him and she heard the key turn in the lock as she bent over the wounded man. He was very pale, and the dark patch of blood on his right shoulder had spread alarmingly. She went back to the door, where she had dropped her bundle, brought it to the table, found the sharp pair of scissors she had wrapped in the sheet and began the awkward job of getting his clothes away from the wound. Her hand shook less now that she was alone and busy, and she took time to think it was lucky for this unknown Frenchman that she was a barbarian of an American girl who had been taught, among other things, how to dress a wound. Inevitably, this made her think of her father—there had been no helping him—but she set her teeth and went on with her work.

At last she straightened up and looked down at him. It was not, after all, so bad as she had feared from the effusion of blood. A clean bullet wound, she thought, and the ball not lodged. He had been lucky. At the thought, his eyes flickered open and he peered up at her in the half dark. "Where am I? What has happened?"

"Quiet!" Her French was as fluent as his. "You are safe . . . for the time being."

"But—you are French? It was all a nightmare then? Where am I?" Feverishly now.

"In England. Not a nightmare, but—you are safe, if you will do as you are bid."

"Of course. For such an angel . . . an angel in a velvet gown . . . not a nightmare. A dream of happiness . . ." His eyes flickered shut again and she smiled sardonically to herself: trust a Frenchman to come up with a compliment. And how remarkably unlike her cousin Ross. Once again that phrase of his echoed in her mind: "Puts off our proposals till the morning." No time to be thinking of that now. They would be lucky if they were not all in Dover Castle by morning.

Several times while she was dressing the Frenchman's wound, she had paused to listen anxiously at the door. Put out the light, Ross had said. Impossible, with the candle lit, to be sure that there was no chink in the apparently windowless room that would betray a light to a search party. And the cloisters so deadened sound that she might well not hear them until they actually emerged from the chapel door. Better safe than sorry. She fetched the tinderbox from its place over the door, put it beside the candle on the table, drew the chair up to it and blew out the candle.

The Frenchman did not stir, but she thought he was sleeping now rather than unconscious; his breathing certainly sounded easier. Anyway, there was nothing more she could do for him, nothing at all to do but think. And not pleasant thoughts either. Was she mad to have obeyed Ross? What was she doing here, hiding a Frenchman, an enemy? Well— she paused at the thought—whose enemy? And, in retrospect, she heard her own voice, over dinner, talking to Richard. Nothing to choose between French and English? Did she really believe that? Of course not—certainly not now, not after living here, understanding what Bonaparte's conquest of Europe really meant. A pity she had said it, but Richard's half truths had infuriated her beyond caution.

Caution. It brought her back to the present. What was she involved in now? What was Ross doing? Was there something worse than smuggling? It almost seemed so, and yet she could not make herself believe it. For the moment, she would give him the benefit of the doubt. If his explanations, when he returned, were not satisfactory, there would still be time to —to do what? Impossible to imagine betraying him. She had chosen her side, that first night on the marsh; too late now to change. But one thing was certain: Ross would have some explaining to do when he came back; and this time she meant to have her questions answered. There would be no putting her off with that easy charm of his.

She stood up, quiet in the darkness. What had she heard? The wind? Imagination? No, now she heard it again, the tramp of feet, voices. . . . She moved over to stand close beside the Frenchman. Keep him quiet, Ross had said, at all costs. And she had understood him. She knew a woman who had smothered her own child rather than let its crying betray her hiding place to the Indians. Well, at least the Frenchman was a stranger. If only she had had the forethought to gag him, instead of sitting dreaming. . . . Do it now? No, he might wake and struggle. Best chance his continuing to sleep.

The voices were nearer now. She wished she dared leave him and listen at the door, but she must not. As best she could judge, the party had just entered the cloisters from the chapel door. She could hear the tramp of booted feet, an unintelligible order, and then, much nearer, Ross's voice. "Never believed it haunted myself, but, dangerous, yes. That's why we don't use it."

"And these doorways?" The strange voice sounded immediately outside and she could see light glancing through crannies in the stonework high up toward the ceiling of the room. Just as well she had put out the candle; though, of course, since they carried lanterns they would probably not have noticed its feeble light.

Ross's voice sounded alarmingly near. "Bricked up behind," he said. "See, it won't move." A hearty shove on the locked door proved his point.

"Safer than to leave it like the other one," said the stranger. So doubtless Ross had already showed him the room on the opposite corner. Had he contrived to arrange a rock fall as he had done for her? Very likely. One should not, it was clear, underestimate Ross.

"And the other corner?" The voice was farther away now and she allowed herself a soundless sigh of relief.

"Bricked up as well." Ross, too, had moved away.

"It's a strange place. No wonder there are rumors. . . . But, just the same, it would make an excellent hiding place. You are sure no one could have got in without passing through the house?"

"Of course. The entrance we used is the only one. The gates to the stable yard are always locked at night. Impossible to reach it save through the house."

"Yes." Thoughtfully. And then, on a note of sudden decision, "One thing we can do, just to make sure. Douse those lights, men! And—silence!"

The streaks of light vanished. It was eerily quiet in the cloisters and Christina found herself holding her breath, as if even its soft whisper might betray her. And as she did so, she realized that the Frenchman on the bed was doing the same thing; he must have been awake all the time. Her hand went

out to touch his sound shoulder in a gesture at once of warning and of reassurance. The silence stretched out endlessly;
then, at last, came a sharp order and the crash of spurred and
booted feet on the paving stones of the cloisters. They were
going away. . . . Were they?

Suddenly, the stranger spoke just outside the door again.
"If I were you, sir, I'd be inclined to have the whole place
closed off. It's hardly safe as it is."

"That's why I have given strict orders that no one is to
come here. Not that the servants are much inclined to, being
convinced that it is haunted. Groans and gibberings are the
least of what they have heard. All nonsense, of course. Well,
what more can I do for you? A drink, at least, before you
go? It's cold work out on the marshes at night."

"I thank you, no. We must not linger. We have lost enough
time as it is. I'll have something to say to Mrs. Emeret in the
morning."

Mrs. Emeret! A cold prickling ran down Christina's spine.

But Ross's voice was casual as ever. "Poor Mrs. Emeret,
do not be too hard on her, Lieutenant. One must make allow-
ances for the spite of a servant dismissed for incompetence.
And, after all, her information paid off to a certain extent.
Your men caught the smuggling vagabonds in the act, you
say."

"But what's the good of that, since they fought their way
out and got away? If I had only sent a larger force—but, to
tell truth, I thought, like you, that it was most likely malice
and moonshine. We all know how active you are with the
Volunteers, sir. It's not likely anyone would dare use the
Grange for smuggling, but you can see what an ideal position
it has. Well, I must not be keeping you any longer from your
bed. My one consolation is that my men are convinced they
wounded one of the miscreants, and pretty sharply, too. They
saw him being carried off. . . . Well, he'll have a hard job to
hide himself, if, as he's sure to be, he's a local man. And,
once we've got him, never fear, we'll make him tell us the
names of his friends."

"I'm sure you will." A leisurely yawn. "But let me give you
something to warm you before you go. We've no housekeeper, and my cousin, who looks after us, is in bed long
since, but I'm sure I could find something for you and your
men."

"No, thank you again. We must be on our way. There'll be the devil to pay in the morning over this night's work." His voice dwindled as he spoke, as if he was leading the way out of the cloisters.

Once again Christina's hand touched the Frenchman's shoulder in silent warning. One could not be sure. . . . But it certainly sounded as if they were going. And, as they went, she could not help a pang of sympathy for the lieutenant. And—how had Ross felt while he made such a fool of him? Unfair that Ross's captaincy in the Volunteers should have given him such an advantage.

"Mademoiselle!" A breathless whisper from the bed. "Are they really gone?"

"I think so." She moved silently back to take his wrist in her cold hand. The pulse was racing. His forehead, when she felt it, was at once hot and clammy. "Try and rest," she whispered. "Anyway, we had best not talk."

"No. But—God bless you, mademoiselle."

She thought he fell into a restless sleep. There was nothing to do but sit on the hard chair, rest her elbows on the table and castigate herself for the fool she was. The silence in the cloisters was absolute. Once, a bat shrieked, and she jumped; once the Frenchman turned over and began an agitated muttering in his sleep and she moved over to put a soothing hand on his brow and murmur, in French, a reassurance that she did not believe. Hours seemed to have passed since the soldiers marched away. What could Ross be doing? Surely he would not leave her here all night? Surely he knew that now, at last, he must explain?

Perhaps he was thinking what lies to tell her. And would she believe him, despite her common sense? Intolerably, desperately, she found herself longing for America, for home, where things were simple, where danger and safety alike were straightforward, recognizable. What was she doing here, in a country she did not understand, among people she could not trust?

Her head went up. Yes, it was the noise of quiet footsteps in the cloister; then she heard the key fitted in the lock. "All's well." Ross's voice. "It's I."

"All's well!" She managed a note of mockery. "I'm delighted you think so."

"In the dark still?" He put down the lantern he carried and turned to look at the Frenchman. "He gave you no trouble?"

"The mildest of men. But . . . ill, Ross. What are we going to do for him?" And, on the words, was angry with herself for this assumption that she was on his side. Before she did anything more, he must explain.

"You seem to have bandaged him very competently. He should do till morning."

"I've done my best. But he's feverish already. He should have a doctor."

"Impossible." The word was bleak in the little room. "I hope he lives, but if he dies, he dies a martyr . . ."

"A martyr? Ross, you must explain. I have gone with you, blindfolded and against my better judgment so far, but I can tell you it's gone against the grain with me. It was touch and go whether I called out when you were bamboozling that poor young lieutenant out there."

"You heard it all?" He sounded merely amused. "I was afraid you must. Is it not a fortunate thing that I have more confidence in you than you have in yourself, Chris? I never thought for a moment you would betray me." And then, unaware of how he had infuriated her, he went on. "We are partners, you and I. It was settled the first time we met. I wish you were a man. You showed a man's courage then— and again tonight. I never had a brother"—he paused oddly for a moment—"never could feel even as a cousin should toward poor flimsy Richard—but you, why, with you at my side I could do anything. You're a friend, Chris. Don't tease me with suggesting I can't trust you. I know it's nonsense. I'd trust you with my life . . . well, in a manner of speaking, I have."

"Manner of speaking!" She picked up the part of his speech that was easiest to answer. "I don't think there's much doubt of what would have happened to you if I had thought fit to scream when that poor young man was outside."

"It would have been monstrous inconvenient, of course, but, no, Chris, it would not have cost me my life. I was afraid I would have to explain to you. Besides, I need a new ally. Parkes is getting too old. Imagine his going to bed before Richard, and letting him lock the back door against me. But, come, it's time we were going."

"Going? But we can't leave this poor man here alone."

"Not 'can't,' must. We must both be on parade in the morning when the story of this night's events comes out. He'll be all right—I hope. Parkes will see to him in the morning. And, if not, well, *à la guerre comme à la guerre,* as he would doubtless say."

"War? That's it, isn't it, Ross? You're not a smuggler at all?"

"Oh yes I am, and a very successful one too. Where do you think Grandfather's brandy comes from? And ask on the marsh about the Captain and you'll hear I'm something of a legend. But . . . there's the difficulty. To my gang, I'm nothing but a smuggler. I can't be protected, not immediately, not openly. If it came to a trial, of course, it would be another matter—and anyway, my usefulness would be exhausted. But, in the meantime, I'm on my own. Or rather"—he held out a firm, brown hand to pull her to her feet—"we are on our own." And then, as an odd *non sequitur,* "I'm glad you're not stupid, Chris."

"Not stupid! Thank you." She looked at the bed. "And this, I take it, is a French spy?"

"Secret agent is a phrase we prefer. Yes, he is a friend of ours from France, and a deuce of a problem, too, just now. He is supposed to go to London tomorrow—and back to France when the next cargo comes. Is there any chance, do you think?"

"Of his going to London? None. Of his returning to France—unlikely. What will you do, Ross?"

"Sleep on it. And so should you. We must be innocent as daisies in the morning."

"It seems profoundly unlikely. I shall not sleep a wink for very terror." But she let him place a pitcher of water by the Frenchman's bed, cover him as best he could with his own greatcoat, and then lead the way down the dark and silent cloister and back to the house.

He paused to light two candles in the kitchen and, by their light, she could see the hands of the big grandfather clock in the hall at three o'clock. It was late indeed. . . . But Ross had paused at the library door. "One moment, Chris. There'll be no chance to talk in the morning, and I did not want to say too much out there."

"Oh?" But she followed him into the library, and sat down

gratefully in an armchair by the hearth, where the embers of a fire still glowed. "You do not trust him then?"

"Not entirely. I trust no one—except you, of course."

"Thank you." Ironically. "But—I'm tired, Ross. What else is there to be said?"

"Plenty. If you're sure M. Tissot won't be fit to travel to-morrow, I shall have to go to London on his errand."

"And who will look after poor M. Tissot—is that his name?"

"Probably not, but it's what he calls himself. And as to looking after him . . ." He paused.

"I know. There's no need to break it to me gently. I will."

"Parkes will help you, but after tonight there's no pretending he's not too old to be trusted with the entire responsibility. Besides, I can see you are an admirable nurse. You speak French, thanks to that mother of yours. It could hardly be better."

"I'm delighted to hear you say so. For my part, I am inclined to think it could hardly be worse. Here am I, with a houseful of visitors already, and you expect me to spend my time running in and out of the cloisters with nourishing broth and cold compresses for a sick man—and to keep it all secret too."

"You'll find it's not so bad. Let him sleep in the daytime, feed him at night, and, whatever you do, don't let him out of the cloisters, Chris. Keep both doors locked, always."

"You don't trust him then?"

"I don't know him. And—better safe than sorry."

"You cheer me more and more. What am I expected to do? Keep a pistol on him all the time I dress his wound?"

"No, no, nothing of the kind. This is merely precautionary. I am sure he knows his own interest too well to give you any trouble. But—I should prefer to find him still here when I return."

"And when will that be?"

"As soon as I can possibly manage. Four days . . . five days. I promise I'll do my best."

"Well, I suppose so shall I. You don't leave me much alternative, do you?"

"Thank you, Chris." She had risen to her feet. "One other thing before you go. I must ride off first thing in the morning. You and Parkes will take care of everything, I know.

But, there's something else . . ." It was the first time she had
seen him unsure of himself. "Christina—I know this is the
worst possible moment, but—you won't accept Richard while
I am away, will you?"

"Accept Richard? What makes you think he is going to ask
me?"

"He'll ask you all right. And, Chris, now at least you can
understand—I have to have the house."

Oh, now she was angry; now she could warm herself at her
own flame of rage. "Are you by any chance proposing for my
hand, Mr. Tretteign?"

"What else can I do? We've been friends, you and I, good
friends, have we not? If I could imagine loving a woman, it
might be you. I can certainly think of no other I could trust
as I have you tonight. But, understand me, Chris, I don't ask
so much of you. It need not, I am sure, come to marriage."

"Oh? And why not, pray? I thought Grandfather had it all
most ingeniously worked out, so that it could come to nothing else."

"We'll get around it somehow, trust me, we will. I will talk
to my friends while I am in London. You must see, I have to
have the house. It's invaluable for my purposes."

"Even if you have to have me too? Is that what it comes
down to, Ross?" Heroic to have kept her voice so light.

"I knew I could count on you! That's it precisely. If the
worst comes to the worst, and we have to marry, I promise it
shall be the merest formality, and when the war is over, I will
see to it the lords grant you a divorce. All I ask is that for
now you consent to the appearance of an engagement to me.
Who knows? The old man might be so pleased he would settle the estate right away?"

"Deluding yourself, Ross, I think." Once again she kept
her voice merely teasing.

"Perhaps . . . or, who knows, the war might end."

"By a miracle? Bonaparte converted to the idea of peace? I
think we had best face facts, Ross. If I should be mad
enough to consent to such an engagement, it would have to
be with the idea of very likely having to go through with it."
Mad was the word—just how mad, she was relieved to think
he had no idea.

"You mean, you'll do it?"

"I mean I'll think about it, Ross, while you are away. At

least I can easily promise you that you won't come back and find me engaged to Richard, woo he ne'er so winningly."

"Thank you, Chris." Surprisingly, he picked up her hand and kissed it. "Thank you for everything."

"I'd wait to thank me, if I were you, till this war is over and we are unhung—and unmarried, too, let us hope."

"Amen to that. Chris, you're a friend in a thousand."

She managed a gallant pretense at a laugh. "My dear Ross, I do recommend that while you are away you study a little how to behave as a courting lover. Not much use our pretending to be engaged if you treat me like something between a younger brother and a valued old retainer."

"Chris! I really believe you will do it!"

"I really believe I have gone stark, staring mad. But, no, I'll decide nothing till you get back. Who knows, with a little bit of luck I may be safely jailed in Dover Castle by then and my problems all solved for me."

"I don't think it for a moment. You and Parkes will manage admirably between you, I am sure."

"Dear Ross, I find your confidence in me more touching than I can say."

Chapter Six

"MISS! MISS CHRISTINA!" Betty's voice dredged Christina up out of a great depth of sleep.

"Yes?" She turned over reluctantly in bed, then sat up suddenly as the girl drew back the curtains and let in a great flood of daylight. "Goodness, what time is it?"

"Late, miss. I didn't have the heart to wake you before. You was dead to the world. But there's the deuce to pay downstairs and Mr. Parkes said I'd best call you."

"Why? What's the matter?" She was out of bed already, afraid she knew.

But Betty's next words were reassuring. "Matter enough! There's a whole troop of soldiers outside wanting to search the house. Proper dragoons they are, miss, you just wait till you see them. They make Mr. Ross and his Volunteers look like a parcel of liverymen. Not but what I wish Mr. Ross was here to deal with them. Old Master's in a proper tearer, Parkes says, and don't want to have them in the house. Which it stands to reason we'll have to, sooner or later."

"Of course. But"—her heart sank—"where is Mr. Ross?"

"Rode off to London at first light. Said he had to have his hair cut, of all things. If you ask me, the lieutenant's not best pleased at finding him gone. Did you hear them last night, miss?"

"Last night? What do you mean?" She let Betty give her the servants' version of last night's events while she helped her dress and was at once shocked and relieved to see how patently Betty was on the smugglers' side. If there had been any suspicious traces in the kitchen this morning, the dragoons were not likely to hear about them.

"But where are the soldiers now?"

"Out front, miss, drawn up ever so regular on the drive, waiting for Old Master to dress and receive 'em. And taking his time something shocking he is, according to his man."

"I'd best go to him. They've not left the lieutenant outside, have they?"

"Oh no, miss, a handsome young man like him. He's in the breakfast room, taking coffee with Mr. Richard."

"Oh, that's all right. Thank you, Betty. Tell Parkes I'll be down as soon as I have seen my grandfather." She crossed the hall and knocked softly on the door of her grandfather's rooms, wishing, as she did so, more than ever that she had been able to see Ross this morning before he left.

"Good morning, miss." She suspected Greg, her grandfather's man, of disliking her, but he concealed it well. "Mr. Tretteign was just asking for you."

"Good. Is he up then?"

"Yes, indeed, miss, with such an upheaval belowstairs." He ushered her through the little antechamber into the luxurious sitting room. Her grandfather was sitting fully dressed in his big chair by the fire, drinking ginger tea.

"There you are at last, girl. Now, tell me what's all this to-do belowstairs." And then, on an even more irritable note, "You may go, Greg, no need to stand there with your great ears agape."

"I only know what Betty's told me." She watched the door close behind the man. "Some affray last night with a gang of smugglers, I understand, and the lieutenant thinks a wounded man might be hiding here. God knows why."

"No need to sound so prissy, girl. You know as well as I do where our brandy comes from—and our tea, for the matter of that. But that's not the question. What I want to know is, do we let them search?"

"Of course we must, Grandfather. They'll find nothing." She hoped she was right. "The sooner we let them search, the sooner we'll be rid of them."

"That's sense." He pulled himself creakily to his feet. "I'll have to see them. Richard's no more use than a tailor's dummy. Trust Ross to be away when he's needed. Gone to London to get his hair cut, of all the mad starts!" But he did not sound displeased. "Making a lady's man of himself, hey? And about time, too. Hasn't got eyes to see the length of his nose, that boy. Well, no wonder. Give me your arm, girl. They'll find nothing, you say?"

"Of course not, Grandfather. Parkes and I will see to them. You need not trouble yourself, beyond speaking to the lieutenant."

"Parkes and you, what?" Now he gave her a very sharp look indeed. "Where's that man of mine? I can't get down stairs with only a chit like you to support me!"

Lieutenant Trevis, growing impatient with the delay and Richard's small talk, emerged into the main hall in time to see old Mr. Tretteign make his laborious way downstairs, supported on one side by his tall granddaughter, on the other by the assiduous Greg. His old-fashioned tie wig, his brown suit made in the old style, with knee breeches and salmon-colored silk stockings, all contributed to a formidable effect. "Well, young man," he paused on the second to bottom step, thus maintaining a slight advantage of height. Christina, standing beside him, also seemed formidable, a tall brown-skinned goddess in gray worsted. "You've got me up five hours early," continued Mr. Tretteign. "What now?"

Lieutenant Trevis had had no intention of apologizing, but found himself doing so just the same as he explained about the man they had chased the night before, their quick search of the outbuildings and subsequent failure to find any trace of the wounded man elsewhere. "He must have had help," he concluded. "With your permission, sir, we'd like to search the house now."

"Or without it, what? I don't know what you expect to find. We lock up tight down here on the marsh. Doors and windows. Ask the butler—it's his job." He raised his voice. "Parkes! Where are you, man?"

"I already have, sir," said the lieutenant as Parkes emerged from the door to the servants' quarters. "He tells me all was locked as usual last night. But, suppose an accomplice inside—"

"One of the servants? Bah—they know better. But search if you must, Lieutenant, quickly . . . and get it over with. Parkes, let them in through the stable yard."

"Thank you, sir." The lieutenant went to the front door to give his orders to the men outside. Christina let out a little, silent breath. All this time she had been holding Richard's eyes with her own, defying him, silently, to mention finding the side door unlocked the night before.

He was looking extremely put out, she noticed, and his first words were reassuring. "I never heard of such an ill-managed business," he said. "Smugglers indeed! If it were to get about town that the house I stayed in had been under suspicion—why, it might cost me my promotion. I suppose you must let them search, Grandfather?"

"Of course I must. It is to all our interests to prove we are not harboring their wounded man."

"Wounded man! If you ask me, it's all a pack of lies. They never even came to grips with the smugglers—if they *were* smugglers and not some innocent night fishermen—and made up the story of wounding one of them to impress their superiors. As for suggesting he might be sheltering here, at Tretteign Grange—why it's unthinkable. And I can tell you I have given that young lieutenant a round warning that if word of this gets about I shall lodge a complaint where it will hurt him most."

"With the Duke of York?" The old man's voice was sardonic. "I did not know he was a friend of yours, Richard. Christina, while this imposition continues, I will drink a cup of bohea in the breakfast room."

"Yes, Grandfather."

The dragoons were quick, courteous and formidably efficient. Christina, who had hurried upstairs to warn her aunt of the impending search, watched with uneasy respect as two of them took the measurements of the upper hall in order to make sure there were no secret rooms or passages.

The lieutenant was directing operations, but turned to Christina as she emerged from her aunt's room. "You're the American young lady, are you not?"

"Yes."

"Would you know if there were any priests' holes or such?"

"I've certainly never heard of any, but of course I've only been here a few weeks."

"Precisely. And you heard nothing last night? This is your room, is it not? You will forgive us, I know, for searching it?" One of his men had just emerged with a shake of his head.

"Yes." She could not help being sorry for the young lieutenant, whose chain of reasoning was obvious: she was a stranger, recently arrived from America; she could not possibly be involved with the gang of smugglers. He thought he could trust her. For a moment, she was angry with herself. He ought to be able to trust her. But, it was no use: she was committed. "Of course you must search everywhere," she went on. "But I am sure you'll find nothing. I was awake for some time last night. I'm sure I should have heard anyone coming across the shingle. You know how noisy it is. And what difficult going. Could a wounded man . . ." She remembered Richard's suggestion. "Are you quite sure someone was wounded?"

For the moment they were alone in the hall, while his men moved systematically from one bedroom to the next. His eyes met her with a frank appeal she found hard to bear. "That's precisely my difficulty," he said. "I was not near enough to see. But my men are positive—"

"Only of course they might be—as a kind of—what do you British call it—point of honor?"

"That's about it. But, of course, we must search. You see, we had had a warning, from a Mrs. Emeret, who used to be housekeeper here. Before your time, I expect."

"On the contrary." Once again she could not help feeling sorry for him as he played into her hand. "I am afraid I was responsible for Mrs. Emeret's dismissal. When I arrived, I found her taking the grossest advantage of my grandfather, who is not, as you will have seen, so young as he was. I am afraid I acted rather high-handedly toward her. It is no wonder she bears us all a grudge."

"You think it merely that?"

"I'm sure of it. She left . . . very angry. And I have taken over her duties. There is not much goes on in this house that I am not aware of." She hoped she would not have to lie to him more directly.

"That is just what I thought. So you would know—"

"Of course I would." To her relief, his sergeant appeared at this point to report that they had found nothing upstairs.

"Have you seen the attics?" asked Christina helpfully.

"No, miss." He sounded at once surprised and taken aback.

"No wonder if you missed the entrance," she said kindly. "It *is* well concealed. I cannot imagine why." And she led them down the hall to the huge oak press where she kept the clean linen. "I'm afraid you have to move this away," she said. "It seems unlikely that it could have been done in the night, but I am sure you would rather . . ." She let the sentence hang, satisfied with having established herself so conclusively as on their side.

It took three men, and a good deal of *sotto voce* swearing, to get the huge cupboard moved aside to reveal the narrow door behind it. "Shall I ring for candles?" asked Christina. "I am afraid you are going to get terribly dirty. So far as I know, the attics have never been cleaned. They run the entire length of the house," she added, "and have been used, I believe, to store everything that was no longer needed downstairs. They should make a quite fascinating historical study. I have kept meaning to go up and take an inventory, only . . . they *are* so dirty."

It took the entire search party two hours to go through the attics, and when they finally emerged their once white trousers bore ample witness to the state of the attics. Downstairs they found Christina waiting for them. "That must have been thirsty work," she said. "There is some of our home brewed in the kitchen for your men, Lieutenant, and I hope you will take a glass of something with me." And then, as a complete afterthought, "You found nothing, of course?"

"Nothing but dust and spiders. Yes, we would be most grateful for some refreshment, Miss Tretteign. I had no idea it would take so long."

"Not Tretteign"—she led him into the morning room— "Tretton. I belong to the American branch of the family. Madeira, Lieutenant, or would you like to try some of our own mead?" She was glad to see that there was no smuggled brandy in evidence. One could rely on Parkes.

"May I try the mead? I've heard of the Romney brew, but never tasted it. I'm a stranger in these parts," he explained, "like you, Miss Tretton." He had changed the pronunciation of her name. Once again, she had got her point across.

"And where are you from, Lieutenant . . . Trevis, is it?" She poured him a brimming glass of mead. "It's strong, I warn you."

"It can't be too strong for me—not after those attics. But I'm obliged to you for telling me of them, just the same. It's good to know there's one member of the household I can trust. I was warned about the marshmen when I was posted here. They'll all hang together—till they all hang together, if you understand me. I'm from the west country, Miss Tretton, from Cornwall. Now, there's a county for you—all friends, all honest, all loyal . . ."

"You make it sound like an earthly paradise."

"Compared with Sussex, it is. You can't trust anyone here, Miss Tretton, not anyone. They're all in league—gentry as well, half the time—drinking run brandy, writing to their friends in France, giving information, I've no doubt, about our state of defense, whether intentionally or otherwise. Why, it's common knowledge there's a traffic with France from Hastings. Smugglers know no law, Miss Tretton, and no loyalty."

She was very much afraid he was right, and it was with considerable relief to her nagging conscience that she saw him rise to his feet. "It's done me good to talk to you, Miss Tretton, thank you. Sometimes I wish . . ." He broke off. "We must be on our way back to headquarters. You'll let me know if you see or hear of anything suspicious?"

"Of course." Hateful to have to lie to this friendly young man.

"Oh—one other thing." He turned back at the door. "Your cousin, Mr. Ross Tretteign. He rode off very suddenly this morning, from what I hear."

She had expected this and managed a laugh. "Yes. He *said* he was going to get his hair cut."

"You don't believe it?"

"Of course not, since he has gone on my business."

"Yours?"

"Yes. You'll not speak of it, I'm sure, since I have reasons for not wanting it discussed in the family, but I have a small estate—left me by my father—and there was some legal business. Ross kindly consented to act for me."

"Oh, I see. Miss Tretton, I am more grateful to you for your frankness than I can say. You'll laugh at me, I know, but his sudden departure—and on such an obvious pretext— you know, it had put the wildest ideas into my head."

She felt very far from laughter, but managed at least a smile. "Oh, poor Ross, did it seem so suspicious?"

They rode away at last. The next thing was to contrive a

word alone with Parkes, but she had had time, while the search continued, to plan for this. "Aunt Tretteign?" She joined her aunt and cousin in the morning room.

"Yes?" Fretfully. "Are they gone at last? I was never so shocked in my life as to have to turn out first thing in the morning for a parcel of filthy dragoons. A most ill-managed business on someone's part."

Christina laughed. "You'd be right to call them filthy after they made the tour of the attics, poor things. I really think we should spring-clean up there next year. Who knows what priceless heirlooms we might find?"

"Heirlooms perhaps," put in Richard, "but not, I am sure, priceless. If they had been, our esteemed grandfather would no doubt have sold them long since to satisfy his passion for gambling on 'change."

"Poor Grandfather," said Christina. "How he must have hated having to admit it."

"'Poor Grandfather' indeed." Mrs. Tretteign had been coming slowly to the boil. "How can you say that, Christina, after his behavior last night! But I suppose it's all of a piece."

"With my being a Yankee, you mean, and devoid of finer feelings?" Christina had grown tired of this favorite phrase of her aunt's. "Frankly I think it's just as well for me that I am."

"But anyone with the slightest perception can see you are not, Cousin Christina." This, with a languishing glance from Richard, made his intentions all too clear. Well, if she could prevent him, she would.

"You know me so well, after twenty-four hours acquaintance? Less, really. Your perceptions must be fine indeed, Cousin." And then, turning back to Mrs. Tretteign, "But I came to consult you, Aunt. Can you see any objection to my taking rubbings of some of the brasses in the old chapel?"

"Rub brasses, child? Today of all days? What in the world will you think of next?"

"But the brasses are beautiful. If I were to succeed in taking their likenesses they would make admirable decorations for this room—and, if well mounted, might even help to keep out some of the worst draughts."

"Well," her aunt cast a dubious look around the room, "if you can make the place look a trifle less Gothic, and maybe hide some of the marks in the plaster, so much the better.

But surely you will freeze to death out there in the chapel at this time of year."

"Oh no," said Christina cheerfully, "I'll wrap up warmly." She rang the bell and when, as she had hoped, Parkes appeared, she explained what she wanted.

He looked very old this morning, she thought, and shaky, but took her point at once with a quick, scarcely perceptible flash of red-rimmed eyes. "Brass rubbings in the chapel? Of course, Miss Christina. I'll make the arrangements directly."

"And I will come and show you what I need." She ran upstairs to put on the warm fur jacket her father had had made for her, and joined Parkes in the chapel. Standing in the doorway so she could make sure no one was near enough to overhear them, she asked, "How is he today, Parkes?"

"Poorly, miss. I'll be right glad to have you take a look at him. Mr. Ross says you're a first-rate nurse and will know what to do."

"I wish I were, but I'll certainly have a look at him, if you will keep watch here."

"Gladly, miss." He handed her the key that unlocked both doors. "You'll be as quick as you can?"

"I will indeed. If anyone comes you'll just have to say I took a fancy to walk in the cloisters—while Ross is not here to prevent it—and stop them coming after me."

"I'll do my best."

"I know you will."

Alone, she found the quiet of the cloisters oddly disconcerting. But there was no time to waste on imaginary ghosts. She hurried down the near side and opened the door to the windowless room where the Frenchman lay. He was unconscious still, but his pulse was steadier and there was little trace of fever. With luck, she thought, he should come about. At least, for today—she was busy removing the dressings from the wound—the question of meals would not arise to trouble them. She was convinced that he would be best without food. Parkes, she saw, had put a fresh jug of water and a solid pewter mug within his reach, and by the look of things he had drunk a little from it. Perhaps, after all, they would be able to pull him through without benefit of a doctor.

The wound was healing nicely. She dusted it with basilicum powder and put on a clean dressing, remembering, as she did

so, her Indian nurse. "Keep 'um plenty clean and dry," old
Nelema had said, "and they mend themselves." This time at
least, it looked as if she might be right.

For a fleeting instant, as she drew the new dressing tight,
Christina had the odd feeling that he was conscious and
watching her from veiled eyes. But why should he? If he remembered anything, he must know her for his friend. Anyway, she had no time to linger. She poured more water into
the mug, settled the blanket around him and hurried back to
the chapel.

And only just in time. She had the chapel door shut behind
her and was turning the key silently in the oiled lock when
she heard Richard's impatient voice from the stable yard.
"What do you think you are doing, blockhead?"

"I'm sure I beg your pardon, Mr. Richard." Now she could
see Parkes standing squarely across the far doorway. "It's
been such a morning, with soldiers all over the house, and
the old master frailer than I've seen him for years. . . . I
really don't know whether I'm on my head or my heels."

"You think old Mr. Tretteign ill?" Richard rose to the bait.

"I'm anxious about him, sir, I truly am. He's too old for
such carryings-on. Stands to reason it's taken it out of him.
I'm just glad you were here, sir, to take charge."

"One does one's best, of course." Richard sounded mollified. "But where's Miss Christina? I came to see how she is
getting on with this mad plan of hers."

"Oh, she's here right enough, Mr. Richard, working away."
And now, at last, he moved aside and let Richard enter the
room to find Christina very busy measuring a sheet of paper
against the largest of the brasses.

"I'd be truly grateful, sir," Parkes went on, "if you were to
give her a hand instead of me. I've got a thousand and one
things to see to after the morning we've had."

"Of course. You may go, Parkes." And then, to Christina,
"That old dodderer gets more intolerable every day. I wish
my grandfather could be persuaded to pension him off. He
might just as well have ordered me to come and help you.
Not that I'm not delighted to do so, of course." A comic
change of tone here. "But surely you should not be out here
in the cold, a delicate young lady like you."

"What's delicate about me?" When she stood up from the
paper she had been measuring, she towered half a head above

him. "But you will be cold, I am afraid, without your great-coat."

"No matter. It would be worth influenza—or even worse —to snatch a word alone with you, and in the house, you know, it's impossible, what with Greg listening at keyholes, and my aunt as inquisitive as she can hold together. How do you bear her, by the way?"

"You should rather ask how does she bear me. She has been wonderfully patient, I think, considering the way I seem to have come in and taken over."

"And about time, too. I tell you, I positively shuddered when last I was here, to think of the waste that went on in the servants' hall."

"Did you really? How very observant of you."

He missed the irony in her tone. "I think you will find, Cousin, that I am a man who can see what's before him as well as the next one. And that brings me to what I have been wishing to say to you. First, let me condole with you about this monstrous proposition of our grandfather's. I had not thought even he could do anything so out of the way. Could he be proved mad, do you think?" He threw it out as an idea that had just occurred to him.

"Of course not. He's as sane as you or I, and you know it."

"All the less excuse for him. To put you—a delicately nur-tured young lady—in so invidious a position—"

"I wish you would stop calling me delicate," she inter-rupted him impatiently. "You must see how far from the mark it is."

"I see that you are magnificent, Cousin Christina. An Am-azon . . . a Penthesilea—"

"I am afraid my classical education has been neglected," she said dryly. "If you wish to pay me compliments, you had best do it in English, Cousin, so I may understand you."

"Compliments! Nothing was further from my thoughts! It is sympathy I am offering, Cousin, in the predicament in which you find yourself. To be given no option but to engage yourself to me—it is an intolerable thing, and what no young lady of spirit, which, compliments apart, I know you to be, could possibly be expected to put up with."

"No option? What, precisely, do you mean by that? Can you be suggesting that our cousin Ross is already married?"

" 'Cousin Ross' indeed!" A dramatic pause. "Has no one told you . . ."

"Told me what?"

"I suppose I should have known. But . . . how can I tell you? It's far from being a proper subject for a . . ."

"Delicately nurtured female?" she put in. "Well, let me reassure you again, Cousin, I'm a woman from the American west. Anything you can bring yourself to say, I shall hear without blushing. But what is this monstrous thing? Tell me quickly."

"I must, I suppose. But believe me, with the greatest possible reluctance."

"Of course. We will assume your reluctance."

"Well, then—but how can I? My grandfather should have told you. It's monstrous—"

"I'm sure it is, but . . . what?"

"Have you not noticed that Ross never calls him grandfather?"

"Yes, I had, as a matter of fact."

"And for reason good." He was fairly into it now, and hurried on. "Because he's no kin of his. Ross was born, Cousin, when my uncle, who should have been his father, had been out of the country twelve months on a diplomatic mission." And then, anxiously, "Do you understand me?"

Try as she would, she could not help a spurt of laughter. "Just, Cousin." And then, sorry for his scandalized expression, "Forgive me. I should be shocked, should I not? Swoon perhaps?"

"It's no laughing matter, Cousin. You have not heard what came of it."

"No. What?"

"A duel, of course. What else? Had you never wondered how my father, and Ross's, both came to such untimely ends?"

Now there was no need to pretend shock. "You cannot mean . . ."

"Ross and I are half brothers. Mr. Tretteign—Aunt Verity's husband—was away for a year in Berlin. My father was" —he colored—"here, with my mother. When my Uncle Tretteign returned from Berlin, Ross was a few days old. Aunt Verity confessed everything . . ." Here a touch of scorn. "Of course a duel was inevitable. They fought in the cloisters, by moonlight . . ."

"And?"

"Ross's supposed father killed his real one—mine. Ours, I should say."

"You're half brothers." It was hard to grasp.

"Precisely. And not proud of it."

"But what happened to Mr. Tretteign?"

"He had to flee the country. Even here on the marsh it was impossible. . . . They fought without seconds . . . madness. He died, not long after, in the West Indies."

"Good God! And your mother?"

"Died soon after, when I was born. So Aunt Tretteign remained, the only female of the family, and brought us both up, Ross and me. It was all hushed up, you see. Grandfather wanted an heir. Ross could bear the name. I could not. But . . . he made his terms. Now you must see how the entail came to be broken. It was a promise made by Aunt Tretteign, on Ross's account."

"Which Ross chose to honor?"

"Well, yes, I suppose you could say that. But for Grandfather to turn round now and give him a chance at it all, and without even telling you that you'd be marrying a—forgive me, Cousin—a bastard! Do you wonder I suspect the old man of being out of his senses?"

"I'm sure my grandfather knew he could rely on you to tell me." Her thoughts were racing. This explained so much that had puzzled her. And something else that she would hardly let herself think. Her father had always been against her coming back, for fear, he had said, that she might marry one of her cousins. "I know it's not forbidden"—she thought she could hear him now—"but marriage between cousins is a mistake, Chris my love. Don't do it." Well, Ross was no kin of hers. The electric shock that had run through her when they first met, when his firm hands held her captive, had had nothing to do with blood relationship.

Richard had gone on talking all this time and she had not heard a word of it. "I . . . I beg your pardon, Cousin. What did you say?"

"No wonder if it disturbs you. I can only ask your pardon, once again, for being the reluctant teller of so sordid a story. But now you will understand that you have no choice in the matter. It was hushed up, of course. Grandfather did his best. But, equally of course, everyone who counts for anything knows all about it."

"I am sure they do."

"So there you are. Even his mother, I am sure, has more niceness of mind than to think it possible for you to marry Ross. And, believe me, Cousin, it is all for the best. He will doubtless propose for you as soon as he comes back from this mad excursion to London, but you must know as well as I do that it is only the Abbey he wants. Absurd that he, who has no claim to it, should pretend to care so much. Working as Grandfather's agent, forsooth! Did you know he sold out of the Thirty-third to do so?"

"No, I had no idea. He talks so little about himself."

"Why do you think he's such a bigwig with the Volunteers? Oh yes, that was part of the price of his waiving the entail. Grandfather bought him his commission in—I don't remember—'94, was it? And of course he's just the kind of daredevil—excuse me, Cousin—the kind of character to do well in the army."

"He did well, did he?"

"Well enough, I believe." Grudgingly. "He served in that unlucky business in the Netherlands. You've never heard of it."

"In '94? You mean

> 'The grand old Duke of York
> With twice ten thousand men—
> He marched them up to the top of the hill
> And he marched them down again'?

I can remember laughing about that when I was in the nursery."

"The Duke of York is our king's son." Stiffly. "And, I can tell you, it was no laughing matter to Ross. He didn't care a rush for his life, they said. I suppose that's how he came to be mentioned in dispatches. An odd business, though. He served right through till 1802 and sold out at the peace of Amiens. Apparently he's been content to lead a slug's life here on the marsh ever since. I thought he was sure to rejoin when war broke out again last year, but not a bit of it. Tired of being a hero, I suppose. At least he seems content enough leading his bumpkin's life of sheep and turnips down here.

And I warn you, that's what you'd find yourself in for if you should be so foolish as to let him talk you round. And—not that he cares a straw for them—he has a way with the girls, I know. I'll not tell tales out of school, but—"

"No, I am sure you will not."

"Quite so. Of course not. I am just trying to show you, Cousin, how fully I sympathize with you in the predicament in which you find yourself. That it is intolerable, we can only admit, and then set about contriving expedients to mend it."

"Expedients?" She might as well get this conversation over with.

"Yes. Of course, I can quite see, that to a young lady of your spirit, the first impulse must be to wash your hands of the whole pack of us. But, what could you do? Where could you go?"

"Where indeed?"

"Of course, the old curmudgeon may change his will, but, frankly, I doubt it. He was always an obstinate old brute."

"You are referring to our grandfather?"

"Who else? He signed that crazy will this morning, you know. Foxton has taken it back to London with him. I rather thought he meant to suggest it would not be safe here. But no use quarreling with him. After all, he may be serving our interest yet."

"Ours?"

"Yes, ours. Yours and mine. Cousin!" Here he caught her reluctant hand. "I know you must have had a young lady's dreams—moonlight, music, the man of your choice. . . . It is our grandfather's fault that we must do it thus in hugger-mugger. But never mind. These days marriage is no bar to romance. . . . That may come later. It's quite the thing, you know. The Duchess of Devonshire has had I don't know how many lovers . . . her husband's just the same. And as for the Oxfords! Well, their children aren't called the Harleian Miscellany for nothing! And you and I will not even have the problem of heirs for an estate, since my plan—and I am sure you will agree with me—will be to sell off the whole place the minute the old tartar is safe in his grave. With what it fetches we should be able to take a house in one of the squares. You shall have your own carriage, your own life—a little entertaining on my account, perhaps. I have no doubt that once I can show a proper face to the world, promotion at the Admiralty will follow. I only get a beggarly two hundred pounds now as a junior clerk. It all goes by favor, of course, and where's my influence? My grandfather never raised a finger to help me. But you—a handsome creature like you—driving your own matched bays in the park, cutting a dash in society. I can just see it. What will they call you, I wonder, if you take? La Belle Sauvage, perhaps? It cannot help but do me good. Melville's an old stick, of course . . . you can hardly hope to catch his fancy, but why look so low? With me to show you the ropes—society's a tricky business—but, who knows, we might even catch one of the royal dukes."

She was so angry she could hardly speak. And yet, would it be wise to quarrel with him? "Why not the prince himself?" she asked.

"Prinney? Why not? He's at outs with both his wife and the Fitzgerald, they say. And he's always liked a fine figure of a woman."

"You really mean it!"

"When you blush, Cousin, you are magnificent. Prinney it shall be."

"I am not blushing." Her control gave with a snap. "I am so angry, I could . . ." She saw him flinch. "Don't worry, Cousin, I would never hit someone smaller than myself. As for your proposition, the kindest thing I can do for you is forget that you ever made it."

His dismay was ludicrous. "But the Abbey? You cannot mean to let it go to the Patriotic Fund? Your family pride must revolt at the idea!"

"Must it? Yours finds no difficulty, it seems, in planning to sell it. Besides, with a little conversion, think what an admirable fortress it should make. Who knows? They might decide to pull it down and use the materials for one of the Martello Towers you keep talking about."

"I wish you would be serious, Cousin."

"Do you? I think you should be grateful I am not. If I were to take you seriously, I believe I should see no alternative but to call you out."

"Fight me? You? A woman? Now I know you are teasing. I should just like to see you handle a gun."

"Would you? What did you call me? La Belle Sauvage? Well, you're right: I've been brought up like one. I can hit a pigeon on the wing, Cousin. I could draw and have you covered before you had so much as closed your snuffbox. Perhaps you will be so good as to remember that before you come to me with any more of your 'propositions.' And now, I should be glad to be left alone. We will forget what has passed, though I confess I should find it easier to do so if urgent business were to call you back to London."

"But what shall I tell the old man?"

"Mr. Tretteign? Oh, if you wish to justify yourself with him by telling him you have tried, and failed, I will be happy to confirm your story. It cannot but do me good in his eyes."

"You're playing for the whole! Infamous."

She had been half leaning, as they talked, against the tomb whose brass top she intended to rub. Now she rose to her full height and towered over him like a fury. But her words, when they came, were mild enough. "Cousin, I do beg you will leave me before I say something I shall regret."

Chapter Seven

RICHARD MARKHAM left for London that evening after a stormy interview with his grandfather. "Failed with you, did he?" The old man had lost no time in sending for Christina. "Well, I thought he would. Thought I could trust your judgment, girl."

"You think I'll marry Ross, bar sinister and all?"

"Richard told you, did he? Trust him to make a mull of things. Made you angry, didn't it? Made you understand a thing or two as well, or you're not the girl I take you for. You see what I'm aiming at now, hey? The name and the blood, at all costs. You and Ross—you're a Tretteign through and through and at least he's a man, not a counter-coxcomb like Richard. You see it now, don't you?"

"Yes, Grandfather, but I don't like it. Please, I beg of you, send for Mr. Foxton again and leave the Grange to Ross outright. That's what you really want . . . you know it is."

"Nonsense. I won't have it go out of the family. If you won't marry Ross, I'd rather it went to Richard. Fool though he is, at least he's my blood, my daughter's son. But what's the matter with you, hey? I didn't think to find you so squeamish. It's no use trying to pretend you don't want Ross, because I've watched you. Well, I've handed him to you, on a slaver. Trouble with him is, he don't much care for women, not in the marrying line, that is, and I can't say I blame him. Maybe you could have brought him round, given time, but time's what I've not got, see? I want it settled before I go. And now, no more argument. I'm tired."

Downstairs, Christina found her aunt on the lookout for her. "There you are at last. Is he very angry?"

"Grandfather? Why?"

"Well, you've refused them both, haven't you? I hope you know what you're doing, Christina, because I am sure I don't. All I ask is that you don't come crying to me for help when you find yourself homeless and the Grange full of soldiers—or worse. . . . Yes, Parkes?"

"If I might have a word with Miss Christina? We're all topsy turvey in the servants' hall I'm afraid."

"The girls crying their eyes out, I expect, because the soldiers are gone. I saw your Betty, Christina, being a good deal more oncoming than I liked, but of course if you will promote a girl from the kitchen—"

"And such a pretty one." Christina had risen to her feet. "But, thank you, Aunt, for warning me. I'll have a word with Betty. I most certainly don't want to lose her now we have got used to one another's ways."

" 'Got used' indeed. I wish you would try to overcome these Republican notions of yours. No wonder if we are under suspicion here with such an arrant Jacobin in our midst."

"I'm sorry, Aunt." Christina had no intention of letting herself be drawn into this kind of discussion. "You will excuse me?"

She led Parkes into the dark little office she had made her own and watched while he took a careful look down the hall and shut the door behind him. "Well, how is he?"

"Feverish, miss. I wish you would make an excuse to come and look at him."

"Oh dear." She looked out at the marsh, where evening shadows were already beginning to thicken. "I can hardly be rubbing brasses in the dark. I know! I have been cooped up indoors all day. And I am terribly afraid of the smugglers."

"No one's going to believe that, miss. Not for a moment."

"No? Well, never mind. Then I am afraid of being bothered again by the military. I shall brave the ghosts and take my walk in the cloisters. And you, Parkes, will be tidying away my things in the chapel. I don't intend to go and see M. Tissot without your being within call."

"Quite right, miss. Jem keeps an eye out in the chapel when I go."

"Jem? He's to be trusted, is he?"

"I should rather think he is, miss. His father—"

She raised a hand. "Don't tell me, Parkes. I'd much rather not know."

She found the Frenchman muttering restlessly on the cot, and wished, when she felt his hot, damp forehead, that it was possible to get a doctor to him. But since this was out of the question, she would just have to do her best with the little kit of medicines she had got used to carrying when she and her father lived miles from medical aid. M. Tissot was not violent, though delirious, and submitted to her ministrations willingly enough, though he gagged at the bitter draught she made him swallow, and then suddenly opened blue eyes very wide. "Ah, the ministering angel," he said in his quick French. "Now I shall recover."

"You will if you do as I tell you."

Parkes was awaiting her anxiously in the chapel. "Will he do, do you think?"

"I hope so. He should really be bled, but that I don't dare do. I suppose there's no one . . ."

"No. Mr. Ross and I discussed it before he left. He must just sink or swim, Mr. Ross said."

"If he dies, it will be our fault."

"Well," Parkes was reasonable, "think, miss. What will happen to him if he is discovered here? And to us, for the matter of that. No, no, believe me, Miss Christina, Mr. Ross knows best. We must just do as he says."

"I suppose we must, but I do devoutly hope he hurries back."

"So do I."

But the days dragged out interminably and still there was no word from Ross. His grandfather was working himself up into a slow dreadful rage because he thought Ross was defying him by staying away. His mother was in a fretful fury for more or less the same reasons. And Christina was beginning to feel the strain of her long bout of secret nursing, particularly as the best time for ministering to M. Tissot was after the family were asleep at night. Worried by Parkes' exhausted look, she had insisted that Jem take his place in standing guard for her when she crept down, with her candle, to change the dressings and administer the Indian draught that was, she hoped, gradually breaking the fever. It was a relief to find Jem a tower of strength, for all his deceptively youthful appearance. "You can rely on me, miss," he had said the first night. "Father says you're a proper Tretteign. Father—"

"Hush." Once again she quenched the confidence before it could be made. But of course, if Jem's father was one of the smuggling band, she had doubtless met him that first night on the marsh. She only hoped his had not been the voice that urged her death.

As if the strain in the house were not bad enough already, a wild northeaster had built itself up and blew in, night and day, day and night, from the Channel, so that even at the Grange, several hundred yards from the sea, the front windows were constantly misted with spray, and the air tasted of salt. Mrs. Tretteign huddled over the fire that blew gusts of smoke into the morning room. "It's an invasion wind," she told Christina. "If only Ross were back! What if they land in the night and he's not here to protect us?"

"If they land," said Christina, "we'll need more than Ross to protect us. But, cheer up, Aunt, it's not an invasion wind, you know. They need a southeaster to get across the Channel. And nothing so rough as this either. Those flat-bottomed boats of theirs wouldn't last half an hour in weather like this."

"Are you sure?" Mrs. Tretteign looked nervously over her shoulder as if she expected to see a Frenchman in the doorway. "Just think what it would be like if they did land—leaving the house, in the middle of the night perhaps . . . jolting across the marsh in the dark. And God knows where to. You know your grandfather won't plan anything."

"I do indeed." Their orders were that, in case of an invasion, the whole marsh was to be evacuated to behind the new military canal that was being dug, but she had tried in vain to persuade old Mr. Tretteign to make any plans for such an eventuality. "I mean to die here where I have lived," was all he would say, but it was no use frightening her aunt still more by telling her this. "Never mind, Aunt," she said instead, "my guess is they won't come till spring—if then."

"And what makes you think that, pray?"

Dangerous ground here. In one of his lucid intervals, Tissot had told her of confusion and sickness in the invasion camps around Boulogne. Did she believe him? She was no more sure of this than she was of the real state of his health. Was he, in fact, better, and shamming it? But why? Parkes, whom she had consulted on this point, was convinced she was mistaken. "He's ill all right, miss. It's just, I think, that he makes a special effort for you. If you had heard him speak, as I have, of his gratitude to you and your medicines . . . but he's very weak still, no doubt of that. He can't move so much as across the room unaided."

Since he and Jem inevitably carried the burden of the heavier nursing, they should certainly know. She was tired, overwrought, doubtless imagining things.

The wind blew more wildly than ever that night, lashing the rain against her windows. Her bed looked almost irresistibly inviting. If only she could lie down and sleep the sleep of exhaustion all night through. But Jem would be waiting for her in the kitchen. She sighed, raked together the embers of her fire and huddled over it, forcing herself to stay awake until she had counted off, one by one, the familiar noises that told of the household's progress toward sleep.

At last it was time. She changed into her warmest morning dress and hurried silently downstairs. Jem was nodding in front of the kitchen fire, but roused instantly at sight of her. "Did you bring the medicine, miss?" He picked up a heavy cloak that was warming by the fire. "You'll need this. It's a dirty night out. Mr. Ross wouldn't mind."

"No. I wish he was back." Absurd comfort in putting on the well-worn cloak.

"So do I. He's worse tonight, Mr. Parkes thinks. Rambling again. Couldn't understand a word of it either, he said."

"I suppose not." A Frenchman's delirium. "Well, let's get it over with, Jem."

Tonight it was too easy to imagine the cloisters haunted. The wind was worrying its way through gaps in the old stonework; water dripped here and there. Christina thought of falling stones and suppressed a shudder.

"Shall I come with you, miss?" Jem asked it anxiously as they stood in the doorway of the chapel. "I doubt if I could hear you call, against the wind."

"Why should I need to call?" But it was tempting. "No," she made herself sound decided, "you know we agreed you should stay here and keep guard."

"Then be as quick as you can."

"Believe me, I will." She took the lantern he had been carrying and scudded, head down, along the side of the cloister. Absurdly, her hands were shaking so that she had to put the lantern down and use them both to fit the heavy key into its lock. The room was dark and silent and she stood for a moment in the doorway, steadying herself, quieting her own breathing so she could listen for the sick man's. Yes, he was breathing fast and irregularly. Now, as she moved forward into the room to put her lantern down on the table, she could see him stirring restlessly on the bed. He began to mutter to himself in French, "Quick, quick, they'll see you . . ." Some nightmare, no doubt, from his past.

She dropped the wet cloak on a chair and moved over to the bed. "M. Tissot!" Surprisingly, his forehead felt cold and damp under her hand. She had expected a renewal of fever. Was this better? If only she could be sure.

Either her voice or her touch had roused him. He sat bolt upright in bed. "Quick!" he said again. "Quick!" And then, "Oh, mademoiselle, it is you! A thousand pardons. I was dreaming. . . ." He pulled the bedclothes around his shoulders as if to hide the borrowed nightshirt.

"You've had a bad day?" She must decide whether to administer her draught or not. If the fever had already broken . . .

"Not so good as I had hoped."

She could feel him shivering under the heavy blanket. "Let me see your wound." And then, as he reluctantly emerged again, "Good God, you're soaking!" The fever must indeed have broken. "Did Parkes leave a dry nightshirt?"

"I . . . I believe so. But I cannot allow you . . ."

"Nonsense." She found the nightshirt where Parkes had hung it and brought it back to the bed. "Gently now." Luckily, the bedclothes among which he continued to huddle as she eased the soaking shirt over his bad shoulder seemed dry. "There. Now you will feel better." The change completed, she dropped the soaking shirt in the corner of the room and proceeded to remove the dressings from the wound. "Ah, splendid. There's nothing wrong with that. I hope, now, you will be as good as new in a few days."

"A few days! But, mademoiselle, are you not aware . . . tomorrow's the night."

"Tomorrow?"

"Yes. Is Monsieur not back yet?"

"No. And no word from him."

"*Mordieu* . . ." And then, "Forgive me . . . but . . . tomorrow. And no word from London?"

"None. But . . . he knows it's tomorrow?"

"Of course."

"Then, never fear, he will come. Or send word. Now, try and get some sleep and don't let yourself worry. It's bad for you."

"Not worry! Mademoiselle, you ask the impossible!"

She must hurry. Parkes might not yet be asleep and she must talk to him tonight. He would know what to do if Ross did not return. Or, at least, she hoped he would.

She was outside, turning her key in the lock when she remembered the shirt, hurriedly dropped in the corner of the room. No time to go back for it now. Parkes would just have to filch another from the chest in Ross's room. She finished turning the key, pulled it out—and stifled a scream.

"Brave girl." Ross's voice, close beside her in the darkness. "I knew I could count on you."

"I'm glad you think so. You frightened me nearly out of my wits, materializing beside me like that. Where on earth did you come from?"

"Nonsense." He ignored her question. "Nerves of steel, Chris, and you know it. How is he?"

"Better . . . but far from well. Thank God you're back. He can't possibly go tomorrow, Ross. It would kill him."

"Tomorrow? Oh . . . he told you?"

"Yes, just now. What will you do?"

"Go myself. There's no alternative."

"To France? Ross—you can't!"

"You think not?" He broke into French as fluently idiomatic as her own. "What a fortunate thing nobody knows I'm back."

"Nobody knows?" It was a momentary distraction from the point at issue. "But, how?"

"A method of my own, with which I do not propose to burden you. There's enough for you to pretend ignorance of already. Who's keeping guard for you?"

"Jem. Parkes is worn out."

"He'll have to be waked just the same. I can't risk trusting Jem with this knowledge. His father . . ." He paused.

"Don't worry. I rather think I know about Jem's father. But, must you go, Ross?"

"If M. Tissot's not well enough, I must. There is too much hangs on this. . . . Is he awake?"

"He was when I left him."

"Come, then." He took the key from her and turned it silently in the lock.

They found M. Tissot stirring and muttering on his bed, half asleep, half awake. He started up at sight of Ross. "At last! You have the packet?"

"Of course. But my friend here tells me you are not well enough to take it."

"Absurd!" He sat up straighter in bed, his flushed cheeks and shaking hand belying his words. "All I need is some air . . . I ask you, cooped up for—how long? I've lost count . . . in a hole like this!" He ran a trembling hand through his hair. "If only I could stop dreaming! Are they dreams? There's blood—oceans of blood, and the guillotine in the middle of it,—Madame la Guillotine herself, crying out for more. Tell me it was merely a nightmare!"

"Of course." Christina's voice was soothing as she laid her hand once more on his brow. It was still surprisingly clammy to the touch. "He has no fever," she said, "but you can see . . . it would never do."

"No." Ross accepted it almost, she thought, with relief. "Very well, then, Chris. Send the boy to bed, wake Parkes, and send him here to me."

"But . . ."

"No buts." He was ushering her out again through the door. "And no time to argue either, or the boy will be coming to find what's keeping you."

It was true. "You'll stay here?"

"Perhaps. I'll lie low at all events. Don't worry."

"No? I'll see you before you go?"

"Best not. You'll look after him for me."

"Of course. But . . . your . . ." She was going to say grandfather, then remembered. "Mr. Tretteign is asking for you. He's getting very angry."

"Oh." He digested this, standing there in the cold darkness. "Very angry?"

"Yes. He thinks you're deliberately flouting him."

"Well, you know what you can do about that, don't you, Chris? Tell him it's been settled between us all the time."

"You can't expect me to!"

"No? You underestimate me, Chris. But I leave it to you. Only, remember, this is not child's play I'm engaged in. If I think it worth the risk of my life, surely you can endure a little temporary inconvenience."

She could not help a quick, sardonic laugh at this description of their engagement. "Well, if I must . . ." She let it hang. "But, Ross, how long will you be gone?"

"Who knows? It depends on the next shipment—and on other things . . ."

"You'll be careful?"

"Of course. I'm always careful. Hush—here he comes." He melted away behind her into the darkness.

"Are you there, miss?" She could hear Jem's voice quite clearly and was not surprised when he went on. "I thought I heard you talking."

"Just wishing M. Tissot good night. The wind's dropped, thank God." She managed an enormous yawn. "Well, bed at last, Jem."

"Should not I see if he needs anything for the night?"

"No. He said he was dropping off to sleep already."

"Lucky him." Jem locked the door behind her and lit her back to the kitchen. There she paused. "You go on up, Jem. I must make myself some hot milk or I'll never sleep."

Luckily Parkes slept downstairs to be near his silver, the only servant who did. She made a little business preparing her hot milk, thus giving Jem plenty of time to get out of earshot to his attic bedroom, then crossed the kitchen to tap lightly on the door of Parkes' room.

He came to the door so quickly—and fully dressed—that she knew he must sit up every night until he heard her come safely back to the house. "What is it, miss?"

"Mr. Ross is back. He wants to see you, Parkes, in the cloisters. No one else is to know. Not even Jem. He says he must go, tomorrow night, in the Frenchman's place. Dissuade him if you can, Parkes."

"Me? Change Mr. Ross's mind for him? Miss Christina! But . . . it's tricky . . . not even Jem? Yes . . . well, that makes sense. The rest of them don't know, of course . . ."

"That he's anything more than a smuggler? No, I thought

not . . ." It explained a good deal. "But, Parkes—to go to France . . ."

"He's been before."

"Does that make it any less dangerous? More so, I should have thought. Oh, if only he'd let me talk to him."

"Wasting your breath, miss." Parkes had by now enveloped himself in his heavy greatcoat and was ready to go. "I'll tell you something he said to me, once, when I was talking much as you are now. 'There are things, Parkes, that are more important than safety.' That's what he said, and there you have it."

"Yes . . . thank you, Parkes. But tell him to be careful. For his own sake."

"Of course. Good night, miss."

But still she lingered, blocking the doorway. "If I could only see him again, before he goes. Ask him, Parkes?"

"I'll *ask* him, if you like. But he said not?"

"Yes."

"Well then?"

She sighed. "I know. Good night, Parkes."

Chapter Eight

NEXT MORNING was sunshine after storm. But the blue prospect of spreading bay and misty cliff was small comfort to Christina. Straining her eyes, she saw, far out to sea, the sails of a small ship.

"Betty!"

"Yes, miss." Betty finished pouring hot water into the rose-wreathed basin and put down her jug.

"Come and look. What's that ship?"

"Ooh." A long sigh of excitement. And then, casually, "One of them French privateers, by the looks of her."

"I thought so. There was one, was there not, the first day I was here?"

"Was there?" More casual than ever, "I'm sure I don't remember."

So Betty knew all about the smuggling too. A father? A brother? Was the whole household in the know? At least it was no wonder that there had been no comment on the steady disappearance of food from the larder. Very likely everyone in the servants' hall knew of the stranger hiding in the cloisters. So long as they thought of him only as a French smuggler . . .

Hurrying downstairs to her solitary breakfast, Christina wondered where Ross was now. In the cloisters still, sharing whatever Jem brought for the Frenchman? No, surely if he had intended spending the day there, he would have let her come to him. Or would he? At all events, without his permission, she knew she could not go. Perhaps he would still be there when she made tonight's visit to M. Tissot. She spilled

102

coffee. Absurd to hope; she knew perfectly well he would be gone.

A summons, immediately after breakfast, to her grandfather's rooms was a relief because it was a distraction. Or, at least, a relief till she got there. He was sitting up in his big four-poster bed, his breakfast tray pushed down toward his feet, the mail bag open on the bed beside him.

"Good morning, Grandfather." She leaned down to kiss the dry cheek. "Is the mail here already?"

"Yesterday's. And still not a word from Ross. I'll not endure it, I tell you! If he thinks he can turn me up sweet by this kind of behavior, he'll soon find his mistake. I want you to write a letter for me, Christina. At once."

"Grandfather—"

"Don't 'Grandfather' me," he interrupted her. "I may be an old man but I know my own mind still, and I know an insult when I get one. How long's he been gone? No—don't tell me, I can count. And not a word. Right—so much for Ross. Sit down, girl. Find pen and paper. The letter's to Foxton, of course. You know how to dear sir him and all that. Put it politely, if you want to, but tell him to come back—at once. And to bring a new will with him, ready drafted. Everything to you, on condition you give no help of any kind to Ross—or Richard, for the matter of that. D'you know what he's planning? Richard! To sell the Grange! Sell it, I tell you, the minute he inherits. I've a letter here from a friend —the young fool's not even got the sense to keep his mouth shut till I'm dead. At least you were right about him, I'll say that for you. And as for Master Ross, you be quiet, girl, and be grateful if I don't brand him a bastard for all the world to know of. Flout my commands, will he? Go off to London in a huff and never write! I'll show him. . . . Now what are you doing?"

She had risen and moved away to the far side of the room. "Fetching you your drops, Grandfather. You will undoubtedly have one of your attacks if you go on shouting so." She poured the drops into a glass and held it out to him with a steady hand. "There, drink that and listen to me for a moment. This is all my fault."

"Your fault? Nonsense!" And then, on a different note, "What do you mean?"

"Just that I engaged myself to Ross the night you made your remarkable proposition."

"What! And never told me!"

"No. Allow me a little pride. I do not really enjoy being put up to the highest bidder, but if it had to be Ross or Richard—well, what would you have done?"

"Just what you have! There's my good girl! Take away those nauseous drops! I don't need drops! This is such a tonic as I've not had these thirty years. I knew I'd bring things about yet, and, by God, I've done it. Engaged yourself to Ross, did you, and never told me! Well, I don't altogether say I blame you for that. A girl must have her pride, what? But where is the wretched boy? Not insulting me, then, but . . . you perhaps? I won't stand for that, and so you may tell him."

"Nothing of the kind, Grandfather. I wish you will try not to jump to conclusions so. Ross is in London on my business . . ."

"*Your* business?"

"Yes. I told that nice young Lieutenant Trevis the day Ross left. He's in town on my account. I had heard, you see, from my father's man of business. There were some loose ends to be tied up. Ross is doing it for me."

"Oh?" A very sharp glance from under the bushy brows. "Should I believe a word you are telling me, do you think?"

"Suit yourself, Grandfather. Lieutenant Trevis did."

"Hmmm . . . I thought him easily satisfied. Made big eyes at him, I suppose, and had him eating out of your hand. Well, just as well, come to that. But when's he coming back?"

"The lieutenant?"

"Don't pretend to be stupid, girl. You know I mean Ross."

"I don't know. I've heard nothing from him. I can only suppose the business took longer than he expected. Or maybe he's not best pleased either to be bullied into matrimony."

"Bullied? Who said anything about bullying? Didn't have to propose to you, did he? Well then . . . anyway, he'll come round, don't you worry, girl. He'll realize soon enough how lucky he is."

"Do you think so?" She could not quite keep the bitterness out of her voice.

"I'm sure of it. Now don't you start getting missish notions into your head. You know as well as I do you're just what

Ross needs, only he's let that mother of his put him off the whole notion of females. And you can't blame him for that either. Give him a little time and he'll come round, sweet as sixpence; you see if he doesn't."

"I thought time was just what you did not propose to give him."

"What? Oh, you mean the proviso about my dying. Yes, but I don't reckon to die yet, girl. So long as my health stays good you can have as long an engagement as you please, and bring Ross round your thumb by easy stages. I tell you, I'll enjoy watching that. It will give me something to live for. Life gets dull, you know, when you're old, and this will be as good as a play to me."

Anger rose to flood tide in her. As good as a play, indeed! He would watch, would he, while she and Ross played out his comedy for him? Almost, she burst out with it all—almost, but not quite. As always, in moments of crisis, she thought of her father. "Think before you speak, Christina." How often he had said it, and how right he had been. The moment had passed. She rose to her feet. "I am glad you find it all so entertaining, Grandfather."

"Still angry with me?" He was no fool. "Never mind, you'll bless me yet, you see if you don't."

Luckily for her, Parkes made an answer unnecessary. "Lieutenant Trevis is here, Miss Christina, asking for you."

"Trevis? Is he . . . alone?"

"Yes, miss." A quick exchange of glances. "No search party this time."

"Well, thank goodness for that. It was quite bad enough clearing up after the last one. You will excuse me, Grandfather?"

"Of course. I told you he was sweet on you. Off you go, girl, and administer the *coup de grâce,* but don't forget Ross."

"Trust me, I won't."

Lieutenant Trevis was awaiting her in the small downstairs room she used as study and office combined. "Miss Tretton!" His color was high as he came forward to greet her. "I was riding by and could not resist the temptation to call and make sure you have forgiven me for the inconvenience we caused you on our last visit. And that you have had no trouble since."

"Trouble?"

"I did wonder. You see, we have found no trace of the wounded man, and no one is missing locally either. You would have let me know, I am sure, if any of your servants had been mysteriously indisposed."

"Of course." She felt a brute. "No, the staff, such as they are, are all present and all well. I was sure, you know, that your men deluded themselves when they thought they had wounded one of the smugglers."

"I suppose that must be it. She's here again. Had you noticed?"

"She?"

"They call her a French privateer, but I'm convinced she's the smugglers' contact. I'm on my way now to alert the shore batteries between here and Rye Harbor. She was here for several days, I remember, hovering on and off, before our last affray. I wish I knew where they got their information. It's always when the Downs Squadron is out at sea, otherwise we'd soon have the lot of them in Dover Castle. She's too fast for any of our small ships, but just let a line of battle ships get after her, and it would be the end of our troubles. I sent an urgent message to the Admiralty this morning. I just hope some good may come of it. But of course there's no chance of getting anything done for a day or so and no doubt by then she'll have landed her cargo and skedaddled. If only I knew where. . . . You've seen nothing suspicious, Miss Tretton? I know you like to walk on the beach."

"Not a thing." This at least was true. "But surely they would never land in the same place twice?"

"Unless as a kind of a double bluff. They're a wily lot, this gang. No good deceiving oneself they're just a parcel of country bumpkins. There's a brain behind them—and all the information they could wish. You'll say nothing to anyone of what I've told you, will you? I have no doubt you have one of their informers right here in this house."

"You terrify me, Mr. Trevis." This, too, was perfectly true.

"Don't expect me to believe that," he said. "You're not one to be afraid of a cowardly gang of smugglers, Miss Tretton. You're . . ." He paused, colored and, greatly to her relief, took his leave.

It went sadly against the grain with her, but as soon as he was gone she rang the bell for Parkes.

"Come in and shut the door," she greeted him. And then, "There's no one outside?"

"No, miss."

"Good. You must tell Mr. Ross they're on the lookout for him. Lieutenant Trevis has recognized the ship . . . the posts will be alerted all along the coast. And—there's worse—he's sent to the Admiralty for a frigate."

"I doubt he'll get one, miss, for a mere privateer. And . . . Mr. Ross has gone. But"—he saw the change in her face— "I'll do my best to get a message to him. It's to be tonight, but not here."

"Thank God for that. I think Lieutenant Trevis is expecting what he calls a double bluff."

"That's just what Mr. Ross said. Now, don't you worry about anything, Miss Christina. It will all go right, I promise you. Mr. Ross is not without friends, you know; powerful ones. It's just that they can't show themselves in the business. If he were so unlucky as to be caught, it would be another matter. Then they would intervene on his behalf. It would be the end of his usefulness, of course."

"I don't care about that. But, Parkes, he might not survive until his powerful friends intervened."

"Mr. Ross? He's got nine lives. Don't you worry yourself about him." And then, "That Frenchman's worse again. Can you come early this evening?"

"I'll do my best. Is it bad enough, do you think, that I should risk a daytime visit?"

"I don't think so, but he's awful restless and muttering away to himself fit to beat the band."

"Oh dear, and I thought he was well on the way to recovery. Parkes . . ."

"Yes, miss?"

Best not ask it. The less she knew, the better. "Nothing. Only . . . I wish it were all over."

"So do we all, miss. But it won't be, not while Boney's running wild over there. Remember, every risk Mr. Ross takes helps to bring the day of his downfall nearer."

"You really think so?"

"I know so, miss. He works direct to Mr. Pitt himself. Many's the war plan has been changed suddenly after Mr. Ross landed one of his cargoes."

"He really does smuggle?" She had somehow hoped against hope that it was merely a false front.

"Course he does. How would he get the help else? Don't look so grave, miss. No one thinks anything of a little smuggling, down here on the marsh." And then, on a totally different note, "Very good, Miss Christina, I'll see to it at once."

He held the door open courteously for Mrs. Tretteign, who rustled into the room with her usual discontented expression. "You might have told me we had a guest, Christina. It is not at all the thing for you to be receiving young men by yourself."

"Young . . . oh, you mean the lieutenant."

"He hasn't got a long gray beard that I have noticed. These hoydenish tricks may be all very well in those United States of yours, but they won't do here, Christina, and so I must warn you."

"Thank you, Aunt." And then, unable to carry meekness any further, "But I did not think you would be dressed for company so early."

"Now was I, or I should have been here sooner. I care about your reputation—and the family's—even if you do not. I have been meaning to have a word with you ever since the young men left. They are your cousins, of course, which is some excuse for the freedom of behavior you allowed yourself with them, but—Lieutenant Trevis! One of the army's new officers, jumped up from God knows where! I've seldom been so shocked in my life."

"You surprise me, Aunt." Best leave it at that.

"Dear Christina." Mrs. Tretteign amazed her by taking her hand and fixing her with a look that was meant to be charged with meaning. If it failed somewhat of its purpose, this was largely because Christina stood a head taller than she. Apparently aware of this difficulty, Mrs. Tretteign pulled gently on the unresisting hand and led her to a small sofa. "There." She settled herself with a pretty rustling of skirts. "Dear Christina, I have so longed for just such a comfortable chat as this. We have so much to say to each other, you and I."

"Have we?" Christina knew she sounded farouche, and did not care.

"Of course we have. Dear child, do you not understand how I feel for you in the appalling position into which Papa has forced you. There is no need for us to beat about the bush is there, my love? If we cannot talk frankly to each other, who can?"

Who indeed? But Christina left the thought unsaid, merely fixing her aunt with a look of what she hoped would be taken for intelligent inquiry.

"The old man's mad, of course," Mrs. Tretteign went on. "But not, I fear, provably so. Mr. Foxton's never cared a rush for the rest of us. It leaves us in a mighty awkward situation."

"Us?" Christina could not help it.

"Of course. Am I not telling you how I feel for you? But don't fret, my dear, it could be much worse. Richard will make an admirably complaisant husband. Really, he's just what a girl like you needs."

"Richard?"

"Well, naturally." A peal of girlish laughter. "You don't think I am going to go down on my bended knees and plead my son's cause, do you? Ross! He cares no more for me, nor for you, nor for anyone than the man in the moon. All he wants is the Grange. Marry him and you'll be condemned to penal servitude for life here on the marsh—and I with you. Surely Richard must have explained to you that his ideas are quite different."

"Yes, he did."

"Well, there you are! It's simple as a-b-c. Marry him, and we're all free. Don't think I shall hang on your coattails. Bath's my plan, or perhaps Cheltenham spa. With money . . ." She stopped, confused, and Christina could hardly help feeling sorry for her.

"You mean," she said, "that Richard has promised you an income out of the estate in return for your support?"

"Richard is a dear boy, and loves his aunt. You think it strange, I can see, that I should prefer him to my own son— well, that's just it. I brought them both up, you know. Richard has been consideration itself always to his old aunt, while as for Ross! Well! His behavior now is all of a piece—rushes off to London, makes his grandfather furious, and never troubles himself with a word to me."

"You're wrong, you know, Aunt Tretteign."

"Wrong?"

"Grandfather's not a bit angry with Ross. On the contrary—"

"What do you mean? What can you mean?" A long pause. And then, "Christina Tretton, if you have gone behind my back and engaged yourself to my son! What are you doing?"

"Ringing for your maid. I was afraid it would be a shock to you, Aunt."

"A shock! Well, you mark my words, girl, it's nothing to what it will be to you. And don't come crying to me for comfort when he ill-uses you. Bad sons make bad husbands, Christina, and that's my last word on the subject." She folded her lips angrily over it.

"Yes, Aunt." Don't say anything about bad mothers. Don't say anything.

The day was endless. Taking her afternoon walk on the beach, Christina was aware of unusual activity at the gun emplacements between there and Rye Harbor. Straining her eyes in the other direction, she thought she could see the flash of arms also at the old batteries on Dungeness, which had recently been overhauled and made fit for service. And, all the time, the French privateer hung on and off the horizon, at once a warning and a challenge.

She shivered in the cold wind. Would Parkes get her message to Ross? And, if he did, what use would it be? The assignation with the French privateer could not be changed. It was all very well for Parkes to talk about powerful friends in London. What would they avail Ross in a running fight between his smuggling band and the soldiers?

Lieutenant Trevis met her on his way back from his round of the batteries, and she forced herself to congratulate him on the stir of activity along the beach. "Yes"—he smiled down at her from his big chestnut—"we're ready for them, all right. Lock up carefully tonight, Miss Tretton, and early."

"Here again?" Surely anyone would ask that question.

"We believe so. We have our sources of information too, I'm glad to say. Money's a powerful argument."

"Yes . . . yes, of course. You'll have a rough night of it, I'm afraid." Huge gray clouds were massed along the horizon, and a sprinkling of rain was beginning to fall.

"Never mind about that, if we catch our men! But you will get wet. Let me have the pleasure of escorting you home,

Miss Tretton. I do not like to see you walking alone here on the beach."

"What, in broad daylight? And with your men everywhere. I cannot tell you how safe I feel."

She had hardly taken off her damp cloak when Greg tapped on her door. "Mr. Tretteign would like a word with you, miss."

Again! She found him dressed in his old-fashioned snuff-colored suit and sitting bolt upright in his big wing chair.

"Christina! I won't be trifled with." He had hardly given Greg time to close the door behind her. "What's this about you and Lieutenant Trevis?"

"Me and—oh, you are well informed, Grandfather."

"I need to be. Seeing him alone this morning, and then running off to the beach for a further assignation this afternoon! It hardly sounds like the conduct of an engaged young lady to me. Mind you, I don't set up for a high stickler like your Aunt Tretteign, but it is no wonder if she is alarmed."

"Alarmed! Aunt Tretteign? On her son's account? Grandfather, you amuse me strangely."

"Amuse you!" Shaggy brows drew together over the angry old eyes. "That is very far from being my intention. Explain yourself, miss, before I lose my temper."

"What have I to explain?" Angry glances met and locked.

His eyes fell first. "Why, your conduct, or lack of it. Your intentions with regard to Lieutenant Trevis, if you want it spelled out for you."

Anger was the best answer. She let it come. "I am twenty-two years old, Grandfather, and have not yet found it necessary to apologize for my conduct to anyone. My aunt has already scolded me for seeing Mr. Trevis alone. I did not take this from her, nor will I from you. I'm not a schoolroom miss who is not to stir without her governess at her side. I'm a free American woman. If you do not like my behavior, I will go away. I warn you, I'm too old to learn new tricks."

"Good girl, good girl!" He rolled his head delightedly from side to side in the big chair. "You sounded just like your father then, in one of his tantrums. Well, I like a bit of spirit —within reason. Gave your aunt a setdown, did you, for finding fault? Well, I can't say I blame you for that. She's a fine one to be talking of conduct. . . . I thought she was pretty quick with her talebearing. But, just the same, what's this about meeting Trevis on the beach, hey? What have you got to say to that, miss?"

"Why, that I met him there by chance. You know as well as I do it's the only place where I can walk. I'm used to an active life, Grandfather. It may satisfy Aunt Tretteign to move no farther than from breakfast room to parlor, but I'd go mad. And don't say I ought to take someone with me either, because you know it's nonsense, and there's no one I could take. If you must know, by the way, Lieutenant Trevis was reading me a lecture on very much the same lines. He thought it his duty to see me safe home. Safe home indeed? I suspect I'm a good deal safer—as a Tretteign—here on the marsh than he is."

He gave a delighted cackle of laughter. "You've hit the nail on the head there, and no mistake. I'll say that for you, girl, you're a Tretteign through and through. Try as I will, I can see no trace of that French mother of yours in you, and thank God for that. Now, now, don't flare up at me again. Kiss and be friends, hey? But I wish, just the same, that Ross would come back."

"So do I, Grandfather." She bent to kiss the papery cheek.

And it was still only dusk. At this time of day, the servants were always particularly busy. Lamps had to be lit, fires made up, bedrooms prepared for the night. It was a time, she knew by experience, when there was no possibility of speaking privately to Parkes. Anyway, she told herself, her second conversation with Trevis had added little to the first one.

She could tell herself that as much as she liked, but churning anxiety still kept her in motion. From her bedroom window, she could peer out over the darkening marsh toward the sea. Fairlight was lost already in cloud and evening shadow and, in the other direction, the Dungeness light was just beginning to show. Out to sea, nothing. The privateer might be there, lying in darkness. . . . If only she knew where the rendezvous was . . . not here, Parkes had said. Then where? Straining her eyes, she could see the lights of the army camp at Fairlight. In the old days, Betty had told her, there had been a lively smugglers' traffic from that series of coves—but now? With the army so near? It would be madness.

The gong, rumbling downstairs, told her that at least another section of this interminable day had been got through. She found her aunt, sharp-eyed, waiting for her in the dining parlor. Of course, in her anxiety about Ross, she had forgotten all about the affair of Lieutenant Trevis.

"Well, Aunt?" She took her place at the oval mahogany table. "I trust you have had a satisfactory day."

"Satisfactory? What can be satisfactory about life in this dismal house?"

"I don't know—Grandfather seems in good spirits tonight."

"You've seen him?"

"Yes. He asked me my intentions with regard to Lieutenant Trevis. I had always thought the boot was on the other foot, but it must be a comfort to you, Aunt, to think that Grandfather has Ross's best interests so close at heart. Won't you try a little of this patty of cockscombs? It's something Cook and I worked out together."

"I thank you, no. It is a lady's duty to think of her figure."

"What a terrible deal of duties ladies have." It had occurred to her that, if her aunt were to go early to bed, she would be free to visit Tissot. But the provocation must be just right. She did not want an hysterical scene, with the entire household upside down, just a small degree of huff would do. "I believe I shall never learn to pass as one." She leaned her elbows negligently on the table and pretended to stifle a yawn with one brown hand. "Ross will just have to put up with me as I am."

"Look at you now!" Her aunt rose to the bait. "My maid Rose would know better. Take your elbows off the table at once, Christina! Did that frippery French mother teach you nothing? I tell you, I begin to think it just as well that you have plumped for Ross rather than Richard. *He* would never be able to bear such common behavior. Ross, I fear, would hardly notice."

This conversation was not going at all as she had intended. What now? "So you will give us your blessing after all? Dear Aunt, I knew your maternal feelings would get the better of you. Ross and I will deal admirably together, I assure you. He is blunt and I am vulgar! Just think what an occupation you will have in trying to see that your grandchildren are not complete little barbarians. Living down here in the country, as we intend to do, you will be their only civilizing influence.

I shall rely on you to make English ladies of all my daughters —and I warn you I intend to have a perfectly enormous family. After all, what else is there to do but breed, down here at the end of nowhere."

"Christina!" Now, at last, Mrs. Tretteign rose to her feet. "Your language appals me. Have you no modesty, no female pride, no shame!"

"Shame, Aunt? You mean, one may do these things, but not speak of them?"

"My God!" Her aunt turned dramatically at the door. "I actually find myself sorry for Ross."

Left alone, Christina found herself, for a moment, sorry for her aunt. She peeled an apple, smiling a little to herself, then twisted her lips, wryly as she remembered her aunt's insulting description of her mother. Her "frippery French mother," indeed, and this from a woman whose misbehavior had caused her own husband's death. Not for the first time, she wondered if the scandal of Ross's birth had been so successfully hushed up that his mother had actually managed to delude herself that none of it had ever happened.

But Mrs. Tretteign had had plenty of time, by now, to get upstairs to the comforts of Rose and *sal volatile*. Christina rang the little silver hand bell.

Parkes should have answered, but instead the footman appeared, looking flustered. "Mrs. Tretteign will not be taking tea tonight," Christina said. "Mr. Parkes is not indisposed, I hope?"

"Miss!" The man became suddenly human. "He's vanished."

"Parkes? What do you mean?"

"Just that, Miss Christina. He served your dessert, just like he always does, and came back with the dishes to the kitchen. One minute he was there, telling Cook what you'd said about the patty—the next, hey presto, he'd gone. I always said this house was full of ghosts." Here an anxious glance over his shoulder to where heavy velvet curtains moved restlessly.

"You mean draughts." But Christina was on her feet. "How long has Parkes been gone, Frank?"

"Well . . ." Time meant little to the lower orders. "Since he brought your dessert, miss."

Twenty minutes or so. Too long merely to have taken food

to M. Tissot. A message from Ross perhaps? "I'd best come out to the kitchen and see what Cook has to say."

"I wish you would, miss, we're all at sixes and sevens there. And short-staffed too."

"Oh?"

"Did you not know? Jem and Thomas have leave for the night. Not that they're much help indoors . . . but if it comes to a search . . ." He held the door for her and followed her down the draughty hall to the servants' quarters.

Here, confusion and anxiety reigned. Meg, the kitchenmaid, who was Parkes' niece, was blubbering over a pile of dirty dishes, while the cook was trying to organize the rest of the staff into a search of the house. "He can't be far," she explained to Christina. "He's only been gone since I put the kettle on." But the huge kettle was boiling furiously. "He'd never be late for serving your tea, not a-purpose he wouldn't."

"No." This had been precisely Christina's thought. Who could she trust here? Nobody. The answer was instantaneous. "I wonder if he can have gone out to the chapel to fetch my drawing materials. I did speak to him about them." It had finally become impossible to carry the brass-rubbing pretense any further, but she had taken the precaution of leaving her crayons there against just such an eventuality as this. "I will go and see."

"Oh, miss, to the cloister! In the dark! Someone should go with you."

Not I, implied the cook's tone, and the faces of the other servants echoed the sentiment.

"D'you think the Abbot's ghost has got him?" This was the kitchenmaid, sobbing harder than ever.

"Nonsense!" said Christina. "But he might have fallen in the dark and hurt himself. Find me a lantern, someone. And one of Mr. Ross's pistols."

"A pistol?" The cook sounded horrified.

"Yes. I can use it, too, if I meet your ghost—or anything else. And a cloak, please, Frank. It's blowing half a gale out."

"Yes," said Cook with grisly relish. "Invasion weather. D'you think the French have landed unbeknownst to us, and caught poor Parkes?"

"Nonsense," said Christina again. "You know as well as I do that those cockleshells they've got at Boulogne wouldn't

stand ten minutes of this. Thank you, Frank." She let the
footman wrap a cloak around her shoulders, then took the
little gun, and the lantern the cook had lit for her.

"I'll come with you, miss." Frank, the footman.

Could she trust him? Better not. "No need. You had much
better set about searching the house."

Chapter Nine

THE FLICKERING LIGHT of her lantern made the darkness of the stable yard seem even more absolute. Should she have made Frank come with her? But—was it hysterical anxiety or something more rational? At all events, she did not trust him. "We have our informants too," Trevis had said, only that afternoon. Monstrous that his informants should be her enemies, but—face it—true. If only Jem were here . . . but Jem, and no doubt Thomas, too, must be out with the smugglers. Knowledge of this had hung heavy in the charged air of the kitchen. No, the pistol, solid in her hand, was her most reliable companion.

The chapel door at last. Nothing here, of course—she had not expected there to be. The door into the cloisters was locked, but this meant nothing. They had agreed that Parkes would always lock it behind him when he went to visit M. Tissot by himself, as Jem's absence must have compelled him to do tonight. She fitted the spare key Ross had given her into the lock and pushed open the door. Thick darkness in the cloisters, and a spatter of raindrops on her face as she passed the place where the roof had fallen away. Don't walk too fast, the lantern might blow out. And yet she badly wanted to hurry. She might not believe in ghosts, but she did not like this place in the dark.

At last her hand found the door of M. Tissot's room—and felt it swing away from her. Unlocked! "Parkes?" she whispered.

Silence. No—heavy breathing. Well, of course, M. Tissot. But she cocked the gun before she moved forward very cautiously into the room. Now her light found the cot in the corner, and the figure on it. White hair! Not M. Tissot, but Parkes, lying very still, his hands, she now saw, tied behind him, his mouth gagged. She freed him, her own hands shaking; found water; found the smelling salts she had used for M. Tissot. Where was he? In the cloisters somewhere? With one quick, anxious movement she was at the door and locking it. Leave the key in the lock: he won't be able to use the other one.

Then back to Parkes with the smelling salts. He stirred as she held them under his nose; his eyelids flickered up, then down again. He looked very old, very frail in the dim light. She should not have let him come here alone. But why should they have mistrusted M. Tissot? She bathed his forehead with cold water, things fitting themselves together in her mind as she did so. She had wondered, once or twice, whether M. Tissot might not be better than he admitted, had even asked herself if he might be trying to avoid returning to France. She must have been right. And, last night, when she had found his clothes wet, he must have been out, exploring the cloisters in the rain, his delirium faked to deceive her. But—more important than any of this—where was he now?

At last, Parkes stirred, raised a feeble hand to his head and opened his eyes. "Miss Christina!" And then, "Where is he?"

"I wish I knew. What happened, Parkes?"

"I don't know. I opened the door, put the lantern down, as usual. Something hit me on the head . . . then, nothing . . . Yes, there." Her gentle fingers had found the lump under the straggling white hair. "Lock the door, Miss Christina!"

"I have. He must be in the cloisters, hiding. . . . The chapel door was locked. He can't have got out that way."

"Unless he found the tunnel."

"Tunnel?"

"Did Mr. Ross not tell you? Should I?" A shaking hand plucked at the blanket she had thrown over him. "I tell you, I don't know what to do for the best . . . but if he's escaped by it . . ."

"Of course you must tell me, Parkes. Mr. Ross would want you to, I'm sure."

"Yes . . . yes, I think so. I wish my head did not ache so. How can a man think?"

"Don't worry, Parkes. It will all come right." How she wished she believed the easy, comforting words. "Only . . . we must think fast." Not just fast—desperately. By his escape, M. Tissot had declared himself an enemy. What might this mean? "Parkes . . ."

"Yes, miss?" He was looking a little better, shocked into self-control.

"Suppose the very worst. Suppose M. Tissot has been shamming it for some time. How much will he know? Mr. Ross came by the tunnel last night, I take it?"

"Yes—and left that way."

"So M. Tissot must have been watching and spotted the entrance. Well then, what may he have heard?"

"My God!" Recollection blanched his face still further. "We made our arrangements, Mr. Ross and I, out there in the cloisters."

"And he heard?"

"He could have. Oh God, what a fool—"

"My fault, Parkes. I was in charge. He fooled me—no time for that now. What were the arrangements?" And, as he hesitated, "You must see, Parkes, you have to tell me now. Otherwise, Ross may walk into a trap."

"You think he'll go to the soldiers, miss?"

"I don't know—I can't imagine—but we must assume he will. Else why has he escaped?"

"I know. If I could only think . . ."

"There's no time, Parkes. Tell me." All the authority she could muster in her voice.

"Yes." He was glad to let her decide for him. "Mr. Ross said a landing tonight would be too dangerous. The signal's to be for them to sink the cargo—"

"Sink it?"

"Yes. They mark it with floats, like lobster pots. Then the fishermen pick it up at leisure."

"I see. But . . . Mr. Ross?"

"Will row himself out, miss, when the *Bel Ami*'s near inshore. Don't look so frightened. It's not so bad as it sounds. He's got friends at one of the batteries. They'll let him through."

"I see." Treachery everywhere. Well—which side was she on? Doubtless the soldiers were heavily bribed. "Parkes, did he mention where or when?"

"No, miss, there was no need."

"Thank God for that. So the worst M. Tissot can do is betray the general plan."

Parkes shook his head gloomily. "That Lieutenant Trevis is no fool, miss. If it gets to him, it's but to move all the defense posts."

"Move them?"

"The guards. To different stations. Don't you see? Mr. Ross will expect to find friends . . ."

"Oh my God! He must be warned."

"Yes, but how! He was spending the day at one of the hideouts on the marsh. He did not tell me which. It's hopeless, miss."

"It can't be." And then, "What's that?" A noise in the cloisters. The scrape of a foot? "M. Tissot?" She breathed it before picking up her gun and bending to blow out the light.

Dead silence for a moment as she moved cautiously in the new darkness toward the door of the room. Now she could hear movement outside. She turned the key, swung the door open. "I've got a pistol. Don't move, or I'll fire."

"Chris!" Ross's voice.

"Oh, thank God, it's you. You're safe!"

"You think so?" His face was haggard, his clothes mud stained, his expression unreadable.

"Ross, what's the matter?"

"Matter! I've been dodging your friend Trevis all over the marsh. How could you, Chris? But—there's no time for that. Only—I must know how bad it is. You let M. Tissot go. How much did you tell him?"

"Tell him? I? Ross, what do you mean?"

"Well—what else can I think?" He sounded as exhausted as he looked. "I was a fool, a crazy fool to trust you. You're American, after all, you said it yourself. Nothing to choose, you said, between the French and the English. Well—you've chosen now. What was the bribe, Chris? Your mother's estates?"

"Ross!" He actually meant it. "If I were only a man, I'd show you." Her voice shook with anger. But there was no time for anger; no time for explanations. Any minute now, the servants would come looking for her. "You're wrong, Ross." She steadied her voice. "We'll talk of that later—there will be time . . . there must. Parkes, you'll explain? I can't stay—the servants will be looking for me. Later, Ross, I'll accept your apology."

"Apology!" He broke off. "What's that?"

"The servants, I expect." She, too, could hear a confused sound of voices at the far end of the cloisters. "I'll get them back to the house if I can. Lucky they're so afraid of ghosts. If you can, get out by the tunnel—both of you . . ." The noise was louder now. "I must go. Parkes, explain!" No time for more. She picked up the lantern she had blown out—no time to relight it. "Here I am," she called, emerging from the little room and pulling the door shut behind her. "Something blew out the light. I've been stumbling about in the dark . . . there's . . . something here. Thank God you've come." She could see them now: Frank in the doorway of the chapel, light in hand, the cook and another man behind him. At all costs she must get them back to the house. "Did you hear it?" As she approached them, she looked fearfully backward over her shoulder.

"What?" Cook asked. "What did you hear?"

"A . . . a kind of groaning . . . and there was a phosphorescent . . . glowing." This just in case Ross should not have thought to put out his dark lantern. "Help me to the house. I think I'm going to faint." And she leaned with all her weight against Frank, compelling him and the other man to pick her up and carry her to the house, while the cook lighted their way with a lantern.

In the kitchen, she subsided with a groan into the cook's armchair by the big stove. "Hartshorn, at once!" She looked nervously over her shoulder. "Shut that door, Frank. It . . . it might follow me."

"Mary and all the saints preserve us." Cook crossed herself. "Meg! The hartshorn!"

"But . . . but my uncle . . . Mr. Parkes?" Meg asked.

"Not a sign of him." Christina had been thinking hard. "He must have gone out the front way, if you've not found him indoors. Or down to the sea perhaps?" Ordinarily fantastic, she knew that tonight of all nights this suggestion must seem reasonable. Tension was expected. Parkes might well have slipped out on some errand in connection with it, and, in that case, would not thank them for making his absence known. She sipped the hartshorn Meg had mixed for her and began to show signs of recovery. "I believe, now, if you were to help me to my study I should feel better."

As she expected, it was a popular suggestion. Her presence in the kitchen was inhibiting, to say the least of it. "Don't tell my aunt." She drooped convincingly between the two men. "I'd be ashamed . . ." She subsided with a sigh of only half-simulated relief on the chaise longue by the embers of the study fire and assured her helpers that she would be better alone. "Only, send Parkes to me the minute he returns. If he's not back soon, we'll have to search outside."

She was alone at last with her anger. Ross had thought her capable of conspiring with M. Tissot to betray him. Her hands clenched and unclenched themselves in her lap. If there had only been time . . . now, the furious things she had not said burned in her throat. She actually thought, for a moment, that she was going to be sick. After all she had done for him . . . and then. . . . Think, she told herself; be calm, be reasonable. Ross thinks all women venal—why not, with his mother always before him as an example? No doubt he had assumed that she consented to their mockery of an engagement entirely for her own selfish reasons. From that, it was only a step to imagining her capable of the kind of conspiracy he had imagined tonight. And, of course, he must be furious with himself for having trusted her. It was anger with himself, as much as with her, that had spoken.

It was thin enough consolation. But by now he would know his mistake: Parkes would have explained it all. He would believe Parkes. He would be sorry for what he had said. It was almost possible to imagine that he would come to her to apologize. For—here was more solid consolation—one good thing, surely, had come out of this evening's work. He must see that it was quite impossible for him to get to France. Any minute, now, she hoped to hear him and Parkes making their official arrival by the front door.

Time was passing. The fire was almost out. Her eyes flickered shut and she dreamed for a moment of accepting Ross's apology. Then they were wide open. A noise in the house? Yes, voices in the hall, then Parkes, alone, very white, very anxious-looking. He was too old for a night like this. But—she sat bolt upright. . . . "Parkes, where is Mr. Ross?"

"Gone, miss. I hope."

"Gone! But, Parkes, it's madness."

"I know, but there was no moving him. He said he had to. He'll be careful, miss, for the sake of his errand. He told me so. He's got a good chance, truly he has . . . one man alone, knowing the marsh, and the soldiers either strangers or, most likely, his friends. He can do it if anyone can." He was talking, she knew, as much to convince himself as her.

"Please God you're right. Parkes, did you tell him?"

"About M. Tissot. I tried, miss, but there was so little time . . . I'm sorry . . . I . . . he . . ." The old man stumbled to a stop, his face whiter than ever. Christina was on her feet in an instant. Monstrous to have forgotten the blow he had received.

"Parkes, you're ill." She half helped, half forced him into a chair. "Sit there, I'll get help. But, first, what do we tell them? You were out taking a breath of air, tripped, fell and hurt your head. It's taken you all this time to get back. They'll think, of course, that it has to do with the smugglers, but no one will say so."

"No, miss." He was looking worse and worse, but made one last effort. "Mr. Ross said . . . tell Jem . . . no one else. Trust him—"

"Not me?"

But his head had dropped forward and he did not even hear the bitter question. By the time she had summoned Frank he was only half conscious, collapsed deep in the chair, muttering to himself.

Frank heard her explanation impassively. "Very good, miss," he said at last. "We'll look after him. Don't you worry."

"I'm sure you will." There was one other thing she must ask, but casually. "Are Jem and Thomas back yet?"

"Yes, miss, just a few minutes ago. Shall I lock up, since Parkes is ill?"

"Please." So many questions she would like to ask. None that she could. Jem and Thomas would be telling the story of the night's events in the servants' hall—but even they would not know what had happened to Ross. For this, there was nothing to do but wait till morning. If he had been caught, they would hear soon enough. Tomorrow, if ever, no news would be good news.

But how endure till then? In the anguish of her fear for

him, she hardly had time to think of Ross's unjust suspicions of herself. If he survived, it would be time enough to think of that.

Betty woke her next morning with an anxious request that she visit Parkes as soon as possible. Glum faces in the servants' hall told her that the news of the sunken cargo was out. And one look at Parkes made it clear that this was not a case for her to handle. Jem must ride to Rye at once for the doctor. She managed a minute alone with him in the stable yard. "Jem?"

"Yes, miss?" Quick intelligence in the open face. Monstrous that this boy should be involved in—no time for that.

"You know . . . about Mr. Ross?" No time for beating about the bush either.

A quick anxious look around. He moved nearer to her and lowered his voice. "Yes, miss. But he wasn't there last night —not at the meeting place—it was the other—"

"Don't tell me who. But, what happened, Jem?"

"A bad night's work. Someone blew the gaff . . . the preventives were out all over, and the soldiers. The *Bel Ami* had to sink her cargo—and they've got gunboats out this morning picking it up. It's more than a man can bear to watch them. And not a sign of Mr. . . . of the Captain either. There are even some say it's his fault."

"Oh!" Danger everywhere. And Ross almost certainly in France, beyond warning, beyond help. How would he get back? Parkes must know his plans, but Parkes was unconscious. "Trust Jem," Ross had said. What else was there to do? "I think he's in France, Jem."

"Mr. . . . the Captain?" A long, low whistle of astonishment. "So that's it. I did wonder. There was talk of a boat. Too much talk, if you ask me." And then, on a different note, "Very good, miss, I'll fetch the doctor for you, all right and tight."

"Thank you, Jem." Frank had appeared in the kitchen doorway. "And all the news from Rye, too."

"Yes, miss." His look showed how well he had understood her.

The whole house was out of sorts that morning. Mrs. Tretteign complained of migraine, refused to go to bed, but sat, very sorry for herself, on the sofa in the morning room, bitterly resenting any attempt of Christina's to leave her and see

how the real invalid, Parkes, was faring. Upstairs, old Mr.
Tretteign had one of his attacks of the gout, and the slightest
noise in the house brought Greg down with a complaint.

At last, late in the afternoon, Jem and the doctor rode into
the stable yard. Christina hurried to meet them, her pretext
being requests from both the old man and Mrs. Tretteign that
Dr. Pembly visit them first. Greeting the doctor with this
news, she managed an exchange of glances with Jem. All's
well, said his look. She was afraid, for a moment, that she
would faint with the relief of it, but bit her lip hard and bus-
ied herself with welcoming the doctor.

Of course he saw his patients in order of rank. A bitter
draught for Mr. Tretteign's gout; headache powders and sympathy for Mrs. Tretteign; then, at last, a visit to the little
downstairs room were Meg watched anxiously over old
Parkes. "Overwork, you think?" He looked at Christina with
sharp eyes that missed little. "And a blow on the head?
Yes . . ." Gentle fingers felt about under the scanty white
hair. "He was lucky. Tripped and fell, did he?" Once again,
his eyes met Christina's, full of implications. "Well, it could
be worse. Only, he's an old man. It will take time . . . and
nursing. Not much I can do." No sympathy here. He followed Christina from the room. "Wild work on the marsh
last night. I wondered, when you sent for me, whether you
had had trouble here." He let it hang, hopefully.

"Oh no." Indifferently. "A glass of something, Doctor, before you go?"

She got rid of him at last, rang and sent for Jem. Inevitably, there were medicines to be fetched from Rye. Having
dealt with this, "Did you learn anything?"

"Not much, miss. There's a lot of talk—angry talk, of
course. But no news of Mr. . . . of the Captain. And there's
talk about that, too, I can tell you. When will he be back,
miss?"

"I wish to God I knew. With the next shipment, I suppose." Fantastic to be talking about it so freely. "Have you
any idea when that will be, Jem?"

"No one has. That I am sure of. We never hear till the day
itself. Less chance of treachery that way."

"Of course." It was elementary sense. "But who gives the
word?"

"Parkes, mostly. He very likely knows now. He's always

been hand in glove with the master and acted as go-between."

"And God knows when he'll be conscious. What are we to do, Jem?"

"Wait, I think, miss. There's nothing else we can do. Very likely Mr. Ross will contrive to get a message through. They often come by way of Jersey. And one thing you can count on—there won't be another shipment for a month . . . the dark of the moon, you see. So at least there's time. . . . Maybe Mr. Parkes will be better."

"I hope to God he is. Oh, one other thing. Is there any news of the Frenchman?"

"Not a word, miss. And I don't like that either."

"No more do I, Jem."

The long, anxious days dragged by and still there was no change in Parkes' condition. Listening to his restless mutterings as he lay somewhere between sleep and unconsciousness, Christina blamed herself bitterly for the burden she and Ross had put on so old a man. Dr. Pembly was puzzled by his slowness to mend, which he considered most unsuitable in a member of the lower orders. But Christina was sure that he was suffering less from the blow he had received than from the long strain of helping nurse M. Tissot and, at the same time, carrying out his usual round of household duties. It was like Ross to be careless on such a point, but there was no excuse for her. Well, she was paid for it now. Tonight, this very minute (she was sitting, at dusk, by Parkes' bed), Ross might be heading to land from the *Bel Ami*—to find no confederates awaiting him. What would happen in such a case? If there was no one to receive the smuggled goods— and, doubtless more important, to pay for them—would the French captain consent to land Ross alone, or would he not hold him as hostage for future payment? Anything might happen—and, worst of all, she might never know.

Over dinner that night her aunt surprised her. "I'm worried about you, Christina."

"About me?" This was a new departure.

"Yes. I wish you would leave the nursing of Parkes to the servants, whose work it is, and take a little care of yourself. You're losing your looks, you know. There used to be—well, call it a kind of healthy glow about you that some men might find attractive. Now look at you! Your grandfather sent for me only this morning to ask what's the matter. He thinks you must be pining for Ross!" His mother's voice made it clear that she found the suggestion nonsensical. "He's getting very impatient himself at Ross's staying away so long."

"I know." This was another cause for anxiety. No wonder if she looked drawn and haggard. And the moon had passed the full; the nights were getting darker. Anytime now, Ross might land and find no one there to meet him. Or—not land at all. Her aunt was looking at her oddly. She picked up fork and spoon and made a gallant pretense of eating trifle.

Chapter Ten

JEM CAME tapping at the door of her study the next afternoon, ostensibly to ask permission to ride into Rye and visit his mother. "Miss! There's been a message."

"At last!"

"Yes, from France, by way of Jersey. It's from Mr. Ross, I think. He says we're to lay off for a while. It's not safe."

"Not safe! Well, you've seen the guards along the coast. But how will he get back? And you're sure it's from Mr. Ross?"

"No, of course not. They come by word of mouth, you see, passed on. The others don't seem too sure of this one."

"But how . . . ?" Best not ask too many questions. And anyway, he had more to say.

"They're not best pleased, the others. Not after losing the lot the last time. They say, if they see her, they'll signal her in just the same."

"Her?"

"You know—the *Bel Ami.*" And then, changing his tone. "Thank you, miss. I'll be sure and be back on time."

"Miss Christina." It was Meg, the kitchenmaid. "Uncle's asking for you. He's better, truly he is. He sat up in bed, large as life, and asked what day of the week it was."

"Did he?" Christina and Jem exchanged glances. "I'll come to him at once."

"I'd be rare pleased if you would, miss. He's in a proper taking about something. 'What's so awful about it being Friday, Uncle?' I asks him, but all he'd do was ask for you, miss."

128

Parkes was indeed better. Sitting up in bed, he greeted Christina with the clear look of returned consciousness. "Thank you for coming so quick, miss." And then to his niece, who was hovering anxiously in the doorway, "Run along, Meg, there's a good girl, and ask Cook for a hot posset for me." He watched the door shut behind her. "Miss, it's tonight."

"No! But . . . there's been a message . . . from France, Jem says, to call it off as being too dangerous. Only . . . he thinks the others may ignore it. They don't seem sure it's genuine."

"How can it be? How would Mr. Ross get back else? But it will be dangerous. There was to be information laid that it would be in Fairlight Cove. And then, someone was to light the beacon there. He said that would cause chaos for a while and he'd slip in here as easy as be damned. Excuse me, miss."

"I see." It was a good plan. She remembered the confusion on November fifth when, despite strict orders to the contrary, half the villages had lit bonfires and burned Guy Fawkes in effigy, and the other half had at once jumped to the conclusion that the invasion had started. On another such night, anything might happen.

"What time is it?" He still looked very frail and ill.

"Early yet. There's time, but not much. Tell me, Parkes, where did he tell you this?"

"In the cloisters, of course. Oh . . . you mean . . ."

"Tissot. Could he have heard you?"

"I—I don't know." His head moved restlessly on the pillow. He was looking worse again.

"Don't worry, Parkes. Jem is riding to Rye to find out what is happening. I'll warn him—"

"He'll need to see Barnes at the George. Tell him I said . . ." His eyelids fell shut.

She found Jem in the stable yard, saddling up the pony he and the other servants rode. Her pretext—a commission for James's powders and tincture of rhubarb from the apothecary —was soon dealt with. She looked around. No one was within earshot, since the gray winter afternoon forbade loitering out of doors. 'She's coming, Jem, the *Bel Ami*. Parkes says it was to be tonight, here. There's to be a false alarm at Fairlight and the beacon there lit. You must see Barnes at the George."

"Barnes! I don't like that. And—the *Bel Ami*'s out there already, miss."

"Oh my God!" It was true then. "Be quick, Jem."

There was one more thing she needed to ask Parkes. She found him still peacefully sleeping with Meg hovering anxiously near the bed, posset in hand. "Should I wake him for it?"

"On no account. Leave it here and I'll see he drinks it as soon as he wakes."

Dark shadows were creeping out from the corners of the room when Parkes stirred at last. "Meg?" His voice was much stronger. She had been right to let him have his sleep out.

"It's I, Miss Tretton." How long would he stay awake this time? "She's there, the *Bel Ami*, and Jem has ridden to Rye to see Barnes. Tell me, Parkes, can they manage without you?"

"Yes. Barnes knows the signals. Mr. Ross said, 'two safer than one.'"

"That's good." She had had an uncomfortable vision of herself down on the beach, flashing a dark lantern and, inevitably, encountering Lieutenant Trevis. Her part would be safer—and worse. She would have nothing to do but stay here and worry. It was almost dark now. She watched Parkes settle back against his pillows, then hurried from the room at the sound of horses' hoofs in the yard outside. Jem was back.

His news did nothing to allay her anxiety. Barnes, it seemed, had listened impassively to the message from Parkes and then sent Jem to the right about. "'What you don't know, won't hurt you. And that goes for old nosy Parkes too. I'll manage tonight my way for once, and so you can tell him from me.'"

"But don't," Christina warned Jem. "I've given him something to make him sleep. So, there's nothing we can do."

"Nothing, miss."

Mrs. Tretteign was unusually gay over dinner that night and teased Christina about her preoccupied silence. "You look worse and worse, my dear. I really think I shall have to suggest to your grandfather that you need a holiday. It's a terrible season for it, of course, but if I were to take you to Bath, or Cheltenham, for the waters . . . or even Tonbridge Wells, perhaps? I'm told there's quite a lively little society there these days. I'm sure if I explained to Papa that your health needs it, he would be reasonable. And besides, it would serve Ross right if he were to return and find no one here to welcome him. You mustn't let him see that you've taken his absence so to heart . . . that would never do, believe me."

"Oh, Aunt, please! There's nothing wrong with me but the blue devils. Does the sun never shine in England?" Rain was lashing against the dining-room windows, and she shivered, thinking of Ross.

Mrs. Tretteign rang the bell. "You need a glass of something to cheer you up, Christina. Now, perhaps, you are beginning to see how I feel about this dead-and-alive house. And it's only December. You wait till you've lived through a whole winter of dark and rain. You'll know, then, why I'd do anything to get away. Oh, Frank, we'll have a bottle of the best claret, if you please."

But Frank was big with news of his own. "Ma'am, Miss Tretton, the beacon's alight on Fairlight cliff. The French must have landed!"

"Good God!" Mrs. Tretteign was on her feet at once. "There's not a moment to be lost. Have the horses put to in the carriage this instant, Frank, and the wagons got out for the rest of you."

This was something that Christina, in her other anxiety, had not thought of. "But, Aunt"—she too had got up and moved to the window to peer out from behind the heavy velvet curtain—"how do we know it is not a false alarm? Don't you remember how some people took flight on Guy Fawkes night, and how silly they looked in the morning."

"But this is not Guy Fawkes!"

"Nor is it invasion weather. Listen to the wind! It's not possible, I tell you. Besides, Parkes is too ill to be moved."

"Well, let that niece of his risk her life looking after him. I know I'm not going to stay and be ravished on his account. I tell you, Frank"—he was still there, hovering by the door—"have the horses put to at once."

"Aren't you forgetting Grandfather?" said Christina. "He must decide. Wait, Frank."

Running upstairs to her grandfather's rooms, she was aware of the rustle of panic through the house and for a moment felt a thrill of pure rage at Ross. What right had he, for his own ends, to plunge a whole district into this abject terror? Old people, loaded hastily into farm wagons, might die of cold tonight; babies be born prematurely on the road, and all because Ross Tretteign needed cover for his return from France.

Her aunt was following her up the stairs; it would make the interview with old Mr. Tretteign that much more difficult. At least he had heard the news already and seemed to be taking it calmly enough. "Another invasion scare, what?" He was still up, sitting in his big chair and drinking one of the three glasses of port he allowed himself a night. "Household in a panic, eh? And you, too, Verity, by the looks of you."

"Nothing of the kind, Papa." Mrs. Tretteign's quick breathing belied her words. "It's not for myself I'm concerned, but for this poor child here. What will Ross say if we let her stay here to be ravished by the French?"

"What will he say if we let her die of cold on the road? I can tell you one thing and that is that I am not going. Not tonight. Greg's been to look out the front windows. There's nothing stirring in the bay—they couldn't land without lights. Well then, they must be beyond Hastings since the beacon's on Fairlight. Even if they have landed, which I very much doubt, they cannot possibly be here before morning. We can sleep peacefully in our beds tonight and leave in good order after breakfast if the morning news warrants it. That's what I am going to do, at all events—and any servant who wishes to keep his place. You ladies, of course, will decide for yourselves, only I must point out that you'll have a cold drive of it, since I shall keep the carriage for myself. You'll not enjoy yourselves much, I think, in Ross's curricle. How about it, Christina? Are you afraid of waking to find six Frenchmen in your bedroom?"

"I'm a good deal more afraid of being lost on the marsh in the dark. I don't for a minute believe it is a genuine alarm. How could they have crossed in this weather? And even if they had, as you say, Grandfather, they must have landed beyond Fairlight. Why should they come here? They'll head straight for London, won't they? Not that I believe they have landed."

"You sound very sure of it." His eyes met hers with one of his piercing glances.

"I am, Grandfather."

"Well, that's settled then. Good night, ladies. Sleep well,

Verity." Mockingly. And then, "Well, Greg, what is it now?"

"If you please, sir, Lieutenant Trevis is below, asking for Miss Christina."

"He is, is he?" Another sharp glance for Christina. "My compliments to Lieutenant Trevis, and perhaps he will step up here."

"Grandfather—"

"Don't look so scared, girl. I won't eat him. But calling on a young lady at this hour of the night—"

"Shows a most lamentable lack of breeding," put in Mrs. Tretteign.

"When I want your opinion, Verity, I'll ask for it. In the meantime, if you wish to stay and hear what Mr. Trevis has to say at this unusual hour of the night, I suggest that you hold your tongue, if you can contrive to. Christina . . ."

"Yes, Grandfather?"

"Did you send for Mr. Trevis?"

"*Send* for him? Oh—in my panic, do you mean? What a poor opinion you have of the female sex."

"Do you blame me? But you have not answered my question."

"I do not intend to. It is insult enough to have been asked it."

Perhaps it was as well that Greg announced Lieutenant Trevis at this point.

"Good evening, sir." Mr. Tretteign pulled himself ramrod straight in his chair. "You will forgive me if I do not rise to greet you. And for sending for you here. Miss Tretton does not receive callers at this hour."

"Of course. I should apologize for disturbing you so late were it not that the news I bring provides its own excuse."

"Not news of an invasion, I trust?" The old man's voice was dry.

"No indeed, sir. But I was afraid—I thought you might think . . ."

"You expected to find us already loading up the family treasures and getting ready to flit? You should have given us credit for stronger nerves, Mr. Trevis. Or some of us. It's all a false alarm, then?"

"Worse. It's a deliberate diversion."

"A what?"

"A decoy. You must know about the smugglers, sir. They

mean to land, here in the bay, tonight. The beacon at Fairlight was intended to draw all our force over there and leave them a clear field here. But they're out of luck this time. They'll find us waiting for them . . . here. That's why I thought it my duty to come to you in case you should hear the fighting on the beach and think the French were landing indeed. Don't worry. Lock your doors tight and take no notice. It will just be the finish of as daring a gang of smugglers as I've ever heard of."

"I . . . see." How much, Christina wondered in her despair, did he see? "Well, it was good of you, Lieutenant, and we are grateful. If we can be of any assistance tonight—in tending the wounded or anything of the kind—you will call on us.

"And now, good night, Mr. Trevis, and, good luck." He waited, silent in his chair, till they had heard Trevis's booted feet clatter down the stairs. Then, "Good night, Verity. You can sleep easy now. Christina, a word with you before you go."

No gainsaying so absolute a command. She moved forward to face the big chair and he went on, watching her closely from under his shaggy brows. "I'm not a fool, even if that young man is. What do you know about tonight's work?"

"I can't tell you."

"You mean, you won't tell me? I think you had better, Christina. I'm a selfish old man, true, but Ross is the last of the Tretteigns. Or"—savagely—"all the last we've got."

"Ross?"

"I told you, I'm not a fool. He's got involved with this gang of ruffians somehow and you've been covering for him. You think I know nothing because I stay up here. I've got a very useful pair of eyes and ears downstairs, in Greg. Just because he keeps himself to himself doesn't mean he's not got his wits about him. Who've you had hidden, since Ross went away, in the cloisters?"

"Good God!" The sharp question had thrown her completely off her guard.

"Yes. And, think again. If I know that, how many other people must know too? Just like Ross, of course. He was always too set on what he was doing to see an inch before his nose. But I'd have thought you had more sense. And as for Ross, don't let him think he can come crying to me for shelter when he gets into trouble. He's made a fool of himself—he must take the consequences."

"What you mean is"—she did not attempt to keep the cold fury out of her voice—"that so long as Ross was getting away with it, you were happy to turn a blind eye and not ask too many questions as to where your brandy and tea came from. But if he's in trouble, so much the worse for him."

"Precisely. I am glad you take my meaning, girl. And, if I were you, I would begin to accustom myself to the idea of Richard Markham as a possible husband. He may be a babbling popinjay, but he's not been in gaol."

"You mean, you'd cut Ross off, just like that?"

"What else d'you expect me to do? He ought to be grateful I didn't say anything to young Trevis tonight, but I won't be the one to queer his pitch for him. If he does it for himself, that's something else again. Understand, girl, the Tretteigns are an ancient and honorable family. The name's not going to be disgraced by anyone—still less by one who has no right to bear it."

"You mean . . . you'd rake that up?"

"Well, of course I would." He thought himself entirely reasonable. "What else could I do? So just pray to God that he's not out there in that *Bel Ami* that's been making herself so conspicuous all day. Because if he is, he's done for."

"You put it very clearly." So much for any idea she had had of telling him the whole story and asking his help. It would be merely to betray Ross's confidence uselessly. "Good night, Grandfather." She moved to the door.

"You've not kissed me good night."

"Nor am I going to." She closed the door very quietly behind her and found Jem hovering anxiously in the hall.

"Miss! What are we to *do?*" Someone, clearly, had contrived to hear what Trevis had said to them. Well, in this house, anything was possible.

"Nothing, Jem, there's nothing we can do. Except pray."

"I'm not much catch at that. But mayn't I go out, and watch? I might have a chance to warn 'em."

"More likely you'd get killed as a traitor for your pains. Besides, it's not so much Barnes and his men I care about, it's the others."

"On board. I know. There's nothing we can do to warn them. Not if Fairlight Beacon was the signal. But, Miss

Christina, I could at least go and see what happens. Then we'd know . . ."

"Oh, Jem"—suddenly the tears she had fought all evening hung heavy in her eyes—"if you'd do that! But be careful, I beg of you. To have you caught . . ."

"I know, we'd be proper sunk. Don't worry, I won't be caught. I know the shingle banks like the back of my hand, which is more than can be said for Mr. Lieutenant Trevis and his men. They'll never so much as get a whiff of me."

"Right, Jem."

Alone in her room at last, Christina carefully put the tinderbox beside the candlestick, then bent to blow out the tiny flame. Darkness was soothing. Perhaps nothing was as bad as she thought. She waited for her eyes to get accustomed to the dark, then moved over to the window and drew back the curtain. At first, there was nothing but absolute blackness, but it was not quite the dark of the moon. Gradually she began to see the hint of shapes. Fairlight was a darker shadow away to the right. They must have got the beacon out by now, and she imagined the cursing, desperate work that would have been. And on the left, Dungeness Light. No other light showed. They went to bed early in the marshland farms and doubtless the men on guard in the batteries along the shore had had orders to show no lights. She shivered, thinking of the men who must be down there in the darkness . . . waiting.

And the *Bel Ami*? No trace of a light out to sea, but that meant nothing. She would come in as darkling as the enemies who waited for her. And there was nothing to be done. Waiting is worst of all. But that was what she must do. She pulled a chair nearer to the window and sat down, the heavy curtains draped around her. It was raining, a light sea drizzle that whispered against the window panes. It seemed, somehow, the last straw. She could think of nothing but Ross landing from the little boat; the sudden volley of shots out of the darkness; rain blurring everything. He might even escape, to lie wounded, dying in the rain, all night on the desolate shore.

Don't think of it. You may need your strength later. Deliberately, she closed her eyes, leaned back in a pretense of comfort in the chair, tried to make herself relax. Impossible, of course. And yet—for how many nights had her sleep been interrupted? Her head fell back into the corner of the chair. She dreamed that Lieutenant Trevis was chasing her across a vast shingle waste . . . her feet could get no purchase . . . she was hardly moving. They were shooting at her. . . .

The shots woke her. Fully conscious in one frantic moment, she leaned forward and peered out of the window in time to see the flashes from a second volley. Now there were lights showing; from time to time she could see a dark figure moving between her and one of them. A fight, of course. But Ross? And to have to sit here, watching, helpless. . . . Her fingernails bit into the palms of her hands. She stood up and opened the window, to lean out into the drizzling rain, but could hear only a confused sound of shouting, and more shots.

Then, like the dream, it was over, so quickly it was hard to believe it had happened. Silence again, and a little group of lights showing, down by the beach, moving about, perhaps in search? Then they formed up with military precision; Trevis's men, no question about it. And their prisoners? No hope that they would come back this way. Trevis would go straight along the shore and take the track up from the first battery. Yes, there they went, flickering, yet in oddly precise formation along the beach. It was all over.

All over but the waiting. She seemed, now, to have been waiting forever. What had Jem seen? And had he been caught too? She found the candle, lit it with a hand that shook so that it took three tries, and opened her bedroom door. Had anyone else heard the affray? Apparently not, since hers was the only room on the front of the house. At least all seemed quiet. Her excuse for going downstairs? Insomnia, and a book from the library.

The air struck cold and damp in this seldom-used room, and she pulled her shawl closely around the low-cut shoulders of her muslin dress. To have changed would have admitted knowledge . . . perhaps it was already too late to pretend ignorance. She moved over to the heavy shutters that covered the window and pulled one ajar. The library, like the Great Hall, faced toward the sea, but down here her view was much more limited. Anyway, there was nothing to be seen but darkness; nothing to do but wait. Light a fire? No, this too would be to admit knowledge. She was just down here on a momentary errand, looking for a book that would send her to sleep. She had long since finished the set of Fielding. What now? *Rasselas?* Or Johnson's *Lives of the Poets?* Volume upon volume of sermons, read perhaps by some more pious generation when the weather was too bad to get from the Dark House to church? This was no time to be reading sermons. Here was something better, an odd volume of Richardson's *Clarissa Harlowe.*

But it was impossible to concentrate on the elaborate, gossipy letters, even more impossible than usual to sympathize with poor Clarissa in her predicament. Besides, was that not a noise? She was back at the window in a flash and opened it a crack. Nothing to be seen, but now, unmistakably, the sound of footsteps, quick and would-be quiet on the shifting shingle. One man, alone. Jem? She picked up her candle and hurried out into the dark hall, where the grandfather clock ticked loud in the midnight stillness.

A scratching at the big door. Suppose it was not Jem? They should have arranged a code of signals, but how could they? She opened it a crack, ready to put all her weight against it. "Jem?"

"Yes, miss."

She pulled it open and he was inside in a flash. "Thank you, miss." He was gasping for breath; the candlelight showed his face pale with fatigue—or with horror?

"What's happened, Jem? Come in here." She led the way into the library, wondering, as she went, what on earth she would say if they were found there. "Sit down. Rest. Tell me . . ."

He half fell into a chair, oblivious of convention. "Miss, it was terrible. And there was nothing I could do . . . nothing. I had to watch . . ." He was still seeing it.

"They caught them?"

"All of them—or nearly. Some got away, I think, in the confusion. Some . . . Barnes is dead, miss. I fell over his body. He should 'a listened to me. But he allays thought he knew best, Barnes did."

"But the boat—the *Bel Ami*? What of her?"

Got clean away. I dunno whether it was a-purpose or not, but the soldiers didn't attack till the goods were all landed. I reckon they thought they'd have it all their own way in the confusion when the loads were being shared. They did too.

Poor Barnes, he was no leader. They know it now, the others, for what it's worth to them. Now Mr. Ross—"

At last. "What of him?" Impossible to keep the tremor out of her voice.

"Nothing, miss. No one stayed from the *Bel Ami* . . . just the goods as usual, that I did see."

"Oh, thank God." Now she, too, sank into a chair. The candle, shaking in her hand, dropped a great gout of wax along the wooden arm. "He didn't come."

"No, miss. And how he will now, God knows."

Chapter Eleven

NEXT DAY, the Dark House was dark indeed. Betty brought Christina the news with her hot water. The battle of Jury's Gut, as it came to be called on the marsh, had been a disaster for the smugglers. "They hadn't got their right leader, miss. No one knows where he is. Everything went wrong." She was so near to tears that Christina did not have the heart to question her further.

At least no one was missing from the staff, but gloomy faces and the subdued tone of the servants' hall told her that many a relative or friend must have been involved in the disaster. The smugglers, apparently, had been taken completely by surprise as they were dividing their haul—quarreling over it, she suspected. Five of them had been killed, including Barnes, and—in some ways even worse—another three had been taken prisoner. Would they betray their friends? The question ran like wildfire across the marsh.

"At least,"—Parkes, who was much better this morning, had a comforting word for Christina—"they can't betray Mr. Ross. Barnes was the only one who knew."

"Thank God for that." Monstrous to be grateful that Barnes had been killed, but how could she help it? She had enough to worry about as it was. Ross was in France, cut off, possibly for the length of the war, by the hostile Channel, and, as if that was not bad enough, his grandfather was getting angrier and angrier at his continued absence. On his instructions, Richard had been invited to come down for Christmas and Christina was afraid she knew what that meant. She threw herself into the preparation of puddings and pies as a distraction as much for herself as for the servants, but with the three smugglers now lodged in Dover Castle, it was going to be a gloomy Christmas on the marsh.

Inevitably, there had been a call from Lieutenant Trevis, very ready to be congratulated on what he called, with a rather uncomfortable attempt at modesty, his good luck. He also wanted to know whether anyone was missing from the staff of the Grange and Christina was glad to be able to reassure him on the point.

"Your man didn't look as if he loved me overmuch, I thought, when he let me in." Trevis was no fool.

"Well"—no use beating about the bush—"you must know by now how they hang together here on the marsh. I ask no questions, but I won't pretend they are happy in the servants' hall. I hope, Lieutenant, that you do not ride alone after dark."

He was so grateful for what he called her concern for his welfare that she wished heartily that she had not spoken. But nothing went right, those bleak December days. The Dark House was in mourning, a state all the more painful because it must not be admitted. Tempers frayed, quarrels flared up about nothing, rain beat day in day out against the window panes.

"If this keeps up"—Mrs. Tretteign's voice was even more querulous than usual—"I doubt if poor Richard will be able to get here for Christmas."

"Really?" Christina had been staring out at the sodden marsh, but turned quickly at this, the first hopeful bit of news since the battle of Jury's Gut.

"The roads will be beyond anything dreadful. There's a proverb, I am sure, about Sussex mud and Sussex clay. I don't quite recall what it is. And poor dear Richard has never been a good traveler. Not at all like Ross, who'd think nothing of riding all day and dancing all night." Her tone suggested that there was something rather vulgar about such practices. "Do you realize how long he has been gone, Christina, and not a word? I tell you, I am out of all patience with him, and as for Papa—I expect a new will daily."

Christina managed a laugh. "If the roads are too bad for Richard, they will certainly prevent Mr. Foxton from coming. Grandfather will have to postpone changing his will till the spring. If it ever comes."

"I knew we should have gone to Bath before it was too late. I get more anxious about you every day, Christina! You were quite a handsome girl, when you came."

"And now!" Christina moved over to peer into the depths of an antique mirror. "Thank God it's too dark to see."

"You should let me lend you some of my rouge. Particularly before Richard comes. We don't want to lose him too."

"Lose him? Oh . . . I see." It had not, before, come quite so brutally clear to her that her aunt thought Ross had gone away because he could not face the idea of their engagement. Now, peering at the haggard face in the glass, she could see Mrs. Tretteign's point. "Well"—she turned away with an impatient shrug—"let us just hope it rains steadily between this and Christmas and gives Richard a good excuse for staying in London, where, I am sure, he would much rather be."

The first part of her wish, at least, was granted. As the days dragged on, water stood higher and higher in the marshland dikes, and the unused gravel pits beyond the house threatened to overflow. Work had had to be abandoned on the military canal, and the foundations of the Martello Towers were all awash. But Richard arrived, just the same, as he had written, on Christmas Eve. And Christina was amazed to find herself actually glad to see him. He might bring new problems, but at least his was a fresh and cheerful face after the gloomy ones that met her at every turn in the Dark House.

"Get here? Of course I managed to get here. It would have taken more than a little mud to keep me away." He dropped his heavy greatcoat on a settle and advanced on Christina with the evident intention of giving her a cousin's kiss. But she withdrew one step up the main stair, and, as he was already half a head shorter than she, he was reduced to planting his kiss somewhere below her left ear.

"Dear Christina." He was imperturbable. "And Aunt Verity!" Another, more successful kiss, which reminded Christina that she had never seen Ross kiss his mother. "And how's Grandfather?"

"Very well." Mrs. Tretteign led the way into the small saloon where she and Christina usually sat. "You got your leave?"

"Of course." He was holding the door for Christina as he spoke and she thought the question had annoyed him.

"Leave?" It was tiresome being taller than he was. She sank into a chair and gazed up at him with questioning eyes.

"Did you not know?" His tone made it clear that he had not expected her to know. "My grandfather has asked me to stay for a month at least. He says he feels unsafe, here in the front lines, as it were, with a houseful of women."

"He does, does he?" She did not try to hide her skepticism. "And the lords of the Admiralty let you go so easily? Hardly flattering, Cousin, surely?"

He colored with anger. "On the contrary, they parted from me with great reluctance and I shall make it clear to my grandfather that I am here at the greatest possible personal sacrifice." A look from his aunt warned him that this was hardly a happy line to take, and he changed his tone abruptly. "Not, of course, that my heart will not always be here."

So that was it. Christina picked up her detested embroidery to mask her face. It was a conspiracy against her. They were all in it. Old Mr. Tretteign had decided that Ross must be written off and had sent for Richard to take his place as her husband. And Aunt Verity—Ross's own mother—had agreed to the plan. Worst of all, Ross would be only too happy to see her safely married off to Richard—were it not for the Grange. More honest than Richard, he had never pretended he wanted her for herself. Well, his honesty, if nothing else, deserved her support.

She smiled up at Richard. "So we are to have the pleasure of your company for a whole month, Cousin Richard. What on earth will you find to do with yourself?"

"God knows." He was very far from being an accomplished play-actor, and she found herself liking him better every time he gave himself away. "There's not even a billiard table fit to play on—not that there'd be anyone to play with, if there was."

"No? My father used to say I played a very reasonable game—for a girl, of course."

"What? Billiards among the savages?"

"Oh"—she retrieved her mistake quickly—"we played at the local saloon, of course. Father did not altogether like my going there"—this in response to a shudder from her aunt—"but it was better than leaving me alone, exposed to who knew what danger, at home."

Richard managed a languishing look. "What a romantic life you have led, Cousin Christina!"

"Have I not?" And then, determinedly practical, "And as to a table, the one in the greenroom here is very far from being beyond repair, if you could but persuade Grandfather to authorize the necessary expense. And I believe you can persuade him to anything, Cousin."

He was delighted. "Do you think so? Then, since you ask it, I will certainly make the attempt."

"Do," she said heartily. "If you do not want us to go melancholy mad. Grandfather does not seem to believe in Christmas. A barbarous survival from classical times, he calls it. I had been looking forward to Drawing the King, and Étrennes and all kinds of quaint English customs, but he seems to think it quite enough if we have roast beef and plum puddings tomorrow—and I achieved them rather by guile than persuasion."

It was not a gay Christmas. But the twelve days dragged by somehow, enlivened by the news that Bonaparte had crowned himself Emperor of France in the Cathedral of Notre Dame.

"Much good may it do him." Richard attempted a cannon off her ball and missed. "This table's terrible." The handyman had just finished working on it.

"It's better than nothing." Christina took careful aim from the awkward position in which he had left her and sank her ball unerringly. "You think it may do him harm?" She returned to the question of Bonaparte, or Napoleon as he now styled himself.

"Good God! What a piece of beginner's luck." In his surprise, he made a botch of his own shot. "Yes, of course it will do him harm. The French won't like it—and the other sovereigns will be furious at having an interloper in their midst."

"I do wonder if you are right." Once again she took careful aim and embarked on a winning break that left him gasping.

"You play like a professional, Cousin." There was a good deal more disapproval than admiration in his tone.

"Oh dear. You find it unladylike? I was Papa's only opponent, you see. I had to study to give him a reasonable game . . . and he was a wonderful teacher."

"I wish you would use that tone when you speak of me, Christina!" He moved around the table toward her, but she, in her turn, dodged to the far side and made a fending off business of chalking her cue.

"Why should I?" She faced him squarely, the cue between them. "Father was everything to me—and I to him." Her voice broke on the words.

"Christina!" He took her moment of weakness for encouragement. "That's just what I want to be to you—everything. Forget Ross, who has all too evidently forgotten you. He's no good for you, I tell you. We grew up together . . . I should know. Women will never be anything but chattels to him. Forget him, Christina—marry me. Your wish shall be my law, my every aim to please you."

"But I don't want a husband like that! Anyway, are you not ashamed to talk to me like this, when you know that I am engaged to Ross?"

"I have our grandfather's permission." He spoke as if that settled it. "As for Ross, God knows where he is by now. Off on one of his mad starts again, I have no doubt. He does it, you know, when things don't go to his liking at home. I remember once, when we were boys, our tutor beat him—unfairly, as he thought. He disappeared for weeks, and returned, when we had almost given him up, with some wild tale of sailing with a gang of smugglers. You can imagine what Grandfather and my aunt had been through, but did he care? Not Ross. He said it had been a very interesting experience and worth a month of Greek grammar. Well . . . I ask you! No doubt this time he's shipped as a foremast hand in a navy ship or something equally fantastic—and, I can tell you, he won't get away from that so easily."

"What makes you think that?"

He hedged at once. "I don't know it for certain, mind you, but there's no doubt it's a very likely probability. And so I told my grandfather. It was my duty to do so."

"And . . ."

Now he had the grace to look a little awkward. "Well . . . you know how it is, Cousin. He wants to see you safely married before he dies—to one of us. If Ross has really volunteered—or even been pressed—for the navy, he's as good as dead for the duration of the war."

"I see." She saw a great deal. Whether he had deceived

himself, or merely his grandfather, made little difference, except in her opinion of him. Worst of all, he might even be right. She did not know that Ross had got to France. Suppose he had been captured—the rest would logically follow from that.

"Dear Christina." He had been quick to spot her moment of hesitation and had crept in, somehow, under her guard. "Stop fighting me!" One hand had got itself around her waist, the other, reaching up, was trying to bend her head to his.

She thought a great many things at what seemed fantastic speed. Rage, her first reaction, was quickly checked. She must not make an enemy of Richard—for Ross's sake, as well as for her own. Exert her full strength, laugh at him, half a head below her there, as she longed to do—and he would hate her. She looked down into his eyes. "Dear Richard." She began, gently, to extricate herself. "Don't."

"But why not? Since I love you, and there is no obstacle?" But he released her with what, laughing to herself, she recognized as relief.

"Nonsense." This much she would allow herself. "You don't love me, Richard, and there is an obstacle—my engagement to Ross, to which I shall stick until he releases me from it."

"Grandfather will be very angry." Here he came to the heart of the matter.

"Leave me to deal with Grandfather." She moved across the room, gave a sharp tug to the bell pull, and, when Frank appeared, "My compliments to Mr. Tretteign," she said, "and would he spare me a few minutes?"

"You're going to tell him you won't?" Richard looked at her almost with awe.

"Yes." What else was she going to tell him? If only she knew. But—sufficient to the crisis were the evils thereof. "I shall have to concede our game, Cousin."

"Well?" Her grandfather looked sharply at her from the depths of his big chair. "Come to announce your engagement, eh?"

"No, Grandfather." But she bent to drop a kiss on his leathery cheek. "I announced that weeks ago, remember?"

"Yes—and much good it's done us. Have you heard what Richard says?"

"About Ross running off and enlisting in the navy? Yes— and give him credit for believing it himself."

"You don't, hey?"

"Of course I don't. Nor do you."

"He might have been pressed."

"A gentleman? Fantastic. Besides, I think I know where he is."

"Oh you do, do you. And where, pray, is that?"

"I'm afraid I can't tell you, Grandfather. It's not my secret."

"You mean it's all moonshine. Now, I'll tell you what I think, girl, and you can just quit arguing and listen to me. Of course you're right on one point—gentlemen don't get pressed. But there might be truth in Richard's story for all that. You know as well as I do that Ross was far more closely involved than I like to think with that rascally band of smugglers."

"From whom we get our tea and brandy? Yes, Grandfather, I have suspected something of the kind."

"Suspected! Pah, girl, don't give me that. If he didn't confide in you, and get your help, too, I'm more senile than I think. Well, then, suppose he was in the gang that day when Trevis caught them. Suppose by some fluke he was not recognized, in his disguise—I have no doubt Ross can look a villainous enough character if he wants to. Might he not then, rather than disgrace himself, and, to be fair to him, us, have stuck to his alias? How do you know he isn't rotting in Dover Castle at this minute?"

"Because I know relatives of all three men who are there."

"Oh." But he returned at once to the attack. "Just the same, he might have traded information for a chance to volunteer for the navy. It's entirely possible, you know, that they'd take him—he's a great brute of a man. He'd make two of Richard."

"And you think that a bad thing. Take a long look at me, Grandfather."

Surprisingly, he chuckled. "Long's the word all right. I know what you're thinking, girl. You're afraid you'll look foolish towering over poor Richard. But it can't be helped. I've borne with Ross all this time, because he had the name —if nothing else. Now, I've had enough. If he's between decks on a man-of-war . . . well, what more suitable place for a bastard? I expect he'll thrive there too. Ross always falls on his feet. Well, now what's the matter, girl?"

She had risen to her feet. "I've had enough. I'm leaving, Grandfather. I engaged myself to Ross, not because either of us wanted it, but to please you. Now, for as little reason, you wish me to break that and make Richard miserable with an engagement as distasteful to him as to me. I came here because my father made me promise, on his deathbed, that I would. It's true that I promised him I'd stay six months, but, if he was alive, I'm sure he'd agree I've done my best. So . . . good-bye, Grandfather."

"What? What?" He gobbled at her in surprise and rage. "Leave! I never heard such nonsense. My granddaughter leave Tretteign Grange! Impossible. Besides"—he was relaxing now, a look of cunning spreading across the blotchy face —"where would you go? Going on the town—hey?—So you'll be fit company for Ross when he gets home?"

"It's lucky you're so old." She stood over him, looking down dispassionately at his crumpled figure in the big chair. "I'm not going to say the things I might, Grandfather. Only this. My father escaped from you. Your other son and your daughter, who stayed at home, do not seem to have made remarkable successes of their lives. I think, even now, old as you are, you are dangerous because you're so selfish and so stupid. Well, you're not going to make a mull of my life, because I won't let you. Father hoped you might have learned something, over the years. He begged me to come back and give you a chance to be my grandfather. 'Family's important,' he said. Well, I've given family a chance for his sake, but now I'm finished. May I have the use of the carriage as far as Rye?" She might have been any guest arranging her departure.

He had shrunk down into the chair, but his voice was still spiteful. "To Rye, hey? And what will you do there? Not set up as one of the muslin company on my very doorstep, I hope."

"What a fool you are, Grandfather." But this time she said it kindly enough. "No, I shall hire a post chaise to take me to London. Has it never occurred to you that my father has friends? The American minister in London is one of them."

"So you'll live on his charity, eh?"

"Rather than on yours—yes. But, in fact, it will not come

to that. You have teased me, I know, about my inheritance from my father, but it should see me through this crisis."

"And set you up, no doubt, in some delicious career—you reckon to commence governess, perhaps?"

"Heaven forbid. But what I do with myself, from now on, is my own affair. You have lost the right even to ask about my plans. So . . . good-bye, Grandfather." She bent to kiss the dry old cheek, and something about the way he had huddled down into his chair moved her to add, "I'm sorry it's had to end like this. I'd have liked to be a granddaughter to you. Father was right, you know, family *is* important. That's just the danger." And then, on an entirely new note, "Grandfather! What's the matter?"

His face was livid and his jaw hung down at one side. "My drops, girl, quick!" He spoke with difficulty.

She poured them with a hand that shook. Monstrous, in her anger, to have forgotten his precarious state of health. But then, to be fair to herself, she had always thought his ill health merely one of his many holds over his family. Now, ringing sharply for Greg, she blamed herself bitterly. After all, he was a very old man. The mere shock of having his wishes crossed—so unusual in his life—might have been too much for him.

But Dr. Pembly, when he came, was less discouraging than Christina had feared. He confirmed that old Mr. Tretteign had suffered a slight stroke. "Been having an argument, had he?" She had been frank with him about the nature of the scene, though not about what had been said. "Well, I've warned him often enough . . . and don't you look so miserable either, Miss Tretton. The truth is, he's been using these seizures of his to rule his family for years. I've warned him often enough . . . but how were you to know?"

"I should have guessed. I'll never forgive myself. But you think he'll recover?"

"Of course he'll recover—with nursing—and be ruling the roost as hard as ever in a week or two. But, that brings me to a point—nursing. Greg's had practice, but I wouldn't trust him with the medicines. And, worthy woman, your aunt . . ." He left silence to speak for itself. "Last time Mr. Tretteign was ill, I sent in a woman I could rely on for sheer good-natured bullying. But she's left the district. Now, you managed Parkes . . ."

Christina had seen this coming. "I was meaning to leave today," she said.

"That's what the row was about, eh? Well, I don't want to pose as your conscience, but won't you feel better if you stay and pull the old man through? It's nothing difficult, mind, just good honest woman's care. But as for your aunt and cousin . . ." It was, she supposed, significant enough that they had left her to deal with him.

"Yes." It hardly took a struggle. "I'll do it."

"Good girl. You won't regret it, I'm sure."

Of course she would not. Had not something, deep down inside her, been glad of a valid excuse for staying? After all, if he came back at all, surely Ross would come back here.

Inevitably, Richard used his grandfather's illness as an excuse to apply for an extension of his leave of absence from the Admiralty. "Do you realize"—he had contrived to corner Christina in her study—"that if the old man were to die now, the whole estate would go to the Patriotic Fund? It doesn't bear thinking of—"

"No?" She rounded on him with pent-up fury. "It doesn't does it, so let's not." And then, more quietly, "Look, Richard . . . for one thing Grandfather is not going to die. For another, I would not have you even if he had just received the last rites of the Church. And, finally, if you so much as hint at this again, I will stop nursing him and let him die." Of course she would do no such thing, but she had Richard's measure by now. He believed her implicitly, and left her alone.

Chapter Twelve

CHRISTINA WAS not so absurd as to expect her grandfather to be an easy invalid. Sometimes she almost suspected him of wanting to die, simply out of bad temper, but, if so, a naturally rugged constitution was too much for him. He began, slowly, reluctantly, ill-temperedly, to recover.

"Well now." He was sitting up in bed for the first time one wild January evening when his rooms were the only draught-free ones in the house. "What's been going on while I've been ill, hey, girl? Richard's still here, I hope."

"Yes, Grandfather." She handed him his glass of medicine. "Still here, and still obeying orders."

"And what, pray, do you mean by that?" He made a disgusted face and put the medicine, untouched, on the table by his bed.

"Why, that he's wooing me as pertinaciously as you could wish. It would be comic if it were not a nuisance." She picked up the glass and offered it to him again. "Dr. Pembly says it's important you should take it regularly."

"Be damned to Pembly. What makes it comic, may I ask?"

"I'll tell you when you've drunk your medicine." She moved away to make up the fire.

"Obstinate bitch aren't you? Damned if you don't remind me of your grandmother." He was looking beyond her now into the remote past. "Everything would have been different if she hadn't died bearing that fool of a girl . . . daughters—pah! Couldn't stop her own husband seducing her brother's wife. That's what all my troubles stem from. God, I could have killed her."

Christina looked at him thoughtfully. He was obviously much better. Well enough to face the truth for once? "Don't you think you probably did?" she said.

"What on earth do you mean?" In his surprise, he drank off his medicine at a gulp.

"Why—just that if you made her the kind of scene you go in for these days, on top of her other troubles, it's no wonder she died in childbirth. Did my grandmother let you bully people?"

"Bully? I?" He was honestly surprised. "Someone's got to keep this family from going to the devil. And I tell you, girl, I mean to do it. And I won't be put off with red herrings either. I want to know what's so comic about Richard's courting you."

"Everything. Poor Richard! He tries so hard. But you're no fool. You must see the absurdity of it. Richard and I? It would be like mating a humming bird and an ostrich, and he knows it."

"Nothing of the kind. And at least he's got more sense than to defy me. I don't suppose there's been any word from Ross while I've been ill?" And then, reading the answer on her face, "Very well then, that settles it. And I'll have no more of *your* bullying either. Send me Greg and write Foxton he's to come at once."

"Very well, Grandfather." She turned to leave the room.

"Too proud even to ask, hey? Well, I'll tell you—a new will . . . everything to Richard—the only one of my grandchildren who obeys me. The only one I can trust."

She looked at him thoughtfully. Remind him of Richard's declared intention to sell the Grange at once? Tell him any marriage between them would have been in name only, with no chance of heirs? Tell him . . . no, there was enough tattle and talebearing in this house already. "Poor Ross," she said instead. And, "Poor Grandfather." She shut the door gently behind her and set about doing his bidding.

She was in her study writing to Foxton when she heard carriage wheels on the drive outside. Who on earth? Dr. Pembly was not due till the next day. Even in fine weather, visitors to the Dark House were few and far between, discouraged equally, she suspected, by her grandfather's bad temper and her aunt's bad name. She was at the window now, peering out through driving rain as a shabby-looking post chaise drew up on the sweep outside the front door. The postboy was still busy with his horses when the carriage door was flung open and a tall figure jumped lightly to the ground. Ross!

She was in the hall in a moment, then, forcing herself to show a calm she was far from feeling, stopped to ring the bell for Parkes. While she awaited his slow approach from the back of the house, she made herself stay away from the windows. Her aunt would think it unladylike if she rushed out to greet Ross. She did not care a straw for that—but Ross would not like it either. She saw that the grandfather clock was five minutes slow and made a little business of reaching up to move its hands.

There, Parkes had appeared at last, and, as he did so, a resounding knock sounded on the heavy front door. "It's Mr. Ross, Parkes." She could at least spare the old man the shock that even such a pleasant surprise must be.

"Ha, Parkes. Good to see you." Ross sounded as matter-of-fact as if he had been merely as far as Rye, or, at most, Hastings. "And Chris." She had let herself come forward now, hands outstretched, a host of silent questions in her eyes. "Good to see you, too." His tone was exactly the same as to Parkes. He took her hands, looked as if he did not quite know what to do with them and compromised by giving them a little, friendly shake and letting go. "Is all well?"

How to answer such a comprehensive question? "Well . . ." she began doubtfully, but he interrupted her. "No matter—there'll be time for that. I've no doubt my grandfather is in a fury, but that can wait too. I've got a surprise for you, Chris, one that will please you."

"A surprise? For me?" But he had turned away and started back down the front steps to the carriage. Following him to the open doorway, she saw movement, faces inside. Ross had opened the door and was carefully, almost tenderly, helping someone to alight. The slight figure—she could not be more than a girl—turned to look at him, laughing, and say something, then ran for it through the rain to the open doorway. "Tina!" She was still laughing as she shook raindrops from her curls. "I'd have known you anywhere." She put up a pointed, delicate little face to be kissed. "I declare, you're taller than ever . . ."

Returning the kiss, "Sophie!" said Christina, "I don't believe it. But how?"

"By a miracle and our cousin Ross." She rolled her r's in the French fashion. "But, come and greet Mamma."

"Mother!"

"Of course. You didn't think I'd trust myself to anyone so dashing as Cousin Ross alone?" They both turned in the doorway in time to see a plump little figure in extravagant widow's weeds make a cautious descent, carefully supported by Ross's arm. Despite the rain, she came up the stairs sedately, looking about her as she came with quick, dark eyes that missed nothing. Now they settled on Christina. "Well, my dear?"

"Well, Mother?" Once again, Christina had to bend to kiss the exquisite maquillage of the cheek. As she did so, a wave of perfume, familiar as the memories of childhood, assailed her; the temptation to make it a real kiss, to throw her arms around her mother and let the tears of welcome come, was strong in her. But, already, her mother had drawn away to look about her at the hall. "I'm delighted to see you, my dear. And this is Tretteign Grange at last. We are exhausted from our journey. Rest first, perhaps, and exclamations later?"

"Mother, you haven't changed a bit!" Christina could not help it. "And Sophie!" She had a hand of each. "Yes, of course you must rest. Come up to my room while I think what's best for you. Ross, if I were you I would go straight to Grandfather. He's very angry. I was just writing Foxton."

"I see." How silent he had been. Tact? It seemed most unlike him. Or could memory of their parting weigh as heavily with him as it did with her? He must know by now that she had had nothing to do with M. Tissot's escape. Could he be trying for the apology she had demanded from him?

"Christina!" His voice made her turn back from the stairs which her mother and sister were already ascending. There was certainly something on his mind. Well, no wonder.

"Yes?" She stopped on the bottom stair to look at him from his own level.

"We have much to talk about."

"Yes."

"And no time yet. Meanwhile . . ." A pause. Something was indeed the matter. "I did not know what to do for the best. I have said nothing—to your Mother—to them."

"Nothing?" She could not help feeling sorry for his obvious embarrassment. "Oh—about our engagement, you mean, such as it is?"

"Yes."

"I see." How much did she see?

"Cousin Ross!" Sophie was leaning over the upstairs banisters. She had snatched off her calash and dark curls fell loose around the little face. "You won't forget your promise?"

"I should think not! Just as soon as you are rested." And then, oddly awkward, to Christina. "I told her about the haunted cloisters."

"And she wants to see them. Of course." She gave him one long, clear look, then turned to follow the others up the stairs.

"That's better." Mrs. Tretton settled back luxuriously against the pillows of Christina's bed. "I shall sleep for two hours. Wake me with a cup of chocolate, like a good child, and tell my father-in-law I will be pleased to wait on him then. He does not leave his rooms, I understand?"

"Not often."

"So much the better. No, child. I said, questions later, or, if you must ask them, ask your cousin." She closed her eyes and relaxed, catlike against the pillows. "Good night, my love. I'm glad to see you."

Christina smiled as she tiptoed from the room. Her mother had always got her own way—except when she wanted father to go back to France with her—and even then she had gone without him. As she paused at the door of the room that had been hurriedly prepared for Sophie, it opened and Betty tiptoed out. "She's fast asleep already, miss. They've traveled night and day, she said. Oh, Miss Christina, ain't it the most romantic thing. You must be struck all of a heap, like."

"I certainly am." It was true enough. And she could feel the whole household stirring with the excitement of the arrivals. How characteristic it was of her mother to have retired so capably until the worst of it was over.

Greg had just emerged from old Mr. Tretteign's suite. "Is Mr. Ross with his grandfather?" Christina asked him.

"Oh no, miss. Not in all his dirt. Mr. Tretteign will see him in an hour's time."

"Oh." This too was characteristic. "I see. Then perhaps

you will ask my grandfather if he will consent to see my mother after that. She is resting at present."

Downstairs, Richard and her Aunt Tretteign fell upon her with questions. They had both missed the actual moment of the arrival since she had been resting and he practicing shots in the billiard room at the back of the house.

"But I know no more than you do," she was protesting when Ross appeared at the top of the stairs.

"Ross! My darling boy!" Mrs. Tretteign could be relied on to act up to an occasion. "I've been in anguish about you. Where in the world have you been?"

"In France, Mother." His dry tone told Christina that he was under no illusions about the extent of his mother's "anguish."

Now the exclamations began in good earnest, and Christina listened with amused respect as he parried some of his mother's volley of questions and answered those that suited him. How he had got to France remained obscure, but he let it seem that his mission had been entirely in connection with his aunt and cousin. Christina's mother, it appeared, had been involved in Moreau's conspiracy against Bonaparte and it had become necessary for her to leave France without delay. She had, however, had influential friends, the Empress Josephine among them, and had contrived to secure papers—under false names—for herself, her daughter and him.

"You mean you left France openly?" Mrs. Tretteign was amazed. "But how?"

"On an American ship. Oh yes, technically they are not supposed to ply directly from a French port to an English one, but of course they do—it suits everyone to close a blind eye to the business. I won't say we didn't have some anxious moments when we were waiting for a fair wind—but, here we are."

"And Mrs. Tretton proposes to stay?" Her sister-in-law sounded less than delighted at the idea.

"Well, I should think so. Where more properly than here? It must make you very happy, Christina"—for the first time he addressed her directly—"to be reunited with them."

"Well, you know, it does," she said.

"How long is it?" Was he digressing on purpose to avoid more difficult questions? "Six years—seven years—since you saw them last? You must find a great change in your sister."

"I certainly do, seeing that she was only twelve when I saw

her last. I'm surprised I recognized her. Mamma has hardly changed at all though. But, poor Mamma, is this the end of her hopes of getting back at least some part of her family's fortune?"

"I'm afraid so."

"You mean, she is penniless?" That was Mrs. Tretteign, sharply.

"Not entirely, I think. But anyway I'm sure Grandfather will do the handsome thing by them. One sight of Sophie! How could he help . . ." He stopped, coloring. "And that reminds me, it is almost my hour to see him. How is he? Greg says he's not been well."

"No, very far from it." Christina put warning into her voice. "He's better, now, but the doctor says any new cause of irritation might prove fatal. So, be careful, Ross."

"I'm always careful. You should know that, Chris."

"Should I?"

"Oh, Ross," his mother echoed Christina's words, "pray be careful. He's been so angry with you. Why did you not even write?"

He laughed. "Dear Mamma, had it not occurred to you that the mail service between France and England has been —shall we say—suspended? But I'll be careful." An impartial smile all around and he turned and left them.

"Well," said Richard, "it doesn't look as if we are to learn a great deal about Ross's adventures in France. How do you think he got there in the first place?" This, with a sharp glance, for Christina.

"I simply cannot imagine. Aunt, where do you think we should put my mother and sister?" She always tried to make a point of consulting Mrs. Tretteign about her domestic arrangements.

"Oh, where you will. I have no doubt you have it all settled long since. But I hope you will make it clear to your grandfather that he will have to increase the housekeeping allowance if he intends to let them stay. I don't propose to go on short commons to feed a couple of refugees."

"You are speaking of my mother and sister." Retreating to her study, Christina was surprised to find herself so angry. But then, the whole day had been one of surprises. Amazing to have felt such a flood of emotion at this reunion. For so long now, her only feeling about her mother had been one of anger. She had been seventeen when the question of a return to France had arisen. Her mother had had letters from her family suggesting that if she returned their chances of salvaging at least part of the family estate would be much improved. Then the arguments had started. She had taken it for granted, at first, that her husband would accompany her, and had been amazed when he had flatly refused. Looking back, Christina could understand that amazement. Her father had always given in on minor points of domestic economy; had equally always been totally firm on the major issues. This time, he was firm.

Quarrels of a dreadfully increasing bitterness had followed. At the time, she had been completely, wholeheartedly on her father's side. Now, looking back across the great chasm of time, she remembered phrases of her mother's: "This barbarous country," "I've done my best for your sake," "No life . . ." and, always recurring, "What about the girls? What future is there here for them?" And, her father, shrugging, "Well, not the guillotine, at all events."

In the end, inevitably, there had been a compromise. Father might be firm, but so was Mother; it must have been, originally, an attraction of similarity between them. She would return to France, with some lip service paid to the idea that, having succeeded in her mission, she might rejoin him. Then, of course, had come the question of the children. This was another evening that Christina remembered with anguished vividness. Twelve-year-old Sophie was already in bed in her curtained cot in the corner of the room. The rest of them had finished their frugal supper and were sitting at the rough log table, pushed close up to the wood fire. Outside, snow was falling as if it would never stop; inside there was the appearance of comfort, of amity.

"I shall take the girls, of course." Her mother had thrown it across the table like a challenge.

"Of course?" Father had put the query lightly enough. "Well—Sophie, I suppose. She is too young to do without a mother. But—Christina? I think she must decide for herself. What do you say, Chris? France and the hope of luxury, or a log cabin and your old father to care for?"

"That's not fair"—she could even remember her mother's tone—"she's too young to decide. It's her whole life, remember. What chance has she of a respectable marriage, out here in the wilds?"

"You'd rather she married a Robespierre or a Danton? But, it's true, it is a hard decision for a child to make. You must think about it, Chris, very carefully."

She had been crying, she remembered, all this time, but had spoken up at once, ignoring the tears that slipped coldly down her cheeks. "I want to stay, Father. I don't need to think about it." And then, a wild appeal to her mother to stay too—wild, and useless. She did not like to remember it . . . or the painful days that followed while her mother made her arrangements, and waited for spring. Had she and her father really believed Mother would go through with it? Maybe not. She remembered another evening, a fine spring one, when, for the first time, they sat down at table alone together and made a gallant pretense at conversation. After that, Father had grown silent, withdrawn, though invariably kind to her. He had always worked hard, now he worked like a madman, and took a madman's risks. Well—they had paid off. Until the last one that had ended in the Indian ambush, the slow and agonizing death. At least she had been there, when they had brought him home, to hold his hand and make him the promises he asked for. And she would keep them.

Betty was tapping on the door to announce that her mother was awake and asking for her. "Miss Sophie's still dead to the world—oh, miss, ain't it the most romantic thing, and her so lovely too!" Was there sympathy, as well as excitement, in Betty's gaze? Very likely. Her grandfather was not a man to keep secrets. Her engagement to Ross, though never formally announced, must have been general knowledge in the servants' hall. And now—what? Had the servants already reached the conclusion that she was trying to hold at arm's length?

No time for these thoughts. "I'll come at once, Betty."

She found her mother already up and dressed in the highly becoming blue gown she had had Betty press for her while she slept. The elegant simplicity of line and cut all said Paris, and, Christina thought wryly, money. No, that was unfair; even in the wilds, when she had been reduced to making her own clothes, her mother had always contrived to look elegant.

"Will I do, love?" Her mother had read her thoughts. And

then, without waiting for the unnecessary answer. "And now, tell me about this old tartar of a grandfather. How is he best handled?"

Christina could not help smiling. There was something admirable, practical and French in the way her mother took first things first. "Well . . ." She thought it over for a moment. "He's used to having his own way, of course, in everything. I think, perhaps, my grandmother could manage him —I suspect he was devoted to her. But she died when Richard's mother was born. I think he's been lonely ever since."

"I see." Mrs. Tretton patted her elegantly smooth coiffure. "And the daughter-in-law, your Aunt Tretteign?"

"Infuriates him. Well," dispassionately, "I'm sorry for her, but she's a very silly woman." She ought to tell her mother about Ross's illegitimacy . . . about Ross . . . but how to begin? Besides, he had made that appeal. At least she must wait till she had talked to him.

"There's a great deal I don't know, isn't there?" Her mother was alarmingly quick. "Never mind, there will be plenty of time . . . too much of it if this place is really the end-of-the-world it seems."

"It is." Christina had already wondered how much better her mother would find the Dark House than the American wilds. But here was Betty again, to summon Mrs. Tretton to old Mr. Tretteign's rooms, and add, with an unbearably knowing look, "And Mr. Ross is in your study, miss."

Ross was prowling about her room, picking up papers and putting them down again. "Oh, there you are, Chris. We must talk, you and I. But, first, how are they? Not too exhausted by their journey, I hope. How gallantly they bore it! Why did you never tell me—"

"Tell you?"

He looked, suddenly, embarrassed. "Why . . . about them. It seems so strange."

"I suppose it does. As to being exhausted, they seem none the worse. Sophie's still asleep."

"That's good. That will do her more good than anything. Chris . . ."

"Yes?"

"There's so much to say."

"Yes." Indeed there was. She thought of their last meeting, of his wild accusations. Was she, at least, to get her apology?

He moved away to the window, then back again. Well, it was no wonder if he found it hard to begin. She took pity on him. "You've heard about Barnes?" Anything to get the talk flowing. "Yes. Poor fool. I sent a message, you know, warning them." He was angry now. "I knew it was unsafe."

"Yes—poor Barnes. And the others—in Dover gaol—can you do nothing for them, Ross?"

"How can I?" And then, at her quick exclamation, "Oh I'll try. I might at least get them pressed for the navy."

"They would think that better?"

"I expect so. But, they're nothing. What about M. Tissot? You're on terms with Trevis. Has he ever spoken of him?"

"Not a word. I can't understand it. If M. Tissot betrayed the rest of your plans, why not you?"

"Some odd notion of gratitude, perhaps. After all, we saved his life, you and I. Oh—and that reminds me, Chris, I owe you an apology, do I not?"

"It's no matter." How trivial it all seemed now. There was worse, she suspected, much worse to come. "But, Ross, what about you? Is it safe for you to be here? Suppose M. Tissot is still lurking somewhere—he can betray you at any moment."

"Let him!" Carelessly. "No need to look so anxious, Chris. I'm in good standing now. I brought Pitt news—bad news, it's true, but what he had to know. Villeneuve's out."

"The French admiral? Good God, where's he bound?"

"To rendezvous with the Spanish Fleet, no doubt, beat Nelson and clear the way for the invasion."

"Dear God."

"Yes. And not a word to a soul, Chris. I should not have told you, but somehow I have a habit of telling you things."

"You can trust me."

"I know. I should always have known. Chris . . ."

"Yes?"

He had moved away to gaze out the window at the gray prospect of marsh and sea. "Grandfather's come round. He's pleased with me—absurdly so. He thinks I've done something romantic—gallant." His voice was bitter. "He does not realize, nor could I tell him, that it was less a question of my rescuing your mother than of her saving me. If her friends had not provided us with papers—it was touch and go for a while there in Paris. She's a wonderful woman, your mother. You never told me."

"I don't think I quite knew."

"And . . . your sister. Sophie." He said the name as if it had a special magic. "You never told me about her."

Christina managed a laugh. "When I last saw her she was twelve years old, with skinny plaits, and puffy-eyed with crying."

"It's hard to imagine . . . but, of course, she's so young . . . a child—an enchanting child. You must be very happy, Chris."

"Yes."

"But . . . this is not what I meant to say. . . . The thing is this. I pointed out to Grandfather that everything is different now. It was monstrous, before, that he should have taken no thought for your mother and sister—in fact"—reproach in his voice now—"I cannot think how you came not to object. But, now they are here, it changes everything."

"Quite so."

"I'm relying on your mother, you know. She'll bring him round, if anyone can. I told him, of course, that she knew nothing about that crackbrained will of his. And, I told him . . ."

"Yes?"

"Why, that it was crackbrained. You can't do things that way, Chris. I can't think why we allowed ourselves even to pretend to conform with his views. It was monstrous. I should not have let you. At least I hope I've made amends now. He tells me, by the way, that Richard is devoted to you."

"Does he?" On monosyllables there was a fair chance of keeping her voice steady.

"Anyway." He came back from the window to stand over her where she sat at her desk, her head bent low over her papers to conceal her face. "I think I've persuaded him that that will of his cannot possibly stand. I am relying on your mother to finish the business. So, it remains only to say how grateful I am to you, Chris. I had no right to ask it—I understand that now. You must forgive me—I think I understood nothing."

"And now—you understand everything?"

"You're not angry, Chris? I thought you'd be so relieved. Oh—it's awkward, I know, but after all there was no official announcement. We're just—back where we started from."

"Precisely." She made a little business of looking for a paper on her desk. "Ah, here it is. I was writing to summon Foxton when you arrived. You think I should finish the letter?"

"I hope so. Ah—what's that?" With a long stride, he was at the door of the room, and now she realized that, all the time they had been talking, he had been listening for something.

Sophie was at the top of the stairs, looking down at Richard, her dark curls framing her little face. "You must be my cousin Richard?" Once again the faintly rolled French r.

"Yes, and most enchanted to make your acquaintance, Cousin Sophie. How barbarous not even to have known . . ." He met her halfway on the stairs and bent to kiss her hand.

"No, no, not like that . . ." A little ripple of laughter. "Have you no graces, you Englishmen? A French *sans-culotte* would do it with more of an air. But Ross is worse—he doesn't even try." And then, as if noticing him for the first time, "Oh, there you are, Ross. You see, I am all ready for my tour of the chateau—what do you call it? Oh—I have it —the Grrrange. Will I do, do you think?" She took two dancing steps off the bottom stair, and whirled to show off the fit of her dark-green walking dress.

"You are far too fine," said Ross. "You'll get your skirts covered in mud, child. And as for those slippers!"

She put a tiny foot on the bottom stair and looked down at it reflectively. "They're pretty, are they not? I brought you a pair, Tina, from Paris. I bought them three sizes larger than mine. I do hope that will be right. They're all the rage there now. As to this dress"—back to Ross—"it's just an old thing —who cares if it gets a little muddy? And you promised me something funny for my feet—I know, don't tell me—pattens, they're called. See what a good pupil I am! Ross has been improving my English for me," she explained to Richard and Christina. "It was shockingly rusty when we first met, was it not, Ross?"

"It was indeed. You used to talk about gentlesmen, I remember, and sing a song about nymphs and sheephards. But, come, let us find you these pattens or it will be dark before we make our tour of the Grrrange." He imitated her pronunciation as best he could.

"*Taquin!* How do you say it? Tease? Is he not a sad tease, our Cousin Ross." Once again this was impartially for Richard and Christina. And then, "But won't you come too, Tina? There's so much to talk about. Just think, I know Cousin Ross better than I do you. He says you're a formidable housekeeper and make them all mind you."

Christina laughed. "That's just why I don't think I'd better come too. I've a million things to see to just now. Besides, Mamma's been with Grandfather for quite half an hour."

"Getting round him, too, I'll be bound. Trust Mamma. Well, come then, Ross. Where's this ghost you promise me? Cousin Richard, had you not best come too, to help protect me? I'm terrified of ghosts! Or will your coat stand the rain? I'm sure it is raining. It has been ever since we landed. Ross cares nothing for his clothes, I know. Mamma was quite shocked when we first met. She will think you very much more the thing, Cousin Richard. And I will teach you to kiss hands properly, since Ross here won't learn. In exchange, you shall tell me all about London society, of which Ross seems to have the most Gothic ideas. I'm sure *you've* been to Almack's, Cousin Richard?"

"Of course I have. And of course I shall join you in your tour of the house. Ross is as likely as not to forget all about you in some confabulation with his groom."

"Do you think so? I wonder . . ." She smiled up at Ross, sparkling, teasing, enchantingly sure of her power. It was no wonder, thought Chris, that both men looked as if they could eat her. There was something irresistible about her happy confidence in her own charms. Now she had put a hand into each of theirs, with a child's gay impatience. "Come on then —I long to meet your ghost. Will he appear for me, do you think?"

"He'll be a brute if he doesn't," said Ross.

But she had drawn back with a little squeak of dismay. "Good God, where are you taking me? Will I be safe, Tina?"

"I'm sure you will." So protected, she might have added, as Ross and Richard followed Sophie into the dark lobby, and she heard them vying with each other for the privilege of adjusting her pattens. It seemed a long time since Ross had done the same thing for her.

Chapter Thirteen

CHRISTINA PAUSED for a moment outside her study door. The party of exploration had still not returned and it was—maddeningly—impossible not to keep following it in her mind. Once, while she was talking to the cook, she had heard Sophie's high, delighted laughter in the stable yard outside, and then her voice. "Oh, Cousin Ross, you are so naughtee . . ."

Ross? Naughty? She had caught Cook's speculative eye fixed upon her, and left the kitchen abruptly. Now she plunged, as for sanctuary, into her study. Inevitably, during his absence, she had taken over Ross's duties about the estate. It was easy to make herself very busy bringing the accounts up to date.

At last her mother put her head around the door. "Ah there you are, my love." Her accent was more marked than Sophie's. "Betty said I would probably find you here. A pleasant enough child, that one, but knows nothing about dress—it's no wonder . . ."

Christina managed a laugh. "I look such a frump? Are you going to take me in hand, Mamma? Don't you despair, just at the size of me?"

"Not a bit of it." She closed the door behind her and settled comfortably in the one easy chair. "I find you striking, Christina—your face has formed itself much better than I expected. As for your height—it's a misfortune, of course, but perhaps not so bad as it might be. I find your grandfather charming." It was clear that she expected Christina to see the connection.

"You've had a long talk."

"Yes. He's lonely, poor old man. He plans to come down to dinner, by the way. He told me to tell you."

"Good gracious! What did you do to him, Mamma?"

"Just let him talk. He seems to have made a sad botch of your affairs, *chérie,* with the best intentions in the world."

"Oh. He told you about that, did he?"

"Of course. I only wish M. Ross had thought fit to do so. It's awkward." And then, with the smile that could not fail to charm. "I am paying you the compliment, love, of speaking to you frankly as woman to woman."

"Yes." Christina managed to smile back. "I'm grateful. But . . . it is awkward, is it not?"

"Men!" Her mother said succinctly. "Well, to be fair—and it must be your greatest comfort, Christina—they are both perfectly convinced—your grandfather and that great stupid Ross—that you agreed to the engagement only from your strong sense of duty." She laughed. "At least I know you better than that. Sense of duty indeed! *Mon Dieu,* how hard I tried to persuade you that it was your duty to come home to France with me." And then, quick to recognize Christina's reaction. "But we'll not talk of that. Not yet, not now. We've more urgent matters to consider. Your poor Ross is head over ears. Well"—fair-mindedly—"my little Sophie's a charming child. Something, I imagine, quite outside his experience."

"Yes." Christina was amazed, and grateful, to find herself discussing it so calmly. "Ross thinks he can persuade Grandfather to consent to an engagement between them."

"He's told you so?"

"Not in so many words."

"Quite so. He's wrong of course. Besides, it's absurd. A folly. Sophie wouldn't have him. And quite right too. It wouldn't last three months. Oh—she's enjoying it, of course —who wouldn't? *Eh bien,* I was afraid I would find myself deadly bored here, but I can see I was quite mistaken. You are to put yourself in my hands, *chérie*—no, wait a moment, there's something that needs saying. You were angry with me, were you not, when I left? You thought I'd betrayed you both, Christopher and you?"

"Yes." At least there would be no pretenses between them.

"Do you understand it better now? I had a life too, do you

see? And a duty, I felt, to you and Sophie. Poor Christopher
—he was always trying to prove something to himself. And
yet he sent you back here in the end?"

"Yes." Christina had thought of this too.

"Well, there you are." For her, this settled it. "Tell me
about Lieutenant Trevis."

"Trevis? There's nothing to tell."

"No? Your Grandfather seemed to think he showed devotion—well, over and above the line of duty."

"My aunt's a terrible gossip.".

"But I notice you don't deny it. Well, let's hope——"

Christina laughed. "That he proves more faithful than
Ross? Mother——"

"No, don't say it." Her mother raised a plump, gracefully
protesting hand. "Don't say any of it. You'll only be sorry,
later. Discussing things hardens them, makes them more real
than they need to be. We're not going to talk about any of
this again. Besides, we've got a great deal else to think of.
Money, to begin with. You've not even asked whether I succeeded in what I went to France for."

"I thought it none of my business."

"Oh dear." An expressive, Gallic shrug. "Do you find
money a dirty subject, too, like my poor Christopher? Well,
I'm sorry, *chérie*, but we've got to discuss it just the same. I
will say for your grandfather, he doesn't suffer in that way. It
was the first thing he wanted to know. We got on famously
once he knew I did not mean to be a charge on him."

"You mean, you did . . . ?"

"Of course. Oh, I see. Ross told you otherwise. Well"—she
laughed—"I thought he had enough on his mind without
knowing what I was smuggling. Yes—I got most of it out of
France with me. It's nothing tremendous, mind you, but
enough to keep me in reasonable comfort—and provide a *dot*
for Sophie. I hope your father's done the same for you. That
was our understanding, you know, when I left. His to you,
mine to Sophie. But by the looks of you I'm afraid his can't
have been much. Is that miserable gown the best you have?"

"I'm afraid so—but you mustn't blame Father. You see, he
made me promise—oh dear, how difficult it is—"

"One more of his crackbrained notions? That poor Christopher. I loved him dearly, you know." And, oddly, Christina
realized it was true.

"So did I," she said.

"And you stayed with him. I know. And made him some absurd quixotic promise, on his deathbed, that is not to be revealed to a soul? Right?"

"Yes, that's about it. But only for six months." Pleading now, for her father rather than herself, "Six months here, as a trial, he said, in my old clothes, dependent . . ." Her voice dwindled away. It had seemed reasonable enough, in the snowbound cabin, with his lifeblood staining the sheets. Now, under her mother's sparkling intelligent eye, it was another matter.

"A trial of you—or of your grandfather? No, no . . . no need to answer that one. He intended it, of course, as a test of your grandfather, and equally, of course, you're the one it's hard on. He left the money—there's a little, I know, your grandfather told me—tied up, I suppose, so you'd be dependent on the family. Lunatic, my poor Christopher, but like him." She said it with such obvious affection that Christina's protest was mild.

"Not tied up," she said. "He just made me promise."

"Precisely. And being the girl you are, you'd keep it, even though it means being as good as invisible in those drab alpacas of yours. And all the time earning double money, as even your grandfather has the grace to admit, as housekeeper and bailiff. Do you ride as well as ever?"

"I suppose so." Surprised. "But there's no sidesaddle. And no horse, for the matter of that."

"No, but there's going to be. I've settled it with the old man. I'm to outfit you. And we'll have no argument about it either. And he's to provide horses for you and Sophie."

"Sophie? But she hates riding."

"Quite so. And does it very badly. It's time she improved, if she's to set up as an English young lady."

"But, Mother—"

"No. I said we'd have no argument. I am your mother after all, and I think, in effect, we understand each other. Now, tell me, is there anything to stop us going to Hastings tomorrow?"

"Hastings? Not if Grandfather lets us use the carriage— and if you don't mind a rough journey. Ross says the roads are terrible. But why?"

"Christina, don't pretend to be more stupid than you are.

Because it's the nearest place where we can buy suitable
materials, of course. I do not propose to have one plain and
one fancy daughter for a moment longer than I can help. Just
think what a monster I must seem to the world at large."

"But there is no world here, Mother. We see no one."

"That's another thing I'm going to change. And, *pour com-
mencer*, we are going to make a party of dinner tonight. That
red velvet in your closet looks as if it came from quite a different stable from the rest of your clothes. You'll wear that,
and I shall do your hair."

Christina had never known the Dark House to seem so
gay. After considering the possibilities of dining in the Great
Hall, her mother had vetoed it, as being Gothic beyond be-
lief. "We'd freeze to death, and your grandfather would probably catch pneumonia." Instead, they had the last leaf put
into the family dining table, a huge fire built up in the hearth
and a screen placed around the head of the table, where old
Mr. Tretteign would sit, to shield him from draughts. Candlesticks from all over the house held a supply of wax candles that made even Christina raise her eyebrows. "I'll pay
for them," said Mrs. Tretton, "if necessary." She was busy
contriving a centerpiece for the table out of shells Christina
had collected on her walks along the beach. "Now—a touch
of color." She stood back to survey her handiwork. "I know.
I saw some colored glass balls somewhere, goodness knows
what they are."

"Net floats," said Christina. "I'll get them."

Satisfied at last with what her neat fingers had made,
Mrs. Tretton turned to Christina. "And now for you."

Christina smiled. "You'll find me less easy material."

"Nonsense. Your bones are admirable—and your figure,
too, if you would only do it justice. But that alpaca . . ."
She shooed Betty and her curling tongs away and arranged
Christina's hair in a series of loose waves. "Mme. Récamier
had her hair so, the last time I saw her." She paused to note
the effect in the glass. "Yes, leave ringlets for the pretty little
girls. This is your style."

Christina managed a grateful smile. "Thank you, Mamma.
You're right, of course." But what's the use, said her voice.

Her mother gave her a little shake. "Courage, *chérie*, it's
never so bad as you think."

"No?" But the gong was ringing. They hurried downstairs

in time to greet old Mr. Tretteign as he came down, very shakily, on Ross's arm. Christina, seeing him for the first time away from the warm chrysalis of his rooms, was shocked at the change his illness had made in him, and doubly grateful for the precautions she and her mother had taken.

Safely settled in the big-armed chair at the head of the table, he looked about him. "Well," with surprised approval, "the old place looks almost civilized." Christina, who knew him well by this time, thought she saw a comment on the extravagant number of candles trembling on his lips, but, if so, he suppressed it. "So you're Sophie." The rest of them had not yet taken their places, and Sophie was standing, somewhat shyly, for once, between Richard and Ross. "Come here, child, and let's have a look at you." And then, as she came forward and dropped him a graceful curtsy. "Well, we've got one beauty in the family at least. I didn't know Christopher had it in him. You are to be congratulated, ma'am."

"Thank you," said Mrs. Tretton. "But I consider that I have two beautiful daughters. Even if Christina does take after my husband's side of the family."

He laughed, the harsh, grating laugh they heard so rarely. "*Touché!* And, tonight, I'll concede your point. You look actually handsome, Christina. I wonder why." A sharp glance from under the shaggy brows told her he wanted to think it was because she was happy at Ross's return. How could he be so blind, with Ross still just a pace behind Sophie, his eyes for her alone? Still—merciful if he continued so.

"My mother has taken me in hand, sir." And much good it would do her, Christina thought bitterly, as they took their places around the table. Since the party consisted of seven people, she and her mother had decided to seat them three a side, with old Mr. Tretteign at the head of the table. Inevitably, since Mrs. Tretton and Sophie, as newcomers, sat on his right and left, Christina and her Aunt Tretteign were at the bottom of the table, with an empty place below them. True, Christina had Ross on her other side, but, after carefully holding her chair for her to sit down, he had leaned instantly across the table to hear what Richard was saying to Sophie. He was questioning her about life in Paris under the new empire and of course the whole table listened to what she had to say. She had actually seen Napoleon on several occasions, but, disappointingly, seemed to remember little about him except the ornate uniforms he liked to wear when holding court. His wife, Josephine, was another matter. "She's beautiful"—Sophie gave her highest praise—"in a lazy sort of way. And dresses superbly. Last time I saw her, she had on a gown of silver tissue, embroidered all over with tiny eagles . . . you never saw anything like it."

"But her character?" asked Ross. "What is she like? Has she any influence over her husband?"

"Character?" Sophie sounded as if the word was too hard for her. "Ask Mamma about that. She certainly helped us, didn't she Mamma?"

"Yes." Mrs. Tretton took over smoothly, as if from long practice. "She can influence her husband, I think, on points he thinks not of the first importance. Otherwise—no. No one can. That's his strength."

"It might be his weakness, too," said Ross.

"You're right of course. But he's an extraordinary man. He really believes, I think, in his destiny—and more important still, can convince other people of it."

"Not everyone, it seems."

"No. That poor Moreau . . ." And then, as if she felt she had neglected him too long, she turned to old Mr. Tretteign. "You must remember some of the great British figures, sir. Christopher used to say what a good friend you were of the first Pitt, the Earl of Chatham. Do tell me what he was like."

"Ah—he was a man. Young Billy's only a shadow of him, whatever you may say, Ross."

"I have said nothing, sir."

"No need to, with that villainous disapproving face. But never mind, I'll take wine with you, boy, and tell you I'm glad to see you home, whatever mischief you may have been up to."

"Thank you, sir." Ross smiled as he lifted his glass.

Inevitably, the talk turned to the chances of invasion, and even Sophie stopped cross-examining Richard about women's fashions in London to let out a little squeak of dismay when Ross explained that it all depended on Napoleon's getting control of the Channel—"Even for so much as a day."

"But he won't, will he?"

"Not if Nelson has any say in the matter."

Listening, Christina remembered the news he had brought

—that Villeneuve was out of Toulon. Suppose he should elude Nelson—or even, by some terrible chance, defeat him?

But Sophie was speaking again. "We must get those horses, Mamma, quickly. Suppose they landed right here, in the bay, there wouldn't be room for us all in the carriage."

"We wouldn't all be going." Did Ross's voice hold less than its usual adoration? "Richard and I would stay to fight."

"But where? Everyone says there's no defending the marsh."

"Everyone may, but we marshmen know better. Oh, it would be guerrilla fighting, I know, but that's what the French soldier is least able to counter. They've found that already over and over again."

"Well," she pouted. "I think it a very depressing subject for our welcome home party, Cousin Ross. Richard, tell me all about the London theater. Is the boy they call the Young Roscius the prodigy they say? Just think, he is younger than I am!"

The conversation became general, to pause for a moment when old Mr. Tretteign cleared his throat and drank Christina's health. "A delicious dinner, my dear."

"Thank you, Grandfather." She sat a little straighter in her chair, squaring her shoulders, almost as if to meet an attack. Sophie was flirting alternately with Ross and Richard. Flirting? The word was unfair. She was trying her strength on them, as a kitten might its claws. And they—don't think about that. Think instead that Aunt Tretteign was looking increasingly put out. Sorry for her, Christina exerted herself to draw her into the conversation and was rewarded, as they rose to leave the room, by an approving look from her mother. "Character tells in the end, *chérie*," she said, as they moved together to the drawing room.

"Do you think so?" Almost the worst of it, in a way, was to find herself, after all this time, so extraordinarily fond of Sophie. She could still remember the bitter, silent tears she had shed after she and her father were left alone. Many of them had been for the little sister she had loved and cared for. She still felt the same—how could she help it? How, even, blame Ross for his devotion? But hating her would have been easier.

Luckily, there was little time for this kind of thinking. It was like having a friendly whirlwind come into the house, Christina thought, dutifully submitting to fittings for the morning dresses, the riding habit and all the other things her mother had insisted on buying her. They were being made up at home, since Mrs. Tretton had no confidence in the Hastings mantua makers, and a great deal in herself. "I'm sorry to say it, *chérie*." She was superintending the second fitting of a dark blue walking dress of *gros de naples*. "But you might as well face it—manners may make the man, but clothes make the woman."

"Oh dear." Christina wriggled among the pins. "I wish I had been a man."

"So you always used to say. But I tell you, love, you will find being a woman pleasant enough if you will only come to terms with it. It's Christopher's fault, of course. He wanted a son so badly—called you Chris, treated you as a boy. Ross does just the same."

"I know. It's my fault, I suppose."

"Of course it's your fault. Your grandfather's getting impatient by the way. Silly old man." She spoke in the same tones of affectionate impatience she used of her dead husband. "He's talking of sending for Foxton again."

"Oh, Mother!"

"Don't worry, I talked him out of it before. I will again. What a fool your Aunt Tretteign is. She could have had such a pleasant life here, with just a bit of management."

Christina laughed as she wriggled into her new riding habit. "Mother, you're a wonder!"

"No—just French, and a little practical. Hurry now, love, or you'll be late for your ride, and you know how men hate that."

"Not when it's Sophie." She was ashamed as she said it, but her mother only laughed.

"Think a little, *chérie*. Would you really like to be Sophie?"

"Of course not."

"Well then—"

"You're right, and I'm a fool." What an immense amount they managed to say to each other without in fact saying anything. "Bless you." She bent to drop an unwonted kiss on her mother's enamelled cheek, then picked up the train of her crimson habit and ran lightly downstairs to find Ross and Richard waiting in the hall.

"There you are at last." Ross was comparing his watch with the grandfather clock.

"Five minutes late. How shocking!"

Richard had been admiring her through his glass. "May I congratulate you on your habit, Cousin Christina? Bond Street surely?"

She could not help laughing. "Hastings' best and my own industrious hands! Your eye must be out, Cousin."

"But where is Sophie? It's past the quarter." Ross closed his watch with a snap.

Hearteningly, Christina found herself irritated with him. "You sound as if you were planning a military operation, not a party of pleasure, Cousin Ross."

"Am I such a martinet?" He rather liked the idea.

"You're a terrible bully, Ross, and you know it." This was Sophie, leaning over the banisters, a vision in blue velvet and swansdown. "Well, was I worth waiting for?" She ran down to join them.

"Forever," said Richard.

"Well, let's lose no more time," said Ross.

Since Richard and Sophie were both cautious riders, Christina soon found herself in the lead with Ross, jumping ditches where the other two took time to go around by the gate. It gave her a chance to ask if there was any news of M. Tissot. "You'll think me a fool, but somehow I don't feel quite safe so long as he is at large."

"Nonsense. A mere man of straw—and why they are making such a dust about him at Whitehall is more than I can understand."

"Whitehall? What do you mean?"

"Merely that they've told me to end the smuggling contact while he is at large. They think it too dangerous. Danger!" Scornfully.

"Oh, poor Ross. And the smugglers?"

"That's just it. I can't stop them. Parkes tells me the gang have elected a new leader and propose to resume operations. It's lucky for me M. Tissot did not choose to betray my identity while he was at it."

"You're sure he did not?"

"Reasonably so. And those three unfortunates in Dover

Castle have been pressed into the navy and shipped out to the West India Station."

"Oh, the poor things. Do their families know?"

"They should by now. I fear it will not make the Captain —as they called me—any more popular on the marsh. It's all blamed on him—on me. Just as well my secret has been so well kept."

"But you warned them."

"I did the best I could." He shrugged. "Well, so long as it's an unknown they're blaming, it provides a harmless enough scapegoat, I suppose. One thing I know will please you. Villeneuve is back in Toulon."

"What! After getting clean away."

"Yes. Napoleon's forgotten that lurking in harbor hardly makes seamen. They met a storm, came to grief and limped back to port to refit. So the news I brought was not so earthshaking after all."

"But it might have been."

"Oh yes. And Pitt's grateful enough. It's just—there's nothing, now, for me to do here. If it were not for . . . tell me, Chris, as my friend, do you think—"

He was interrupted by a shout from Richard. "Ross! Christina! Here, quick."

They exchanged startled glances, wheeled their horses and set them to gallop back across two long fields. "Dear God!" Ross turned back to Christina, as he entered the third field and saw Richard, dismounted, bending over Sophie, who lay half in, half out of a drainage ditch, while their horses grazed peacefully close by.

"Hold my horse." Christina pulled level with him and jumped down as she spoke. Hurrying forward, she was relieved to hear a passion of sobs and furious, incoherent speech from Sophie. "It's all your fault, Richard. You should have told me . . . and my habit, my lovely habit, it's ruined."

"But are you hurt, love?" As Christina bent over her, Richard withdrew, she thought with a touch of relief, to explain the circumstances of the accident to Ross.

"Hurt?" Sophie let Christina put a supporting arm around her. "I'm furious! He should have told me. How could anyone jump a great river like that?" She picked up her plumed riding hat, which lay in the mud beside her. "And look at my hat—my best hat!"

"But you're all right? You don't hurt anywhere? Try and stand up, pet, do."

Ross and Richard moved at once to help, and Sophie was set on her feet, only to exclaim again at the state of her habit. "All over mud—and look at my poor feathers. I'll never ride on the marsh again. I hate it! And it's raining too! It always rains here. I hate it, I tell you. I hate it, I hate it!"

"Quietly, love." Christina had almost forgotten Sophie's tendency to hysterical outbursts, but now flashed a warning glance to Ross and Richard. "It's only a little velvet, after all. I'm sure we can get you another habit just as good."

"Just as good! Don't make me laugh." A shrewish note marred the pretty voice. "This habit was made by Leroy himself. I expect it cost more than your whole wardrobe put together. And you talk of getting me another one here! Oh, I wish I had never left France. I'm sick of mud, and rain, and horses." The tears were coming freely now.

"There, love, there." She pulled a handkerchief out of her pocket. "You'll feel better directly. It's the shock of the fall," she explained for the benefit of Ross and Richard, who had withdrawn to a slight distance and were being very busy with the horses. "We must get her home."

"Of course. The shock." Ross sounded relieved. "Never mind, infant, we'll have you home in no time." He brought her horse forward.

"You don't expect me to get back on that brute?"

"Well," he said reasonably, "how else can we get you home?"

"Home!" The tantrum broke. "Home, you call it! I wish I'd never seen your dark old house, with its draughts and its damp and its dreariness!" She was sobbing harder than ever.

"I'm sorry you find it so." Something in his tone startled her. She stopped crying and put out a shaking hand for Christina's handkerchief.

"I'm s . . . s . . . sorry." She raised big eyes, still all afloat with tears, to his. "I'm being very naughty, aren't I? If *you* will help me, Ross, I'm sure I can manage to ride home."

"We'll all help you," said Ross.

Chapter Fourteen

JUST THE SAME, it was quite a little business to get Sophie back onto her quiet horse, and Christina watched with wry amusement as she shook her disheveled curls at the two men and thanked them prettily for their help. As a child, she had always been extra good after one of her tantrums, and now, laughing and cajoling, she soon had them apparently her slaves again. Christina, meanwhile, had quietly led her own horse over to the field gate and remounted.

"Chris—I'm so sorry." Ross had remembered her at last.

"No need. Father made me learn to mount unaided. He said anyone as large as I was must learn to be self-sufficient."

"You're splendid." But already he was pushing his horse forward to ride close beside Sophie.

It was the same when they reached home. Sophie was soon lying on the morning-room sofa, with Ross on one side and Richard on the other. Christina looked in at the door, then turned away, fighting a pang of bad temper that made her ashamed. Busy with Sophie, no one had seen her. Suddenly, intolerably, she was tired of it all, tired, more than anything, of herself. On an impulse, she crossed the hall to the cloakroom, wrapped a shabby old waterproof cloak around her, pulled its hood up over her head and let herself quietly out the side door on to the terrace. It was raining harder than ever and the wind worried at the skirts of her cloak, pushed the hood back from her face, teased out tendrils of damp hair. This was a kind of attack she could bear, even enjoy. She leaned forward against the power of the wind and took the path to the beach. Today, surely, it would be deserted.

Trevis was a man of sense. He did not force his men to unnecessary duties. With this wind blowing, and from this direction, nothing could cross the Channel. The coastal guards would be snug by fires at headquarters.

Yes, the curve of the beach stretched gray and empty at her feet as if not a soul was stirring between Fairlight and Dungeness. She loved it like this. Salt spray mixed with rain on her face. For miles around, people huddled over fires; only, here, among the lashing elements, she was free for a while from the burden of the Dark House.

All alone. She lifted damp skirts and ran, scudding sideways against the wind, to where a long groin reached out to sea. A quick, high step and she was on it and walking down to where she could watch the green waves growling below her, feel the wind in her hair, listen to the mixed voices of sea and storm.

A light, suddenly lurid, behind a cloud far out to sea warned her that somewhere, in majesty, the sun was setting. Soon it would be night. Time to go back to the Dark House, and all the misery it held for her.

She turned to edge her way back along the narrow groin, the wind behind her now, trying to push her off. Suddenly, she paused. A man was coming down the beach toward her, carefully close in to the groin so as to be as little visible as possible. Lurking? Skulking? The unpleasant words fretted at the edge of her mind as she made herself go calmly forward as if nothing was the matter. A smuggler perhaps on his way to pick up some sunken cargo when the tide was low enough? If so, he would be more afraid of her than she need be of him. But then, why was he coming so definitely toward her?

Now, at last, the shingle was nearly level with the groin on the side away from him. She jumped down and made herself start steadily up the slope, but his voice halted her. "Mademoiselle, a moment, please."

French. And, on the moment, recognition. M. Tissot! No need—or was there?—to be afraid of him. She turned and waited for him to come up with her. But once again his voice came, anxiously, from the far side of the groin. "Mademoiselle—if you would come here to me? It's as much as my life's worth to be seen talking to you. It's urgent—a matter of life and death."

It sounded even more melodramatic in French. She did not

much want to go back and join him on the sheltered side of the groin. But yet—a matter of life and death, he had said. Whose? She climbed back onto the groin and stood there above him, looking down. "This is near enough," she said. "Speak from there."

He shrugged. "I don't blame you, mamselle, I'm afraid I played you a low enough trick before, but, believe me, it was necessary—"

"For you, perhaps. But, come, I should be home. What is it that it is so urgent?"

"You must believe me, mamselle." He had recognized skepticism in her tone. "It's life and death, as I said, for all of you. Word's got out that it is monsieur up there at the house who led the smugglers. Among the smugglers themselves, you understand? They blame him for everything, for the *débacle* here on the beach, the death of their friends. They know, too, that the survivors—the prisoners—have been pressed into the navy. Worse than death, mamselle, or so they feel it."

"How do they know all this?" She looked down at him, clear-eyed in the twilight.

"It's not my fault." Defensively. "I had my orders. To break up this channel of communication. I'm a Frenchman, mamselle. I do my duty as it comes. Only when I told them —I had not intended murder."

"Murder?"

"They mean to attack the Grange tonight. They're—very angry. They'll burn it down. You'll all be killed. Worse. I couldn't let it happen to you, mamselle, who nursed me. Besides"—he seemed to be talking as much to himself as to her —"it's not necessary. The gang's broken up. M. Tretteign will never be able to use them again for his own purposes."

She was not interested in his self-justification. "When will they come?"

"As soon as it's full dark, I think. There's not much time, mamselle."

"No." She was thinking at frantic speed. Ross would want M. Tissot caught and held. But she had no possible chance of doing so. Forget about that. Think only of the Grange, her mother, Sophie, the old man. . . . Go straight along the beach to Trevis for help? No—first she must consult with Ross. Besides, it would be quicker to ride—quicker for Richard to ride than for her, granted that Ross must stay and organize the defense of the Grange in case help should be slow in coming. She looked up and down the beach. Lights showed now at Rye Harbor, and, the other way, at the gun emplacements on Dungeness. "Could you not go for help?"

"No." It was final. "I have risked more than I should already for your sake. Now, I must go." He turned and ran, slipping and stumbling on the loose shingle, and still keeping as much as possible under the shelter of the groin. Where could he be hiding? No time to think about that now. Nor to wonder what purpose of his own he meant to serve by this warning. It was nearly dark. And at first full dark, according to him, the attackers would come. Fantastic—the marshmen, attacking Tretteign Grange. But—in these circumstances— possible.

She lifted her skirts and ran up the shingle slope and along the path to the Grange. In at the side door; it was quickest. Where would she find Ross? She looked into her study, where he often sat, partly to catch up on the work she had done while he was away, partly, she suspected, to be away from the clatter of female tongues in the rest of the house. But today, the room was empty.

In the saloon, her Aunt Tretteign was talking about her migraines. From the look of her mother and Sophie, she had been doing it for some time. "Always come on when something unexpected happens," she said. "So inconsiderate of Richard."

"Richard?" Christina interrupted unceremoniously. "What's he done?"

"Gone back to London." Aunt Tretteign took it as a personal grievance. "Tomorrow would have been quite soon enough. And as for riding all night—I never heard such a lunatic notion. It will bring on one of his bilious attacks, and so I told him." And then, really looking at Christina for the first time, "My dear child, that is hardly the costume, surely, for the drawing room."

In her haste, Christina had not even paused to throw off her wet cloak. "No," she said. "I must find Ross, at once."

"He could have stopped him." Mrs. Tretteign was still concerned with her own grievance. "Richard always minds Ross —I can't think why. But all he said was something about an urgent summons being an urgent summons. Not even sense."

"I think Ross went out to see Richard on his way." Mrs. Tretton had been studying Christina closely. "I don't think he intended to go far. You would probably meet him."

"Thank you, Mamma." What else should she say? She looked at Sophie, bent gracefully over her work, her accident apparently quite forgotten. No need to frighten them yet. But —a long, speaking look from her mother. "I'll go to meet him. You'll be here?"

"Of course." Her mother's voice was calm, as always, but told her she knew something was afoot.

"Good." She hurried out into the hall, threw open the front door and peered anxiously out into the gathering darkness. Suppose Ross should meet the advancing smugglers, all by himself? It did not bear thinking of. At all costs, he must be warned. She listened, desperately, for the sound of horses' hoofs, returning. Nothing but the wind wailing over the marsh and the steady growl of the sea. Ross must have gone farther than he meant with Richard. What would they be talking of? Sophie?

No time for thoughts like these. She turned and ran through the side way to the stables. "How long have the gentlemen been gone?" Jem was whistling as he groomed her mare.

Absurd question. Time meant nothing to him. But he came up, just the same, with a helpful answer. "Time enough for me to sweep out the stable where Mr. Richard kept his horse. If you can call it a horse." With fine scorn. "I don't wonder Mr. Ross said he'd be right back. No pleasure in riding alongside of a slug like that one."

Christina's heart leapt with relief. "He said that, did he?"

"Yes, miss. Told me to wait on and stable Arab for him when he gets back. All the others is gone, see." The yard was indeed unusually quiet. "He won't be long, not Mr. Ross."

Christina knew Ross's consideration for the servants well enough to be sure of this herself. Fantastic that his enemies might even now be closing in on the Grange, perhaps finding him on the marsh, all unawares. She had made up her mind. "Saddle Honey for me—quick. I'll ride out to meet him."

"Yes, miss."

Take no notice of his knowing look. Just hurry .... hurry. "Hurry." She put it into words.

"Yes, miss, but you ain't dressed . . ."

Nor was she; not for riding. No matter; seconds might be precious. But suppose Ross had ridden farther than he meant. She must warn someone before she left. Who? With the question, came its answer. A back door opened and her mother looked out. "There you are, Christina. Can I help?"

"Thank God. Yes." She joined her mother and explained in quick, disjointed sentences about M. Tissot's warning. "They may come any time. I can't leave Ross out there, unsuspecting. Besides, when I've warned him, I'll ride on along the beach for help."

"Yes. Should I prepare the others for flight, do you think?"

"No." Christina had been thinking hard. "For one thing, neither Ross nor Grandfather would consent to leave the Grange to its fate. Besides—imagine an encounter out on the marsh. It would be worse than anything. . . . No, we must just pray God and hold out here till help comes."

"You're right, of course. Go carefully, love."

"Be sure I will."

Chapter Fifteen

DUSK WAS thickening over the marsh, and Christina, taking Honey down the rough drive at as fast a pace as she dared, congratulated herself that there could be not the slightest doubt on the way Ross would come. He would have set Richard on the road to Rye and would come back the shortest way. No anxiety there; and no use worrying about anything else. She had done, was doing, what she could. Nothing else for it but to ride steadily on, while raindrops seeped through her drenched cloak. But surely the weather was on their side. Might not such a night discourage the less bellicose of the smugglers? She should have asked M. Tissot how many the gang numbered. No use fretting about that now. Ride on . . . ride hard. If possible, she wanted to meet Ross close to where a side track ran down to the beach—that would be her quickest way to Trevis's headquarters.

How quickly it was getting dark. Surely she must meet Ross soon. If not, it would mean he had decided to ride on to Rye with Richard. What then? Cross that bridge when you come to it. She needed all her concentration to keep Honey going steadily along the rough, half-visible road.

Ah—she lifted her head. Yes—at last, the sound of a horse coming rapidly toward her. A single horse—anyway, the smugglers would hardly be riding. They would come secretly, quietly, by ones and twos across the marsh. Thank God this was Ross, reining in Arab at sight of her.

"Chris! What in the world?"

"The smugglers! They're going to attack the Grange." She

183

told her story as concisely as possible, helped along by his quick, pertinent questions.

"I've seen nothing," he answered her final question. "But then, I wouldn't have. They won't come this way. You should be safe enough, riding along the beach." He sounded as if trying to convince himself. "But I'd best see you down there."

"Nonsense. There's no time. And, besides, it's you they're after. They might well let me by."

"That's true. They love you, don't they?"

"Well—the women, some of them, I think, are grateful to me. Ross! We've no time to be talking here."

"You're right. Good luck, Chris."

"And to you." She had already turned Honey away from him and threw the words back over her shoulder. Don't think that they might never meet again. Very likely it would all prove a false alarm. But—here was the turnoff for the beach —Ross had never even suggested such a possibility, and he, surely, should know to what lengths the smugglers were capable of going. Stories she herself had heard of the famous—or infamous—Hawkhurst gang would keep coming into her head. There had been cases enough of horrible vengeance exacted for betrayal—or simply of the murder of riding officers who had been too hot on their trail.

Maddening to have to go so slowly, but this was a mere track, and, worse still, one she had hardly ever used. She dared not risk a fall, the chance of laming Honey. Slow and steady, she told herself, steady does it. It had stopped raining. Good? More likely bad, though undoubtedly a relief to have only wind in her face. Where would M. Tissot be by now? Doubtless snug by the fire in some hiding place or other. She should be grateful to him, but felt only anger, a cold determination that sometime, somehow, he must be caught and made to pay for his treachery.

Thank God, here was the steep slope of the sea wall. She dismounted, to lead Honey carefully up it, and then slowly, step by careful step, down the sliding shingle. And here, by mere good luck, was a groin from which to remount. She was up in a bound and guiding Honey down to the waterline. The tide had fallen fast since she had met M. Tissot; now it was well below the bottom of the breakwaters. Safe enough to let Honey out at last, and exhilarating to feel the wind of her own movement. Ahead—a long way ahead—she could see the lights of the little camp by the first gun emplacement—her destination. Suppose Trevis was not there. Well, there would be someone in authority.

How long had it been since she had left the house? And how successful would her mother have been in organizing its defense? But at least, Ross should be there by now. Aunt Tretteign, of course, would be in hysterics—and Sophie? An odd flash of memory took her back to a day long ago in America when there had been rumors of an Indian attack. Sophie had been little more than a baby then—a terrified baby who did not understand—and it had been Christina's task to look after her and, at all costs, to keep her quiet. She should be at the Grange now, doing the same thing. Would it always be her task to look after Sophie, at whatever cost to herself?

The lights were very near now. She turned Honey's head inland and, once more, was forced to dismount and lead her carefully over the treacherous shingle.

"Who goes there?" Although she had expected it, the welcome challenge made her jump.

"Friend." She found Trevis himself in the disused farmhouse that served as headquarters for the gun crews. He would have liked to waste time exclaiming over her drenched condition, but she would not let him. "No time for that." She held on to her drenched cloak. "Besides, I mean to go back with you."

"Back?"

Telling her story yet again, she began to feel herself in some recurring nightmare, the kind where movement becomes impossible, and feet cannot touch the ground. And yet, he, too, was quick to grasp the situation, and equally quick to act on it. As he listened, he was scribbling orders, sending out messengers for reinforcements, throwing questions at her as he did so. Of course, it had not occurred to her before, in her private anxiety, but for him this was a golden opportunity to make an end, once and for all, of the smugglers. Preoccupied with this chance, he did not, to her relief, think to ask why they should attack the Grange.

Suddenly, absurdly, deplorably, she felt sorry for them, moving as they were, all unawares, into a trap. She tried to shake off the feeling, but could not. After all, they were not just smugglers, they were Jem's uncle, Betty's cousin, lord knew who else. If only it would all prove a nightmare.

Trevis had finished his arrangements and was putting on his heavy military greatcoat. "You'll wait here, of course."

"No." She had been ready for this. "They may need me. Please let me come too. I'll be no trouble, I promise you." And then, when he still looked doubtful, "Besides, if I understand your plan aright, you intend to catch the smugglers unawares. What more natural than that you should escort me back and stay for dinner? With your men posted outside—it can't fail."

"I suppose it should be safe enough." Doubtfully.

"Of course it will. I can't believe they'll attack so early—well, it stands to reason they'll wait till the house is quiet. And, besides, what would I do here?"

"It's true." This argument struck home. "It's very far from being a fit place for a young lady."

She took this, with a sigh of relief, as capitulation, and followed him outside to where a little party of soldiers was drawn up, mounted and ready. The smallest possible delay while Honey was fetched for her, and they were riding back the way she had come, along the beach. "Much less chance of encountering the gang this way," said Trevis.

"Yes." Once again, the cold question nibbled in her mind: how many of her friends—or her friends' friends—would be found among the smugglers?

It was just perceptibly lighter now than it had been when she came. From time to time a rag of moon showed among hurrying clouds. "There'll be light enough to recognize them," said Trevis, with a cheerful ferocity that chilled her blood. And then, "Best ride in silence now."

They stopped, at last, down on the beach, where the path turned off for the Grange. Trevis made his final plans with a quick certainty that Christina found formidable. The rest of the troop were to dismount here, leaving their horses in charge of one of their number, and spread out to surround the house. Another contingent should arrive, soon, from the far side. "Don't worry, we'll be ready for them when they come," said Trevis, as he and Christina started on the short ride up to the house.

No noise but the wind and the sea. Christina breathed a

sigh of relief as they came up over the sea wall; there lay the house, quiet as usual, lights showing in a few windows.

"Good," said Trevis.

"Yes." She had been too fully occupied to realize just how anxious she was. Had she really expected to find the house a smouldering ruin?

Just the same, it was an eerie feeling to come in among the outbuildings, as she led the way around to the front of the house, and wonder whether dark figures were crouching there, watching her every move. Be natural—at all costs be natural. "I'm grateful to you for escorting me home." She made her voice loud on purpose. "I rode farther than I meant."

"You certainly must have." Trevis had jumped down and held her horse for her to dismount.

"If you'll hold them a moment"—she moved up the front steps—"I'll send the boy." The door would be locked, of course, an elementary precaution. She beat a resounding tattoo on the knocker.

"Who's there?" Ross's voice. Doubtless he had been following their approach through the darkness.

"It's I, Chris. And Lieutenant Trevis. Could you send Jem to stable the horses?"

The door swung open. "I'm glad to see you." Ross raised his voice, to shout the order back to the servants' quarters.

"All's well?"

"Quiet as the grave." And then, on a more prosaic note, "We've been waiting dinner for you."

"Good. I'm famished."

It was not Jem, she noticed, who came running to take the horses, but a new boy they had recently taken on. Now Trevis came up the steps to join them, and to ask, "No trouble yet?"

"Nothing."

"Good. The house should be surrounded by now. There'll be a hot welcome for them when they get here. This should be the end of the whole rascally pack of them."

"Yes." An odd note in Ross's voice. Well—no wonder. If she had qualms about the smugglers' fate, how much more must he? "You're drenched, Chris." He turned to her. "Hurry and change. Dinner can wait."

She smiled at him. "It must be spoiled already. Very well, then, if you'll excuse me."

When she entered the drawing room ten minutes later, she was at once aware of tension crackling in the air. Her mother, of course, greeted her imperturbably as always. "There you are, *chérie*. We were getting almost anxious about you. Lieutenant Trevis tells me you rode farther than you meant."

"Yes. I must apologize for delaying dinner." How right her mother was to behave as if nothing was amiss.

But Mrs. Tretteign's hands were working in her lap, and there were spots of disastrous red high up on her cheekbones. "Food!" Petulantly. "I couldn't eat a thing. Not now . . ."

"You must," said her sister-in-law. "Lieutenant Trevis, if you will come with me?" She led the way across the big hall to the dining room, and Christina, watching her Aunt Tretteign flutter anxiously after her, took time to breathe a question to Ross. "Grandfather?"

"Knows nothing."

"Good." But here was Sophie, deathly white, emerging from the shadowed corner by the piano, where she had been pretending to look over some music.

"Tina, you're all right?" she asked.

"Of course I am, goose. I'm sorry if I've kept you all waiting for your dinner."

"Oh . . . don't. Tina, I'm frightened . . ."

"Nonsense." This was Ross, robustly, as he took an arm of each of them. "You're hungry, that's all."

It was a strange enough travesty of a dinner party. Mrs. Tretteign was in one of her crises of the nerves, and Christina, watching her sniff into her handkerchief, sigh gustily and pick at her food, could only congratulate herself that these were enough of a commonplace to cause no comment. But Sophie was another matter. She, too, was silent. Her pale face and reddened eyes suggested a recent storm of tears; there were red spots on her cheekbones and even her dark hair seemed to have lost something of its usual luster. Drained of its animation, her face was pitiful and almost plain, and Lieutenant Trevis, who had not met her before, treated her merely with the careless courtesy due to the insignificant child she looked.

Ross, too, was withdrawn, and Christina, helping her

mother to carry on a routine conversation with Lieutenant Trevis, wondered what pangs he must be suffering on the smugglers' account. After all, he could not help but feel the whole thing his fault.

They were all strained, listening, in the many pauses in the conversation, for sounds from outside. Once, Mrs. Tretteign half rose to her feet. "Shots!" she said. "I hear firing."

Trevis and Ross both rose and moved to the window to listen. "You're imagining things, Mother," said Ross coldly. "It's only the wind on the marsh."

"The wind, indeed! As if I hadn't heard that nights enough to be able to tell it from gunfire. But I suppose I'm just an hysterical female, too." A glance for Sophie suggested the point of this remark and Christina wondered more than ever what kind of scene she had missed.

Sophie sniffed loudly into a tiny lace-trimmed handkerchief. "We can't all be heroines," she said. "And as for me, I always understood ladies were not supposed to go riding in the dark alone. I'm sure, Mamma, if you've told me once—"

"I've told you a thousand times, Sophie," interposed her mother, "not to speak about what you don't understand." And then, rising, "You will not be long over your wine, Ross?"

"Of course not. But Trevis and I intend to make a circuit of the house before we rejoin you ladies. It's getting late."

"Yes." They had, indeed, dined very late, and Christina, her ears at a stretch like the others', had been expecting the attack momentarily and wishing she had had a moment to find out what plans had been made for the defense of the house.

But now, at last, the four women were alone in the saloon. "I'll ring when we wish for tea," her mother had told Parkes. "Till then, we do not wish to be disturbed."

"Poor old thing," said Christina, when he had closed the door behind him. "I wish we could persuade him to go to bed. He looks like death."

"Oh really, Tina," burst out Sophie. "I've no patience with you. Here we are, about to be murdered in our beds—if not worse—and all you can think of is the butler's health. Have you no finer feelings?"

"Not many, I'm afraid, love," said Christina cheerfully. "And, really, it seems to me most unlikely that we are to be murdered in our beds—or worse, as you suggest. After all, there are I don't know how many troopers out there guarding the house."

"Gallantly fetched by you. Not at all the thing, I should have thought, to be riding about the marsh like that, but I seem to be in a minority."

"Yes you are, aren't you, pet." Her mother spoke with cheerful firmness. "It was foolish, you know, to break out at your Cousin Ross like that. I've yet to meet the man who can bear female tantrums. Oh well, come and sit down, and tell yourself that at least you've learned a useful lesson tonight."

"Lesson! I've learned that Ross Tretteign has the manners of a backwoods lumberman. He slapped my face." One little hand went up to the red spot on her cheek. "I'll never forgive him."

"And he'll never forget how badly you behaved," said her mother with undiminished cheerfulness. "You've lost a beau, pet, the quickest way you could do it. And as to the slap, I'd have done it myself if I'd been near enough. Two more of those hysterical screams of yours and the whole house would have been in an uproar and your grandfather would likely have had another stroke. You must learn, *chérie,* that there is a time and a place for all things. Hysterics are all very charming and ladylike over a mouse, or a dead bird, but in a real crisis a lady should behave like—"

"Like Christina, I suppose you mean to say."

"Well, since you suggest it, yes, like Christina. And, another thing, my angel, while we're on the subject, no lady ever did herself any good by criticizing another in front of the gentlemen. It won't do, you know. It won't do at all. It's lucky for you your Cousin Richard was not here. He has very high standards of courtesy."

"Mother, please." Christina was alarmed at the fixed look in Sophie's eyes. But it was too late. Sophie had jumped to her feet. "Cousin Ross! Cousin Richard!" she screamed. "A couple of country bumpkins! As if I was to care what they thought of anything. Oh, God, I wish I were dead—or in Paris." The door slammed behind her.

"Tant pis," sighed her mother, "how stupid of me. I should have waited. I suppose we're all a little on edge tonight."

"She'll have one of her crying fits," said Christina. "I'd best go after her. She might bear me more easily than you, Mamma, just now."

"Yes, I suppose so. I'm sorry, love, but she made me angry."

Christina laughed. "I can see she did. But"—before her mother could speak—"don't tell me about it. I'd much rather not know."

The old house was strangely quiet, as if suspended, waiting. . . . She moved over to the ledge in the hall where bedroom candles stood ready and was surprised to find that none of them had been taken. Oh well—Sophie had doubtless been in such a passion that she had run upstairs in the dark.

But when she reached Sophie's bedroom, she found it empty. Where could she have gone? A quick survey of the downstairs rooms showed no trace of her and she hurried back to the saloon. "Mamma, I can't find Sophie."

"Oh no!" A look of appalled comprehension crossed Mrs. Tretton's face. "She can't have—"

"I didn't like to say anything," put in Aunt Tretteign from her seat in the chimney corner, "but I thought I heard the front door slam, after the child ran out just now. But of course if I'd have mentioned it, I'd merely have been told it was my nerves, so I stayed quiet."

"How could you—" began Mrs. Tretton, but Christina stopped her. "No time for that," she said. "We must find Ross and Trevis and go after her. She's done this before, Mother?"

"Yes, when she thought she was—well—misunderstood. But never under circumstances like these. I never thought . . . if harm comes to her I'll never forgive myself."

"I don't suppose it will." Christina managed a calm she was far from feeling. "She'll probably give one of the troopers a terrible fright."

"Heartless!" sniffed Aunt Tretteign. "Quite heartless. That poor child, goaded, teased into this madness, and all you talk about is fright. But of course you two would never understand what it is to be highly strung."

"No," said Christina, ringing a loud peal on the bell, "I believe I never shall."

Ross and Trevis were still outside, none of the servants knew just where, so Christina began to organize a search party of the men, one group to go with her mother, the other with herself. "I'll take the cloisters party, Mother, do you work your way round the front." As she spoke, the front door swung open and Lieutenant Trevis ushered in Ross, who was carrying Sophie. It made a most romantic picture as she clung around his neck, her curls brushing his cheek. Then, he deposited her, unceremoniously, on a settle in the hall. "Can you walk now, do you think?" His voice was coldly furious.

"I . . . I don't know." She bent to rub a slender ankle, just apparent below the hem of her dress. But he had turned away to speak to her mother.

"Lunacy, ma'am, and I hope you'll give her the scold she deserves. A few years younger and I'd beat her myself. This is no time to be indulging in tantrums. She nearly got herself shot by the trooper on guard at the front. And can you blame him? It would have served her right if she'd been killed, instead of merely twisting her ankle."

"And the shot may well have given warning to the smugglers." Trevis, too, was furious.

"There's no sign of them?" Christina did her best to deflect the men's attention from Sophie, who sat there, a child's tears streaming down her cheeks.

"None yet," said Trevis. "But we should be getting back . . . if you really want to come?" This to Ross.

"Of course I do."

"But, Cousin Ross." Sophie put her foot to the ground and winced. "I can't walk—how shall I get upstairs to bed?"

"Frank can carry you," said Ross. "Come, Trevis."

"Well," said Mrs. Tretton, as the big door closed behind them, "I did warn you, love. How bad is it?" Christina had already bent to examine the ankle.

"It's hard to tell," said Christina fair-mindedly, seeing nothing. "I'll fetch some cold compresses."

"And *sal volatile*," suggested her mother. "The child's had a hard day. Don't take on so, pet. There's as good fish in the sea as ever came out of it."

"Will Ross ever forgive me? He was so angry!" Sophie was badly shaken—as much, Christina thought, looking back down the stairs, by Ross's anger as by her injury. Returning with cold bandages and the *sal volatile*, she found her sister cheering up under the sympathy of her mother and aunt. Mrs. Tretteign was in her element, and had fetched a salve of her own—sovereign, she maintained, against bruising. "We wouldn't want to have one ankle larger than the other."

"D'you think I might?" Now Sophie sounded really frightened.

"Of course not," Christina intervened. "I can't see much wrong with it, to tell you the truth. Don't you think, with an effort, you could walk on my arm as far as the fire in the saloon? You'd be so much more comfortable there."

"Anything rather than have Frank carry me." Sophie let Christina help her to her feet and limped, with a good many groans, to the sofa nearest the fire. Once established there, with cushions and *sal volatile*, she put an anxious hand to her tousled curls, and admitted herself to be feeling better. "But what a brute Ross is," she broke out. "Oh—excuse me, Aunt Tretteign, I quite forgot. But can you imagine anything so unkind as to give me such a scold, at such a time?"

"Quite heartless," sighed his mother. "But, I tell you, my dear, Ross never had the slightest feeling for a female's susceptibilities. Many's the time I've been prostrate with one of my migraines, or suffering with my nerves, and got no more sympathy from him than you have tonight. Now, Richard's quite another matter, he understands about these things. Why—he even suffers with the migraine himself."

"Very creditable, I'm sure," said Christina dryly.

But her aunt was not listening, she had turned toward the window. "What was that? I'm sure I heard something!"

"Nonsense." Christina was very near losing her temper. "How should we hear anything at this side of the house?" And then, with an effort at a lighter tone. "Really, Sophie, love, we should be grateful to you—since it's no worse. Do you know, worrying about you, I had quite forgotten the smugglers. If they really meant to get here at first dark, they're very late. Do you think perhaps they have changed their minds?"

"I only know I'm dying for sleep," said her mother. "Shall we leave them to the tender mercies of the military and retire to bed, do you think?"

"What?" This was practically a squawk from Mrs. Tretteign. "And be ravished in our beds!"

"You have less confidence in Lieutenant Trevis than I, Aunt," said Christina. "To tell you the truth, I merely feel sorry for those poor smugglers, walking into such a trap."

"Sorry! Christina, how can you speak so? It will serve you right if they fool the soldiers in some way—you know how stupid they are—and reach the house. How do you know there is not a secret passage leading into this very room? At any moment a whole gang of them may burst in here, and then what use will Lieutenant Trevis and his soldiers be?" She looked nervously around, having succeeded in frightening herself quite as much as she had Sophie, who burst into a fresh flood of tears.

"I told you we should have gone at once," said Sophie, through her sobs. "If you'd only listened to me, we'd have been safe in Rye by now."

"And you know what Ross said to that," said her mother.

"Ross is a brute. I really believe he values his moldy old Grange more than the lives of the lot of us."

Christina was beginning to understand what had gone on while she was away. "I hope you didn't say that, love."

"Of course I did. Why not?"

"Well, mainly because I think it's true, and you know how the truth hurts."

"Well," said Sophie unanswerably, "I wanted to hurt Ross."

"I think"—this was Mrs. Tretton, who had been sitting placidly netting all this time—"that we should have some entertainment. Christina, love, would you rather read aloud or sing for us?"

"I'll gladly sing," said Christina, "if you can bear to listen." And she moved over to the piano, ignoring a mutter of "fiddling while Rome burns" from her aunt.

When Trevis and Ross came back, around eleven o'clock, the first thing they heard was her voice, cool and deep, in "Jesu Joy of Man's Desiring."

"Admirable girl," said Ross. "I knew she'd keep the others from panicking."

"I imagine she's had her work cut out, just the same." Trevis followed him into the saloon.

"Well?" Christina swept her hands up the piano in a soft, conclusive chord. "Are we to be burned in our beds?" She spoke quietly, and, following her eyes, they saw Sophie fast asleep and Mrs. Tretton nodding in her chair. "There's nothing like music for a sedative." Still speaking softly, Christina moved forward to greet them.

"Not a sign of them." Trevis sounded simply disappointed. "It's getting very late, too. Can they have been warned?"

"Well"—Ross had hardly spared a glance for Sophie, all

flushed cheeks and tangling curls on the sofa—"it's possible, I suppose. With the best will in the world, one can't move even a small body of troops about in the dark without some noise."

"You think they heard us?"

"Most likely. After all, it's life and death to them to know every sound of the marsh." And then, to Christina, "I really think you ladies could safely call it a day now, and go to bed."

"Do you?" Her eyes met his speculatively. "I'm sure you know best." She was indeed. There had been no sign of the boy, Jem, all evening. Doubtless Ross had sent him off, as soon as he got back, to warn the gang that they had been betrayed. Well, in a way she could scarcely blame him, but it seemed hard on Lieutenant Trevis. And on the rest of them. So it had been merely a comedy they had played out all evening. Well, poor Sophie. She gave Ross a chilly look.

"A storm in a teacup, I suppose. And I thought I was being such a heroine. What do you say, Mamma, shall we cut short the melodrama and go to bed?"

"You really think it safe?" Mrs. Tretton addressed the two men equally.

"I believe you should, ma'am." It was Trevis who answered. "We shall be on guard all night, of course, but I really hardly hope, any longer, that the attack will be made."

"Hope!" she said. "Thank you, Lieutenant! I'm not sure I altogether like playing bait for your trap."

"Trap?" Mrs. Tretteign snorted awake. "What's that? What's happened? Have they come?"

"No, Aunt," said Christina. "Lieutenant Trevis was just saying he had given up hope of them. We are going to bed as if nothing had happened, and in the morning, no doubt, it will all seem like a bad dream." She moved over to where Sophie still lay curled up, fast asleep. "Come, pet, time for bed, and here's Cousin Ross to carry you up." It's the least you can do, her eyes challenged him across the sofa.

"Oh! I had such a dream!" Sophie woke all at once, like a child, bright-eyed and smiling. And then, looking around, "No—it wasn't a dream? Tina?"

"It's all right, pet. It's all over. Either a false alarm, or they heard the soldiers and thought better of it. How's your foot?

Can you walk, do you think, or shall Cousin Ross carry you up?"

"I shall walk." She had remembered it all now. "No need to trouble Cousin Ross." She spoke as if he was miles away, and pulled herself upright, holding on to the end of the sofa.

"Nonsense." Like Christina, Ross had seen her wince as she put her weight on the bad foot. He picked her up as if she weighed nothing and moved toward the door. "It's been a bad evening for us all. Forgive me, infant, if I was cross?"

"I suppose so. But you were, you know, dreadfully!" She smiled up at him.

"Well, of course I was. Chris, you're coming?"

"Yes." It was odd how the atmosphere had changed. It was all over. Good nights were quickly, almost shamefacedly said. Ross was going to watch all night with Trevis. For nothing, Christina thought sardonically. And yet, but for M. Tissot, how different it might have been. The Dark House might be in flames by now. So why could she not feel grateful to him? Impossible, somehow, to believe in his protestations of gratitude, his concern for her safety. What kind of double game, she wondered, was he playing now?

Chapter Sixteen

"WELL, WHAT NOW?" It was not until late next day that Christina contrived a word alone with Ross.

"How do you mean, what now?" He still looked drawn with fatigue from his night's vigil.

"Well—suppose they try again?"

"Oh, I don't think they will."

"You sent Jem to warn them." It was hardly a question.

"Yes." He had the grace to look apologetic. "It was the least I could do."

"I suppose so. A pretty parcel of fools we must all have looked, being heroic. You might have told us."

"You know I couldn't."

"No." She conceded it reluctantly. "Poor Lieutenant Trevis."

"Yes. I'm beginning to hate this double game. Chris—you could run the estate perfectly well on your own, could you not?"

"Well—I did, while you were away."

"Exactly. Will you help me persuade Grandfather to let me go?"

"Go?"

"Back to the army. Pitt as good as said, last time I saw him, that my usefulness here was finished. He told me too that my old regiment is in training for a continental venture. And that friend of mine I told you about, Arthur Wellesley, is on his way back from India to take a new command. Pitt told me that too. I could see he thought I would rejoin there and then. He even gave me a bonus, since spying is not gen-

197

erally well paid, which I am sure he intended to cover the price of a commission. And, of course, he was right. I'm useless here—specially after last night. But—Chris, what a fool you must think me. I—who had no use for women—to be so besotted, and for a child with no more sense . . . oh, I'm sorry"—he had seen her expression—"it's hard to remember she's your sister. You're so unlike, the two of you. Chris, I think I've been a little mad. I couldn't go away—can you understand that? Specially not when Richard was here. Do you think she cares for him?"

"I doubt if she cares for anyone. You're perfectly right, she's a child still. Why should she not behave like one? I thought you were brutal to her last night."

"I knew you were angry."

"I intended you to."

"But, Chris, you must try to understand. I had imagined her—fool that I was—I had dreamed her into everything I had always wanted. And she's so lovely—you must see that. Like a nymph, a fairy-tale princess. I think I went a little mad the first time I saw her. They were coming back from a ball . . . she was in silver . . . there were raindrops in her hair. And she smiled at me, as if I was—I don't know—the only person in the world. And all the time, she's nothing, cares for nothing but dress, thinks of nothing—and a coward, too!"

"She's my sister." Oh, how it helped to be angry with him. "You've no right to speak of her like that. Just because you put her on some absurd pedestal of your own imagining—"

"God, what a fool you must think me!"

"No, why?"

"An infatuated fool! I suppose I took it for granted that she had all your qualities as well—"

"As being so lovely?"

"Well, she is, isn't she, Chris? Exquisite. You should have seen her in her ball gown . . . something so precious. And so silly. Well . . ." He turned away from her, to stand with his back half turned, looking out at the gray marsh. "At least I can thank God for a rapid cure."

"If you are cured."

"Oh, I'm cured all right. She's confirmed everything I always felt about women—fainting, hysterics, and—I ask you —the crowning folly of rushing out of the house like that. It would have served her right if she had encountered the smugglers. Still, I must admit it was useful to me. I think I have contrived to convince Trevis that it was the stir she caused that alarmed them. He did not much like to think his men had been noisy, and I was beginning to be afraid he might look about for other explanations—"

"Like your having sent Jem?"

"Quite so. Well, Chris, what else could I do? I led them, they're my responsibility."

"I know, Ross."

"You really do, don't you? You understand so much. You should have been a man, Chris."

"I've often thought so."

"You're the only woman I've ever respected. When you came out to meet me last night . . . well, all the time I've known I could trust you. Taken it for granted, I suppose. You've no idea what that's meant to me. To know, all the time I was in France, that you were here, looking after things. Do you know, Chris, you're the first real friend I've had? You don't know what it was like, growing up here, on the marsh, and knowing the whispers that went on behind my back. Oh—I knew all right—trust my mother for that."

"You've never forgiven her?"

"Why should I?"

"Because she is your mother. Family's important, Ross. I've been learning that. It means something. Oh—I can't explain . . ."

"Family? A mother like mine! As silly—do you know, last night, when Sophie had hysterics—oh, you weren't here, but she did, you know. Suddenly, I saw—she's just like my mother."

"Oh, poor Ross . . ."

"You may well say so. Chris! Come back, look at me." She had moved a little away from him to gaze in her turn out the window at drizzling rain. Now, he took her hand and pulled her around to face him.

An involuntary shiver ran through her at his touch, and at the same time she knew that he felt nothing. She threw back her head to look him in the eyes. "Yes?"

"I know what a fool I've been. At least, give me credit for that. And somehow, my very madness has made me see things more clearly. I never meant to marry, you know. The idea was intolerable. Now—I don't know—everything seems different. There are . . . responsibilities . . . the marshmen . . . the place . . . the family—you're right about that, Chris. Oh, I know I'm a fine one to talk. I, the living blot on the family scutcheon to be talking of family! But someone must think of it. You know as well as I do, Richard thinks of this place merely in terms of money."

"And you love it."

"Yes . . . yes, I do. Well, you know how it is. I've worked for it, and that's what makes you love something. You must understand that. You've done the same thing. And that's why, Chris . . . I'll be honest with you. I can't offer you love, but . . . marry me, and I promise you a full life's partnership. You're the best friend I've ever had. Be mine. Be my wife."

Oh God, but she was tempted. "Ross—I don't know—I must think—"

"Of course. There's no hurry. Think about it, Chris, think what a partnership we'd make, you and I, how much we could do. But . . . take your time, Chris. I've spoken too soon, I know. We could not, decently, announce our engagement for a while anyway, for that poor child's sake. Is she very cut up today?"

She dropped his hand as if it burned her. "She's very snug in bed, eating comfits and crying over *Clarissa Harlowe*. And as for us, Ross, I can give you your answer now. You do me great honor in even considering marrying me, when, as you yourself say, you have always found the idea of marriage intolerable. Well, so do I. To marry without love, to make myself a slave for no reason. Why should I, Ross? Answer me that, why should I?"

"Oh, God, Chris, I don't know. What can I say to you?"

"Nothing to the purpose, that's certain." Anger had carried her so far . . . now, suddenly, it failed her. He looked, in his bafflement, so lost, so strangely young. . . . She reached for a memory that would blow the saving anger hot again. "How can you, Ross? Ask me to marry you, to be your partner, when, not so long ago, you thought me capable of betraying you to M. Tissot?"

"Of betraying . . ." He had forgotten all about it. "Oh that! I did not know you, Chris. I've told you, I've been a fool. Do you know, I'm even grateful to Sophie. That madness of mine, that infatuation with her, it's taught me a great deal. I see more, somehow, than I used to."

"Oh well." She managed a shrug. "Perhaps in the end, you will manage to see your way to marrying her."

"Never! Chris, I know I've done this all wrong . . ."

She smiled at him. "You have, haven't you? But never mind, Ross, nothing you said could have made any difference. There's no right way to a marriage without love. Now, come, sit down, forget all about it, and let us think what we are to do about Grandfather."

"Your grandfather, not mine."

"Oh, must you be so tiresome!" Again, anger was a relief.

"I'm sorry, Chris, but, you know, my life's not been an easy one."

"Frankly, Ross, nor has mine. Whose is, come to that? So let's leave being sorry for ourselves, shall we, and consider what's best to do next. And, to begin with, you are really set on rejoining the army?"

"More than anything in the world. It's the answer to everything. With the least bit of luck I'll be killed."

"And that, of course, will be the greatest comfort to us all! In the meantime, I believe I have an idea of how to deal with Grandfather. You'll leave it to me?"

"Gladly. You cannot possibly make more of a botch of things than I have contrived to. But what will you tell him?"

"The truth, to begin with. He must know that our engagement's off. We've sailed under false colors long enough. It's my fault. I should never have agreed in the first place."

"I should never have asked you."

She laughed. "No, but it's a little late in the day now to be worrying about that. Let us think, instead, on what grounds we are to break it off. Shall we quarrel, Ross?" Miraculous to keep her voice so light. "Or—better, surely—why don't you plead guilty to your passion for Sophie?"

"No!" Explosively. "I tell you, that's over. It doesn't exist."

"That's what you think today. But tomorrow?"

"Don't, Chris. I know I've been a fool, but even my folly has its limits. Not tomorrow, not ever. No, we must tell the truth."

"It will make a change." And then, recovering the lighter note. "It will also make Grandfather furious. It might even kill him. You know what Dr. Pembly said. No, Ross, let me handle this. It will be better so."

"But what will you say?"

"I shall tell him enough of the truth—that I've changed my mind. It's a woman's privilege, after all. And God knows there are grounds enough ready to my hand. Grandfather's no fool. He's seen you mooning after Sophie . . . everyone has. He may be angry, but he won't be surprised."

"Mooning?" Ross was angry now, and she was glad. "Not a pretty word."

"No." She left it at that.

"Oh, you're right, of course. I deserve nothing better. But that's just it. I've behaved monstrously enough to you already. How can I let you take the blame for breaking off our engagement? Grandfather will be furious."

"And you think I'd rather be publicly jilted than face his rage? I thank you, Ross . . . no. You are going to be thrown over, and like it. I'm not sure that I shall not make you a public scene." She could not help smiling at his appalled expression. "Don't worry, I doubt if I could rely on you to do it right. It's a pity though." Thoughtfully. "I rather fancy myself in the part. No, we'll have our quarrel in private—we've just had it now, in fact, and I will take the next opportunity to break the news to Grandfather. Have I your permission, if the chance serves, to tell him of your plan to rejoin your regiment?"

"Whatever you think best, Chris. I'm in your hands. And how I'm to thank you—"

"Oh, at least, Cousin, spare me that."

It was a day for confrontations. She had hardly escaped from Ross when her Aunt Tretteign cornered her in the still-room. "Christina!"

"Yes, Aunt?"

"I have been wishing for a word with you."

"Oh?" It was the last thing she wanted. "Will you not find it cold in here?"

For once, the appeal to hypochondria failed. "Yes, but it can't be helped. I know my duty, Christina, and I intend to do it."

"Oh?" This was a new departure.

"Yes. How long do you expect me to sit back and watch you pulling the wool over your grandfather's eyes? Fooling him to the top of his bent, the whole lot of you, that's what you're doing. And it's time it stopped. You know as well as I do that Ross and Richard are both mad for that little hussy Sophie—"

"You mean my sister?"

"Come now, Christina, no need to play the stoic with me. You know as well as I do how she's put your nose out of joint. Well, I mean, just look at it. Before she arrived, you had your choice of Ross and Richard. And now . . ."

"I look like wearing the willow. You are perfectly right, of course, Aunt. My only question is, what concern is it of yours?"

"What concern! Be a little reasonable, girl. Can you pretend to have forgotten the terms of your grandfather's will? If he were to die now, the Grange would go to the Patriotic Fund, and then where would we be—any of us?"

"Where indeed? But, tell me, Aunt, what do you expect me to do about it?"

"God knows! But something. I always thought you a girl of resource, Christina, but now—the way you have lain down and let that mother and sister of yours ride roughshod over you—why, I find it merely pitiful."

"What a strange thing. Now, I feel quite differently about them."

"Oh . . . you . . . you're just a born victim. I suppose it's because of having no finer feelings. Now, if you had my sensibilities—"

"How glad I am, Aunt, that I have not. Do you really think life would be any happier for us all if I were to take up hysteria? But, let's not be angry with each other. You're right of course. It's time my grandfather understood how the land lies, and, indeed, I have just had it out with Ross." Now was the moment to promulgate the idea of a quarrel between them.

"Had it out? That sounds ominous." Mrs. Tretteign breathed curiosity.

"Yes. I hope I have given Ross something to think about over and above poor Sophie's charms."

"You mean you have actually sent him to the right-about. Oh, good girl, good girl! I truly did not think you had it in you."

"You mean you are pleased?" Impossible not to be disconcerted.

"Of course I am, child. It was the most ridiculous arrangement from the start. Well—I mean, anyone could see you and Ross didn't care a rush for each other—why should you, two such strong characters?" She did not make it sound a virtue. "But if you have pulled yourself together at last, and given him his *congé*—why, the way is open for us all to be happy."

"I'm glad you think so, though I fail to see quite how."

"But it's so obvious, child. Ross and Sophie, you and Richard. Impossible for your grandfather to object to that."

"And Richard?"

"Well . . ." She had the grace to blush. "Of course, he has been dangling rather after Sophie, but then, he thought he had no chance with you. I tell you, love, Richard's a man of the world. And, of course, no question about it, if you and he marry, you'll get the Grange. Old Mr. Tretteign is angry enough with Ross as it is. Once tell him you've broken your engagement, and he can whistle for his inheritance."

"You think so?" It was exactly what she herself feared.

"Of course. He's a bad man to cross, your grandfather. Well—there you are. You and I know Richard's plans for the Grange. He'll sell it, and we will all be happy. Only, my love, you will be careful how you break the news to your grandfather, won't you? Just think if it should kill him."

Christina had had enough. "The Patriotic Fund would be the gainer," she said shortly. "And now, if you will excuse me, Aunt, I really must get back to my housekeeping."

"Such a capable girl!" Sudden venom in her aunt's voice told Christina how much she had been resented. "Bailiff, and housekeeper, and all. And as for this idea of yours of commencing school mistress, of all the crackbrained notions—I warn you that there are not many gentlemen who can abide a bluestocking. You would do better, if you ask me, to apply yourself to more feminine pursuits. I rather think the gentlemen—"

"Would prefer it if I took up swooning? Well, Aunt, I'm sorry to disappoint you and them, but it's not a thing I'm capable of—I hope." And she put an effective end to the conversation by climbing a stepladder and beginning an exhaus-

tive, if enraged, inventory of the household's supply of pre-
serves.

She was sure she could rely on her aunt to spread the news
of her supposed quarrel with Ross; it was merely a question
of how long it would take. She was therefore not surprised to
be summoned into her mother's bedroom just as the changing
bell was ringing.

"What's this about you and Ross?" Mrs. Tretton came
straight to the point.

"I've broken our engagement—if you could ever call it
one."

Her mother nodded. "Wise, I think." Thank God, she
could be relied on to avoid intolerable sympathy. "But the
old man will be very angry."

"Yes—that's my next problem."

"What will you tell him?"

"As little as I can manage. . . . Ross means to rejoin the
army."

Mrs. Tretton threw back her head and laughed. "Of
course! And leave you to sort out the muddle he has made of
his life. He's quite disillusioned with my poor Sophie, is he
not?"

"For the moment."

"Yes. Let us hope he does not leave too soon. We must
certainly have a few more riding parties before he goes."

"Mother!" But Christina could not help laughing. "You
don't mean you intended poor Sophie to have that fall!"

"Well, so long as she was not hurt. No, of course I did not
mean that. I just thought that out riding . . . if things won't
arrange themselves, love, one has to give them a little push
here and there. That's a woman's way. And, as for Sophie,
don't fret about her. She'll be all the better . . . I've my
plans for her, too, you know."

"I'm sure you have. But—Ross and Richard—you don't
think . . ." Impossible quite to get it into words.

"She cares for either of them? Nonsense. Of course she
doesn't. Between ourselves, I'm not sure, dear child, that she
is capable of caring very strongly for anyone but herself.
That is why I am so sure of a good match for her. She'll do
what I tell her, that one, which is more than I have ever been
able to say for you, love."

"No—and look where it has got me."

"Don't, *chérie*. It's not worth it." But she passed her a clean handkerchief. "I'm sure you did not let him see you cared."

"Ross? Of course not. He's no more idea of it than the man in the moon." She dabbed at her eyes angrily.

"Good girl. If you can keep it like that . . . he's vulnerable now, you know. Passion leaves room for passion."

"I wish I was dead."

"Nonsense. And if you're not careful, you'll be late for dinner. Wear your red tonight, love, it will put some color into your cheeks."

"Go down with all flags flying?" But she did as her mother suggested and was glad of the consciousness of looking her best when, immediately after dinner, she and Ross were summoned to old Mr. Tretteign's room.

His first words were hardly encouraging. "I've sent for you to hear your wedding plans. It's been shill-I, shall-I long enough. Now, I want to see something settled."

"But, Grandfather." Christina was ready for this. "I don't want to get married yet."

"Don't want, eh? And what has 'don't want' to do with it?"

"A good deal, Grandfather. I'm of age, you know, and more. I can't be forced into anything."

"I doubt if you ever could." Grudging respect in his tone.

She laughed. "Thank you. So—Ross, you'll not mind if I speak plainly?"

"Of course not." But he looked alarmed.

She had thought hard during the afternoon and had changed her plan for dealing with the old man. Ross's very surprise at the line she took would lend it conviction. And there would even be a tenuous thread of satisfaction in it for her. "Well then," she plunged in, "how can you expect me, an American girl, with a mind of my own, to consider marrying someone who just stays at home like a tame cat about the house, when the future of the world is being settled, in blood and tears? Send Ross away. Make him rejoin the army and do something in the world! Then, when he comes back, I'll marry him, if he wants me to." A challenging look told Ross not to believe this.

"Well I'll be damned." The old man believed her and his words came out like an explosion. "What do you think you are, girl, a Roman matron?"

"No, just a woman who wants to marry a man, not a puppet. You know I can run the estate as well as Ross. How can I respect him if that's all he does? And, I tell you, I won't marry a man I can't respect. Well, why should I?"

"Because you'll starve if you don't."

"You've forgotten my father's estate. And my mother's not exactly a pauper, you know." And then, appealingly, "Dear Grandfather, don't let's quarrel. You know I've promised to do as you wish—in the end."

"In your own time! But how much time have I? Answer me that, girl, if you can."

"The doctor was very pleased with you, last time he came."

"Doctors! Pah! I tell you, I may die any day, any hour, any minute—and, before I do, I want the future of the Grange settled. A grandchild would be best . . ." And then, "That's it—and be damned to the lot of you. Christina, write Foxton to come at once. The Grange goes to the first grandson bearing the name of Tretteign." He was shaking with excitement now. "And as for you, Ross, join the army, if you like, but don't expect a penny-worth of help from me."

"Grandfather, that's not fair." This was Christina. "You know how hard he's worked for you here."

"Keep quiet, girl. He's had his board and lodging, hasn't he? Horses to ride? Clothes to wear? Stay here, Ross, do the work you're fit for, and your allowance continues. Go haring off to London on this crackbrained scheme of yours and— phut . . . finish."

"Very well." Ross stood up. "I'm sorry, sir, but . . . finish it is."

"You'll starve." Was the old man already wishing he had been less definite?

"I doubt that. And if I do, I promise you I'll do it quietly, not to disgrace the name"—a cloud crossed his face—"the name I bear. And that reminds me, sir, you'd best think hard and draw your new will carefully. Suppose I were to marry the first girl I met on the way to London. Her son would be called Tretteign, and, in the world's sight, your grandson."

"Ross—don't." Christina's voice was pleading, her anxious eyes fixed on the old man, who looked ready to burst with rage. "I think it an admirable idea, Grandfather, and I'm sure Mr. Foxton will draw up just the kind of will you want. I'll write him at once. Come, Ross, we've been tiring Grandfather."

"Your grandfather." But, mercifully, Ross waited till they were outside to say it. "No kin of mine, I'm glad to say . . . the old bully. How can you bear him, Chris?"

"Why—because he is my grandfather, I suppose, and because, oddly enough, I love him. There's a lot you don't understand about love, Ross."

"I begin to think you are right."

Chapter Seventeen

ROSS MADE his announcement at lunch the next day. "Mother"—how seldom he called her that—"I've applied to have my commission reinstated."

"You've done what?"

"I've asked for my commission back." And then, with an effort, as if he found the explanation distasteful, "You must see that I cannot do otherwise. There's talk that my regiment is shortly to be ordered abroad—how can I stay here—"

"How can you do anything else?" Mrs. Tretteign's voice rose. "Of all the monstrous, inconsiderate, ungrateful . . ." She buried her face for a moment in a lace-trimmed handkerchief, but watched him over it with a pair of bright, tearless eyes. "You can't do it, Ross. To leave us here alone . . . unprotected . . . practically in the front line! And besides"—for her, this evidently settled it—"what will your grandfather say?"

"I've told him. He's furious. I can't help it. And, Mother, I'm sorry, it's no use arguing. The letters have gone. Now it's only a question of time."

"You mean you did not even consult me—"

"What would have been the use? Remember, I'm a man, ma'am, with a man's responsibilities."

"Responsibilities!" This made her angrier than ever. "To yourself, I collect! I do not see much sign of your responsibility for us. What about me? I suppose I'm just a useless old woman—what matter if I'm raped by the whole French Army—don't pretend to be shocked, Ross, this is no time for mincing words. But have you thought what will happen to the girls if you leave us here alone? To Sophie?" Here, said her voice, was another powerful argument.

"Of course I've thought. In a way, that's why I'm going. This war must be finished, ma'am, this constant threat removed. If every man in England only felt as I do, it would be over soon enough."

"I'm glad you think so." Spitefully. "Your rejoining will make the whole difference, I take it?"

"It's my duty, Mother." And then, turning to Christina and Sophie, who had sat, so far, silent and embarrassed auditors, "You do understand, don't you? You think I'm right to go."

"Of course," said Christina.

"Well," Sophie's voice was petulant, "I suppose if you are set on it—it seems monstrous foolish to me, I confess. From all you have told me, campaigning is nothing but a dead bore: short commons, mud and a strong chance of death at the end of it."

"That must be my consolation, Sophie."

She looked merely puzzled; it was Christina who understood and answered him. "Ross! If you speak like that, I shall think you wrong to go."

"I'm sorry, Chris, and—I take it back."

"You promise?" Oddly, as her clear eyes met his, they might have been alone in the room.

"I promise."

"I wish I knew what you two were talking about," said Mrs. Tretteign crossly. "It would be more sense to promise not to go, Ross! Even if the letters have gone off, I'm sure Richard would use his influence to have them stopped. Sophie, try to persuade him."

"Of course!" Sophie raised reproachful eyes to Ross. "You cannot be so cruel, Cousin Ross. To leave us here all alone, Tina and me, with no cavalier—it does not bear thinking of! Besides, you cannot have forgotten"—she spoke as one bringing forth a final argument—"you promised to take me to the Spring Assembly at Rye!"

"I'm sorry, Sophie. It's true—I did promise. You will have to hold me excused."

"And if I do not?" Sparkling now, teasing, challenging, sure of her power.

"I shall be sorry." And then, seeing her color change at the flat rebuff, "But never mind, infant, they are not renowned

for speed and efficiency at the Horse Guards. Who knows?
My commission may not come through before the Spring Assembly."

But already the evenings were drawing out. Coarse gray
marsh grass seemed to turn green overnight and was embroidered here and there with tiny yellow flowers Christina had
never seen before. There was a new quality in the light, too,
and a soft freshness in the air. The lambing had started all
over the estate and Ross was out most of the day superintending it, while Christina occupied herself with fighting
moth and mildew in his uniform jacket and pelisse.

He found her busy in her office one evening of watery sunlight and sun-spangled showers. "There you are, Tina. I've
been looking all over for you. You should not be working
here in the dusk. Oh"—awkwardly—"I've got a present for
you, from an admirer—"

"Oh?" She rose to meet him, oddly confused by his use of
Sophie's pet name for her.

"Yes, Jem's younger brother. He picked them for you specially. Here . . ." Their hands touched for a moment as he
gave her the little bunch of ivory-colored flowers.

"Thank you. But what are they?" She bent her head over
them to conceal a rising tide of color. "They smell of
heaven."

"Your first primroses, barbarian! Yes—I'd forgotten how
good they smell." He, too, bent down and for a moment his
dark hair brushed hers. "We used to ride over to Starlock
every spring, Richard and I, to pick them under the hill.
They don't grow on the marsh."

"They're lovely, Ross. Thank you . . ."

"Thank Jem's brother." Once again an odd awkwardness in
his tone. "Or—thank me, if you will, for bringing them to
you. A fine booby I felt, riding about the marsh with a lady's
nosegay in my hand."

"Poor Ross. I hope you met no one."

"Not a soul. I hear you are thinking of setting up a school.
Jem's mother is in a seventh heaven of expectation."

"I do hope I do not disappoint her. You do not mind,
Ross?"

"Mind? Because you do what my mother has so signally

failed to? I hope you don't think me so poor-spirited as that, Chris. It just seems one more debt that I owe you."

"Oh, don't talk of debts . . ."

"But I must. You've changed my life, Chris, by your coming. You must let me tell you what it means . . . to be free at last to have my own life . . . to be able to think of a future. . . . You've done all this for me, and given me the courage to face it. . . . Chris!" And then, "Damnation! Yes, Parkes?"

"There's an urgent messenger from London, sir."

"Tell him to wait!"

"Yes, sir." And then, "It's Mr. Pitt's livery, sir, white and blue."

"Oh—in that case—confound it—you'll excuse me, Chris?"

"Of course." In the twilight, their eyes met for one unfathomable glance, then, alone again, she bent her head to drop a light kiss on the flowers she held. "Chris!" He had begun . . . what next? Maybe nothing . . . maybe. . . . No, she dared not even imagine it. She went out to the pantry and made a long, delicious business of putting her flowers in water.

Returning, she met Ross in the hall. "Chris!" He came toward her. "I have to leave at once!"

"Tonight?"

"I'm afraid so. Pitt's sent for me to London—urgently. I don't know what it's about, but of course I must go."

"Of course." Why was he speaking so loudly? What was the message his eyes were trying to give her? "What can I do to help?"

"Nothing, thank you. I've told Jem to saddle up."

"You're riding?"

"Yes. I'll not be gone long—I hope. No need for heavy luggage. I'll just take a cloak bag behind my saddle."

What was he trying to tell her? "You're starting at once?"

"In ten minutes. My good-byes will be soon said."

"Will you see Grandfather?"

"What's the use? Chris . . ."

"Yes?" And then, suddenly daring, "Let me ride a little way with you. I've an errand to do at East Guldeford."

"So late?" He looked, at first, doubtful, and then, she thought, relieved. "Well, why not? No one would harm *you*,

Chris. But no errands tonight, it's too late for that. Only, if you felt like setting me a little on my way . . ."

"I should like to. I'll run and change." No time to ring for Betty, no time to think as she huddled herself into her riding habit. Fifteen minutes later they were riding side by side down the drive.

"Chris!" He turned toward her, his face dimly seen in the failing light. "I'm glad you chose to come. There's so much I'd like to say to you—so much . . ." He stopped. "I've no right. If I come back—"

"If! What do you mean, Ross?" She was shivering now with a chill that had nothing to do with the coming of dusk.

"I ought not to tell you. Pitt said—but I must—I—there are limits. I cannot just disappear."

"Disappear? Ross, what do you mean?"

"Pitt is sending me to France. Something's gone wrong with his chain of agents. He's had no word from there for weeks. And, it's spring, Chris. Any moment, Villeneuve may be out again. If he eludes Nelson this time, the invasion we've laughed about may be a reality. Bonaparte needs only two days—twenty-four hours, perhaps—in control of the Channel, with the weather fair. You must see, I've got to go . . ."

"Yes." She saw, too, the risks he ran. "But how?"

"A fast carriage is waiting for me beyond Rye. I'll be in Portsmouth by morning. A British frigate is standing by to land me on a bit of coast I know in Brittany. After that . . . well, I've always been lucky."

"But how will you get back?"

"The same way I go over—if I'm lucky. If not, well, there are always ways. It's getting the news back that matters."

"How long?" She tried to match his deliberately casual tone.

"A week, with luck. Less, perhaps. The frigate's to stand in every night, waiting for my signal. So, you see, I'm probably making a to-do about nothing. I'll be back next week, and no call for farewells. But—if not, Chris, if something should go wrong, you'll say the right things? To my mother, to Sophie, to the old man?"

"Yes, Ross. And . . . to myself?"

"Ah, Chris. If we'd only had more time. But no, I've no right. I—the fool you've seen me, the besotted fool I've been.

I can't . . . and with my name, my scandal-spotted name! No, if I come back, if I can do what Pitt wants, do something, however little, that matters, something for liberty and the hope of man, then, perhaps . . . but it's no use. Things don't happen like that. No, Chris, this is the answer to everything. You're all the heir the old man needs. You'll look after the place, be good to my mother, be everything I've not been. Think of me kindly, sometimes, as of a fool who was wise enough to see his own folly."

"Ross!" Now she was frightened. "You do mean to come back?"

"Of course. It's my duty. And, besides, Chris, I want to—more than anything, I want to. When I do—if I do . . ." He stopped, changed his tone. "Dear Chris. Let me call you that, just once. But—it's time you were turning back. There must be nothing odd about my leaving tonight, and, besides, it's getting dark. You should not be out alone."

"As if I cared." Words choked in her throat. "Ross, be careful. For all our sakes. And for England's."

"I will. And now—good-bye, Chris."

"Good luck." She must not delay him, even for a moment. And already, it was too late. One long, strange look back at her in the dusk, and he was spurring on his horse toward Rye. She allowed herself the small indulgence of sitting quietly where she was, watching him disappear, with never another backward glance, into the low-lying mist. Something cold and wet fell on the hand that held her reins. Well, it did not matter now if unfamiliar tears were streaming down her cheeks.

But she must not look as if this had been anything but the casual farewell of a few days. Deliberately, she got herself under control before she turned homeward to face the battery of eyes and questions at the Dark House.

Luckily, no one seemed much interested. Mrs. Tretteign was only concerned with the shock her son's sudden departure had given to her nervous system. Sophie was cross because he had left before she could give him various commissions to the London shops. "After all, if he is coming back in a few days, he could easily have matched my ribbons for me."

Only Mrs. Tretton's observant eyes saw Christina's hands tighten on fork and knife. She intervened with a deliberate change of subject, and, later, when the evening seemed to stretch interminably with anxiety and small talk, she gave Christina her chance to escape. "You look to me, child, as if you had the headache. Why not make an early night of it?"

Christina was glad to get away, and yet the solitude of her room was torture. She had sent Betty off to bed, and now sat by the window, gazing across the bay, past the light on Fairlight Cliff, toward Portsmouth where, tomorrow, Ross would embark for France, and probable death. He had made light of the risk he ran, but now, alone in the dark, she faced it all. If he was caught, it would be as a spy, with death the only end. And—they might never know. The deaths of spies are private ones, unhonored, unreported. She jumped to her feet to prowl restlessly about the room. Suppose she had thrown everything to the winds—pride, modesty, all of it. Suppose she had said, "I love you, Ross, come back for my sake." Might it have made a difference? She would probably never know.

Chapter Eighteen

ALL THAT LONG WEEK it rained. Not the mild marsh drizzle Christina was used to ignoring, but wildly, with winds of gale force, exacerbating her anxiety for Ross. Suppose he had not even been landed yet, but was beating about out there in the Channel, risking death equally by shipwreck and by capture? Haunted by thoughts like this, she felt it the last straw to be cooped up in the Dark House the target of so many observant pairs of female eyes. But the weather was too bad even for her. To go out for her usual evening walk in a full gale must arouse comment, and comment was of all things to be avoided. Everything must go on as calmly at the Grange as if Ross was indeed in London, playing too high at Brooks', as his mother seemed to think.

"Of course, it is tedious down here for him, with only us females," sighed Mrs. Tretteign. "No wonder if he makes an excuse from time to time to run away to London."

An excuse! Christina clenched her teeth to avoid speaking, and moved over to the window. The small saloon they were sitting in looked out on to the stable yard, but even here she could see the reflection of a red glow in the sky. "It's clearing up at last," she said. "It looks like a splendid sunset. I think I'll just go down to the beach for a breath of air."

"To the shore? So late? Not by yourself, surely?" But Aunt Tretteign had finally given in about what she called this unladylike habit. Her protest was merely formal and Christina made her escape without more ado.

It was good to be outside, wonderfully good to be alone at last, free to indulge the anxiety that had haunted her for seven dragging days. Out here, in the wind, nothing seemed quite so bad. The sun was setting in glory over Fairlight. Tomorrow should be a fine day. Perhaps it was a good omen; perhaps tonight Ross would come secretly down to a Brittany beach and be picked up by the frigate's boat. He might even be home tomorrow.

Or—he might not. He might already have died a spy's quick death in France. Down on the damp, gray sand, she shivered a little as the wind blew her hair this way and that about her face. The sky beyond Fairlight was fading fast. Now only a few crimson streaks remained, reflected high up among the clouds. With the sun's going, color ebbed from everything. The marsh lay dun and secret behind her, the sea dark and sullen in front. It was time to be going back to the Dark House—would she ever come to think of it as home?

She turned, when she got to the top of the beach, to look back across the darkening sea toward where, sometimes, she had been told, you could see the lights of Gris Nez, then climbed with quick, sure steps up the shingle bank, down the slope of the sea wall on the other side and past the battered old hut, where, when they were boys, Ross and Richard had kept a boat.

What was that noise? Ross? Here? Absurd! She had paused instinctively at what had seemed the sound of movement in the hut, was moving forward again, when a voice—M. Tissot's voice—said, "A moment, mademoiselle. And silently, I beg." He moved out from the doorway of the hut. "I'm armed, you see, and will shoot if you scream or run."

"Why should I?" She wished she felt as confident as she made herself sound. Half a mile to the house. No hope of help; and the shadows thickening fast.

"Why indeed? It is but to do me the favor of a small visit in return for all the hospitality you have shown me. Be a little reasonable, and you shall come to no harm, I promise. You'll do as I tell you?" A little movement of the gun he held underlined the seemingly courteous request.

One quick look around. Nothing but the silent marsh, a light showing, now, high up at the Grange—in her own room, perhaps, where Betty would be laying out her dress for dinner. And all, so far as she was concerned, as distant as the moon. Two men had detached themselves from the shadows behind M. Tissot and moved toward her.

"They'll only tie your hands," said Tissot. "And see you do as you are bid."

"Gag her?" asked one of them. An Englishman. A stranger, with an accent she did not recognize.

"No." M. Tissot had taken a moment to think about it. "She is a young woman of good sense. She does not wish to be shot in the leg. Do you, mademoiselle?"

"Frankly, no." She kept her voice casual, while concentrating all her attention on her hands, which one of the men had pulled, with a kind of firm courtesy behind her back. It seemed several lifetimes ago that her Indian blood-brother had showed her the trick. "You hold them—thus." His English had been as quick and fluent as her own. "They tie you up, and, look, when you wish it, you are free." Did she remember? Had she done it right? Don't test it now, and risk discovery. Wait. Wait . . .

"Not a very long walk," M. Tissot was saying. "And we know what a good walker you are, mademoiselle. I was beginning to think you would never come. Imagine our discomfort. A whole week in that deplorable hut."

A whole week. Now she was cold with fear, not for herself, but for Ross. They had been waiting for her since he left. They must have seen her start off with him. What did they know? What did they want to know?

Don't show you're afraid. Don't show you understand anything. She swallowed a lump of something in her throat, and said, "A whole week in that place! Waiting for me! M. Tissot I am excessively flattered, but, do tell me, why?"

"All in good time. She's safely tied? Very well then, *allons*. One on each side, and, mademoiselle, I am three paces behind you, with the gun in my hand. If we should meet anyone, we are taking you to see an old woman, who is very ill, in her cottage on Dungeness. If you value your questioner's life, you will let him go."

But they met no one on that walk that seemed as if it would never end. This was a path she had not known existed, cutting right across the marsh to somewhere inland from Dungeness. Once, they all stopped for an interminable few moments, before crossing the road that ran down to the gun emplacements on the shore. For an instant she let herself hope. Lieutenant Trevis, if they should encounter him, would never believe M. Tissot's story. But Tissot was taking good care that they meet no one. Her hands were tied; she could not even drop her handkerchief as they crossed the deserted road and plunged back into the dark heart of the marsh.

"Faster, mademoiselle." M. Tissot's voice, courteous as ever, from behind. "We do not wish to be benighted here." And then, a few minutes later. "Halt!" And to the men who had walked silently on either side of her. "Blindfold her now. You see, mademoiselle, I hope to be able to set you free, presently. The less you know, the better."

He hoped! But there was nothing for it but to stand passively while a silk scarf was bound tightly around her eyes; to submit to being led forward again, more slowly, along the rough track.

Surely they would have missed her at the Grange by now? But what good would that be? They would go down to the beach and find nothing. What on earth would they think? Her mother, she knew, could be relied on for quick, sensible action. She would send for Lieutenant Trevis. And, by the time he arrived, it would be full dark. Any traces they might have left on the muddy paths would be invisible till morning.

"*Bien.*" Tissot might have been reading her thoughts. "It is starting to rain again."

So much for that. There would be no tracks in the morning. So—she was on her own. Think . . . plan . . . don't waste a moment on fright; there's no time for that. And even with the thought came inspiration. Of course, she ought to appear frightened. Could she manage hysterics, quietly, so that M. Tissot would think her negligible, a panic-stricken woman. But—the thoughts were surging through her brain now—it would be difficult to convince Tissot of this. A pity he knew her so well. Still—give it a try, just the same.

She slumped heavily against the man on her right. "I can't walk another step." The quaver in her voice was too convincing for comfort. "Where are you taking me? My grandfather will pay you well, if you will only let me go. I promise you he'll give you whatever you want."

"Not money, mademoiselle." Tissot's voice, skeptical, from behind her. "Something much more valuable—information. Oblige us with that and you shall go free in the morning."

"Information? What can you mean? I don't understand!" And then, "In the morning? But you can't keep me all night. Imagine my reputation!"

"Your reputation, mademoiselle? Be thinking, rather, of your life. I should be sorry to see you come to harm, but I warn you . . ." He let it hang, ominously, in the darkness, and she knew that here, at last, was the real Tissot—a man who would stop at nothing.

But at all costs she must keep up the pretense of imbecility, remain the girl who, faced with death, thought only of reputation. "I'm frightened. Where are you taking me? I want to go home!" Once again, the quiver in her voice was too realistic for her own comfort.

"Not much farther now." At last, a note of contempt in Tissot's voice. He thought she was cracking. Thank God for that. But—be careful. Pretended cowardice could so easily slide over into the real thing. She stumbled along between her two guards, keeping up her Aunt Tretteign's kind of low, despondent monologue. And, always, the burden of it, "But, *why?* I don't understand."

"You will soon enough. And—in good time—here we are." The sound of a door creaking open. A smell of damp and dry rot.

"Where are we?" She let her voice rise almost to a scream, and one of her guards tightened a warning grip on her arm.

"Let be," said Tissot. "No one can hear her now. Scream if you must, mademoiselle. There's not a soul for miles." He sounded pleased with himself. Doubtless he thought her spirit completely broken.

Well, so it must seem. She sobbed convincingly all the way up the narrow, tumble-down stairway, for which, at least, they had removed the bandage from her eyes. In the room at the top, she looked about her with genuine horror, by the light of the lantern Tissot carried. "You can't make me stay here! There'll be rats!"

"No need to stay. Just sit down, relax, calm yourself, and answer a few simple questions, and you shall be home before the search for you has really begun."

Her guards were tying her to a chair, and once again she had to concentrate, for a few moments, remembering what Little Eagle had taught her. Then she resumed her babble of inane protest, with its catchphrase, "I don't understand." And all the time, somewhere behind the simulated panic, a part of her mind was thinking coldly, clearly, at express speed. Even if she did answer his question—which she never would—she did not think M. Tissot would let her go. Why should he? It would merely increase the risks he ran. And doubtless this tumble-down farmhouse had cellars . . . a well. . . . No one would ever know what had happened to her.

"There." They had finished tying her up and stepped back from the hard chair on which they had set her. "She's all yours, monsieur."

"Good. You'll find food in the room below. No drink, mind you, and no lights. There'll be work to do later on."

Yes—burying her. The shudder that ran through her was all too genuine, but she managed to make the most of it just the same. "Grandfather will be very angry." Again that horribly convincing quiver in her voice.

"He will, won't he?" Tissot sounded amused. "All the more reason for telling me what I want to know and getting home quickly."

"Yes, of course, anything—but what do you mean? What do you want to know? Grandfather will pay—pay well—to have me back unharmed."

"I am sure he would." She noticed the telltale use of the conditional, but gave no sign. "But I'm not a vulgar kidnaper, mademoiselle. I serve a great cause—the cause of France. And you, who are half French, should understand, should sympathize. We are going to make the world a better—a happier place. Freedom for all! Is not that an inspiring cry?"

"Yes." She managed a tone of simple perplexity. "But what has that to do with me?"

"Why—everything, mademoiselle. You are fortunate enough to be able to help us—oh, just in a small, an unimportant way, with a piece of information we could easily get elsewhere. But you are the nearest, the quickest, source. Tell me what I need to know, and you shall find yourself one of the heroines of the new empire."

Well—it was thin consolation—her acted hysteria must have convinced him. Otherwise he would never expect her to believe that. "I see." She sounded puzzled. "There's something I know that's important? But what on earth? What should I know, living down here, a nun's life, on the marsh?"

"And suffering from a nun's *ennui,* I've no doubt. . . . Tell me, mademoiselle, how would you like to find yourself carried across the sea and launched in society at Paris? You'd have twice the success your sister did."

How terrifyingly much he knew. But, "Paris? Could you? Oh, M. Tissot!" Would you really swallow that girlish enthusiasm?

Apparently he would. "Of course I could." His voice was patronizing now. "If I chose. But, first, you must show yourself ready to oblige me."

"And then you'll untie me? Take me away from this horrible place?"

"At once. There *are* rats, by the way. You'd hear them soon enough if I were to take away the light—and feel them too, I've no doubt. Have you ever seen a prisoner from Newgate, with his ears all nibbled away? Not exactly the beauty treatment for a handsome girl like you." The contempt in his voice was open now.

"Ugh . . ." She managed a long, low convincing shudder. "Only tell me what you want of me, quickly."

"A trifle, no more. But first, as a token of good faith, tell me something else. Something, I warn you, that I already know. Answer me truly in this, and I shall know I can trust you on the more important issue."

"Trust me!" She made it almost a squeak. "But of course you can trust me! I don't want to have my ears gnawed by rats." How difficult it was to sob convincingly when one could not put one's hands in front of one's eyes. But she did her best. And all the time, the undercurrent of rapid calculation continued. What was his game? What was this question of which, he said, he already knew the answer? Was this not, in all probability, a trick to make her think it unimportant?

The next moment, she knew this guess was right. "Very well, then," he said. "If you are ready to help me, tell me, first, where M. Ross Tretteign has gone. Answer that right, and I shall know I can trust you."

Ross! There it was. And no time for thought either. "Ross?" A triumph of childish amazement in her voice. "But that's too easy! He's gone to London. Mr. Pitt sent for him in a great hurry, last week, and he went off without more than a clean shirt in his saddlebag. And left me with all the worry of the lambing, too." Now she was plaintive, ill-used . . .

But M. Tissot's face had hardened, set to stone. "Come, mademoiselle, you can do better than that." He moved toward her, as she sat, helpless, tied to her straight-backed chair, raised his hand, watched her eyes follow it, and struck her, with cool violence, full across the face.

Now the tears came easily, tears of rage and pain and fright. If it had not been already decided, that blow had sealed her fate. He could not let her go now, whatever tales he might tell of trips to Paris. What a fool he must think her! Well, so much the better. "Why did you do that?" She looked up at him with, she hoped, the expression of a child unjustly punished. "I said I'd tell you whatever I know. Ross rode away last Tuesday. I rode with him almost as far as East Guldeford, but then he made me turn back because he said I was slowing him down and he must reach London as soon as possible. Cousin Ross doesn't like women much, you know. He let me come that far because he had things to tell me about the estate. He thought Mr. Pitt had some special service for him. Is that what you want to know about?"

Thank God, he was looking at her doubtfully. "Is that really all he told you?"

"What else was there to tell? Do you know more about it than I do? If so, I wish you would tell me, because Grandfather is getting very impatient about Ross's being away again. If I could tell him . . . explain to him . . ." She let her voice dwindle away.

"*Sapristi!*" He was angry now, but as much with himself as with her. "He told you nothing?"

"But—I keep asking you . . . what was there to tell?"

"And you pretend you don't know a closed carriage was waiting for him on the other side of Rye?"

"A carriage? But where's his horse?"

"Stabled at the George."

How careless of Ross, she thought, and how like him. But she must keep up her part. "At the George? M. Tissot, I don't understand anything. I suppose Mr. Pitt might send a carriage for Ross, if he wanted him in a great hurry—but why not send Arab back to the Grange? Grandfather hates paying livery bills—he'll be very angry." She managed to make this sound the most pressing of her worries.

"But the carriage did not go to London, mademoiselle." He was watching her more closely than ever. "It took him to Portsmouth."

"To Portsmouth?" What a fool she sounded, parroting his words. But that was what she wanted. Folly was her only hope. "Good God!" Here, suddenly, was inspiration. "I knew he was restless, since Mr. Pitt said he was no use down here any more. Can he have decided to join the navy instead of the army? M. Tissot, you don't think that? Oh—Ross—we'll never see him again."

He had turned away from her and was pacing up and down the room. Now he turned suddenly to loom over her, hand upraised. "He told you nothing?"

Her face burned where he had already struck her and it was easy to flinch. "He told me to ride over to Pett and see how the lambing was going there. But it's rained so hard, I could not venture. I'm afraid he'll be angry when he gets back." Oh, Ross, she prayed, if you only do get back . . .

"Goddamn!" In his fury, he swore in French and English equally. "You really don't know?"

"Don't know what, M. Tissot?" Here was the crisis. If she contrived to convince him that she knew nothing, would he not kill her on the spot, so that she could be buried before morning? She must fight for herself, as well as for Ross. Living is pleasant, the sun in the morning, and small flowers in the grass, sea winds, and cloud patterns at dusk. . . . Think, think quickly, think for your life. "He did say one thing." She brought it out doubtfully, as if searching back through memory.

"Yes?" He was close above her now, hand poised, reminding her of the blow that still smarted across her cheekbone.

"Let me get it right . . ." Her mind was racing. M. Tissot knew Ross had gone to Portsmouth. He would inevitably have deduced that this meant France. Right—she had it. "He said—something I did not understand. Something about the beach. I walk there most evenings you know." Of course he knew. Why else had he waited for her there? But keep up— at all costs keep up the pretense of stupidity.

"The beach?" His voice was contemptuous. "When he was going to London?"

"That's what I did not understand. He said something about my evening walks—about waving to me. Oh . . ." She looked up at him, all eagerness, as if it had just occurred to her. "You say he went to Portsmouth? Can he have been going to France all the time? To somewhere round Gris-Nez?" And then, on a note of horror, "Oh—I should not have told you. Oh, Ross . . . you'll not hurt him?"

"Hurt him? Of course not." He had what he wanted now. "We just want to talk to him."

Yes, she thought, as you are talking to me. Oh God, let this be right . . . let them search as hard as they please for Ross on the northern coast, while he was picked up safely from some Brittany beach.

"Anything else?" He had turned away to conceal, she suspected, a look of triumph. "What about when he was coming back? He must have said something about that."

"Let me think." A week, Ross had said, "If I'm lucky." Well, then, "He did say something to Grandfather. It made him angry, I remember. Things do make Grandfather angry these days. He's getting old, you know, and it's a mistake to cross him." She was a silly babbling girl who might betray a man's life in innocent gossip. Had she done it right?

His expression as he turned impatiently to stand over her again told her that she had. "Yes . . . yes . . . I know all about your old fool of a grandfather. But what was it that made him angry?"

"Why, Ross planning to spend a whole month in London. Drink, and gambling and more debts, Grandfather said, and probably no commission to show for it in the end. Ross wants to go back into the army, you know, now Pitt thinks he's no use down here any more." And then, on a note of hysteria, "Oh! I should not have said that." And, gathering some tattered shreds of would-be dignity about her, as a girl might, "That's all I can tell you, M. Tissot." Let a little doubt creep into her voice. It might mean one more night of living. "I won't say another word. And now, you promised you would send me home." An artistic trembling on the last word. "Aunt Tretteign will be so cross."

"Yes, yes. All in good time, mademoiselle. I have some arrangements to make first. You shall have something to eat and drink—you must be famished. And then, when I return, I will see you safely home."

"Oh, thank you." He was going to organize the hunt for Ross. Meanwhile—what did he plan for her? Already, she could see, his mind was far away, weaving a net for Ross.

"You won't be long? I don't like it here . . ." A nervous glance around the room, trying, at the same time, to make a note of every detail, in case he should take away the lantern.

And then, as he picked it up, "Oh, please, leave the light. I'm so frightened!"

He shrugged—"If you like"—and opened the door. "Here," he called down the stairs. "One of you come and keep mamselle company. She's frightened on her own."

"Oh, please!" She made it a girl's plea. "I'm scared of them. Can't I lock myself in and wait till you get back?"

"Well." As he pretended to consider it, something sardonic in his expression told her that he was not coming back. He would leave the job of disposing of her to the others. Now he pretended to come to a decision. "The trouble is"—he said it with an engaging frankness that might have deceived her once—"the door does not lock. Don't worry, they won't molest you, I promise. They have their orders."

Not including rape? Impossible to suppress a shiver. But —why believe a word he said? Time was running out for her, faster than she had expected. "Oh, take the light away," she whimpered as he moved toward the door. "It hurts my eyes. If you'd only untie my hands, so I could move about a bit . . ."

"I'm sorry." He picked up the light. "But I'll take this, if you prefer the dark, and the rats."

"Don't!" It was almost a shriek, which she let dwindle off into a bout of hysteria that would have done Aunt Tretteign credit. And all the time, as he moved, lantern in hand, toward the door and out of sight, her hands were frantically busy behind her back, remembering what Little Eagle had taught her. These few moments, while he was giving the men downstairs their orders, were probably all the chance she would get. Now, more than ever (was the knot working loose?) how pleasant living seemed. Just breathing, and eating—even being unhappy, being in despair seemed a privilege. To be alive . . . to suffer . . . to know, this is I, Christina. Irreplaceable. Irreplaceable. What would Ross think if he came back to find her vanished? Would he guess what had happened to her? Would he know that she had died for him? Probably not. Ah! There! The knot had given. Blood brother, Little Eagle, you could not save my father's life, but you may save mine. The knots that tied her to the chair were easier, since the man who had tied them had already dismissed her as negligible. Free, she made herself sit for a moment, massaging life into her stiff limbs, before she risked slipping out of her shoes, standing up and moving, soft-footed, to the door. Thank God, at least this much of what he had told her had been true. The door did not lock. Very gently, she pulled it open. Darkness, and the sound of voices below.

M. Tissot was giving his orders. "Wait for full dark." He sounded impatient to be off. "In the meantime, she's yours."

"Full dark? Dawn more like. There's life in that one. No, no. We'll see all's right and tight before dawn. But in the meantime . . ."

Cold shivers ran down her spine at his tone. No use hoping to bribe these two with promises. No time to be lost either. Willing it to silence, she pulled the door farther open. Now, she could see a gleam of light, thrown up from the bottom of the stairway that faced her. Very cautiously, she slipped out into the hall, blessing the silent floorboards. Downstairs, one of the men laughed. "A hard night's work," he said.

She had been in many marsh cottages like this one—small farmhouses, they had been once, when the wool trade was at its height. There would be one other bedroom on this floor. Yes, here was its door, and ajar, thank God. The voices downstairs sounded further off as she tiptoed in. The chances of being betrayed by a creaking floorboard were so much less. And her eyes were used to the darkness now; she half felt, half saw her way to the window, which should look out over the back of the house.

It was stuck fast with years of disuse. Wait for the bustle of M. Tissot's leaving? No, time was running out too fast for her already. She found her way back across the room and tied the rope that had bound her to what seemed the only piece of furniture, a musty cot. No way of telling, in the dark, what kind of condition it was in. No time to wonder. It was, simply, her only chance. She moved to the window again, the rope end in her hand. Most of the tiny panes of glass had been broken long since—there would be no shatter of glass below. Now! The violence of the push she gave almost sent her out through the window as it swung open with a loud creak of rusted hinges. No time to think; no time to listen. Already, she was on the window sill, the cord in her hand. Not too far down, surely? These marsh houses were built low, crouching close to the ground to be out of the wind. Anyway—the rope burned her hands. She landed, jarred but unhurt, in what must once have been the cottage garden. A rank smell of nettles and something prickly under her stockinged feet. Fool . . . she had left her shoes behind. No time to be thinking of that. How could she listen when her heart beat so loudly? She made herself stand for a moment; made herself breathe slow and even. Yes—around at the front, M. Tissot was mounting his horse. With luck he would be gone before the others discovered her escape. From what she had seen of them, their pursuit would be very much less dangerous than his.

Her breathing was easier now, and she could just make out the shapes of things. Not quite dark yet, thank God. It had seemed an age since they caught her, but it could not be all that long. The search would only just be out at the Grange. And how far away was she? She did not even know what direction to take, and there were no stars to guide her. But— away. Already she was half walking, half crawling through the undergrowth of the desolate garden. Briars scratched her face. Raspberry canes? Here was a tangle of undergrowth that must once have been a hedge around the little garden, but ragged, now, and blown sideways by the wind, so that she struggled through it without too much difficulty. On the other side, of course, would be a ditch.

Yes, her foot slipped down—far down in the darkness— and she caught a thorny branch of the hedge to steady herself. The ditch would not—probably—be very wide, or very deep. How much time had she? She turned to peer back toward the house. No sounds, yet, of discovery or pursuit. Instead, M. Tissot's voice, raised in farewell at the front of the house, and then the noise of a horse being ridden off, fast, in the other direction. So much for Tissot. But—it meant that time was running out for her. Any minute now, the men would go upstairs and find her gone. What would they do? They were English—probably Londoners—but stupid; followers rather than framers of orders. They would find her gone, find the broken window, search the garden. This was elementary.

She had decided already. No time to work around the house to the front where the road lay. Besides, this was probably what they would expect her to do. Instead, she let herself down, gently, into the ditch, and found, as she expected, a bottom of about a foot and a half of water and a great deal of mud that sucked around her stockinged feet. Under normal circumstances, it would have been horrible.

Tall reeds brushed against her face. She had a struggle to get through them, but at least they helped her to keep upright. And—here was the other side. She climbed out and found—thank God—a typical field of marsh grass. But—which way to go? She had lost all sense of direction during that interminable blindfolded walk. A shout from the house settled the question for her. They had discovered her escape. Direction, for the moment, mattered little as long as it was away.

She did not dare run, for fear of falling and twisting an ankle, but set forward across the field at a brisk walk, straining her ears as she went to try and make out what was happening back at the house. They were blundering about now in the garden, shouting and swearing. With luck, they would assume she was hidden somewhere there, and lose time searching.

But—take nothing for granted. She kept moving steadily away from the house, tripping from time to time on a patch of rough grass, or a hole in the ground, grateful for the sure touch of her stockinged feet. Something was trickling down her face. Blood, of course. She must have scratched herself many times in that wild dash through the hedge. But that—like her drenched and muddy skirts—was trivial compared with the vital question of . . . which way? She had crossed the field now and come, inevitably, to another ditch. Foolish, surely, to cross this one in blind flight as she had the last? Or—cross this one, and then try to find a path? Yes—a moment's consideration settled it. She was only a field's width from her pursuers. No time, yet, for lingering.

She set her teeth and struggled down the steep bank. This ditch was deeper; the mud sucked at her knees; something rustled close by. A water rat, she told herself, just as frightened as she was. Don't think about fright. Don't think about snakes underfoot. The ditch was wider, too, than the other one, but here at last, was the other bank and another field of grass. And—a sudden scurry of movement around her stopped the thudding of her heart for a moment. Absurd— these were sheep. And—if her pursuers were listening, were intelligent, the sheeps' outraged baaing as they woke and scattered would tell them where she was.

Thank God M. Tissot was not there. She moved forward steadily. Her feet had found a sheep track. Follow it. It might lead nowhere, but, equally, it might lead to a gate, a real path.

In fact, it led to another ditch. Could she be walking around in circles? Suppose this new ditch was, in fact, the one she had already crossed. Don't think like that—defeated thinking. But, it was true; already she was not quite sure which way she had come—where the house was. At the realization, she made herself stop and listen. No lights anywhere, no sound but a sheep, quite near her, munching away at the grass. No, she was wrong. Now she could hear, not very far off, the steady growl of the sea. And then, a new sound: horses' hoofs. Had one of the men ridden after M. Tissot? Most likely. Well, then, that was the direction of the road, and she was still steadily getting away from the house.

But—if she was to continue to do so, she must find a path. This time she turned along beside the ditch. If she kept going around the field, presently she must find a way out and a path. Don't think that it would very likely lead back to the house. If she found nothing at the corner, where the ditch turned, she would have to go back and try the other way.

It was awkward keeping along the side of the ditch in the dark. Once, she slipped, nearly fell in and had to stand for a minute or two, fighting down panic. No time for that. No time even to think about lying down on the soft, damp grass and waiting for morning. In the morning, it was true, she would be able to see her way, but so would they. And—this stretch of land behind Dungeness was the wildest, the most deserted of the whole bleak marsh. No use thinking daylight would bring help. Her help must come from herself.

Here was the corner of the ditch, and here—her tired feet slipped in the mud—was a real path. She went forward, hands outstretched. Yes, the ditch was bridged with earth here, and a rickety gate barred the way. She kilted drenched petticoats and climbed precariously up. It swayed under her weight, but held, and she paused to look about her from this point of slight vantage. Yes, there, behind her, all too near, still, was a light that must be in the house she had left. Nothing else. No glint of lanterns between it and her. Doubtless while one of the men went after M. Tissot, the other was contenting himself with a new search of the house and garden.

She had a little time then, and at last she was on a path—doubtless the one the sheep used. So—in the end it should take her to some lonely marshland farm. Unlucky that the Tretteign land was all the other way, toward Rye, so that she had had no reason to visit these parts.

Lord, she was tired. Once again, the idea of lying down, here, in the field, and sleeping, surged up to tempt her. Lunacy. She made herself walk steadily on. With luck, M. Tissot would be too occupied with his pursuit of Ross to care much about her escape. But—don't count on it. Here was another gate, rather more solid than the last one. Don't let yourself linger, sitting in precarious comfort on the top of it. Down again, and on . . .

And so for three more fields, while the blood dried on her face and little shivers of cold and fatigue began to run through her. How much longer could she go on? Madness to think of resting—the clammy touch of her wet petticoats was a reminder of what she would suffer if she stopped. No—at all costs she must find help, shelter . . .

Was she talking to herself? Whispering, "Help, shelter," to the time of her stumbling feet? Well, if it kept her going . . . and here was another gate. As before, she let herself pause for a moment on top to look about. No sign, now, of the house she had left, no sound but the mutter of the sea and a sudden shriek that tore along her nerves. But it was only some small marsh creature caught by a stoat—a ferret? She shivered in sympathy and climbed tiredly down from the gate. Here was a new surface for her bruised feet. Gravel, surely; almost a road? The one that led to the house? It might be. Go slowly, carefully. Listen, keep listening . . .

The gravel was noisy torture, but she found a grass verge and pushed herself steadily along, pausing from time to time to quiet her ragged breathing and listen for the sound of a horse. A small doubt nagged at her. How sure was she of her direction? Suppose this was indeed the road to the house she had left—and she was going toward it? Possible? Likely? Probable? And—would she know the house?

The answer, of course, was, bleakly, no. They had taken off her blindfold inside. If she was not careful, she might knock on her captors' door, asking for help. This was defeated thinking again. Don't let yourself . . .

Anyway, she would soon know. Something was looming up ahead of her, blacker than the general blackness of the night. No light showed anywhere. Well—it must be very late. No wonder if there was no one stirring. People kept early hours, out here on the marsh. And, surely, this total darkness and silence must be a good sign. Back at the house she had left, they would still be searching for her. And she was almost sure that the road had stopped at that house; here, it went past.

Then, why was she so reluctant to turn off it, to knock on the door and ask for help? Was it merely fatigue, dulling thought and clouding judgment that made this dark group of buildings seem so sinister, crouched, waiting by the road? Of course it was. In a minute she would be warm by a fire, telling her story to some sleepy farmer. She turned off the road past the dark shape of an outbuilding, and moved toward the house, feeling her way carefully over the surface of a neglected courtyard. And now, too late, she realized in a flash what had made her afraid of the house. Her quick ears had told her that there was something—someone—stirring in the dark courtyard, but her slow mind had refused to take in the message. She whirled at a movement behind her, felt a violent blow on the back of her head and fell into blackness.

Chapter Nineteen

HER HEAD was splitting. Where was she? She moved, feebly, on the narrow bed, and pain and memory seared through her. She had walked straight back into M. Tissot's trap. Absurd—lunatic—pitiful. But—why was she alive? And unbound? It would hurt horribly to open her eyes. It did.

For a few seconds, the room swam in front of them, then, with a painful effort, she made them focus. A different room. Hope surged up in her. Surely, a different house? Lived in, this one, though on a level of penurious poverty. Where, then; why?

She must have spoken the last word aloud, for it brought a rustling from the corner of the room behind the bed. Too painful to turn her head. She waited, and a woman moved forward into her line of vision. "Hush." An urgent finger on pale lips enforced the whispered command, but the tired face seemed friendly enough, only anxious, desperately anxious—frightened? She might be any age—very likely was little older than Christina herself, but dragged down by poverty, beyond caring about herself, a slattern with great clumps of dark, neglected hair falling around the haggard face.

"Hush!" she said again and moved forward close to the bed, to lean down and whisper, "If you're lucky, they'll forget about you. If not, I'll do what I can."

"They?" But as she whispered it, Christina was afraid she knew, and the woman's obvious fright at the question confirmed her fear. She had escaped from M. Tissot, only to stumble on one of the smugglers' marshland hideouts. Miraculous that they had not killed her at once.

The woman had moved away toward the door. She opened it, very carefully, just a crack, and they both strained their ears, listening to the mumble of voices below. Men—a great many of them, by the sound of it. A meeting of the whole gang? Disastrous. The woman sighed, shrugged and closed the door as carefully as she had opened it.

Close to the bed again, she whispered as carefully as before.

"They're still arguing. My Pete's taking your part. The others . . ." She let it hang. "One thing—there's not much time. "They'll have to get going. There aren't very many more hours of full dark and some of them have got to get clear up to the weald." A look of terror gave life to the weary face. "Don't tell them I said that. They'd kill me."

"Of course not." It was all horribly clear now. She had stumbled on the gang in the very act of sharing out a haul and making off with it on the dangerous journey down the dark ways inland and so to London.

"What—" The woman's upraised hand stopped her. Someone was coming upstairs.

"Shut your eyes." It was the merest breath. "You've not waked."

Good advice, surely? She closed her eyes and made herself lie limp on the bed as the door was flung open and a man's rough voice said, "Well, how is she?"

"Dead, by the looks of her. I don't know what Mr. Ross will say."

So they knew who she was. Was that good, or bad? Very likely it had saved her life so far.

So far. The man was swearing at the woman in a tone that suggested she was his wife. "To hell with Mr. Ross," he concluded. "The question is, what's to do with her?" From the sound of his voice he was moving forward, nearer to the bed. "The only secret woman's a dead one."

"No!" She must have flung herself between him and the bed. "What's she seen? Nothing! Anyway—you know she said nothing, before. Why should she now? Let me keep her here till all's safe. Pete— I know about her. Betty tells me things. She's good. Pete, she's going to start a school for the children, so they needn't grow up as we have, with nothing. You can't let them kill her."

"The children again! Can you think of nothing else!" But his voice was no nearer. "I suppose we could keep her here. I'm not on the run tonight. You'd look after her?"

"Of course. Pete—they'd pay. I'm sure they would."

"The old man?" This was clearly a new idea. "I reckon you might have something there." A shout from downstairs. "Right, I'm coming. . . . I've to see them on the way. Shouldn't be too long. You won't mind being locked in with her."

"Locked? But Pete, if the children wake?"

"To hell with the children. Just make up your mind, Madge. D'you want to keep her alive—or not?"

"Oh, Pete, I do. Betty says—"

"Damn Betty. Right, then. No nonsense, mind, and no talking. I'll be back before dawn. With luck, she'll be dead by then anyway."

Lying at once rigid and apparently limp, Christina heard the door close at last, the grinding of a heavy key in the lock. Odd to have a door here that locked. Or—not so odd? Had this room been used as a prison before? There were stories enough, she knew, of people who had crossed the smugglers' path—and never been seen again. Faced with transportation for life, the gangs might well think murder a cheap price to pay for possible freedom. She shivered, and opened her eyes. The woman—Madge, he had called her—was standing close by the bed, candle in hand, looking at her anxiously. Once again, her first word was whispered. "Hush."

Christina nodded wordlessly. Sounds of bustle downstairs suggested that the gang were getting ready to leave. Now, voices were raised, apparently in argument—they came nearer—to the foot of the stairs? The woman—Madge—stood rigid, listening, the candle shaking in her hand so that great gobbets of tallow fell on the floor. Then the voices died away again, a door closed somewhere in the house and presently there were sounds of talk and movement outside.

"Thank God," Madge whispered. "They're going. But— wait." She put the candle down on the window ledge and subsided limply on to a piece of wood that served as a stool. She was shaking all over, now the crisis was past, and Christina, watching her, realized what a risk she had taken. Nor was it over yet. They were locked in here, waiting for the man—Pete—to come back. Her eyes went to the window.

Madge must have been watching her. "No," she whispered. "It's barred. Besides—he'd kill me."

"You could come too."

"And the children? Anyway, it's hopeless. I know . . ." She moved over to listen at the window. "They're gone now." But she kept her voice low. "Pete said he'd be back at dawn. He'll have to tell the new leader about you. He wasn't there tonight. They'll do what he says."

"Even if it's murder?"

"Oh—I hope it won't be. Why should it?" She was trying to convince herself. "You didn't see them, after all. That's what Pete always tells me . . . don't look, don't hear, don't know. I stay up here, when they come, with the children, and watch the wall—and pray. Betty's my cousin," she explained. "She's talked about you. I'll do what I can."

But what could she do? Christina made herself sit up, made herself think, defying the pain in her head. "Who is he?" she asked. "The new leader?"

"I don't know." The quick disclaimer carried conviction. "A stranger. French, Pete thinks, an *emigré*—but for God's sake don't say I told you. I'm not supposed to know that, but Pete talks, sometimes, when they've been drinking."

"I won't tell." Had she managed to keep her voice steady? A stranger—and French. Don't let Madge see what a blow this was. But—face it just the same. Every logic indicated that the smugglers' new leader was M. Tissot himself. If he was—don't think about that, but make sure, if possible. "Has he been leader long?" She made the question casual.

"Oh no. There's been so many. They keep changing, since they lost the Captain. This one took over after the attack on the Grange—the one that didn't come off."

"I see." She did indeed. M. Tissot had betrayed the gang's plans, and taken advantage of the consequent panic and confusion to get control. Useless to tell Madge this—but, her husband? Would he believe her? She had better be convincing . . . her life depended on it, and very likely his, too, and the rest of the gang's. For if M. Tissot had taken control of the smugglers, it could only be for his own purposes—and Napoleon's. Try to explain this to Madge? No—useless. Wait, and pray that Pete came back before he saw M. Tissot. Here was

a glimmer of hope. With luck, M. Tissot would be busy looking for her. Ironically, Pete might not find him to tell him
where she was.

"How do you feel?" Madge's question interrupted her
thoughts.

"Better." Surprisingly, it was true. "But you look exhausted. Lie down here and rest." She was only a little un-
steady on her feet as she moved over to the window. "I'll sit
here and watch. I must speak to your husband the moment
he gets back. I think I can tell him something about his new
leader. Something he should know at once."

"Something bad? Pete said no good would come of a
Frenchman . . ." Her voice dwindled off. She had indeed
been exhausted.

Christina blew out the stub of candle and settled herself as
comfortably as she could on the floor below the window. She,
too, was tired out—or would be if she let herself think of it.
The scratches on her face hurt, her bruised feet ached and
the clammy touch of her drenched skirts sent an occasional
long shiver through her. But she had more urgent things to
think about. She must work out how to convince Pete that
his new leader was, in fact, a French agent. More lives than
her own depended on that. For she did not like to think of
the part M. Tissot and the smugglers might play in an invasion. Not that the men would intentionally act the part of
traitors, but they might easily not understand what they were
doing until it was too late. So—at all costs—she must convince them. She sat stiffly upright to keep awake, and mar-
shaled her arguments as time dragged by, punctuated by little
gurgling snores from Madge and the occasional cry of a night
bird out there free in the dark.

She must, in the end, have dozed off, for when she opened
her eyes gray daylight was filtering into the room through the
broken panes of a filthy window. What had waked her? Now
she heard it again—cautious movement downstairs. Pete? Or
M. Tissot? In one silent movement, she was by the bed, shaking Madge awake. "Someone's downstairs," she whispered,
but the woman only groaned, and muttered something, and
buried her face more deeply in the ragged bedclothes.

Footsteps on the stairs, now, and the sound of the key in
the lock. "Madge?" Pete's voice, surely—who else would call
her by name?

"She's fast asleep." Christina moved over to the door. "You're her husband? I must talk to you. It's a matter of life and death—yours."

"Dammit, you're alive then. What d'you mean, life and death?" He swung the door open and stood facing her, a huge shadow in the half light. "No tricks, now."

"Of course not." If she could only see his face. "Have you seen your leader yet?"

"Our leader? Goddamn the bitch. What's she been tattling about?" He moved threateningly forward into the room and a pale ray of light caught his face. It was coarse, but not brutal —and, thank God, not stupid either.

"You'll live to be grateful to her." Take and keep a tone of command. "You've not seen him, have you? He wasn't where you expected him to be?" His expression told her that she was right. "I'll tell you why not." She pursued her advantage. "Because he's a French agent, using you and the gang for his own purposes. No—listen! You remember the attack that was planned on the Grange? And that I was the one who gave the alarm?"

"Yes—what of it?" She had his attention now.

"It was a Frenchman who told me about it. M. Tissot, he called himself. He was wounded on the beach last autumn. Mr. Ross brought him back to the Grange and I nursed him in the cloisters. Only—he tricked me and escaped. A slight man, with a sallow face, speaks English perfectly, with the faintest trace of an accent, poses as an *emigré*, of course, but, I tell you, he's Boney's agent. He's making you traitors, the lot of you. You'll find yourselves helping in the invasion."

"No!" It was an automatic reaction and he followed it with a string of oaths, covering, she suspected, desperate thought. "You're sure?" he asked at last.

How to convince him? Aware all the time of the minutes running by, she made herself go over all the evidence with him, patiently and slowly. "It must be him," she concluded. "Don't you see? It all fits together."

"I dunno." He scratched his head dubiously. "I'm sure I dunno what to do for the best. If he's really playing Boney's game . . ." Another string of oaths underlined his position as a loyal Englishman. "Hanging's too good for him. But"—a gleam in sharp little eyes—"he brings in the stuff all right, and tight. We'd need to be precious sure—"

"Of course he brings in the stuff. More than you've ever had before?" she hazarded.

"Yes—and cheaper." A doubtful note in his voice here. Had this caused speculation already in the gang?

"Well, naturally. It's the bait—and you've taken it, hook, line, and sinker. What has he asked you about the defenses, here on the marsh?"

"Well—o' course he needed to know what to expect." But she had him shaken now; his slow brain was coming around to accepting the idea of M. Tissot as an enemy agent. "What's to do?" he asked at last.

"If you were to catch him, and hand him over to the army . . ." She knew at once that she had gone too far.

"Us! And be transported for our pains? Thank you, no."

"Let me go then and I'll—"

Again she had gone too far. "So that's your game." He backed away from her, his hand on the door. "Not likely. You may be right about the frog—I won't say yes, I won't say no; but one thing I do know and that's that you're staying right here. My life wouldn't be worth a minute's purchase if I let you go. You're worth money, see—"

"But how long? What are you going to do? You'll not tell him?"

"Not yet anyhow. Here . . ." A sudden lunge caught her wrist and held it in a grip of iron as he dragged her over to the cot where Madge lay in deep sleep. Still holding Christina in a grip that hurt, he shook his wife roughly awake and told her to stir herself and get some breakfast. "I'm starved. As for you"—he gave Christina's wrist a last warning squeeze that brought angry blood to her face—"just keep quiet, will you, and thank God you're alive."

He slammed the door behind them and Christina sat down shakily on the bed. Had she achieved anything? Impossible to tell. A little time, perhaps? Fatigue washed over her in great waves. Give up? Lie down, and sleep and sleep and sleep. No, there was one thing to do first. She moved over to the window to peer out into the dim gray morning. A derelict farmyard, and beyond it, all awash with mist, the marsh. And, on the window, heavy iron bars. No hope of escape this way; the room had indeed been used as a prison before. Well then . . . she moved like an automaton back to the bed, fell across it and was asleep.

When she woke, evening sunshine showed up in the film of dust over the room. She was stiff and chilled, but her head had stopped aching and she was ravenously hungry. It was agony to put her feet to the floor, but she made herself do so and moved stiffly over to listen at the locked door. Silence. No—somewhere a child was crying. A door banged and she heard a man's voice raised in anger. Almost certainly, Madge's husband, Pete. She tiptoed back to the bed. This was no time to call attention to herself.

Much later, there came a little tapping at the door. "How are you?" Madge's voice.

"Starving."

"I'll tell him." She came back a few minutes later. "He says"—in this house there was obviously only one "he"— "he's got to go out. I can feed you, but if you escape, he'll kill me. D'you understand?"

"Yes, of course. I promise I'll do nothing."

"He said I could trust you. If you promised—word of a Tretteign—I'll bring you something. When he's gone. You're to stay up here, though." She anticipated Christina's next request. "Safer, he says."

Safer? Had he at last believed what she had told him about Tissot? Madge, when she returned had no idea. "He tells me nothing. Not when he's sober. I'm sorry it's no better." She put down a plate of bread and cheese and a mug of filmy water.

Both plate and mug were cracked and filthy. Christina, concentrating on making herself eat slowly, hardly noticed. As she was eating, a boy and girl came and peered cautiously around the corner of the door. Unlike their mother, they were almost clean and their hair showed signs of careful combing. Madge might have given up for herself, but for her children she still had hope. "They're too young to talk about you," she explained. "Not that there's anyone for them to talk to, down here on the marsh. Oh—how I hate it." It was a cry from the heart.

"You don't come from round here?"

"No—I'm London-born. If I'd only known . . ." She saw that Christina had finished and reached out to pick up the plate and mug. "Pete says I'm to lock you up again between whiles," she explained. "Safer so. You don't mind?"

Christina could not help smiling. "I won't have to. But—could I have some water? My feet—"

Madge exclaimed with horror at sight of them and went off to fetch a bucket of water from the well and a handful of fairly clean rags. "You should have the doctor. I wish I knew when Pete would be back."

Or what he's doing, thought Christina. "He gave you no idea?" she asked.

"No. He often leaves us like this. I hate it . . ." She shivered. "I hate the marsh, and the quietness, and that everlasting sea. Oh, I wish we was back in London!"

"If I escape from here alive, I'll see you get there. What would you like to do, you and Pete, if you could?"

"Oh—run a little inn, miss. On one of the main roads out of town. He's that good with horses, and I'm a fair cook. But what use is that down here on the marsh? We were mad when we came here. He don't want"—she lowered her voice and looked around nervously—"He don't want to smuggle, miss, but we were starving when the offer came. What could he do? You can't just listen to the children crying, not when you know it's hunger. But, miss, you're not having me on? You might really be able to set us up in London, where they couldn't get at us?"

"The gang, you mean? I think you'd do better to leave with their consent. From the stories one hears . . ." No need to finish the sentence. "But as to setting you up in an inn—yes, if you get me out of here alive, I promise you, I'll do it."

"Oh, miss! To get away from the marsh . . . back to town, where there are people, talk, lights at night. You don't know what it means. I hardly dare think about it. But—could you?"

"You're wondering if I can afford it." This was no time to beat about the bush. "I promise you, I can. My father left me some money of my own. You shall have your inn wherever you choose. I promise—word of a Tretteign." And then, "Good God! How could I forget! Do you know what the date is?"

"No, miss." But Christina was not listening. A date she had been looking forward to all winter had slipped by unnoticed. She had been six months at the Dark House and was free, at last, of her promise to her father. When she got back, everything would be different. When? *If* she got back.

Chapter Twenty

NIGHT AGAIN, and the moon a mere rag among hurrying clouds. Alone in the dark little room, Christina jumped up suddenly, alerted by a sound below. Merely the clink of metal on stone—a simple little domestic sound, but it must mean that the moment of crisis had come. The gang were here, digging up their second load of smuggled goods.

Was Tissot with them? If he was, she might as well say her prayers; he could not afford to let her survive. If he was not, she had a chance, a slender one, if she could only convince them as she thought she had Pete. Well, at least it would not be long. She felt along the window ledge for the broken-toothed comb Madge had lent her, and tidied her hair as best she might. The look of a lady and an air of command might help her—if she was not already beyond help.

Time ebbed by. Presently there was a commotion in the yard below. The train of borrowed pack animals must be getting under way. Many a marshland farmer would wake to-morrow morning to find one of his horses missing—and the next day find it back, with an offering of brandy or tea as pay for its use. Would she wake tomorrow morning?

Could they have forgotten all about her? There were unmistakable noises now of the convoy getting started. Or—was M. Tissot waiting, so that the smallest number of men would witness her murder, before he disposed of her? Now—now there was a noise on the stairs, the key turned heavily in the lock, Pete stood outside, lantern in hand. "Come," he said, "we want to talk to you."

"And about time too." Behave as if nothing was the matter. Sweep past him and walk downstairs, head high, as if he was bound to stand back for her.

He did. She led the way, pushed open the door at the foot of the little stairs and found three masked men waiting in the main room of the house. Her heart leapt. Surely the masks spelt hope? And at least from their build she was sure that none of them was Tissot. Having observed this, she moved forward with apparent calm into the room. It looked unwontedly comfortable, with a fire blazing on the hearth, tallow dips in bottles casting a comparatively good light, food and a squat bottle on the makeshift table. A quick glance at the three men showed them flushed under their masks, but probably not drunk—yet.

She moved over to the room's one passable chair and sat down. No sign of Madge. Doubtless she had been shut in with the children when the gang arrived. "Well?" she said.

"These are my friends." Pete had closed the door of the stair behind him and put down his lantern. "They want to hear what you have to say—about him."

"The Frenchman? Gladly." She told it over again in full, calm detail. At last, she spoke directly to the tall mask she had recognized as the leader among them. "I'm a Tretteign. I know my friends. I've promised Madge"—here a glance for Pete—"I've promised her an inn on one of the roads into town. If we can all forget what has happened, I think I can offer you something still better."

"Prove it." This was, comparatively speaking, an educated man, and her task so much the easier.

"You're all patriotic Englishmen, I know. That's why I've told you about M. Tissot, about what you have unwittingly got yourselves into. Well—don't you see, here's your chance of free pardons for anything you may have done . . ." Leave it as vague as possible, pretend to know nothing of the loaded beasts that were now making their darkling way across the marsh. "The whole country is invasion mad—and with cause. Catch M. Tissot—a known French agent, hand him over to the authorities as publicly as possible—you'll be the heroes of the hour—everything else forgotten. Would you be glad of a chance to turn"—what word to use? Well—chance it—"respectable?"

At least, she had made them think. They were conferring together now in voices so low that she could hear nothing, try as she would. But—she heard something else that they missed in their preoccupation. Someone was moving about, very stealthily, outside. M. Tissot himself? Madge, perhaps, or one of the gang on some nefarious purpose of his own? Or—Ross, come to look for her? Against all reason she believed this. Useless to tell herself that Ross was in France, very likely dead or in prison. . . . Something in her was perfectly sure that he was outside that window now, a darker shade in the darkness, looking in.

Suppose she was wrong. Suppose it was Tissot who would fling open the door any minute now. She clenched her teeth. Get it wrong and she was as good as dead. But her mind had made itself up. Resolutely, she looked away from the window, with its telltale flicker of movement, lest her eyes should draw someone else's to it.

The conference in the corner was growing more heated. Voices rose. "Too dangerous," said one. "She knows me," growled Pete. So much for Madge's little inn on the London road. They were advancing on her now; she rose to her feet to meet them.

"I'm sorry." The one who acted the leader sounded as if he might even mean it. "You must see that you know too much."

"Nothing I can't forget." Play it out to the last moment, keep their attention on her and believe . . . believe with all her heart that Ross was outside, waiting the moment to burst in. No hope, judging by the slow, reluctant advance upon her, but in him.

"An accident," said the leader. "One of the gravel pits. So —handle her carefully." Again that note of regret, almost of apology. "We'll make it quick." They were all around her now, and she could smell fatigue and fear, sour from their bodies. One of them caught her hands and twisted them expertly behind her back. "Drowning," said the leader. "A bucketful of water. Quick."

If she could only see their eyes. Something inhuman about these masked faces made appealing to them doubly hard. "It's all true, what I've told you." She kept her voice steady. "Word of a Tretteign. I'm giving you the chance of your lives. You're fools if you let it slip."

"Then—we're fools." It was final. "Quick, you."

Movement behind her. The bucket of water? With a sudden wrench she pulled free of the hands that held her, stood clear and stared them down with huge, contemptuous eyes. "Fools!" She spat it at them. "And murderers. Who shall have the privilege of drowning me? I'll not make it easy for you, I promise. I'll make it something you'll remember as long as you live. We Tretteigns walk, you know. One of us haunts the Dark House already. I shall walk always beside you, reminding you of the chance I gave you, that you had not the wits to take. Your hands will tremble, you'll remember me and miss your aim when you most need to be steady. Then you'll know I am there, with the curse of the Tretteigns upon you."

"Damn you." For a moment, she had shaken them, but she had also made them angry enough to kill. She could see it in the way they moved forward.

Glass crashed behind her. "Very still, all of you." Ross's voice. "I'll shoot the first man who moves. Quick, Chris, here to me."

She was there already, where he leaned in through the window that was too small for him to pass. "Take the pistol from my belt. Steady now." He had felt her tremble, but could not know that it was less from fear than from the electric shock of his touch. "Don't get between me and them. I thought you'd never give me a clear line of fire. That's it." She had done as he told her. "Now, you cover those two."

"Yes." She had the gun cocked and ready in a hand as firm as his own.

"My cousin's as good a shot as I am." His voice controlled a little ripple of movement in the room. "I'd go on keeping still, if I were you."

"That's all very fine." The leader was standing rigid where Ross's voice had halted him. "But you know you can't get her out of here."

It was all too evidently true. To get to the door, Christina would have to move between Ross and the smugglers. They would have her instantly as a hostage.

"No," Ross said cheerfully. "It's too bad, isn't it? I can really see no alternative to shooting the lot of you. Unless, perhaps, you can suggest one? I find myself less cold-blooded than you. I don't mind letting you live, if you can show me how I can safely do so."

"Be damned to you!" As the leader sprang forward, Christina shot him in the leg.

"Admirable." Not a tone's difference in Ross's voice. "I'll cover the rest of them, Chris, while you reload. And now, my friends, I hope you see that we mean what we say. There are only three of you now, to all intents and purposes. Do you want to go on till there is only one?"

"Let them go, I say." This was Pete. "You wouldn't really hurt us, Mr. Ross? I never wanted to harm her, I promise I didn't."

"No? You just went with the crowd?" His voice was deadly. "Then you can go with the crowd now." He was taking aim.

"No, Ross, wait." Christina kept her steady aim fixed on the man who had fallen to her share. "His wife's been good to me. I'd like to spare him, if you think we can."

"Do you hear her?" Ross spoke directly to Pete. "You were fetching a bucket of water to drown her, like a sick kitten, and she would like to spare you. Well—will you make it possible for us?"

"God, yes. What must I do?"

"Tie up your friends. Then we can talk." And, when Pete hesitated for a moment. "Or be shot, all of you, as your leader has. He looks as if he could do with some help, by the way. He's bleeding fast. If you care."

"I care about myself." Pete again.

"Good. Then move forward, take the rope that lies so conveniently ready on the table—for you, I suppose, Chris?—and tie them carefully. Very carefully. Remember, we are watching."

The others swore at Pete horribly as he went to work, and Chris, watching, thought that poor Madge would need to go farther than London if she was to be safe in her little inn. "Don't worry, Pete," she said. "You shall go to America, you and your family. You'll not regret this day's work, I promise."

Beside her, Ross laughed. "You're incorrigible, Chris. Think about yourself, for a change. As for these curs, I like your plan for them best."

"Mine?"

"I've been listening for some time, waiting my chance. You're right, of course. They're fools, and murderous ones, but they're marshmen, for all that. And—Chris—I got them into this—it's my duty to get them out."

"Duty of a Tretteign?" She could not keep the smile out of her voice.

"Yes, if you like. Ah, that's better." The two remaining masked men were now securely tied, while their leader lay on the floor, blood pouring from the wound in his leg. "Now, you"—to Pete—"sit down on that chair, your hands on the table, and listen as if your life depended on it. Which it does."

"Yes, sir." But his eyes kept flickering toward where Ross still leaned in at the window, as if they expected something.

"Ross! He's watching for someone." And then, to Pete. "You sent for M. Tissot?"

"He did." Pete glanced toward the wounded man.

"He may be quite near," Christina said. "And—not alone."

"Quite so. And very convenient—for us. Keep him covered, Chris, I'm coming in."

Absurd to feel so bereft when the comforting warmth of his shoulder moved away from beside her. But she held her gun steady on Pete, keeping an eye at the same time on the wounded leader. "Don't move." She had seen him gather himself together. "I mean it." A crash in the next room told her that Ross had burst in a window. Now he opened the door and came to stand beside her.

"So Tissot's coming here. Very well, now's the time to make up your minds." He spoke to the three men impartially, ignoring their wounded leader on the floor. "Which side are you on? French or English?"

"He's really one of their's?" Pete was now the spokesman.

"Yes. You should have believed Miss Tretton. I can give you no better proof than she did, but I advise you to accept it. And—time's running out. Do I tie you up too?"

"No, dammit. I'll believe *you*, Mr. Ross. What do we do?"

"How soon will he be here?"

"Any moment now."

"And how many?"

"Only two others."

"Good. In that case I think we'll need no help from our friends here. Help me get them out of sight, will you?" And, when they had been stowed, protesting, in the dark and noisome scullery, "Now, Chris, you're a prisoner, remember. Sitting at the table, very despondent, with Pete guarding you. The pistol under the table where it won't show but ready cocked. Pete, you'll stand by to let them in and tie them up as I disarm them. And, one more thing, I promise you, word of a Tretteign, if you betray me, I'll kill you."

"He won't," said Christina. "His wife and children are upstairs. Are they safely locked in, by the way?"

"Of course. What d'you take me for?"

"A fool." But she said it without malice.

"Hush!" Ross had already placed himself in the corner of a big cupboard where he would be invisible from the window. "Here they come."

No secrecy about his arrival. M. Tissot expected nothing but friends. They could hear horses ridden rapidly up to the house, a little bustle of dismounting, and then a loud knocking on the door that led directly into the kitchen.

"Don't forget that I've got you covered." Ross whispered his warning as Pete moved across the room to open the door.

In a few moments, Tissot and another man entered the room—doubtless the third would be out holding the horses. "Where are the others?" Tissot had taken in Christina's forlorn appearance with a glance and moved forward confidently into the room.

"Where you'll soon join them. That's right." Ross's gun had sent both men's hands automatically into the air.

"The devil! When did you get back?" You had to admire Tissot's coolness.

"Last night. Tie them up, Pete. Obliging of you to bring horses. Do any of the rooms in this wretched house lock, Christina?"

"There's one upstairs." She shivered a little at the memory. "And, I suppose, the one Madge is in."

"Yes. Fetch her, would you, and the children?"

"What about the man outside?"

"You're right. We should deal with him first. You keep watch here while I bring him in. There must be something I can tie the horses to."

Twenty minutes later, it was all settled. The two sets of prisoners were securely tied and deposited in separate locked rooms, with Madge downstairs as guard. Christina had offered to stay with her, since Ross refused to trust Pete so far, but he had been firm. "You're taking no more risks tonight, Chris. I never want to go through a day like this one again. I don't care if the whole lot of them escape, so long as I have you safe."

"They won't escape." Madge had settled her two sleepy children in blankets on the floor. "I'll kill them first." She meant it. "You'll not forget my inn, Miss Tretton?"

"Don't worry, I won't. I owe her my life," she explained to Ross. "They'd have killed me when they caught me, but for her."

"Don't speak of it. When I got back and found you missing . . ." He stopped. "There'll be time to talk of that. The question now is, how are we to get you to Trevis's headquarters?"

"I'll ride of course. What a fortunate thing it's dark. You and Pete will just have to ride on ahead. This dress is past praying for anyway. Don't look so worried. I've ridden astride often enough when I was a girl. I can manage."

"I think you can do anything." Pete was busy untying the horses and, just for a moment, they were alone together. "Chris! When I thought you dead—I wanted nothing but to die too. I've been—almost mad, I think, all day, looking for you from one of the smugglers' hideouts to the next. If I'd not found you—"

"I'm very glad you did." Pete had the horses ready now. "I would have been dead, I think, in five minutes. And drowned in a bucket, too, like that poor Duke of Clarence. Only water instead of wine. A dreary end."

"Don't talk about it. I don't believe I'll ever feel safe to let you out of my sight again."

"That's going to present its problems. Oh, thank you, Pete . . ." He had brought the smallest of the three marsh ponies for her to mount. "I can manage perfectly by myself." This to Ross, who was still close beside her.

"That's the worst of it. I know you can. But you're not going to, Chris. Here. Up with those skirts." And as she obediently scooped up tattered muslin, he lifted her in strong arms that made nothing of her, and set her in the saddle. Then, instead of letting her go, he pulled her close against him. "I've done a lifetime's thinking today, Chris." Pete had gone back into the house and the two of them were alone there in the dark. "You're what I need. You're all I need. Be honest with me, Chris, here in the shadow of death. Tell me you feel it too. It can't be one-sided, this passion that runs through me when I hold you thus. Admit it, Chris! Tell me it's not."

"Dear lunatic . . ." She stopped. Almost, with his arms close around her, she had poured it all out, had said, "I've loved you always," but something female, something she owed to her mother, stopped the words on her tongue. "And Sophie?" She made it light, teasing.

"Sophie!" His arm, closer still around her waist, told her he knew she had yielded. "How dare you, Chris! That was a folly, a nothing. . . . What did you call me? Lunatic? Well, that's about it. I was moonstruck, crazy . . . If you'll just forgive me, Chris, and bear with me . . ."

"Well . . . I'll try." Teasing now.

"You'll do nothing of the kind." His arm moved up, to find her head and bring it ruthlessly down to meet his. "I'm not asking you, Chris, I'm telling you." His lips left hers at last. "You're mine. To hold you like this—God, Chris, if you knew what it cost me not to speak before I left for France. But I had no right."

"And now?"

"I'm past caring. When I found you missing—thought I'd never see you again—everything was suddenly quite simple. Horribly simple. Nothing else matters, now I've found you. We're part of each other, you and I. It's a fact . . . there's nothing to be done about it."

"No?" Again she kept it light, would not let herself tell him how long she had felt this.

"Do you know"—oddly, his next words echoed her thoughts—"the strange thing is—I know now—it's all been madness. I've been yours ever since that first night we met. Do you remember, Chris?"

"Of course I do. I bit you."

"Vixen! Bite me now, if you dare." Once again, she surrendered, was engulfed in his kiss. Emerging, shaken and with lips that hurt, she was aware for the first time of Pete, now anxiously hovering.

"Ross! Darling! We should be going."

"My dear"—for a moment longer he held her close—"call me that, and I'll do anything in the world—except leave you. But, you're right. Here, Pete, my horse!"

"I'm sure I wish you very happy, the both of you." Pete

brought the third horse forward. "If I'd only a'known, miss, I'd never a'let it happen—any of it. Mr. Ross's young lady . . ."

Christina could not help laughing. "Madge saved me because she thought I'd start a school for her children, and Pete would have because I was your young lady, Ross. Can no one love me for myself alone?"

"No one but me, and I, poor fool, can't help myself."

"I said you were a lunatic. But, Ross, what are we going to do?"

"Marry."

"Yes, love—and then?"

"Oh—I see." He seemed to come back from a distance. "Of course, you don't know. I came back by way of London. Ride on a little, Pete." And then, when he was out of earshot. "I've done what Pitt wanted. Re-established his chain of agents and brought him news. Villeneuve will be out again any time now, but, please God, he'll find Nelson ready for him. And—I've got my commission. That's why we must be married at once. I may have to go any day."

"Then I'll come too."

"What? Impossible. The ardors of a campaign—"

"Well, really, love, look at me now. Don't you think I might be safer, with the British Army to protect me, than here on the marsh with your smuggler friends about?"

"Oh—as to them. We're going to take care of that. Pete and his friends caught Tissot, remember."

"Oh they did, did they? How odd, I thought it came about quite otherwise."

"I can't help that. Here, Pete, I want to talk to you." And from then until they reached the army post he coached them ruthlessly in the story they were to tell. "You, of course, my love," he concluded, "are much too gravely shaken by your experience to say anything at all. You will leave it to Pete and me."

"Should I have a mild case of hysterics, do you think, for good measure?"

"If you do, I promise I'll beat you, there and then. You should have seen the hysterics Sophie was having when I got to the Grange."

"Oh dear—they must be so anxious. Let's get home as soon as we can."

"I promise you, love, we will."

He was as good as his word. Christina had refused even to dismount, pleading that remounting would be too much to bear. "Besides, something tells me I'm best out here, in the dark."

It seemed hardly any time that she sat her tired horse, exhausted herself, but inexpressibly content. Then Ross was back, with Trevis full of anxious inquiry at his side. She brushed it away. "There's nothing wrong with me that a good night's sleep won't cure."

"Gallant!" said Trevis. "At least, thank God, we can send you home by carriage. Here it comes."

"Now that is good news." Ross was already beside her, to lift her in one powerful movement from the saddle and carry her over to the carriage that had drawn up beside them.

"There." He deposited her with loving lack of ceremony on the seat and turned back to Trevis. "You'll lose no time?"

"We march directly."

"Good. You'll let me know—I only wish I could come too."

"In the morning. And I shall hope for good reports of you, Miss Tretton."

"Thank you." The carriage was moving forward at last. Ross's arm reached out, found her in the darkness and pulled her against him so that her head rested against his shoulder. She let out a little sigh of pure happiness as its current ran strong between them once more. Almost too strong. "Ross?" Her voice was teasing.

"Yes, love?"

"Did you really want to go with Trevis and his men?"

"Well—yes"—the strong arm held her closer than ever—"and no. I would not leave you now for anything in the world—but, I confess I would be relieved to know that that woman had obeyed orders."

"Madge? What orders?"

"I told her to let the smugglers free when she heard the soldiers coming. It will rather spoil our story if she fails to do so."

"So it will." She could not make herself care about it. Her head drooped lower on his shoulder. "What a waste . . ." She was asleep.

She waked when the carriage stopped, and was vaguely aware of Ross carrying her indoors, of anxious faces, of exclamations, and, above all, of Ross, ruthlessly making his way through the little crowd of excited, questioning women and up the stairs to her room, where he deposited her on her bed. "Sleep well, my love." Their third kiss—ecstasy—but she could not keep her eyes open. Someone pulled off the shoes Madge had lent her. More exclamations, and Ross's voice, "In the morning. Leave her in peace now." Then blessed darkness to plunge fathoms down in sleep.

Waking at last to happiness and broad daylight, she winced as her bruised feet felt the floor, and limped across to the window. The marsh below was awash with sunshine, the sea sparkled, the old house was warm with the feeling of another winter safely over. "It's spring," she thought, "and I'm home. And . . . Ross." Now, thinking of him, she could not dress fast enough. No time to ring, and wait, and answer Betty's questions. So much to do today, so much to settle, and through it all, the warm glow of happiness, and Ross.

Now, surely, she heard his voice. But raised in anger, in her grandfather's room. Ross, angry, today? No time to wince as she forced swollen feet into her softest pair of kid slippers. She opened her door and heard her grandfather's furious voice:

"This is no time for marrying, for engagements . . . Pah! I tell you, we've lost the Grange!"

"I don't understand." This was Ross, calmer now, his voice raised to carry above a babble of female ones. Were they all there then? Greg was hanging about outside the half-open door of her grandfather's rooms. His anxious face lit up at sight of her. "Miss Christina! He ought to be stopped. He's had bad news. I'm afraid . . ."

"Yes. I can hear." Greg stood aside and she crossed the room to put a gentle hand on her grandfather's shoulder as he made to rise from his chair, his own hands shaking on the cane he used to steady himself. "Don't, Grandfather. It'll be all right, I promise you."

" 'All right!' she says. Because you and Ross are in a fool's paradise of happiness everything in the world must be rosy. But you're wrong, girl. I tell you, as I've just told them, we've lost the Grange. Here, read it if you don't believe me, and mock me if you must." He pushed a letter into her hand. "But I say again, I'd a right to do what I wished with my own. It's not my fault if it's all gone wrong. How was I to know this cursed war would drag on forever? We're ruined, I tell you, ruined."

"Don't, Grandfather." She could feel him shaking under her steadying hand. "Aunt Tretteign, hush! There's no need for hysterics. Sophie, fetch Grandfather his pills."

"No! I tell you, I want to die. All my life I've worked for the Grange, loved it, lived for it when none of you thought of anything but yourselves, and now—this. I'll not live to see it go."

"But, Grandfather, it's not going. Here, for my sake, take your pill, drink this and listen to me."

"What do you mean, it's not going? Can't you read, girl?" But he took the pill in his shaking hand and swallowed it with a little of the water she held for him.

"It looks bad, I agree." She dropped the letter carelessly on a side table. "But I promise you, it's not so bad as it looks. Do you feel better now? Can you stand another shock—a pleasant one, I hope you'll think it?"

"What do you mean?" His voice was easier. She had contrived, as she intended, to lower the tension in the room.

"That I've a confession to make." Her eyes met Ross's across the room. "I had meant to tell Ross first, since it concerns him. You'll forgive me, Ross?"

"Anything."

"Well then." It was oddly difficult to say it now. "Grandfather, you must forgive me too. You see, I promised Father. He . . . he wanted, more than anything for me to be happy. He said that to be sure, to be safe, I must come and live here for six months before I told you."

"Told me what, girl?" He was beginning to shake again. She must make it quick.

"Grandfather, that I'm rich, quite dreadfully rich. Will you forgive me?"

"I don't understand." He had aged appallingly since she saw him last. "Rich? You can't be. How?"

"D'you remember how Father used to go off to Battle to work in the iron mines there?"

"Of course I do! Quite unsuitable for a Tretteign, and so I told him. But what's that to the purpose?"

"Just this." There was no way she could sweeten it for

him. "After Mother went, he gave up trapping. I don't think he could bear it any more, alone in the wilds. I'm sorry, Mother." Their eyes met in friendly comprehension across the room. "He went down to Pennsylvania. And, Grandfather, he discovered an iron mine. When he died he was one of the richest men in the Union. It's all right, Grandfather. We can pay off this"—a light tap made the letter unimportant—"buy back the land you've had to part with—we'll still be dreadfully rich. I don't entirely understand about iron, but it seems to be excessively important."

"It's important all right." This was Ross. "Have you still control, Chris?"

"Through my man of business. Yes. You must advise me what I should do."

"Wash your hands of the lot of us!" Violently. "You're an heiress. What should you be doing here?"

"Ross! I came home, don't you understand?" And I met you on the marsh. But don't say that. Just give him time.

"He's right." Explosively from the old man. "What have we done for you, that you should spend your fortune on the Dark House?"

"Taken me in. Liked me a little, I hope. Don't you see—I came here, an American, a stranger. Now—I knew it when I thought I might never see it again—the Dark House is my home. It doesn't matter what you say, Grandfather, we're going to keep it. If we can keep the iron mine, too, so much the better, but what's an iron mine compared to the Dark House?"

"But—for me? I can't let you." He was shaking again.

"I didn't say for you." She had thought hard about this. Her eyes appealed to Ross for understanding. "For all of us, the Tretteigns. You made Ross and me get engaged, remember, back before Christmas, because you wanted an heir for the Grange. Well, we save the Grange . . . for the heir."

"Well I'll be damned," said Ross. For a moment his eyes met hers, angry and challenging. Then, deliciously, like sunshine, laughter crept into them. "Chris." He came across the room to her. "You ought to be ashamed of yourself." But his arm was around her again, warm as sunlight, warm as happiness.

"Oh, I am." She raised her face to his. "Forgive me, Ross?"

"Well . . ." Slowly, as his head bent to hers. "What else can I do?"

"Upon my soul," said Mrs. Tretteign, "I was never so shocked in my life."